D0462826

Praise for the novels of Nancy Fisher

Code Red

"Don't miss *Code Red*, a medical thriller that will keep you hyperventilating." —Catherine Coulter

"Nancy Fisher, author of great medical thrillers . . . has written another chiller. . . . Fans of the subgenre will feel the afterglow of a winning tale."
—*The Midwest Book Review*

Special Treatment

"Nancy Fisher is a fine writer and fills her book with real medical interest." —*Publishers Weekly*

Side Effects

"This medical thriller maintains a fast pace until its satisfying denouement. . . . Realistic in both scope and description, Fisher has created likable characters and thrown in just the right amount of anthropology, biomedicine, ecology, pharmacology, romance, and intrigue." —*Publishers Weekly*

Vital Parts

"Fisher's fast-paced, credible tale should give Robin Cook a run for his money."
—*Orlando Sentinel*

"Nancy Fisher is breathing hotly down the neck of Robin Cook, and if he doesn't look out, she'll leave him standing." —Stuart Woods

Praise for the novels of
Nancy Fisher

Cut & Run

"Nancy Fisher... a medical thriller that will
keep readers turning..." —Gothic Journal

"Nancy Fisher, author of great medical thrillers,
has written another thriller.... Fans of this subgenre
will find themselves in a twisting tale."
—The Mystery Book Review

Special Treatment

"Nancy Fisher's a sure writer and this one book
will well enthrall intense..." —Rendezvous

Side Effects

"This medical thriller maintains a fast pace with the
satisfying denouement.... Realistic in both
scope and description. Suspenseful and full of
characters and thrown in just the right amount
of... romance, honest, and added by a fortunate
of... romance and intrigue." —Publishers Weekly

Vital Parts

"Fisher's fast-paced, credible tale should give
Robin Cook a run for his money."
—Orlando Sentinel

"Nancy Fisher is breaking hotly down the track of
Robin Cook, and if he doesn't look out, she'll
leave him behind." —Span Week

CODE BLUE

Nancy Fisher

AN ONYX BOOK

ONYX
Published by New American Library, a division of
Penguin Putnam Inc., 375 Hudson Street,
New York, New York 10014, U.S.A.
Penguin Books Ltd, 27 Wrights Lane,
London W8 5TZ, England
Penguin Books Australia Ltd, Ringwood,
Victoria, Australia
Penguin Books Canada Ltd, 10 Alcorn Avenue,
Toronto, Ontario, Canada M4V 3B2
Penguin Books (N.Z.) Ltd, 182±190 Wairau Road,
Auckland 10, New Zealand

Penguin Books Ltd, Registered OfÆces:
Harmondsworth, Middlesex, England

Copyright © Nancy Fisher, 2000
All rights reserved

 REGISTERED TRADEMARK–MARCA REGISTRADA

Printed in the United States of America

Without limiting the rights under copyright reserved above, no part of this
publication may be reproduced, stored in or introduced into a retrieval system, or transmitted, in any form, or by any means (electronic, mechanical,
photocopying, recording, or otherwise), without the prior written permission
of both the copyright owner and the above publisher of this book.

PUBLISHER'S NOTE
This is a work of Æction.Names, characters, places, and incidents either are
the product of the author's imagination or are used Æctitiouslyand any resemblance to actual persons, living or dead, business establishments, events, or
locales is entirely coincidental.

ISBN 0-7394-0693-0

For Ann, Barbara, Carol, Jane, Joann,
Joyce, Leslie, Lenore, Roberta, and Sheila—
friends forever

ACKNOWLEDGMENTS

Many thanks, as always, to my brother Dr. Robert Fisher of Minneapolis, for sharing his impressive medical expertise with me. I'm grateful to the Alcor Life Extension Foundation [(877) 462-5267], of which I am a member, for much valuable information, and also to Dale Burg. Any errors are mine alone. The contributions of my agent, Bob Diforio, and my editor, Hilary Ross, are much appreciated. And my daughter, Sarah, and my mother, Tema, lavished upon me their usual love and encouragement.

Do not go gentle into that good night . . .
—Dylan Thomas

Prologue

Consciousness returned gradually, like a fog slowly lifting. He was aware of a cool rush of air against his face. He sensed he was in motion, swaying, gliding. He rolled his head to one side and commanded his eyes to open, but the lids felt too heavy.

Voices spoke softly. "He's coming around."

"Tighten the strap."

He felt a pressure around his midsection. What was happening? He opened his eyes and blinked in the semidarkness. He seemed to be in some sort of tunnel. How odd, he thought fuzzily. He watched the black walls rush past, and began to feel slightly sick.

"Where am I?" he murmured, but it came out as a thin moan.

"Hang on," someone told him. "Almost there."

Almost where? he wondered, but his lips refused to form the words. The swaying movement stopped, and he felt a series of bumps.

"Easy, now," a voice said.

The gliding motion recommenced, but more slowly. He heard a series of metallic clangs.

Hands adjusted the sheets that covered him. Whose hands? What sheets? What was going on?

"They'll look for him," said someone.

"Let them," came the reply.

He sensed a change of light beyond his closed eyelids, and the air on his cheek turned frigid. Look for whom? he mused hazily, then realized they were talking about him. Alarm thrilled through his body, and he forced his eyelids open.

"Good morning, Dr. Harland."

His dilated pupils widened further as his eyes flicked from one strangely garbed figure to the other. "What . . . ?"

"Don't try to speak. It's too late."

The man squinted, desperately trying to focus on the face that swam above him, silhouetted against the light. "You!" he exclaimed softly.

"Yes, me. I'm afraid your career at Greenvale is at an end, doctor. You can't be allowed to do any more damage."

"Damage?" The man frowned. "I don't know what you mean." He felt disoriented and very cold.

"Oh, I think you do."

The figure stepped away, and the man found himself staring into a bright round light. Full moon, he thought muzzily.

"Good-bye, doctor."

Good-bye? He felt a prick of pain as the needle went in. "No," he cried. "Wait—" Then the fog came down again, and he knew no more.

Chapter One

An icy wind swept in from the ocean, hurrying the loose flotsam of civilization before it as it swept inland. Pregnant clouds scudded across the sky, obscuring the sliver of new moon. The woman was shrouded against the coming rain in a hooded coat that obscured her thickening body and pale, anxious face. A passerby would have been struck by her panicky haste as she hurried along the darkened street. But no such passerby appeared. It was late by New Chatham standards, after eleven, and tomorrow was a working day. The few cars that sped past her along the county road were intent on beating the storm home.

Jagged lightning provided sudden, brief illumination as the woman scurried around to the back of the modest colonial-style house. Her hand on the doorknob, she glanced over her shoulder at the snowy field beyond the garden, staring for a moment at the stark silhouette of a large, gabled mansion. Then she opened the door and slipped inside.

The hallway, papered in fresh green and white, was bright and welcoming. Halfway along it, the woman turned right through a modest archway and entered a denlike sitting room painted a soft sage. The room was crowded with furniture. Twelve men and women of various ages were crammed into the small space, conversing softly.

At an oak trestle table, a woman with a red silk

shawl around her shoulders was stirring the contents of a highly polished silver punch bowl. "We were about to start without you," she said, looking up from her work. Her smile took the sting from her words.

"Sorry," the latecomer apologized, slinging her coat over the back of a chair. "We're shorthanded this week, and I—"

"Never mind. You're here now." The woman glanced at her watch. "We'd better get started."

The new arrival perched on an arm of the sofa, smiling a greeting at the others as punch was ladled into paper cups and handed around. Then, having poured one for herself, the shawled woman seated herself in the rocker.

"Welcome, friends, to this extraordinary meeting of the Gaia Society," she began, surveying the room with satisfaction. " 'Extraordinary' in the sense that it's not one of our regularly scheduled meetings. And that we're not"—she gestured at the window—"out there; not with this storm. But the most extraordinary thing about this meeting is what we are here to celebrate. As you know."

A satisfied murmur greeted her words.

"After years of protests and picketing," she went on, "we are at last having an effect." She paused. "It has been said that a hundred fully conscious people can change the world. Well, we're doing it with a lot fewer than that." She waited for the smattering of self-congratulatory applause to finish. "We've seen many changes in our town in a few short years, all of them crimes against nature. Economic and ecological changes, starting with the building of Greenvale Hospital five years ago on land that had been set aside for a town park and nature preserve."

An angry buzzing broke out, and she raised her hand for silence. "But giving away our natural heritage wasn't enough for the bankers and politicians," she continued, her voice rising. "They also gave the hospital special dispensations in their disposal of sewage and bio-trash. They gave them big tax incentives. And they welcomed the rich and famous who came to our town, changing its very nature."

She paused and drank off the last of her punch. "We fought the building of the hospital and lost. But we did not and we will not stop fighting." She turned to a bearded young man on a straight-back chair. "Are the leaflets ready for next Sunday's march?"

"We're running them off tomorrow," he assured her. "Two thousand copies."

"Good. Did you have any luck with the posters, Annie?"

"Herbs & Scents took one," came the reply. "And Tea for Two. And the high school's ecology club. But the chains—The Gap, Starbucks—all said it was against company policy to put posters in their windows."

"Well, concentrate on the smaller stores." The leader turned to another member. "I'm still hoping you'll change your mind and speak at the rally at the library. People respect you."

"Which is precisely why I can't." The man smiled ruefully. "You know that."

"You should stand up and be counted," a wiry little woman told him angrily.

But the leader shook her head. "That's not fair," she said firmly. "We all contribute in different ways. He does his part."

"I still think—"

"We shouldn't argue," another participant interrupted, his voice charged with emotion. "Not tonight."

"That's right," the leader said. "Tonight we must unite our cosmic energies, not diffuse them." She glanced at several undrained cups. "Drink up."

The room seemed to be growing warmer. Hands pushed damp hair away from flushed, eager faces.

· "We warned them." The leader's face was moist, her eyes overbright. "We who are committed to natural living, to fighting the wrongful changes being perpetrated upon our town, we warned them." Her passion brought her unsteadily to her feet. "We warned them not to build the hospital here. Heal yourself with herbs, we told them. Don't pollute your bodies with unnatural poisons the doctors call drugs. Don't submit to the surgeon's knife. Live according to Nature's will. But again, they ignored us."

This time she did nothing to quell the furious voices.

"For five years we have protested the presence of Greenvale Hospital and the evil it has brought." Her voice became strident. "For five years we marched and picketed. But our peaceful protests did not work. So we united our spirits, here in this room, and called upon the forces of Nature to come to our aid. And those forces heard us."

A clap of thunder echoed through the small room, and hail rattled against the uncurtained windows.

"Thanks to you, the committed core of our organization, Dr. Ward Harland is no longer chief of cosmetic surgery at Greenvale." She paused for the cheer that went up. "The pain of his disappearance is already being felt," she continued. "Many expensive cosmetic procedures—the financial lifeblood of the hospital—have already been canceled. If the situation continues, Greenvale will be bankrupt."

"Lord, let it be," a woman murmured fervently.

"But won't Greenvale's chief administrator step in?" someone asked. "Slater made his name in cosmetic surgery, after all."

"Strangely enough, Slater's refused to go back into the OR." The leader pulled the fringed shawl from around her shoulders. "For which we should give thanks," she added, "since our efforts against *him* have not been successful." A frown passed across her flushed brow as she thought of the celebrated surgeon who had brought Greenvale Hospital to New Chatham. "So we must continue to focus our cosmic energies on those who do *not* refuse to perform surgery. And now it is time for us to strengthen those energies."

People were loosening collars, unbuttoning buttons, pulses racing, faces feverish.

"As we do so, let us also give thanks to our new sisters and brothers in arms, Humans for Humanity, for their financial and psychic support of our cause. Their national demonstrations against genetic tinkering and other ungodly research should inspire us all. It is an honor to be recognized by them, and to become a part of their national coalition."

Carrying her shawl, the leader crossed to the punch bowl with uncertain steps. The others murmured excitedly, eyes burning with expectation as they stood and began pushing back the furniture. When they had cleared a sufficiently large space, they joined hands and formed a circle in the center of the small room.

Thunder rolled as the leader draped her shawl around the silver bowl. Lifting the bowl in both hands, she turned toward the circle, which opened to allow her to move into its center.

"To the heart of Gaia, mother of the earth," she intoned, lowering the bowl toward the floor.

"To the heart of Gaia . . ." the group repeated, swaying ecstatically.

"To the stars above you, Gaia." As she raised the bowl high in the air, a stab of reflected lightning touched its silver with an eerie glow.

"To the stars above . . ."

"And to all that lies between that we must protect." The leader carried the bowl around the circle, tilting it to allow each person to drink. When it was empty, she set it carefully on the floor, then began circling the bowl slowly, facing outward to the ring of celebrants, her arms outstretched. "Hear us, Gaia. We invoke the Natural Way."

". . . the Natural Way." The group circled around her revolving figure, echoing her chant.

"Hear us, Gaia. We invoke the powers of the earth."

". . . the powers of the earth."

"Hear us, Gaia. We invoke the spirits of the cosmos."

". . . the spirits of the cosmos."

"Hear us, Gaia. We invoke the forces of the darkness." Eyes wide and unfocused, the leader began to spin, her arms windmilling. She stumbled, recovered, spun faster, ripping at her blouse.

"Gaia . . . Gaia . . ." The celebrants were pulling at each other's clothing, grabbing at breasts and groins in a drugged frenzy.

Amid the chaos, the leader revolved alone, bare to the waist, head thrown back, breasts rising and falling as she gasped for breath. "We give thanks for the casting down of Ward Harland," she cried, her slurred words raised above the beating of the rain. "And we call upon the power of Gaia to kill whoever comes to take his place."

"Kill whoever comes . . ."

A flash of lightning lit the room, followed by a deafening roll of thunder. "Gaia has heard us," the leader shouted, raising her arms to the storm as the cult gyrated in drugged ecstasy around her. "Gaia is angry."

Chapter Two

She swung off the interstate, glancing at the driving directions Samuel Slater's secretary had faxed her. Left at the exit ramp, right at the light . . . It had been eleven years since she'd visited her parents in New Chatham, longer still since she'd been a teenager there. In the interim, she'd gone off to college and then medical school, Mom and Dad had retired to Santa Fe, and the sleepy, economically depressed riverside town she'd once called home had grown into a modern, thriving community, thanks to the man she was on her way to see.

The winter day was crisp and bright, the sky cloudless. She rolled down the window and inhaled the scents of wood smoke and salt air. After so many years in New York City, she found the smells intriguingly foreign. She drove slowly through the outskirts of town, took a wrong turn, cut through the parking lot of a large shopping center, and backtracked. She'd expected changes, but she was truly surprised at the extent of them. New roads had sprung up, a multiplex, a marina, several luxury condominium developments, a sprawling new high school.

Headed in the right direction again, she concentrated on the road and tried not to think how good a vodka and tonic would taste. It's like they said in rehab, she reflected: you'll always be an alcoholic. The trick is not to give in to it.

Dr. Taylor Barnes had just driven the eighty-eight miles between New York and New Chatham in an attempt to rebuild her life. A successful, sought-after cosmetic surgeon at thirty-four, she'd been unable to cope with so much success so soon. The stress of her practice, coupled with the failure of a seven-year marriage to a dermatologist who resented the "twenty-four-seven" schedule of her surgical residency, and later, the high-powered career she was building had turned her social drinking into a serious problem that effectively ended her meteoric rise and put her, at age thirty-six, into the Caron Foundation treatment center.

She'd emerged to find, not surprisingly, that no one would hire her. She'd come to New Chatham today in the hope that Dr. Samuel Slater, the founder, chairman, and driving force of Greenvale Hospital, would feel differently.

And she had reason for hope, because the situation at Greenvale was unusual. A private hospital, Greenvale had been specifically created to attract socialites and celebrities, to provide a luxurious facility where the wealthy and well-known could check in for discreet face-lifts, liposuction, and tummy tucks. Here, they could dry out, lose weight, or undergo more standard medical treatment away from the prying eyes of the press. Backed by local bankers and politicians who were now reaping the financial benefits Greenvale had brought to their town, Slater had full administrative control. If Taylor could convince him to take her on as his new chief of cosmetic and reconstructive surgery, no board of directors would go against his decision.

And why should they? Taylor thought as she drove slowly along the waterfront. Look what he's done for the place.

A large sailboat was being hoisted out of the newly dredged harbor; other yachts were under cover in what had once been Eddie's Boatyard, now rebuilt, expanded, and christened "Chatham Cove Marina."

Large homes, some guarded by high ironwork gates, dotted the low-lying hills, their manicured lawns flowing down to the sea. Even the smaller houses she drove past had been gentrified. The peeling paint and ramshackle front yards of her childhood were gone.

The revival of New Chatham had been featured in everything from the *New York Times* to *Architectural Digest*. The influx of wealthy folk from New York and Boston and Los Angeles had produced a real estate boom. "Discovering" the area during their stays at Greenvale, they'd bought or built second homes here, and more than a few had made New Chatham their permanent residence. This sudden rise in the tax base had funded major civic development, which in turn had drawn a host of middle- and upper-middle income families to the town. National retailers as well as local entrepreneurs were enjoying the boom.

And so are developers and home owners, Taylor thought. From the look of things, she doubted she could afford to buy the house her parents had counted themselves lucky to have sold cheaply, nine years earlier.

When she'd first contemplated this shot at a comeback in her old hometown, it had seemed bittersweet. Driving over the Triborough Bridge that morning, she'd even felt a little apprehensive. But seeing it now made her feel a lot better. New Chatham had become a completely different place. Naturally, there would be a few familiar faces, but relocating here would have no more emotional impact than moving to Chicago or Dallas—

Her foot hit the brake before her mind said stop. What the—?

She pulled over and gazed up at the old Victorian mansion, feeling the same frisson of fear she'd felt as a child. The Haunted House, they'd called it then, daring each other to pound on its door with the rusty metal knocker. Now the Rockingham House stood weather-beaten, shuttered, and obviously empty, but still scary as hell. Why was that?

And why was the property still undeveloped when so much of New Chatham had been gentrified? She glanced at the gated cemetery directly across the road from the Rockingham House. Surely it couldn't be that; developers wouldn't be frightened off by a cemetery. The house was large, with an extensive garden behind it, and thanks to all the new development, it was no longer on the outskirts of town. It didn't make sense that it should be standing empty.

She sat staring at the place. It looked just as frightening as she remembered it. A strong sense of foreboding came over her, and she shivered.

Oh, come on, she told herself firmly. It's just an old house. You're not a child anymore.

She pulled down the vanity mirror and smoothed her tawny hair, then applied fresh lipstick. With a glance at the driving directions—she was actually quite close to Greenvale, though the route was convoluted—she pulled out onto the asphalt. She had just five minutes to find the hospital, and arriving late was not a great way to start a job interview.

"Congratulations, Sam," Garrison Potter said with enthusiasm. "Great news." He rubbed his hands together in an unconscious gesture that had always seemed to Slater a mix of brisk efficiency and rampant ambition.

"Don't open the champagne yet," Slater told him. "There are plenty of other worthy contenders."

"But the Larrabee! You know what kind of P.R. mileage we can get out of an award like that? 'The American Nobel.' Hell, it'll open up a whole new area of fund-raising for us."

"*If* I get it." Slater smiled at the energetic young man behind the desk. "That's a big if." Not for the first time, he reflected on his good fortune at recruiting

Garrison as the hospital's combination CFO and director of development.

"You know who else is up for it?"

Slater shook his neat gray head. "They keep the list of nominees a secret until the awards dinner. Not that some of the names won't get out before that. But at this point, no, I don't."

"Excuse me, Sam." Slater's administrative assistant, an attractive fortyish woman whom Slater had brought with him from Boston, stuck her head around the partly open door. "Dr. Barnes is here."

"Take her into my office, Penny, and get her some coffee," Slater replied. "I'll just be a minute. Harland's replacement," he told Garrison. "Maybe."

"About time," Garrison said. "We're hurting. So what's he like?"

"She. Helluva surgeon. Had some problems in the past but resolved them, so I'm told."

"What kind of problems?" Garrison frowned.

Slater opened his mouth and closed it again. Why worry Garrison before he'd made up his mind about Barnes? "Nothing we can't handle."

"So where's she working now?"

"Nowhere, I'm afraid. But a couple of years ago, she was a hotshot cosmetic surgeon in New York City. I've talked to a number of her former patients, and they sing her praises."

"That part sounds good. But . . . Greenvale's become well-known. And we've got plenty of money in the budget. You can have your pick of surgeons. If this Barnes is such a hotshot, how come we're the only place that wants her?"

Slater's eyes flashed. "Let me worry about that," he snapped.

"I only—"

"I know. I'm sorry. The thing is, I'm looking for a very special sort of person. Surgical skills are only part of it. There's also personality, directability . . . I think Taylor Barnes may be just what I'm looking for."

"I still don't know, Sam. Will our patients accept a woman cosmetic surgeon?"

"They will if I tell them to," Slater said firmly.

Garrison frowned. "New Chatham's quite a change from New York. Does she know what she's in for, coming to a small town?"

"I think so. She grew up here."

"Really? Hey, you think maybe hiring a native daughter might help us with those damn protesters?"

"I doubt it," Slater told him. "Pete Ohlmeyer's lived here for years, but having him as head of cardiothoracic hasn't helped us any."

"He was also on call when Maggie McCormick's husband died, don't forget." Slater gave a resigned shrug. "Besides, *nobody* likes Pete Ohlmeyer."

"He's very good at what he does."

"If you say so. Still, a woman might be more useful. How old is she? Any chance she knew Maggie Kay McCormick when she lived here?"

"I think Maggie's a year or two older."

"Close enough. If Barnes did know her, and if she could get to her—"

"I doubt they would have had much in common, even back then. Besides," Slater added, "Maggie has too much invested in the movement to back down just because an old acquaintance tells her to."

"Invested?"

"Sure. Look at it from her side. She worked for years to get this land turned into a park, and then we came along and turned it into a hospital. A few years later, her husband comes in for routine surgery and dies of cardiac arrest. She's not the brightest woman in the world, and suddenly she's a widow, she's all alone. The Gaia people take her under their wing, tell her the hospital is the villain, that it destroyed her town, killed her husband . . . Don't get me wrong," Slater continued. "She makes me furious with her protests and her speeches and those damn posters she sticks on our windows. But she's a little . . . unbalanced, I think. And the movement's all she's got, poor woman."

"Poor woman my ass," Garrison snorted. "She's dangerous. They say those people are into some weird stuff."

"Weird? Like what?"

"Drugs, spells, secret ceremonies . . . Don't tell me you haven't heard the rumors." Slater was silent. "You have, haven't you?"

Slater sighed. "Rumors," he said. "If I believed every rumor I hear in this town . . ." He rose from the upholstered side chair and stretched. "Come and meet Dr. Barnes." Garrison followed him out into the corridor.

In Slater's large, well-appointed office, a taffy-haired woman in a well-cut dark suit and pale silk shirt was reading last month's *Lancet* and idly petting a small white Scottie.

"Dr. Barnes?" The woman looked up. Reassuringly pretty, Slater decided, but not so gorgeous she'd scare away the female clients. "Sam Slater," he said. "Welcome to Greenvale."

"Thank you," Taylor said, surprised that Slater looked closer to sixty than the fifty-four stated in the hospital public relations packet she'd been sent. She stood and extended her hand, and Slater enveloped it briefly in his own slim palm. "I've heard so much about you and your work here at Greenvale," she enthused. "It's a real pleasure to finally meet you . . ." She trailed off, thinking, Jeez, you don't sound too desperate, do you?

But Slater appeared to find her effusiveness charming. "And I've heard so much about *you*," he said. "I appreciate your making the trip out here. I see you've met Snowball."

Taylor glanced over at the dog. "He's sweet. It's"— she chose her words carefully—"unusual to allow a dog into a hospital."

"This is an unusual hospital." Slater reached down

and scratched the animal behind the ears. "He's a stray. He adopted me, and I don't have the heart to leave him at home all day. Oh, this is Garrison Potter, our chief financial officer."

"Ah, the money man. Nice to meet you." Taylor smiled at the intense, dark-haired man in the expensively cut suit and Harvard tie and thought, Nobody would dare call you Gary.

"Nice to meet you, too, doctor," Garrison replied, surprised at how young she looked. He wondered what the problems were that Slater had referred to.

"Garrison and I worked together when I was chief of cosmetic and reconstructive surgery at Boston General," Slater was saying. "Best damn hospital administrator I ever met. Please sit down, Dr. Barnes."

"Taylor," said Taylor.

"Taylor." Slater seated himself in the leather swivel chair behind his wide oak desk. "Want a refill on that coffee? No?" He turned to Garrison. "See what you can find out about the other nominees."

"I'll get right on it." Effectively dismissed, Garrison nodded at Taylor and left the office, closing the door softly behind him.

"Any trouble finding the place?" Slater asked.

"A little," Taylor admitted. "Everything's changed so much."

"For the better?" Slater reached down to pat Snowball, who had settled himself on the physician's narrow lap.

"Definitely. Peeling paint and ramshackle buildings are only picturesque if you're passing through."

"I agree." He paused. "Unfortunately, not everyone does."

"Oh?"

"Most of the people here in town are supportive of Greenvale. They're grateful, and they're glad we're here. They're already planning a big celebration in April to mark our fifth anniversary. But you can't please everyone. There's a small but vocal protest group that prefers things the way they were."

"Peeling and ramshackle?" Taylor asked with a smile.

Her smile was not returned. "Low-key," Slater said seriously. "Rustic. Inexpensive." He sighed. "They claim that the coming of Greenvale Hospital has changed the character of New Chatham. It has; I can't deny it. Real estate *is* more expensive. The chains *have* replaced many of the old family-run stores. But there's also a new high school. A new library. An expanded public beach. For most people, quality of life has improved."

"Sounds good to me."

"And to a lot of other people. But not to everyone. The protest group continues to picket and protest and make trouble for us. Maggie Kay McCormick plastered our ground-floor windows with posters last week—"

"I went to high school with a Maggie Kay," Taylor said slowly. "Short, chubby, snub-nosed?" She smiled. "I can't imagine her involved in a protest movement. All she was interested in was boys."

"Well, she's changed. How well did you know her?"

"Not very. We were in the same grade, but we hung out with different crowds. I seem to remember she got married right after graduation. A guy who worked in the local garage."

"Jack McCormick. He died two years ago."

"I'm sorry to hear that."

"He died here at Greenvale," Slater said meaningfully. "That's when she got involved with the protesters."

"I see." Taylor paused. "Well, I'm sorry for Maggie, but those things happen. And as you said, you can't please everyone."

"Exactly." Slater studied her for a moment. "So you have no problem coming back here? That 'you can't go home again' stuff doesn't worry you?"

"Not at all. It's been many years since I lived in
New Chatham. It's changed completely. And the job
would be a great opportunity for me." She paused.
"It's no secret why my career went sour. But things
are different, now. *I'm* different. And I need to work."

Slater nodded. "You were an excellent surgeon.
You had a great reputation. The truth is, I've been
curious about you for some time. A woman cosmetic
surgeon's a rarity, even in New York City. Not that I
have to tell *you* that." Snowball shifted in his lap, and
he patted the dog fondly. "Of the five hundred or so
board certified plastic surgeons who practice in Manhat-
tan," he continued, "how many are women? Twelve?"

"I believe we're up to fourteen now," she said with
a smile.

"And your clientele was very similar to ours. That's
important to me. Catering to the rich and famous is
an art. And frankly, it's what butters our bread."

"I understand."

"And allows us to fund the free clinic. We're not
just a bunch of society doctors here," he continued
defensively, "and this is not just a celebrity hospital,
although some people in this town insist on forgetting
that. The quality of medical care at Greenvale is on
a par with the best hospitals in the country."

"So I've heard," Taylor said. "Would I be working
with clinic patients, too?"

"From time to time. But it's your expertise with our
other clientele base that interests me."

"People like Lynda North?" Taylor glanced toward
a signed photograph of the famous actress that formed
the centerpiece of the group of photos hanging behind
Slater's desk.

"Do you know her?"

"Only her work. She's wonderful, isn't she? Have
you seen 'Blue Dusk' yet?"

Slater nodded. "Very impressive. And she's never
looked better," he added archly.

"Your work?"

"Ward Harland's." His smile faded. "The man I'm looking to replace. And soon, I hope. I'm being pressured to start operating again. So far I've refused."

"But why?" Taylor blurted. "You're famous for your surgical skill—" She broke off. It was really none of her business.

"Once I go back into the OR," Slater explained, "I'll never get out again. And frankly, my priorities and interests have changed. These days, I prefer to concentrate on running the hospital and doing research." He paused. "In fact, I've been nominated for a Larrabee."

"That's wonderful!"

"I doubt I'll actually get it," he said modestly. "But just to be nominated . . ."

"A real honor. What kind of research are you doing?"

"I'm developing new perfusion solutions for the preservation of transplant organs . . . Are you interested in research?"

Taylor shook her head. From the first time she'd picked up a scalpel, she'd loved the action and immediacy of surgery. Research had never held any appeal for her. "I'm afraid my talents are more cut-and-paste," she answered diplomatically.

"Which is exactly what we need here," Slater said. "And fast."

"I hope you don't mind my asking," Taylor said carefully, "but I was wondering why Dr. Harland left so suddenly. It seems rather . . ."

"Unprofessional." Slater finished her sentence for her. "He talked about opening a private practice in Los Angeles. With contacts he made here, presumably," he added bitterly. "One day, he just took off."

"But . . . didn't he have a contract?"

"Of course. But if he didn't want to be here, I sure didn't want to keep him." He spoke calmly, but his trembling hands betrayed his anger.

Unsure of what to say, Taylor sipped her now-tepid

coffee in silence. She had hoped Slater would suggest she call Harland to get some background on the job, but now she felt it would be less than politic to ask for it. Never mind, she thought; I'll find him through the A.M.A.

"New blood's what we need here," Slater said, his anger dissipating. He stood, gently depositing the Scottie on the floor beside his chair. "How about a tour of the place?"

"I'd like that."

"Penny's put together a packet of information on Greenvale for you. The piece about Harland is out of date, of course," he added, ushering her out into the common area, where his administrative assistant was working. "Oh, your office would be just over there," he said, pointing. "And you'd have your own secretary. Thanks, Penny." He took the envelope of material his assistant held out to him and handed it to Taylor.

"Thanks," Taylor told the woman. "Nice meeting you."

"Nice to meet you, too."

"I have a good feeling about this, Taylor," Slater told her as they walked out into the hallway. "I think we'd work well together."

"I think so, too." God, please let me get this job.

"You'll work your butt off," he warned.

"Suits me fine." Whatever it takes, she thought; whatever I need to do to prove to the world I'm still a surgeon. And to prove to myself that I can stay sober under pressure.

He nodded as though reading her thoughts. At that moment, a tall, red-haired nursing aide in a crisp pink uniform came flying around the corner, jostling Taylor, who fell against Slater.

Braking sharply, the woman turned back, contrite. "Gosh, I'm sorry, Dr. Slater."

"Slow down, Janice," Slater ordered as Taylor

righted herself. "Don't kill off my new staff before I hire them."

"New staff?"

But Slater was already steering Taylor around the corner to the main corridor.

The nursing assistant continued along the hallway to the common area where Slater's assistant sat working at her computer. "Who's that with Dr. Slater, Penny?"

Penny looked up. "Dr. Barnes. Why?"

"She looks familiar. Who is she?"

"A cosmetic surgeon from New York. Sam's considering her for Ward Harland's job."

"A woman department chief? That's great. Think she'll get it?"

"Could be. Sam was very impressed with her credentials."

"Well, here's hoping." Janice gave Penny a thumbs-up, then turned away, her smile fading.

Chapter Three

It was after midnight, and Lynda was weary. She'd been hanging around, her hair in rollers, since three that afternoon, running lines with Andrew, discussing a possible project with her agent at ICM, nibbling a salad and washing it down with bottled water. Rigging the car had taken longer than anticipated, the walk-through had started late, and they hadn't begun shooting until nearly nine.

Now she sat at the dressing table in her trailer, wiping off her makeup and studying her reflection. Harland had done a beautiful job; despite the long shooting day, she looked terrific. It wasn't vanity that drove her to examine her face. Like her talent, her looks were part of her working equipment.

A knock at the trailer door. "Your car is here, Ms. North."

"Thanks, Bob. Tell him I'll be a few minutes."

"Will do."

As a rule, Lynda shunned the studio car and driver, preferring to drive herself to and from location in her sporty new Mercedes. But lately her night vision wasn't what it used to be. She finished her toilette and ran a brush through her short blonde hair, then rose and went to the tiny kitchenette. From the small fridge she took a bottle of Evian and set it on the counter. The cupboard above was stocked with a variety of glassware but she selected her usual water tumbler.

No wineglass for her because she drank no wine. Or whiskey. Or coffee or tea. She consumed no meat or dairy products. She exercised daily, took three yoga classes a week, and swallowed so many vitamins and herbal supplements her friends claimed she rattled when she walked. Lynda was serious—some said nutty—about her health. "I plan on living forever," she'd answer lightly when people teased her about her spartan lifestyle. Only her closest confidants realized she was absolutely serious.

Sipping the water, she went to the portable metal clothes rack. Pushing aside the various costumes that hung there, she located the blue sweater and jeans she'd worn to the set that afternoon and pulled them from their hangers. She set down the glass, dropped her robe in the linen bin, and got dressed.

A canvas briefcase lay on the sofa, loose script pages beside it. She picked it up, stuffed the papers inside, and headed for the door. She had her hand on the knob when she remembered something, and paused.

Returning to the makeup table, she surveyed the jumble on its surface, frowning. Where the hell was it? She tossed a scarf aside, moved a tissue box. A gleam of metal caught her eye. She reached for the thin silver chain with its flat, inscribed pendant and held it in front of her for a moment, studying the image of the staff with its entwined serpent. Then she lifted the necklace over her head and let it drop around her neck, tucking the pendant carefully out of sight under her sweater. It really was nobody's business but her own, she reflected. Besides, if word got around, it could hurt her career.

It had been two weeks since he'd made love to her, and he was nearly frantic with desire. Sure, there were plenty of women at the annual sales convention who would have loved to screw the chairman of Polaris Technology. But it was Lydia he'd wanted, and

wanted badly. Their affair was still new enough to
excite him to fever pitch, even over the phone. First
time I've done *that,* he thought, pulse racing as he
remembered.

She opened the door wearing only the skimpy panties and bra he'd sent her from Las Vegas.

"Look what I brought you," he murmured, pressing
her hand to his erection.

In minutes they were sprawled together on the bed,
his clothes scattered like leaves. On the way over, he'd
pictured her nipples pressing against the thin fabric of
the bra, imagined the feel of the panties' wet crotch.
He'd had two weeks to think about the things he
would do to her; he'd even described some of them
on the phone, to her delight. But now that he was
with her, he couldn't wait. Ripping off the panties,
he shoved himself inside her. She cried out, her hips
pumping to drive him deeper. Faster and faster . . .

"Ow! That hurts, dammit."

He hesitated in mid-stroke, gasping. What was she
talking about? Why was she stopping?

"What the hell *is* that thing?" she gasped.

He opened his eyes and looked down. She was holding the flat pendant that hung from a thin chain
around his neck.

"It keeps hitting me in the face," she complained,
turning it over in her fingers. "What is this, a medical
alert?" She looked up at him, concern on her flushed
face. "You okay?"

"It's nothing. I'm fine."

"But it says, 'In case of—' "

He grabbed the pendant from her hand. "It's nothing, I said." He pulled the chain up over his head and
tossed it across the room, watching it pool on the floor
beside his pants.

"It can't be nothing, Herb. Not if it's a medical
alert—"

"Relax. I only have to wear it because of some huge

life insurance policy the Board's insisting on. Pain in the ass. Doesn't mean a thing."

"Really?"

"Really." He smiled reassuringly.

Her face relaxed. "Good. Now, where were we . . . ? Oh."

He sighed. Interruptions were a killer at his age. Well, it would give him a chance to do some of those things he'd been thinking about, the last few weeks. "Turn over, baby," he told her.

Chapter Four

Taylor sipped her coffee, wishing it were something stronger and feeling proud that it wasn't. The Science Section of the *New York Times* lay open on the kitchen table in front of her, but her thoughts were far away.

When she and Slater had parted after the hospital tour, he'd strongly hinted that he'd be calling her with an offer by the end of the week. All during the first half of the drive back home, she was elated. But by the time she crossed the New York state line, she was full of self-doubt. Maybe it was too soon to go back into the OR. Could she handle the pressure without resorting to the booze? What if she cracked? And what about New Chatham itself? Was a small town the right place for her?

If only she could discuss it with someone active in the world of medicine, she thought; somebody who'd have the perspective she lacked. Trouble was, most of her recent professional contacts probably wouldn't take her very seriously. Too many of them had known her primarily as a drunk.

As she turned back to the paper, her eye was caught by a name she recognized. "Dr. Kipling Lawrence," she read. "Brilliant biotech breakthrough." She scanned the article, which detailed his successful career to date, enumerating the offers he'd received from a number of distinguished research facilities a year earlier and his ultimate selection of the renowned Emerson Institute, which had promptly built him a state-of-the-art lab in their new facility.

Good for him, she thought, a little surprised. Not that he wasn't brilliant. But this kind of success so early in his career . . . well, she'd had that, too, and she'd thrown it away. Kip had obviously handled it better. Of course, he'd known wealth and privilege all his life. But in her heart of hearts, she realized it wasn't that simple.

Taylor had worked with Kip early in her training, when he was a charismatic senior resident at Memorial and she was a fourth-year medical student. Unlike some of the residents, Kip was patient with the new doctors who rotated onto his service, using his impressive intellect to teach rather than terrorize. And he hadn't bought into the widespread but subtle discrimination against female surgeons. Instead, he'd applauded Taylor's decision to specialize in surgery, and had given her a glowing recommendation.

Even then he'd never really liked dealing with patients, preferring the lab to the examining room. Despite this difference in their attitudes toward medicine, Kip and Taylor had become good friends, and one evening, in the backseat of a taxi, it seemed as if their friendship was about to evolve into something more. But it hadn't, and soon after, Taylor had met Paul.

She and Kip had remained friends through the early years of her marriage, and then lost touch. She'd always felt Kip disliked her husband—ex-husband now, so maybe Kip had been right. And she'd also suspected Kip had regretted what had failed to happen between them, that long-ago night.

The photo accompanying the article showed a handsome, light-haired man nearing forty, with strong, regular features and a boyish smile. Perhaps she should call him, she thought. *I saw the article in the* Times. *How have you been? I'd like to get your thinking on something.* It had been a long time, but somehow she felt Kip wouldn't judge her as harshly as the others might.

And he was every bit as attractive as she remembered.

Calling Kip Lawrence was an interesting idea on a number of levels, she decided. She reached for the phone.

"As you can see, they made me an offer I couldn't refuse," Kip said, leading Taylor through the laboratory suite. "The whole facility is purpose-built, and the equipment is state-of-the-art." He looked over at her, grinning gleefully. Like a little boy with a new toy, she reflected. A damn expensive toy.

He was even better-looking than she remembered. The crisp striped shirt beneath his lab coat looked custom-tailored—no surprise there, she thought—and he carried his tall, lanky frame with an easy confidence.

"We share the use of an animal lab on the third floor," he was saying, "and an electron microscope in the basement."

"Very impressive. But tell me more about this biotech breakthrough of yours. The article made it sound like you're re-creating the stuff of life."

"It's not quite like that, although it *is* very exciting. My team and I are attempting to assemble strands of human DNA into artificial chromosomes."

"It's not my field, of course, but . . . aren't we already doing that?"

He shook his head. "I think you're confusing my work with existing gene therapy, where they use viruses to add genes onto existing chromosomes."

"Dr. Lawrence?" A young man in a lab coat approached with a sheaf of papers. "Sorry to interrupt, but Ronnie double-checked the data and got the same replication rate. That would mean—"

"Yes, I know. You want me to go over it?"

"I think you'd better."

Kip took the papers. "I'll do it tonight," he promised.

"Thanks." Flashing Taylor a curious glance, the man retreated.

"Another breakthrough?" Taylor asked with a smile.

"Another mathematical error, more likely," he said, steering her back toward his office. "Two steps forward, one step back." He paused. "What were we saying?"

"You were telling me about using viruses in gene therapy."

"And probably boring the hell out of you."

"No, I'm interested. Go on."

"Okay. The problems with using viruses to add genes to existing chromosomes are: One, the viruses can change the function of the chromosome. Two, they sometimes cause mutations. Three, the new genes don't always replicate as the cell divides, so you lose them. But my research seems to indicate that artificial chromosomes may bypass those problems. In fact, we've managed to replicate a few of our artificial chromosomes in culture for almost two months now."

"Sounds pretty impressive. Your father must be pleased," she added. Kip had often complained that his father, a wealthy, socially connected investment banker, had been disappointed by Kip's choice of medicine over a partnership with the family firm.

"Dad paid my tuition at Harvard Med," Kip said, "but he's never really made his peace with it."

Taylor turned back toward the busy men and women in lab coats. "You've been working here, how long?"

"Just over a year."

"You've been amazingly successful in just one year."

He smiled. "Emerson gives us excellent financial support. And I've been very lucky." He paused. "We've had our share of problems, of course. Publicity's good for fund-raising, but it also brings out the crazies. We were picketed for two weeks by some anti-gene-research group when the article in the *Times* came out; blocked the whole damned sidewalk. And a bomb threat last month—false, thank God."

"How awful."

Kip shrugged. "It seems to have died down for the moment."

"Excuse me, Dr. Lawrence." An intense man with spiky blond hair stood in the doorway. "You wanted these printouts?"

"Thanks, Sergei. Just drop them on the counter, will you?" As the man hurried away, Kip turned back to Taylor with a smile. "That 'Dr. Lawrence' was for you," he said. "Usually they call me Kip."

"You have a large staff for a new lab. And a lot of them look old enough to be post-docs."

Kip nodded. "I've been lucky there, too. My people are great. We're seventeen at the moment, and growing. In fact, we're adding someone next week. I get résumés from California, Boston, Toronto, Europe, the Pacific Rim. It's very flattering that so many talented people want to participate in my work."

"Modest as well as brilliant."

"Don't forget 'good-looking.' " He grinned at her and retrieved their coats from the hook behind his office door. "Hungry, too. I hope you are. There's a French place around the corner, if that's okay."

"Fine."

He held her coat, and she wriggled into it, inhaling the subtle, masculine scent of his expensive cologne. "God, it's wonderful to see you," he said. He stood for a moment, his hands resting lightly on her shoulders, then released her. "I'm really glad you called. We have a lot of catching up to do."

"More than you can imagine," Taylor replied, turning to face him, her eyes serious.

Kip studied her. "I heard rumors about . . ." He broke off.

"About my becoming a lush."

"I wouldn't have put it quite like that."

"*I* would," Taylor said. "It was pretty bad. But it's getting better. I can control it. At least, I think I can."

"Tell me about it over something with a cream sauce," he said kindly, and led her from the room.

Although the restaurant *was* just around the corner from Emerson's laboratory complex, Kip had obviously chosen it with care. From the richly paneled walls and expensive floral arrangements to the classic French menu and attentive staff, it bespoke money and taste. Of which, Taylor recalled, Kip had both.

"Something to drink, madam?"

"A ginger ale," said Taylor.

"I'll have the same," Kip said.

"Please don't feel you can't have a glass of wine because of me," Taylor said quickly.

"I never drink at lunch," he assured her. "Kills the rest of the work day."

The waiter arrived with menus, and they studied them in silence until the drinks arrived.

"To friendship," Taylor proposed.

"To friendship," Kip agreed. They clinked glasses and drank. "Now, why don't you tell me why you really called."

Taylor flushed. "I told you. I saw the article in the paper, and I thought how long it had been . . ."

"It *has* been a long time," Kip said. "But I still know you better than that."

Taylor sighed. "I need to ask your advice about something."

"Order the Chicken Divan."

"No, I'm serious. I think I'm about to be offered a job."

"Congratulations!"

"And I don't know whether or not to take it."

"How does it stack up against your other offers?"

"There *are* no other offers. Nobody else is willing to hire me."

"What would you be doing?"

"I'd be chief of cosmetic surgery. I'd get to do a lot of procedures. It's a chance to rebuild my confidence, my reputation. It's perfect."

"So what's the problem?"

"I'm afraid." Taylor took a deep breath. "I'm terrified I'll blow it."

Kip nodded. "You know, when I came to Emerson, I was a little nervous myself. They were putting so much money behind me, so much faith in what I could do. I know it's not the same," he said quickly as she started to protest, "but I can empathize." He paused. "You did strong work before. You can do strong work again."

"As long as I stay off the sauce."

"That's right. Can you?"

"I think so. But stress is what drove me beyond social drinking, once. What if it does again?"

"Look, Taylor. There's stress and there's stress. You had a rotten marriage—hell, I could see from the start that he was jealous of you—on top of which a surgical residency is not exactly compatible with any kind of personal life. After that, you were building a high-profile practice and trying to work things out with Paul. You were being pulled in a million directions at once. The stress in the OR was only part of the pressure you were feeling."

"Actually, the OR was the only place I *didn't* feel stressed out." She hesitated. "So you're saying it's different this time."

"I'm saying it could be, yes. Hell, everyone deserves a second chance. It's a dream job. I say go for it." He started to reach for a piece of bread, winced, and withdrew his hand.

"Something wrong?"

Flushing, Kip took a small vial from his jacket pocket and shook a pill into his palm. "It's nothing."

"Your hand is shaking. Are you ill?"

"Incipient ulcer," he said shortly. He popped the

pill in his mouth and washed it down with a swallow of ginger ale.

"Talk about stress," Taylor teased.

Kip shrugged, obviously unwilling to discuss it, then forced a smile. "Occupational hazard," he said lightly.

Their food came, and Taylor realized she was hungry. In her drinking days, she'd gotten into the habit of skipping breakfast, and although she tried not to do that anymore, a slice of toast was still about all she could manage.

"Guess I was right about the chicken," Kip said, watching her dig in.

"You were. It's delicious." She broke off a piece of crusty roll. "Let's talk about *your* life, for a change. Married? Divorced? Taking up skydiving? Running for President?"

He laughed. "I'm afraid my life is very dull these days." He hesitated. "Although there is this rather amazing thing that's just happened . . ."

"Yes?"

He put down his knife and fork. "I've been nominated for a Larrabee Award."

"A Larrabee! That's fabulous."

"It's not a done deal. I suspect it depends on how well my current research pans out. If we can expand our chromosome-building and increase our replication time . . . but it looks good." His eyes sparkled.

"That should please your dad."

Kip nodded. "Funny how the approval of one's parents still matters, even at our age." He paused. "Of course, I don't know who the other contenders are, so it's kind of hard to rate my chances. They keep the list very hush-hush—"

"I know who one of them is," Taylor said.

"You do? Who?"

"Sam Slater."

"Shit." Taylor stared at him. "You sure about that?" he asked her, frowning.

"He told me himself." She hesitated. "Do you know him?"

"He founded Greenvale Hospital, up in New Chatham," Kip said. "How do *you* know him?"

"I don't. That is, I only met him a couple days ago when he interviewed me. Didn't I tell you? Slater's the person I'd be working for. Chief of cosmetic surgery at Greenvale." She studied Kip. "Is there something I should know about him? About Greenvale?"

"No, not at all," he said quickly. "Take the job, by all means. It's just—the idea of a society doctor being nominated for a Larrabee doesn't sit well with me."

"Don't let him hear you call him that," Taylor said. "He's very defensive about his celebrity practice. And to be fair, Greenvale does operate a free clinic for the town's residents. Slater's doing some kind of research, too," she added. "Something to do with organ transplants."

Kip shrugged. "The Larrabee committee knows what it's doing, I suppose. Actually, I should be pleased." He grinned at her, his mood bright again. "If the rest of the competition is like Slater, I'll be a shoo-in."

The waiter took away their empty plates, and they ordered coffee.

"So you think I should take this job," Taylor said. "Assuming I'm offered it."

"Why not? It sounds like a great opportunity. And New Chatham's supposed to be a charming place."

"It is *now*. I grew up there, and believe me, it didn't used to be."

"So you're from New Chatham. Any problems going home again?"

"That's what Slater asked. No, my only concern is about small-town life generally. Privacy issues, things like that."

"Does Slater know about your drinking problem?"

Taylor nodded, impressed that Kip had immediately understood her worry. "He seems to be okay with it."

"Then it won't matter," he assured her. "People will take their cue from him." He set down his glass, and checked his watch. "I don't mean to be rude. It's just that I have an appointment at two o'clock that I can't miss." He frowned. "Not that I wouldn't *like* to. Never mind, we still have some time." He sipped his coffee. "If you get the job, when will you start?"

"Soon, I think. Slater's being pressured to do procedures again, and he doesn't want to."

"Why not?"

"Different priorities, he says. The point is, he needs somebody there yesterday. If he hires me, I'll have to start right away."

The bill came and Taylor reached for her handbag, but Kip shook his head. "I'll get this."

"But I called you."

"And I'm glad you did. But I'd like to treat. Besides," he added with a smile, "you're the one who's out of work."

"Not for long, I hope," Taylor replied. "But if you insist . . ."

"I do."

"Well, thank you."

"My pleasure. Really." He took out his wallet. "Let me know what happens with the job."

"I will."

"New Chatham real estate is still a good investment, so I hear," he mused. "I've been thinking about buying a weekend house. Maybe I'll come up and look around, see how you're getting on." He looked at her. "We could have dinner."

"I'd like that."

He reached across to put his platinum American Express credit card in the bill tray, and his hand brushed hers. Inadvertent or deliberate? she wondered.

Outside the restaurant, Kip hailed a cab and offered her a lift, but although the weather was cold, Taylor decided she felt like walking.

"Call me when you hear something," he told her, opening the taxi door.

"*If* I hear something."

"You will." He smiled warmly. "Don't sell yourself short." They looked at each other for a long moment. "If you're sure I can't drop you somewhere . . ." She shook her head. Kip folded himself into the taxi's narrow backseat and closed the door, turning back to look at her as the cab pulled away, his smile fading. It could be useful having Taylor Barnes in New Chatham, he thought; very useful indeed.

Taylor took her time, ambling along Madison Avenue, playing back the lunch in her mind. A thrill coursed through her as she thought of Kip's hand touching hers. Whoa, she told herself. Slow it down, kid. He's just a friend, remember? Besides, you need to save your psychic energy for the essentials: getting a job and staying sober. Everything else takes a backseat.

Still, a backseat could be a very interesting place.

It was nearly three o'clock. The blood had been drawn, the physical examination finished. The patient, dressed again in his street clothes, appeared in the doorway of the specialist's private office.

"Please come in," the specialist said, looking up from the chart on his desk.

The man dropped heavily into a chair. "It's getting worse, isn't it?"

The specialist nodded; they both knew the truth. "It's worsening, yes," he said cautiously.

"It's progressing faster than we expected. Isn't that right?"

"A little faster. But—"

"A lot faster. Don't lie to me, Dave. We've known each other too long for that."

The specialist sighed. "A lot faster, yes."

"How significant is that?" The specialist shrugged. "How much time do I have? Two years? Three?"

The specialist shook his head. "Six, eight months," he said softly. "A year at most."

The man rocked back as if physically assaulted. "Only a year? Are you sure?"

"At the most." The specialist hesitated. "I'm so sorry."

"A year. It's not enough."

"If there's anything I can do. For you personally, I mean—"

"I need more time," the man said.

"I wish I could give it to you."

"You don't understand," the man said angrily. "I need more time—" He broke off. "I'm sorry. I didn't mean to bark at you."

"Perfectly understandable under the circumstances."

"Dave?"

"Yes?"

"This is just between us, right? It's very important that nobody finds out."

"Of course. Doctor-patient confidentiality—"

"Not your wife, not your partner . . . nobody can know."

"Absolutely. I understand."

"No, you don't, but it doesn't matter." The man levered himself upright. "Thanks for everything. I'd better be getting back."

His brow furrowed with concern, the specialist rose, too. "Will you be all right?"

"Oh, yeah," the man said bitterly. "I'll be just fine."

The message light on her phone was blinking when Taylor got home. Slinging her parka over the back of a chair, she hurried over and pressed the playback button, her heart thumping.

"Dr. Barnes? This is Dr. Slater's secretary at Greenvale Hospital. Dr. Slater would like to discuss the terms of your employment here, and your start date."

Yes, Taylor thought fiercely. Yes.

"It's one-thirty now, and he has a two o'clock appointment out of the office. So I suggest you call back sometime after three." A phone number followed, and the machine clicked off.

Taylor checked her watch—two forty-five. Twenty minutes or so to wait. She hunted up the Post-it with Kip's number and dialed, eager to share the good news. Then she remembered that he, too, had a two o'clock appointment, and hung up again.

Go for it, he'd said. It's a dream job. But would she measure up? Was it too soon for her? Was it too late? Get a grip, she told herself firmly. You can do this. You want to do this. You *have* to do this.

God, I could use a little liquid courage right now, she thought; just a small one to keep my spirits up . . .

What you need right now, she told herself sternly, is a tall, cold celebratory glass of—club soda. Feeling shaky but virtuous, she headed for the kitchen.

The steaks were well aged, the potatoes smothered in sour cream, and the baked Alaska impressive. It wasn't the Ritz, and it wasn't dietarily sound, but it was the sort of menu the bankers of New Chatham preferred at their monthly luncheons. And these days, what the bankers wanted, the bankers got.

Calvin Mayhew, president of the recently formed bankers association, tapped on his wineglass with his fork. "Gentlemen," he said as the room quieted, "before we go back to our respective offices and pretend to get some work done this afternoon—" general light laughter "—I'd like to propose a toast." He raised his half-empty goblet. "I give you Donald Potter. A man with the vision to see a good thing and grab ahold of it!" More laughter, light applause. "More importantly, a man generous enough to cut his friends in." Loud applause, a few guffaws, several hear-hears.

Donald Potter smiled, rose, looked around him. "It's Garrison you should be thanking," he said. "I just did what my son told me to do." More laughter;

Donald Potter had never been one to follow any star but his own. "Although I would remind you," the banker continued, "that not everyone here was quite so enthusiastic in the beginning. You, Barry, and Ed over there."

"Yeah," Ed, a large, florid man, responded. "But after you kidnapped our wives and kids . . ." More laughter; Slater and Garrison's joint proposal for funding the building of Greenvale Hospital had been approved only after some serious arm wrestling.

"Well, that's all water over the bridge." A titter of laughter from those who got the weak joke. "Working together, we have created a new New Chatham, a town on the move. Prosperous. Famous. Growing."

"And providing an excellent return on our investment," Calvin chimed in, to prolonged applause.

"And so, gentlemen, let us raise our glasses to Samuel Slater," Donald Potter proclaimed, "and to the continued success of Greenvale Hospital."

Loud huzzahs and the clink of glasses, followed by the hush of bankers mentally counting their money.

Chapter Five

Kip sat, his chin in his hands, staring at the screen of the imaging microscope.

Two weeks had passed since his lunch with Taylor and her subsequent acceptance of the position at Greenvale. Twice during the few days before her hurried relocation, they'd tried to fit their schedules together and failed. Now she was eighty miles away, and from the sound of things, the only way he'd see her was if he held to his promise of making a trip to New Chatham.

Which, much as he wanted to, would be difficult, especially since he was already scheduled to be out of the lab for two days next week. The real possibility of a Larrabee gave his research priority, and projects like his didn't end on Fridays at five p.m. Nor did they start at ten in the morning, which was why he and most of his research team were already hard at work at eight this morning.

"Coffee, Kip?" Ronnie stood behind him, the communal coffeepot in one hand, a small tray in the other.

"Yes, thank you," he said in halting Mandarin, turning away from the monitor screen.

The pretty Chinese research assistant laughed. "You're getting better," she said. Although she'd only recently arrived in the United States, her charmingly accented English was far better than the few words of Mandarin she'd taught him.

The imaging microscope was housed in an open cubicle along one side of the lab. Turned as he was, Kip could see several other researchers sipping from paper cups. "That was nice of you, Ronnie," he told her in English.

"My pleasure." She filled one of the paper cups and placed it near his elbow. "Don't knock it over," she admonished. "Milk? Sugar?"

"Both." He added milk from the carton on the tray, then took two sugar packets and a stirrer. "Thanks again."

"No problem. Hey, Frances? Coffee?" Retrieving the tray, the Chinese woman moved off.

Kip ripped open one of the small packets and stirred sugar into the hot brown liquid. He lifted it to his lips, but feeling the steam against his face, set it down again. Better let it cool a little. He turned to the screen, almost knocking the coffee over onto the keyboard with his elbow. Shit, he thought, that's all I need, and moved the cup well back on the table alongside the monitor.

Kip was famous for his tendency to become totally absorbed in his work. Colleagues often teased him that earthquakes could rock the lab, the building could be on fire, but Kip would remain oblivious.

Which was why his coffee sat half hidden behind the monitor, congealed and forgotten. And why it took him so long to realize what was going on behind him.

The sounds reached him slowly, seeping into his consciousness. His fingers paused on the keyboard, he frowned, he turned around.

Sergei was throwing up in his wastebasket.

Kip rose, immediately concerned. "You okay?" he asked, then felt stupid. Of course the man wasn't okay; he was sick as hell. "What's wrong?" he asked, then realized the lab was nearly deserted. "Where is everybody?"

"All sick." Ronnie approached, looking shaken.

"Gene and Arthur and Pat . . . They're all in the bathroom. Everybody who . . . oh, God . . . everybody who drank the coffee. I'm so sorry."

"Sorry? Why?"

"It was me who took the coffee around, remember? But I didn't make it, Kip, I swear. The pot was already filled." She hesitated. "You think the milk might have been bad?"

"Did everyone who got sick have milk in their coffee?"

"No, not everyone." She frowned. "How do *you* feel?"

"Fine." Kip glanced behind him. "I didn't drink any coffee," he said. "I forgot it was there. How about you?"

"I didn't have any, either. The coffee ran out."

"Sergei?" Kip went and put a hand on the man's shoulder. "How you doing, buddy?"

"Better." But the scientist was very pale. "I think it's passing—" Suddenly he doubled over, clutching his stomach. His eyes widened, and he struggled from his chair. Still holding his abdomen, he hurried off in the direction of the lavatory.

Kip looked at Ronnie. "They all have the same symptoms?" he asked.

"They seem to, yes. Vomiting, diarrhea, stomach pains . . ." Tears stood in her eyes.

"It's not your fault," Kip told her. "Something must have been accidentally contaminated. The sugar packets, or the coffee . . . Or maybe the milk *was* bad."

Tom and Gene returned from the bathroom, pale and unsteady. "I will *never* drink coffee again," Gene declared, falling into a chair.

"Better let me take a look at you." Kip did a quick exam, palpating the man's stomach, checking his pulse and his pupils. Nothing unusual. "How do you feel now?"

"Weak," Gene said. "But a lot better."

"It was intense," Tom said. "But it passed quickly."

"Mind if I look you over?"

"Go ahead."

Tom, too, checked out.

Slowly, the remainder of the nine affected staffers straggled back from the rest rooms, shaken but recovering.

"What do you think it was?" Tom asked.

"Could have been anything," Kip said. "Something in the storage closet could have leaked into the sugar packets . . ."

"But we don't store lab chemicals in there," Gene said.

"Perhaps one of the cleaning staff spilled cleaning solution on them," Sergei offered.

"Or something got into the coffeepot by accident," Pat suggested.

"Whatever it was, we don't have to worry about it anymore," Ronnie announced, reentering the lab. "I threw everything out. The milk, the coffee, the sugar, the unused cups. I collected everybody's used cups, too. I bagged everything and put it down the trash chute. And I washed the coffeepot about a million times. I'm really sorry, guys. How could I know . . . ?"

"Nobody blames you, Ronnie," said Pat kindly.

"Thanks, Pat."

"Hell, you've had a week to poison us," Gene teased her. "You wouldn't wait this long."

"Well, I'm glad you're feeling better." Ronnie looked around at her lab mates. "They say coffee's good for settling the stomach. Anybody want a cup?"

Sergei groaned, Pat told her she was nuts, and Gene balled up some paper and threw it at her.

"Just kidding, guys," she said.

Slowly, people settled down and the work resumed. Kip went back to the microscope screen, typed in an instruction, then stopped. At the back of the work-table, shielded from view by the monitor, sat a cup of cold coffee. He rose and went to the storage cabinet, removed several glass test tubes with stoppers, and slipped them into his pocket. He returned to the microscope workstation and, working quickly, his back to the room, filled each vial with coffee and shoved the stoppers home. Placing the used cup in the wastebasket beneath the table, he palmed the tubes and carried them to his office, where he tucked them inside a manila envelope. Tonight, after everyone else had left, he'd pack them up properly and send them for analysis.

He slid the envelope into a desk drawer and stood up, glancng idly out of his office window at the drizzle that had begun to fall. A flash of color caught his eye, bright against the grayness. Frowning, he watched a woman in a red shawl scurry along the sidewalk. He couldn't read the placard she carried, but he'd lay odds as to what it said. The woman turned and looked up at the window where he stood, and Kip instinctively drew back. Feeling a little silly, he moved to the window again in time to see her disappear around the corner. So the protesters were back.

Frowning, he glanced toward the drawer that held the vials of coffee. There was no way the woman could have gotten inside the lab, was there? No, of course not, he decided. Still, it was a very unsettling thought.

Chapter Six

Taylor swam slowly up from a deep sleep, fumbling for the shrilling clock, feeling around for the bedside lamp. Nothing seemed to be where it was supposed to be. She peered into the darkness, thoroughly disoriented, then remembered where she was. Her new condominium home.

She glanced at the clock's lighted dial and fell back against the pillows again, closing her eyes. Six in the morning: too damn early. Why in hell had the alarm gone off at this hour? She rarely got up before eight, these days. There was no reason—

With one swift movement she was out of bed, her feet on the carpet, her heart pounding, horrified at how close she'd come to going back to sleep. Today was her first surgical procedure at Greenvale Hospital. She was due in the OR at seven.

She found the light switch and flicked it on, pausing for a moment to look around. The condo rental was expensive, and the bedroom was well furnished and decorated, although the pink and green color scheme was a little much for her taste. The living room downstairs was better, mostly beiges and creams, the polished floors set off by softly patterned area rugs.

The bathroom, tiled in a pale pink, was en suite. She showered quickly and returned to the bedroom. The last of the still-to-be-unpacked cartons were pushed against the wall under one of the windows, and she leaned across them to peek between the lattices of the Levolor blinds. Streetlights, set far apart, glowed in the darkness. Nothing was moving, and no lights showed in any of the windows of the houses across the way. She let the slat drop and began to dress. It wasn't New York City, that was for sure.

The gray Lexus she'd hurriedly leased was waiting in the freestanding garage. Using her remote control, she keyed the garage door open. Tossing her medical bag and coat onto the car's rear seat, she got in and drove out into a new day that thought it was still an old night.

She parked in her assigned spot in the underground hospital garage and took the elevator up to the second floor, where most of the physicians' offices were. The hospital seemed much calmer than she was used to hospitals being, even at this early hour, and the emergency room was weirdly silent, dramatic proof that she'd truly left the Big Apple behind.

In her office, she hung up her coat, locked her handbag away, and checked her desk and phone for messages, then headed down the hall again toward the elevator that would take her up to the OR suites on the third floor.

"Dr. Barnes?"

She turned. Garrison Potter was hurrying down the hall toward her.

"You're here early," she said with a smile.

"It's surprising how much work you can get done when the phones don't ring," he replied. "You've got Mrs. Lacey this morning, I understand."

"Right." She stabbed at the elevator call button.

"Well . . ." He hesitated. Slater was still refusing to tell him about that mysterious problem he'd referred to, saying he preferred the staff get comfortable with Taylor first; after that, it wouldn't matter. Now Garrison studied her carefully. Irene Lacey was an important personage. If Barnes screwed up—

The elevator arrived. "This is me," Taylor said, getting in. "See you around."

"I'll ride up with you." He followed her into the elevator.

Taylor hit the button for "three," then looked over at him. "Don't worry," she said with a confidence she only partly felt—it had been a long time since she'd performed surgery completely sober—"I've done this procedure a hundred times."

"Was it that obvious?"

"Yes, but that's okay. I'm the new girl, after all."

The elevator door opened and Taylor stepped out. Garrison put his hand out to stop the door from closing. "What time do you think you'll finish?"

Taylor considered. "Between eleven and eleven-thirty would be my guess."

"Well, how about my buying you an early lunch? To celebrate your first case here?"

"Sure. That would be nice."

"Good. I'll come by your office around noon." The door slid closed.

As Taylor put on the blue surgical scrubs for the first time in seven months, her old self-assurance returned. This was what she loved, what she had always loved, from her first surgical rotation as a medical student. She felt strong and confident. She went through to the sink area to scrub in. I'm back, she exulted. I'm back where I belong.

"I'm afraid it's not up to New York standards," Garrison apologized as they opened their menus, "but the chef did train there. His New American dishes are particularly good."

"The chili shrimp sounds good," Taylor said. "Especially in this weather." Beyond the large picture window at the front of the restaurant, a light snow was beginning to fall.

"Oh, it's excellent," he assured her. "I eat here a lot," he continued. "Partly because it's the best place

in town, but also because I feel as if I have a vested
interest in its success."

"Oh?"

"As soon as I heard Trevor was looking for financing to start his own place, I told my father to back
him."

"Is your father in the restaurant business?" Taylor
asked.

Garrison laughed. "He's in the everything business.
He's a banker. He provided loans to half the new
businesses in this town. Greenvale Hospital, too. He's
the first person Sam and I approached for funding."

"I'm surprised a Boston banker would invest in
New Chatham," Taylor said, thinking, Sam and I?

Garrison looked surprised. "Boston?"

"I thought you were from Boston."

"I am, yes. But my dad lives here." Seeing Taylor's
confusion, he explained. "My folks were divorced
when I was small, and I stayed in Boston with my
mom. Dad was working for Citibank at the time, and
he decided to go international. Did very well, too. He
ran the Far East out of Singapore for fifteen years,
then they sent him to New York to head the corporate
division worldwide. About ten years ago, he decided
he'd made his pile, and he wanted a bank of his own.
He'd made up his mind to stay in the northeast, but
a New York City acquisition was out of the question,
of course. So he did some research, looked around,
and ended up buying First Federal here in New
Chatham."

The waiter arrived. "What are you drinking?" Garrison asked Taylor. "The house white is excellent. Or
we could look at the wine list."

"Just a Coke, thanks."

He smiled. "You're not doing any more surgery
today. I checked."

"Soda will be fine."

"Really? I thought all you sophisticated New York-
ers drank wine at lunch."

"Not all of us," Taylor said lightly.

"Suit yourself," Garrison said, and ordered the pinot grigio, pointedly addressing the waiter by name. "You really ought to taste it," he told her when the drinks arrived. "So you'll know for next time, when you're in a more festive mood." And he pushed the wine toward her.

Taylor took a deep breath. "Please don't be embarrassed," she said, "but I'm a recovering alcoholic." Seeing him flush, she added, "I take it Sam didn't tell you."

"No." Wine sloshed onto the tablecloth as he hastened to retrieve the glass. So that was the problem Sam had alluded to, Garrison thought. Christ; he hoped the old man knew what he was doing. Although she did appear to have it under control. "I *am* embarrassed," he told Taylor. "I never would have suggested—"

"Please. It's okay. I just thought, since we're going to be working together, you ought to know."

He nodded. "I guess life in the fast lane can do that to you," he said, and instantly regretted it.

"Fast lane?" She frowned.

"I meant your being a celebrated New York City cosmetic surgeon. Look, none of this is coming out right." He sighed. "Let's start over."

Taylor smiled at him. "From where you ply me with wine?"

"From where I welcome you to the Greenvale family." He raised his glass. "Here's to you, Dr. Barnes. I'm glad you're with us."

"Thank you."

They sipped their respective drinks. "I suppose Sam told you we have another New Chathamite at Greenvale?"

"Peter Ohlmeyer, cardiothoracic; yes."

"You know him?"

"Hardly. I was only a teenager when I went off to college. Ohlmeyer's what, sixty or so?" She took a roll from the basket and broke off a piece. "Although I

keep feeling that there's something about him I ought
to remember." She frowned, beset by an uneasy sensa-
tion that whatever it was, it wasn't very pleasant. "I
suppose I should find him and say hello."

"I believe he's away this week on personal business," Garrison said. "But you're bound to run into
him sooner or later. Unfortunately."

"I take it you don't like him much."

"Nobody does. Please don't repeat that," he added
quickly. "Sam's a big fan of his. Of course, Ohlmeyer
isn't nearly as abrasive with Sam as he is with the rest
of us."

"I see." Hospital politics, Taylor thought; I will not
be drawn into them.

"I hear the Lacey procedure went very well," Garrison said quickly, sensing her thought. "Sam's been
singing your praises."

"It was pretty straightforward," Taylor said modestly, but he could tell she was pleased.

The waiter appeared again to take their order, and
Garrison studied Taylor from behind his menu. Intelli-
gent *and* attractive, he thought. Great hair, nice
clothes. Good mind. The first woman in this town
who's classy enough for me to take seriously. I wonder
if she's seeing anyone.

Amused, Taylor pretended not to notice him checking her out. Despite his stuffiness and his drive to
impress, she found Garrison oddly appealing. There
was a certain puppy-dog quality to his eagerness to
make sure that she noticed his French cuffs, that she
realized what movers and shakers he and his father
were. And he was obviously no dummy. The restaurant was packed; he'd been right to get his father to
back it. And if he'd really been responsible for bringing Greenvale Hospital to New Chatham, he had
every reason to be pleased with himself.

"So you went to Harvard," she said.

"Harvard Business School. How did you guess?" he
asked, looking pleased.

"The tie you wore, when we met in Sam's office."

"Oh." A look of disappointment flashed across his face.

"I'm impressed," Taylor told him. She wasn't, particularly, but it was obviously what he wanted to hear. "And you met Sam at Boston General?"

"That's right. We hit it off right away. Despite our different backgrounds."

"He didn't go to Harvard?" Taylor asked wickedly, then felt guilty. Taking the mickey out of Garrison was like shooting fish in a barrel.

But he didn't seem to notice. "Sam couldn't afford a place like Harvard," he said seriously. "He worked his way through the state university. Through medical school, too. He came from nothing, but look what's he's accomplished. I admire him for that."

Their food arrived, carefully prepared and beautifully presented. "I have enormous respect for Sam," Garrison said, slicing into a grilled Portobello mushroom. "As a professional, as a businessman, as a visionary. Consider what he's done for this town."

"What the two of you have done."

"Oh, I just pointed him toward the financing," Garrison said, suddenly modest.

"And he made you his chief financial officer."

"Yes. One of the great things about Sam is, once he trusts your abilities, he lets you run."

"So I've noticed," Taylor said. "I was pleased that he didn't scrub in with me on Lacey. Although he did insist on reviewing the photos with me beforehand, and he wanted a full debriefing afterward."

"Not surprising when you consider how important a happy Irene Lacey is to this hospital. But you'll have plenty of autonomy when he gets to know you better. Which he will, with all the procedures you've got coming up; Reardon, Kenneson . . ."

"You're keeping track of my schedule?" Taylor smiled.

"Absolutely. Every satisfied customer has referral

potential. I have big plans for the future of Greenvale,"
he continued enthusiastically, his food cooling on his
plate. "A major institutional fund-raising program, an
expansion of the hospital's physical plant . . ." He
broke off. "Sorry. I get a little intense sometimes. But
it's unusual for me to find someone my own age whom
I can talk to, in this town. Someone smart, who's involved in the same industry."

"I wouldn't call medicine an industry, exactly—"

Garrison waved a dismissive hand. "You know what
I mean." He picked up his fork, put it down again.
"Do you think we could have dinner together some-
time? Maybe go to a movie?"

"That sounds like fun," Taylor said carefully. "I
could use a friend in this town. It's been years since
I lived here, and I don't know a soul. Yes, I'd like us
to be friends."

Friends, Garrison thought; she must be seeing someone. He wondered who it could be. Well, he could
use a friend, too. And who knew where friendship
could lead?

"Deal," he said.

"Dr. Barnes."

"Taylor? It's Mom."

"Oh, hi, Mom. I got your message. I was going to
call you tonight."

"Well, now you don't have to. Your father and I
were just wondering how you're settling in. Does it
feel strange to be back?"

"Not really. The town's so different now."

"And how's the job going?"

"Pretty well, I think. I did my first surgery today.
It felt great to be back in the OR."

"That's wonderful, dear. We're both so glad. And
you're . . . all right?"

"Clean and sober. How are you and Dad?"

"We're both fine dear. I'll let you get back to work
now. We just wanted to say hi."

"I love you, Mom. And give Dad a hug for me."
"We love you, too, dear. And, Taylor?"
"Yes?"
"We're both very proud of you."

Chapter Seven

He paid off the taxi and did the last four and a half blocks on foot. Cheng's instructions had been very specific, as always, and it would have been foolish, perhaps even suicidal, to disobey. The elderly Chinese billionaire spoke quietly, but his calm demeanor concealed a ruthlessness verging on cruelty that was still legendary in the Hong Kong he'd left in 1995, two years ahead of the British.

The man strolled past smoked ducks hanging from hooks, outdoor bins filled with strange tuberous vegetables, an ornate cinema showing an old Bruce Lee film. San Francisco's Chinatown was a major tourist attraction, and he gazed at the scene around him, trying to appear a casual visitor. But his step was a little too purposeful, his expression a little too focused.

At the end of the tourist section, he turned one corner, then another, and found himself in a drab and narrow working-class street. A little way along, he stopped at a nondescript flat-fronted building, its windows opaque, its steel door a riot of Chinese graffiti. A small plaque identified it as the office of the Formosa Trading Company. Not, by all appearances, a particularly profitable enterprise.

To one side of the door was a lock plate, red alert light glowing warningly, to the other, a push-button intercom with a small video camera mounted above it. He pressed the intercom button. "It's Forewing," he said.

"Please do come in, Forewing."

Did he detect a faint note of derision in the Chinese voice with the British accent that bade him enter? He'd always felt Cheng had been laughing up his silken sleeve when he'd insisted the non-Chinese members use Chinese code names. The movie mogul had been dubbed "Kung Wu," although his real name was well-known to them all, and Cheng had given the much-photographed European princess the code name "Lop-yen." Both had wealth beyond avarice, yet they had meekly agreed. Such was the power of quiet Mr. Cheng.

The security plate light changed from bloodred to bilious green, and the man known as Forewing pushed through the door and mounted the dingy, poorly lighted stairs. At the second-floor landing, another lock light glowed. As he approached, it too changed color, accompanied by a loud click signaling the unlocking of the plain metal door set flat into the rust-stained wall.

Beyond the door was another world.

An antique Chinese carpet, deep-piled and subtly colored, covered the polished floor of the entrance gallery. Heavily lined drapes of creamy silk masked the windows of the luxurious room beyond, in which priceless furniture, centuries old, gleamed with lacquer and polish.

Cheng's bulky Chinese manservant-cum-bodyguard stood aside as "Forewing" entered. "Good afternoon, Fong," Forewing said with punctilious courtesy, acutely aware that Fong could kill him with one quick jab of his stiffened hand—and would, should Cheng order it. Fong bowed slightly but didn't reply. An orphan, rescued by Cheng as a child from the back alleys of Hong Kong, Fong was a mute.

Kung Wu and Lop-yen were already seated on low cushioned chairs set around the ornately carved table on which delicate jade-green porcelain dishes were set out in anticipation of the banquet that would eventually follow. Cheng, resplendent in a black and silver ceremonial robe, his long shining silver hair tied back in a ponytail, extended his arms, and the wide sleeves opened like the wings of a giant butterfly.

"Sorry I'm late," Forewing said.

"Of course you are," Cheng agreed pleasantly. "You followed my instructions?"

"As always," Forewing answered.

Cheng nodded. "Please to sit. There, next to the lovely Lop-yen." The princess smiled at Forewing, who lowered himself into the chair beside her. "So. We are ready to begin," Cheng said softly. He nodded at Fong, who glided swiftly from the room.

Cheng settled himself in his own chair, higher than the others, and clasped his hands in front of him. "Thank you for your presence here today. To heighten our powers of concentration, we will, as always, start with a short period of meditation. I have always believed that meditation is more effective on an empty stomach. As is the consideration of business matters. Therefore, no food or drink will be served until after we have finished. Kindly close your eyes." He reached for the tiny gold bell beside his plate and rang it once.

The first time he'd attended one of these meetings, Forewing had been rather amused at this practice of Cheng's. But he soon found that he enjoyed the feelings of intense calm and heightened awareness that invariably followed.

Cheng led them through the ten-minute meditation, signaling its end by ringing the gold bell.

"Now we are ready to deal with the business at hand," he said. "Forewing? Perhaps you would be good enough to report on your progress to date."

"It would be my pleasure," Forewing replied formally. "My research results are very promising. There is still much work to do, of course, but I am very hopeful . . ." He trailed off.

"Hope is not enough," Cheng said. "What I require is the fulfillment of hope."

"That's what I'm after, too," Forewing said quickly. More than you know, he thought. "And, as I said, the research is very promising." Cheng was still scowling. "It's so promising," Forewing added, "that I'm being considered for a Larrabee Award. Very prestigious."

"Fool!" Cheng spat. "You show our work to the world?"

My work, old man, Forewing thought. "No, of course not," he said aloud. "The research is the key to what we hope to do, but it's also useful in other, more public ways. No one will suspect."

"You are sure of this?"

"Absolutely. And a Larrabee will bring more research grants. Money to finance our work."

"Money is not an issue," Cheng told him, but Forewing could practically see the man's brain churning. Cheng's attitude toward money was simple: No matter how many billions a man had, he could always use a couple more. "So the research goes well. And the women I have provided? They are satisfactory?"

"Yes," Forewing said. "They're fine."

"Good. Should you need more, or wish to replace them with others, you will please tell me."

"Thank you, Mr. Cheng."

Cheng turned his attention to Kung Wu. "Please favor us with a recruitment update."

"Even better than we expected." The slim, sandy-haired mogul spoke with the confidence of a man in possession of eleven Oscars, an open prescription for Viagra, and a beach house in Malibu that had not yet fallen into the sea. "Nearly two hundred and climbing."

"And the, um, process?"

Kung Wu shrugged. "As good as can be expected. Given the current technology," he added, glancing over at Forewing, who bristled.

Cheng smiled. A little competition among the ranks

was no bad thing. Impassively he turned to question Lop-yen.

Forewing had ceased to listen. The others played important roles, of course. But it was his own discoveries that were allowing them to do what they did. And it was his ongoing research that would eventually enable them to do it better. Much better.

Some twenty minutes later, business concluded, Cheng again rang his little bell. Fong entered, carrying a painted tray on which stood an unlabeled bottle of unusual design and four delicate cups of gold-laced crystal. Fong placed the tray gently on the low table in front of Cheng, bowed, and withdrew.

Reverently, Cheng drew the bottle toward him. The cork had already been loosened, and he pulled it free without a sound. He poured a thimbleful of pale wine into each of the crystal cups, then handed them around the table. Only Forewing knew what they were about to taste, its rarity, its monumental cost.

Cheng raised his cup, and the others followed suit. "To hope."

"To hope," they echoed.

Cheng smiled. "And also to us, my friends." He tilted his glass, and a shaft of sunlight flashed through the fabled Chinese wine, striping his face with a rainbow of reflected color. "May you live a thousand years."

Chapter Eight

Taylor stood staring out of the picture window, sipping a cup of cranberry tea. With no procedures that day, she'd treated herself to a late start; her first in-hospital meeting, with a potential patient, was at eleven, her first clinic appointment, at three.

A late February thaw had set in, washing away the last in a series of snowfalls and drenching the sidewalk in front of her town house complex with lawn runoff. The sun was bright, the sky a hopeful blue. Equally hopeful, Taylor decided to forsake her down jacket for a dark wool coat.

She went to the kitchen and rinsed out the cup, placing it neatly in the drying rack. Back in her drinking days, cups and glasses would pile up in the kitchen sink for days on end. Six months sober and counting, she thought. It wasn't so long ago that six months sober would have seemed an impossibility.

She retrieved some files from the den, feeling pleased with her progress. Once again, life had at least the potential for being good. She was very glad she'd come to Greenvale, although New Chatham itself felt a little strange at times. Many places she remembered from childhood had been gentrified and housed new occupants, but they were still evocative. Occasionally she saw a face she recognized but couldn't place. And, although most of the townspeople were newcomers, several people from her past had come up and introduced themselves: a grade-school classmate, a former friend of her mother's. As predicted, she'd run into Peter Ohlmeyer, the cardiothoracic chief. He'd been lunching with Sam Slater in the hospital cafeteria, and Sam had called her over and introduced them. Still unable to bring forth the memory that tickled in the back of her mind, she'd smiled and held out her hand. He'd taken it in a firm grip and given her a restrained smile as he brushed back his shaggy white hair with surprisingly thick and stubby fingers and peered at her through steel-rimmed spectacles, the barest hint of a question in his eyes. I must ask Mom if she remembers anything about him, Taylor had thought and then promptly forgot all about it.

She packed the files into her briefcase. It felt good to be working again. The hospital staff had taken a wait-and-see attitude at first, but once she'd proven herself in the OR, they seemed happy to have her there. She'd found the OR nurses especially nice. Professional, too. Yesterday's facial reconstruction had been long and complicated, but the team had done strong work. She decided to pick up some muffins at Starbucks and leave them at the nurses' station for everyone.

Carrying the briefcase, she got her wool coat from the hall closet and put it on, then dug her leather gloves out of the pockets of her down jacket. Today felt like it was going to be a good one.

She stepped out onto the brick landing in front of the door and turned back to lock it, juggling her briefcase and gloves while fumbling with the two sets of keys. She was attempting to replace the house keys in her bag when they slipped from her hand, hitting a corner of the top stair and ricocheting onto the walk below.

With a sigh, Taylor went down the two brick steps to the walk, pausing as she felt an odd rocking under her shoe. She knelt and retrieved the keys, then examined the stair. Yes, one of the bricks was loose. She'd have to tell the managing agent, she thought, wiggling it. Someone could trip. She pulled a little harder, twisting slightly. Perhaps she could reposition the brick more safely until someone came to fix it. All at once the brick came away in her hand.

There was something underneath.

She leaned closer. A cavity had been hollowed out beneath where the brick had been. In it lay a small, carved figure. She drew it out and gasped. Obviously female, with long, tawny hair and carefully painted features, it was dressed in a miniature set of surgeon's scrubs. A knife was stuck through the figure's back.

Feeling suddenly cold, she shoved the brick back in position and stood up, the figure still in her hand. The knife was real, and sharp. Careful not to touch the haft, she placed the figure, still impaled by the knife, inside her briefcase.

Maybe it wasn't going to be such a terrific day after all. Well, she'd dealt with harassment before, she reminded herself. She could deal with it again.

On her way to becoming a cosmetic surgeon, Taylor had experienced a range of discrimination, both subtle and obvious. Surgery was traditionally a boy's club, and most of her medical school supervisors had tried to discourage her choice of the specialty, citing the rigor, the stress, the masculinity of the training environment. Surgical residency programs strongly favored male applicants while just as strongly denying such favoritism. Throughout her five-year general surgical residency and two-year plastic surgery residency, not all her fellow residents had been supportive. But she knew what she wanted, and developed a thick skin. When some joker stole a penis from the autopsy room and slipped it inside the pocket of her lab coat, she'd casually pulled it out, waved it around, and asked whether someone had lost something. She liked to think that such experiences had made her stronger. They'd certainly hardened her determination to be the best damn cosmetic surgeon in the program, and the most successful one afterwards.

Her initial shock at finding the knifed figure beneath the brick was quickly turning to feelings of anger and resentment she'd thought were behind her. So somebody in town didn't like female surgeons, she thought. Well, screw 'em.

Starbucks was crowded, as it always was at that hour, and that helped restore a sense of normalcy. Still, the clerk had to ask her for her order twice before she heard him.

"Two cranberry muffins, three pumpkin, two apple-raisin," she told him.

"You want those to go?"

Taylor rolled her eyes. In a better mood, she would have been tempted to tell him no, she'd eat them here, but all she said was "Yes."

"Taylor? Taylor Barnes?" Taylor turned. A dark-haired woman in a long black skirt, her loose-fitting nubby-weave blouse set off by a large silver and turquoise necklace and a sweeping scarf, waved at her from a nearby table, her silver bracelets jangling merrily. "See, Ben?" The woman turned to the beefy, pale-haired man seated across from her. "I told you it was Taylor."

Taylor had no idea who the two people were, but she smiled perfunctorily and turned back to pay for her muffins, then started for the door.

The woman stood and intercepted her. "Olive Erbach," she told Taylor. "And this is Ben. Guess we've changed. But not as much as you," she added, laughing.

Ben Erbach . . . The name sounded sort of familiar, but Taylor still couldn't place it.

"I taught chemistry at New Chatham High," the man said almost apologetically. "Wouldn't expect you to remember me, it's been so long. But you were one of my best students. I always said you were destined for medicine."

"Dr. Erbach. Of course," Taylor exclaimed, remembering the chunky blond man who had taught one of her favorite subjects. He certainly *had* changed. "Are you still teaching?"

"Oh, yes, indeed. I do the odd bit of research, too. You should see our new science labs."

"I never had the pleasure of teaching you," Olive chimed in. "At least, I don't recall . . ."

"Olive teaches art," Ben explained. "I seem to remember she joined the staff at the start of your senior year." He smiled at Olive. "That's how we met."

"Come and sit with us," Olive said eagerly. "We'd love to hear all about what you've been doing."

"Maybe just for a minute," Taylor said, sliding into a chair. The warmth of their welcome was comforting after finding her murdered effigy.

"Ben was so pleased to hear you'd come back home," Olive told her. "We've been meaning to call you."

"How are your parents?" Ben asked.

"Fine. They live in Santa Fe now."

"Oh, I love Santa Fe," Olive enthused, fingering her necklace. "It's so . . . artistic."

"So what's it like, coming home again?" Ben asked.

"A little strange sometimes," Taylor admitted, "but fine. The work at the hospital is going well." She paused. "Everything's changed so much."

"That's certainly true," Ben said. "In some ways, it was kind of sad to see the old places go out of business. But," he added, brightening, "Starbucks is a vast improvement over the greasy spoon that used to be here."

"There's been so much new construction," Taylor said. "Although the Rockingham place looks as grim as ever. But that big open lot down near Eddie's— Chatham Cove Marina, I mean—is all condominiums now."

"Is that where you're staying?" Ben asked.

"No, I'm in a complex just off West Lake Road," Taylor said.

"I know where you mean," Olive said. "It's new; built last year. You like it there?"

"It's okay." Taylor thought of the carved figure in her briefcase and frowned. "At least it was, until this morning."

"What happened this morning?" Olive asked solicitously. Seeing Taylor hesitate, she added, "Why don't you tell us? Maybe we can help."

"Someone left me a little gift," Taylor said slowly. "Under the front steps." She took the figure from her briefcase and set it on the table.

Ben drew back, and Olive's eyes opened wide. "What the hell is that?" she exclaimed, reaching for it.

"Careful," Taylor warned. "The knife is very sharp."

Olive examined the figure carefully. "It's like . . . a voodoo doll or something. You say you found it under your front step?"

"One of the bricks was loose. It was underneath."

Olive nodded to herself. "That's where they'd put it," she said. She looked up at Taylor. "Under the steps to your house. To make you go away."

"What? Who would?"

"Someone who wished you harm."

Ben took the figure from Olive's hands. "Don't listen to her," he told Taylor firmly. "It's probably just some prankster."

"I figured it was a bit of harassment by someone who didn't like women surgeons," Taylor said. "I've experienced that before. Although nothing quite like this," she added with a weak smile.

"That's probably it," Ben agreed.

But Olive shook her head. "We've all heard the rumors, Ben. Don't deny it."

"I've heard them, but I don't believe them," Ben said stoutly. "Cults, spells . . . I'm a scientist. I don't

buy any of that shit. And you shouldn't, either," he
told Taylor firmly. "Don't scare her like that, Olive."

Olive sighed. "Ben's probably right," she conceded.
"It's just . . . there are a lot of people in this town
who don't like the hospital being here, don't like the
changes it's brought. Sometimes they get . . . violent."

"Sam—Dr. Slater—mentioned the protests. He said
Maggie Kay McCormick is one of the leaders."

"Maggie McCormick their leader?" Olive scoffed.
"Now, that *is* silly. You know Maggie, Ben. She
couldn't lead the way to the bathroom." Ben
shrugged. "Anyway," she continued, "the point I'm
trying to make is that these people can be dangerous."

"To me? I didn't bring Greenvale to New
Chatham."

"No, but you're helping to keep it here. You're
doing surgery, bringing in money to keep the hospital
going. Some people might not like that."

"So they put voodoo dolls under her front step?"
said Ben incredulously. "Come on, Olive. If those people really wanted to do Taylor harm, they'd go right
for the jugular. They wouldn't mess around with
dolls."

"Well, it could be a warning," Olive said. "Of things
to come."

Taylor shivered.

"Nonsense," Ben retorted. "This is just some silly
prank. The best thing you can do, Taylor, is to put it
out of your mind." Picking up the effigy, he went to
a large covered trash bin by the counter and thrust
the figure deep down into the soggy mess. "That takes
care of that," he announced, returning to the table.
"Drink up, Olive. I have a class in fifteen minutes."

"Are you sure that was wise?" Taylor asked, staring
indecisively at the trash bin. "Maybe I should have
shown it to the police."

Ben shrugged. "I can get it out again if you want,"
he offered. "But why give whoever put it there the
satisfaction of taking it seriously? Damn pranksters."

"Ben's probably right," said Olive. She swallowed the last of her coffee and stood up. "Just put it out of your mind." She embraced Taylor warmly. "It was wonderful to see you. And you will come to dinner soon, I hope?" she added, releasing her. "I'll call you."

Ben gave Taylor a thumbs-up. "Hang in there," he said, helping Olive on with her coat.

With a jangle of jewelry, they were gone.

Chapter Nine

The black-clad figure crept along the darkened hallway, a small satchel slung over one shoulder. Stepping carefully around the large canisters that lined the walls, the intruder headed for the red and white glow of an exit sign, pausing at the door to ease it open. A dimly lit flight of cement steps led upward. The figure ran lightly up the first flight, then hesitated. From the darkened hallway beyond the landing came the sound of voices. The intruder stepped back against the wall in position to be hidden by the door, should it open. The voices slowly receded down the corridor; the landing door remained closed. With visible relief, the figure continued up the stairs.

Kip jabbed the elevator's up button impatiently as he scanned the sheaf of printouts he carried, his overcoat slung around his shoulders: Let's go, let's go, let's go.

Like most electron microscopes, Emerson's was ensconced in a special room in the basement in order to diminish vibrations. Working in a research facility that could afford its own wildly expensive electron microscope was highly advantageous, but its basement location meant a certain amount of up-and-down commuting.

Which was why Kip had taken to coming in around 5:00 A.M., when the facility was nearly deserted. It was a lot easier to get things done. And the elevator was almost always there when he needed it. So where the hell, he wondered impatiently, had it got to this morning? He'd come directly down there, not stopping at his office first, to continue the work he'd started the day before. Now he was eager to analyze the printouts.

A faint light leaked through the glass-paneled doors of the side offices as the intruder slid along the wall. A car horn sounded outside, and the shadowy figure jumped, then moved slowly forward again, withdrawing a small metal object from the satchel.

A pneumatic rumble heralded the elevator's approach. About time, Kip groused to himself, shifting the stack of printouts from one arm to the other. The door slid open. He got in and punched the button for his floor. The car, notoriously slow, began to rise. As he rode upward, his thoughts drifted to Taylor. Seeing her again had awakened all the old feelings for her he'd managed to conceal, years ago. Maybe this time he'd have the courage to act on them.

Casting hurried looks to the right and left, the interloper stepped inside the lab, carefully shutting the door. A quick look around and the intruder moved silently into the main work area. The metal object flashed in the dim light from the street as a gloved hand extended it toward the monitor screen. Working quickly, the black-clad figure went from computer to computer, the metal object flashing.

The elevator wheezed to a stop, and Kip got out and started down the darkened hall. As he came around the corner, he froze as a faint movement caught his eye. He frowned, then realized the door to his lab stood open.

"Hey!" He ran forward. "Who's there?" But the

corridor was now empty. Had he imagined the shadow? But he'd been the last to leave the night before, and he knew he hadn't left the lab unlocked. He went in and flicked on the lights.

And gasped.

Every monitor screen bore a death threat, scrawled in bright red lipstick.

He went through to his office and dropped the printouts on his desk. The vandalism was more extensive here. Not only his monitor but the window and two walls were smeared with the sticky red cosmetic. Sinking into his chair, he reached for the phone.

"Chris? This is Kip Lawrence. It's about five-fifteen, and I know you're not in yet, but you better come up here as soon as you get in. We've had a visitor."

He disconnected, then called the security desk in the lobby. "No," the guard told him. "No one's been in except a few regular staffers."

"How about people leaving? I thought I saw whoever did this running down the hall as I came in."

The guard consulted his book. "No one's signed out since eleven-fourteen last night," he said. "I've been on since midnight, and I'd have seen anyone leave."

Kip thanked him and replaced the receiver. There wasn't much he could do until the head of security came in and got his message. He tilted back in his chair. This was all he needed right now. With a sigh, he reached for the printouts, then paused. He hadn't yet had a report on those coffee samples. He'd have to remember to give them a call.

"Jesus," Chris said. "What a mess."

"Tell me about it."

Outside in the corridor, various members of Kip's staff milled about, waiting for the custodial staff to finish cleaning up.

" 'Death to those who play with the seeds of life,' " Chris said. "What the hell does that mean?"

"Sounds like an indictment of masturbation," Gene said, entering the office.

"Very funny," Kip said tiredly.

"They've finished in my section," Gene said. "Is it okay if I go in? I've got a ton of stuff to do."

Kip looked at Chris, who nodded, and Gene hurried away.

"What now?" Kip asked.

Chris shrugged. "We can tighten security on this floor, put an extra man on to do a walk-through every hour, that sort of thing. But frankly, we have no leads."

"We have *one*," Kip said, "although I'm not sure what it means. Have a look at this." He pulled a crumpled piece of paper from his desk drawer. "It was stuck on the coat hook behind my door."

Chris took the paper gingerly so as not to smear the dark red lipstick. " 'Gaia is angry,' " he read aloud. He looked up at Kip. "Who the hell is Gaia?"

Chapter Ten

Taylor initialed the page, closed the folder, reached for another from the stack at her left elbow, opened it, scanned the top sheet, made several notes in the margin, turned the page, yawned mightily, stretched, and leaned back in her chair. She shifted her gaze to the half-moon hanging low over the dark landscape beyond her office window. The past two days, she'd spent more time inside the OR than out of it, and she was bone-weary. She closed her eyes, rubbed them, opened them, yawned again.

"How about a nice hot dinner? You look like you could use one." She turned around. Garrison, his coat over his arm, stood in the doorway.

"I've got all these files . . ." she protested weakly.

"Do 'em in the morning."

"I've got surgery in the morning."

"Then do them in the afternoon. It's after nine, kid; time to go home. You look beat."

Taylor sighed. "I am."

"A little Mexican food will revive you. I know a place that makes the best strawberry daiquiris on the East Coast." He smiled. "Even the virgin ones are great."

Taylor hesitated. She was spending an awful lot of time with Garrison, one way or another. Still, it was good to have a pal. "You're on," she said. "But my

treat, for a change. Just give me ten minutes to finish
up here."

"I'll meet you in the lobby." He went to her, taking
her wrist in his hand. "Now, the big hand's on the
'one,' " he said, pointing at her watch. "If you're not
downstairs by the time it gets to 'three,' I'm coming
back up to get you." He held her wrist just a beat
longer than necessary, released her, smiled, and
disappeared.

Taylor sat for a moment, her wrist still warm from
his hand. Maybe she *had* been seeing too much of
Garrison. I really do like you, friend, she thought, but
not that way.

She finished reviewing the open file, closed it, and
got her coat from the narrow built-in closet. February's promise of an early spring had proved false, and
the first of March had brought flurries flying in on a
cold wind. She put the coat on, reaching her hands
down into its deep pockets for the black leather gloves
she'd worn that morning.

One was missing.

Odd, she thought; she was sure she remembered
having both gloves with her when she'd arrived at the
hospital that morning.

She checked the pockets again, and the floor of the
closet; no glove. She must have dropped it somewhere.
Damn, she thought, frowning; those gloves were expensive.

Chanting, the leader revolved slowly, lifting the silver bowl to the east, the north, the west, the south.
Reflected moonlight flashed from its highly polished
surface as she tilted it first one way, then another.
Around her, feverish cult members swayed, impervi-
ous to the biting cold, the flurries that raced across
the icy field. They wore stout shoes or boots, and
heavy wool capes with cowls that covered their heads.
Beneath the capes, they were naked in anticipation of

the orgy to follow, back in the leader's over-warm, incense-fragrant house.

It was an ancient belief, this conviction that sexual energy promoted psychic energy, older than the cult of Gaia itself. From the Bacchus fertility rites of ancient Athens to the infamous Gilles de Rais circle in fifteenth-century France, the combination of sex and drugs had long been used to produce a transcendental state believers considered a divine madness.

The leader set the bowl carefully on a wide, flat stone and, arms outstretched, began to shuffle around it, her gaze on the sky above. Her hood fell back, revealing a face distorted by fierce emotion. "In the name of Gaia . . ." she chanted, her hair streaming in the wind. "In the name of Gaia, we will destroy her."

"In the name of Gaia . . ." the others repeated.

"We will destroy her."

". . . destroy her . . ."

From the pocket of her cape, the leader drew a small bottle and held it aloft. "Alcohol was her downfall," she proclaimed. She unscrewed the top of the bottle, pouring a thin stream of liquid in a tight circle around the silver bowl. "We will use her weakness against her. We will tempt her, force her, if necessary. She will start drinking again, and Slater will fire her."

Setting the nearly empty bottle on the ground, she took a lighted taper from a thickset man, his face shrouded by his cowl, and touched the alcohol; a circle of blue flame leapt up.

She watched them blaze and subside, then turned back to the group. "Maggie Kay, you went to school with her. You must befriend her, and then tempt her."

"I didn't really know her," a short, plump young woman protested a little tentatively. "Anyhow, it doesn't seem right to make her start drinking again now that she's—"

The leader took hold of the woman's shoulders and stared angrily into her eyes. "You dare to question me?" Her voice was low and threatening.

"Of course not," Maggie said quickly. "I just thought—"

"Don't think. Act. The only way to destroy the hospital is to destroy the doctors who bring in the money. Have you forgotten that the hospital killed your husband? How many times have you told me you want vengeance for his death? Well, here's your chance." She went and picked up the bottle of spirits.

"What if I can't? Uh, what if I really try but I can't?"

"If you fail," the leader told her, "other . . . options are available." She added the remaining drops of the alcohol to the contents of the bowl and tossed the bottle away.

"But why me? I don't want to—"

Clutching the bowl, the leader swung back, fixing Maggie with a terrible look. "Those same options," she snarled, "can be used against any of our members whose loyalty is in question. Do you understand?"

Maggie nodded, too frightened to speak.

Satisfied, the leader began to circle again, holding the bowl aloft. "Destroy her, Gaia," she chanted loudly.

"Destroy her, Gaia . . ." Their voices rang out above the rising wind.

With a flick of her wrists, the leader upended the silver bowl. Something dark and squishy dropped onto the frozen ground, accompanied by the reek of alcohol and a thick, viscous liquid that pooled dark red in the light of the moon.

"Did your father finance this place, too?" Taylor asked, forking up the last of her burrito.

"No, *I* did," Garrison told her. She looked up from her plate, eyebrows raised questioningly. "I came into a small inheritance, a few years back. New Chatham seemed like a good place to invest it."

Taylor looked around; the small, pink-walled restau-

rant was crowded even at this late hour. "Looks like
you picked a winner."

"I usually do," he told her, gazing at her meaningfully.

Should she ignore it, she wondered, or make a big
speech about their just being friends? She took a sip
of her virgin daiquiri. Ignore it, she decided; it's late,
and I'm too damn tired for speechifying.

But Garrison was no dummy. Seeing her look away
from him, he immediately launched into an amusing
story about the difficulties he'd had in finding a local
decorator who understood Mexican style. "Of course,
we get our pick of designers up here these days," he
concluded, "now that New Chatham's been featured
in the shelter books."

"Shelter books?"

"*House & Garden, Better Homes . . .*"

The waiter came, offering flan and coffee. "Not for
me, thanks," Taylor said. "It's getting late."

"Just the check," Garrison told the waiter.

"This dinner's on me, remember?" Taylor said.

"In my own restaurant?" Garrison smiled at her. "I
don't think so. Besides, I want to." Again, he looked
deep into her eyes.

Looks like I'm going to have to make that speech
after all, Taylor thought. "I'd really feel more comfortable if you weren't always the one who paid," she
said. "Otherwise, it makes our relationship seem
like . . . something it isn't."

"How do you mean?" he asked, all innocence.

You know damn well, she thought. She took a deep
breath. Okay, you asked for it. "I really like you, Gar,
but I like you as a friend. Not as a . . . a boyfriend."

"That could change."

"I don't think so."

"I'm a big boy," Garrison told her. "I'll take my
chances."

"But I'm not comfortable being with you if you're
going to be hoping for something more. Besides, I'm

sort of seeing someone in New York." Not quite accurate, but a useful half-truth.

"I see."

They were quiet for a moment. "So, are you okay with that?" she asked him. "Our being friends, not lovers?"

"I can work on it," he said lightly.

"Good. Because I really do want you as a friend, Gar," Taylor said. She thought of the surgeon figure with the knife in its back. "I need friends, at the moment."

Garrison nodded. "Sam told me about that doll thing you found under the steps."

"Really? I'm surprised."

"Are you? Why?"

"Well, he made so little of it when I told him about it. Said it was just some stupid prank." She paused. "Ben Erbach said the same thing."

"Who?"

"My old high school chemistry teacher. I ran into him and his wife at Starbucks right after I found the doll." She drained her glass and set it down. "What did Sam say about it to you?"

"Same thing he said to you, but . . ."

"Something's bothering you. What is it?"

Garrison hesitated. "There are rumors—have been, for as long as I've been here in town—about some sort of cult associated with the protesters. Rituals, spells. Directed against the hospital."

"Well, they don't seem to have worked," Taylor said more bravely than she felt.

"That's what Sam's always said before."

"Well, he's right. I mean, he's still here, the hospital's still here . . ." And Ward Harland, the man she'd replaced, was gone. But there was no mystery there, she reminded herself; according to Sam, the man had relocated to L.A. No—rumors of spells and voodoo dolls under the stairs were simply scare tactics. Sam had been honest with her; he'd told her about the protesters during her job interview. If she let them scare her now, she'd be playing right into their hands. Which she couldn't afford to do; she needed this job.

"I'm sorry I brought it up," Garrison was saying. "*I* certainly didn't intend to scare you away." He grinned at her. "You're good for business, doctor. Anyway," he added more seriously, "I can use a friend, too. There aren't a whole lot of people in this town with whom I feel an affinity."

The waiter arrived with two small glasses of Kahlúa—"Compliments of the house"—and the bill.

"One of the perks of ownership." Garrison laughed, reaching for his glass.

"None for me, thanks," Taylor told the waiter, then turned to Garrison. "Won't you let me pay for dinner?"

"Not on my turf." He signed the bill and replaced it on the small pewter tray.

"But the whole town's your turf," Taylor protested, laughing. "I'm going to have to cook dinner for you."

"I'll take you up on that." He took a long pull at his drink and set it down. "Shall we go?"

"Don't you want the rest of your Kahlúa?"

Garrison shook his head. "It really is getting late." They retrieved their coats and went out into the chilly night.

They'd convoyed from the hospital to the restaurant. But the tiny parking lot had been nearly full, and Garrison had had to park on the street.

"May I walk you to your car, madam?" he offered, draping a pseudo-casual arm around her shoulder.

"No need," she said lightly, wondering how many times she was going to have to make that speech about just being friends. "I'll be fine."

"Are you sure?"

"Absolutely," she assured him, stepping back. "I'm a New Yorker, remember?"

"Well . . . see you in the morning, then."

Regretting her missing glove, Taylor buttoned her coat and started up the gravel driveway that led around to the parking lot in back of the restaurant. Patchy illumination from the side windows provided sufficient light to see her way along the path, but once she reached the lot itself, there was only the glow of a decorative streetlamp set well off to the side.

She located her car, fumbling in her purse for her keys, suddenly spooked by the darkness. She was sliding in behind the wheel when the smell hit her: alcohol fumes. With an undertone of something else.

And what was that thing on the dashboard? Without thinking, she reached for it, then gave a little scream of disgust as her fingers connected. The object was cold and spongy. Wet. Sticky.

Swallowing her distaste, she examined it in the car's interior light.

It was her missing glove. And it was drenched in blood and booze.

Chapter Eleven

The duty sergeant opened the passenger door and peered in. "What the hell is that?"

"My glove. Somebody put it in my car that way."

"Any sign of forced entry?"

"You tell me," Taylor said irritably. She'd driven straight to the police station from the restaurant parking lot, shock and disgust at her discovery quickly giving way to anger. "But first, please get that damn thing out of my car." He looked up at her, frowning, and she added, "I assume you'll want it for evidence."

"Evidence of what?" The night was bitter, and the officer blew on his hands to warm them.

"Of harassment," Taylor exclaimed impatiently. She'd heard about small town cops, but this was just silly. "Obviously, I'm being harassed."

"There won't be any usable prints," he said doubtfully. "Not soaked like that." But he went and got a plastic evidence bag and sealed the noxious glove inside. He set the bag on the ground and pulled out his flashlight. "This the first time something like this happened?" he asked, leaning over to examine the driver's door for scratches.

"I found a sort of voodoo doll under the steps of the town house I'm renting," Taylor told him.

"Really? When was this?"

"A couple of weeks ago. I'm afraid I threw it away," she added ruefully.

He stood up. "No marks. No sign of a break-in. You wouldn't happen to be missing a car key?"

"I only have two, the one in the ignition and the one in the glove compartment. It's still there. I checked."

"You have any thoughts about who might be doing these things?" the officer asked, reholstering his flashlight.

"Someone who doesn't like women surgeons would be my guess. I've experienced that before. I haven't been in town long enough to make any personal enemies." She thought for a moment. "Do you know whether my predecessor, Dr. Harland, ever reported being harassed like this?"

"I'm sure he didn't. I'd remember it, believe me." He glanced at the evidence bag with distaste.

"So what do we do now?"

"I suppose the lab could run some tests," he said dubiously. "Of course, no crime's been committed per se. You weren't attacked, your car wasn't broken into. Lab time's expensive."

"I could take it to the hospital lab, if you'd prefer," Taylor said, keeping her tone light.

"Oh, that won't be necessary," he said quickly. "We'll do what we can. I just don't think it will amount to much."

"But you'll let me know what you find?"

"Sure. Give us a call in a couple of days."

"Will do." Taylor opened the door and slid in behind the wheel. The car still smelled awful, and despite the cold, she lowered all the windows.

"You okay? You're shivering."

"I'm shivering because it's freezing," Taylor retorted. She switched on the engine and turned the heat up full.

"Well, I wouldn't lose any sleep over it, doctor," he told her, bending down to speak through the open window. "I'm sure it's just some dumb prank."

"You really think so?" Taylor raised a sardonic eyebrow.

"Absolutely." The officer smiled reassuringly. "This
isn't New York City, you know. New Chatham is a
very safe place."

The phone was ringing as she came through the
door. Chucking her coat over a chair, she hurried to
answer it.

"I just finished up here, and felt like talking to you,"
Kip said. "Hope it's not too late to be calling."

"It would have been, if I hadn't had to stop at the
police station," Taylor replied. "As it is, I'm glad to
hear a friendly voice." She told him what she'd found
in her car and the duty sergeant's reaction to it, then
described the voodoo doll with the knife in its back.

"Sounds spooky," Kip said when she'd finished.

"The spookiness isn't what's bothering me," Taylor
said, carrying the phone into the bedroom and plop-
ping herself on the bed. "Hell, I'm a scientist, Kip. I
don't believe in that mumbo jumbo. And Lord knows
I've experienced harassment before. No, it's the sense
of . . . malevolence that I don't like."

A pause. "How are you . . . holding up?" he
asked carefully.

He means, am I drinking again. Taylor shivered
slightly. God knew, she'd thought about it. Driving
home from the police station, she'd had a palpable
need for a drink, a physical urge she'd found hard to
control. "I'm hanging in there," she told him.

"Glad to hear it. Uh, Taylor?"

"Hmm?"

"You do know you can call me anytime you need
to talk."

"Well . . ."

"You can."

"Thanks. That's good to know. And now let's talk
about anything else, okay? How's your work going?"

"Really well. Busy as hell, though." He considered
telling her about the incidents at the lab, but decided
it would only add to her worries. Besides, Davis

Leeds, Emerson's director of research, had made it very clear that the incidents were not to be mentioned outside Emerson. "I keep hoping to grab a few days to come and see you," he said. "But the project's at a critical stage. Maybe in a couple of weeks." He paused. "It may not seem that way, but I'm really looking forward to seeing you."

"So am I." They were both silent for a moment. "Well, I guess I ought to get some sleep," Taylor said at last. "I have to be up at six."

"I've got an early start, too. Sleep tight."

"You, too."

"Taylor? Don't let this nonsense scare you away."

"No chance of that," she assured him. "I need this job too much."

She hung up, changed into the T-shirt she slept in, performed her evening ablutions, and climbed into bed. She turned out the bedside light, eyeing the shadows that painted the darkened walls. Somewhere a board creaked in the wind. She drew the covers higher.

Someone was trying to frighten her away from New Chatham, that was obvious. But who and why? Was it really because she was a woman? Or would any new doctor have gotten the same treatment? Had Ward Harland? The police officer had said her predecessor had never reported any such harassment, but that didn't mean it hadn't happened. Harland might simply have chosen not to report it.

She closed her eyes and burrowed deeper under the covers. Just as she'd refused to allow harassment to deter her from becoming a surgeon, she was now determined to keep this job and redeem her career.

Sure, this stuff was more malevolent than the discrimination she'd experienced during her training. But she'd been completely truthful in what she'd told Kip. The theatricality of the bloody glove didn't scare her, nor did the voodoo aspect of the hidden doll. She was a scientist: pragmatic, educated. Cultist trappings held no terrors for her.

But someone had impaled that doll and placed it within a few feet of her front door. Someone had drenched her glove in blood and alcohol and gotten inside her car with it. And that was frightening indeed.

Chapter Twelve

The sun was streaming through the curtains when Taylor awoke early the next morning, its cheery brightness somehow diminishing the previous night's events.

The temperature had moderated slightly, and the sky was cloudless as she drove through the tree-lined streets to Greenvale Hospital, her spirits rising. She parked her car in the underground garage and stopped at the hospital cafeteria for a bagel and coffee, feeling positive and determined.

Only one cashier was on duty at that early hour, and a short line had formed behind an intern fumbling for change. Taylor positioned herself at the end of the queue. Just ahead of her, a stocky, white-haired man was eyeing the transaction impatiently and muttering to himself.

"Dr. Ohlmeyer?" The man turned. His eyes were stormy, and his cheeks were flushed. "I'm Taylor Barnes," she reminded him. "Sam introduced us."

"Yes, of course. My fellow New Chathamite. This is unbelievable, isn't it?" His arm swept toward the cashier in a large gesture. "There's simply no excuse for such inefficiency. Doctors should have a separate line." The cashier shot him a baleful glance, and a passing nurse caught Taylor's eye and shook her head tiredly.

"They don't get much of a crowd before eight," Taylor pointed out, refusing to tackle the issue of elitism he'd raised. "Anyway, we're moving now," she added as the intern hoisted his tray and moved past the cashier.

"So we are, at long, long last. Here, let me buy you breakfast." He slid his tray toward the cashier and reached for his wallet.

"That's not really necessary—"

"To welcome you to Greenvale." He was smiling now, all charm, the flush of irritation fading. "We townies have to stick together. Take both trays out of this," he told the cashier brusquely, handing her a crisp new fifty.

"Well, if you insist," Taylor said awkwardly. "Thanks."

"Sam asked if I remembered you," he said as they moved past the register toward the tables, "but of course I didn't. Why should I?"

"Quite right," Taylor agreed pleasantly. "I left New Chatham as a teenager."

"Precisely. Our paths wouldn't have crossed. I wouldn't have known you, and you wouldn't have known me."

"Actually, your name did ring a bell."

"Really?" Something flickered in his eyes. "Perhaps someone in your family consulted me?"

"No, that wasn't it." Taylor frowned slightly. "I've been trying to remember . . ." She trailed off. "Shall we sit here?" She set down her tray and pulled out one of the gray plastic chairs.

"Remember what?" He slid into a chair across from her.

"That's what I can't remember." Taylor gave a little laugh.

Ohlmeyer didn't seem to find it amusing. "New Chatham's a real gossip mill. That's what *I* remember about this place. Can't say I missed that."

Taylor frowned. "But . . . I thought you'd always lived here."

"No, I left, oh, nearly twenty-five years ago, set up

a practice in Hartford. I'd been renting out the family house for years, and I finally decided to sell it. So I moved back in to fix the place up. It happened to be around the time Greenvale was being built. And when I saw what Sam was doing, and understood the changes it would bring to the town, I decided to hold on a little longer."

"Good decision."

"You bet. Anyway, I met Sam, we got along, and he hired me. You?"

"I had a cosmetic surgery practice in New York City," Taylor said slowly. "Then"—she smiled—"I met Sam, we got along, and he hired me."

"And in between, you developed a drinking problem."

"Which I got help for," she replied, surprised. "Did Sam tell you?"

Ohlmeyer nodded. "Don't worry. I'll keep your secret." He winked.

"It's not a secret."

"It ought to be. That kind of thing scares the hell out of patients. Can't say I blame them." He leaned over and patted her hand paternally. "You can trust me not to say anything. We physicians have to support each other." He flashed her a conspiratorial smile.

"Actually, I've already told a few people," Taylor said, affronted. "I think it's better to get the truth out in the open. Secrets tend to turn around and bite you in the ass."

Ohlmeyer's smile faded. He stared at her moodily. "You think that, do you?"

"Yes, I do."

"Then you're very naive."

"Excuse me?"

"Some things have to be kept secret. When you've had more life experience, you'll learn it's the truth that can turn around and, as you so colorfully put it, bite you in the ass."

Taylor frowned. "You can't really believe that."

"Oh, but I do. Wholeheartedly." He sighed. "Women are often unrealistic in their appraisal of the big picture. Perhaps that's because they approach things emotionally rather than rationally—"

"Excuse me," Taylor said rising. "I'm expecting a patient." She grabbed her tray and headed for the exit.

Ohlmeyer stared darkly after her, his hands unconsciously curling themselves into tight, white-knuckled fists.

No wonder people didn't like the sexist bastard, Taylor thought as she rode the elevator to her office. Well, they could add her name to the list.

She finished the bagel at her desk while thumbing through a local Yellow Pages for car alarm installers. She chose one and made the appropriate arrangements. Then with twenty minutes in hand before her first meeting, she sipped the last of the coffee while paging through her notes on the patient she was expecting. She was already well versed in the information they contained, and soon set them aside. Her thoughts drifted to her predecessor.

Before Slater had offered her the job, she'd considered trying to locate Ward Harland for a little background, but in her rush to accept and relocate, she hadn't bothered. Now, however . . .

She started with the American Medical Association, identifying herself and requesting Harland's current business address and phone number. "Chief of Cosmetic Surgery, Greenvale Hospital," the records clerk told her. "New Chatham, Connecticut."

"No, that was his previous position," Taylor corrected the woman. "Where's he working now?"

"That's all I have," the clerk said. "That plus a home address and phone number, also in New Chatham. You want that?"

Taylor took down the information, thinking there

might be a forwarding number on the line, but when she called it, the phone just rang and rang.

Strange that he wouldn't have notified the AMA of his change of venue. Well, it had only been a couple of months. Maybe he was still getting his practice organized.

She tried the American Society of Plastic and Reconstructive Surgeons, and the American Society for Aesthetic Plastic Surgery. Both had only Harland's New Chatham address. Neither knew of any more recent affiliation, in Los Angeles or elsewhere.

She hung up, sipped her coffee, and picked up the phone again. Even if Harland hadn't bothered to change his address with the AMA et al., surely he'd have a telephone. She called Directory Assistance for Los Angeles, trying the four major area codes. No business phone. No home phone.

She was debating whether to try the L.A. hospitals when a knock at her half-closed door interrupted her thoughts. "Yes?"

Slater popped his head in. "Got a minute?"

"Of course," Taylor said. "Pamela Reese is due at eleven to talk about a bleph and a rhinoplasty, but until then I'm yours."

"Heard you had a little, uh, car trouble last night," Slater said, sliding into the guest chair across from her. Taylor's eyebrows rose in surprise; she'd told no one but Kip. "Police chief's a friend of mine," he explained, placing the file he carried onto her desk. "He thought I'd want to know. I asked him to keep mum about it—no sense giving the nutcase responsible the satisfaction—but I urged him to do everything he could to find out who's doing this stuff. He didn't seem very hopeful." He leaned back and folded his hands in his lap. "Helluva business, finding that glove. Especially after that doll thing under your front step. Must have been very unnerving."

"What's really unnerving is how they got it inside my car. I'm having an alarm installed this afternoon."

"Good idea. Such things aren't pleasant, of course, but as I said when we first met, not everyone's a fan of Greenvale."

"Or of female surgeons, perhaps."

"Could be."

He studied her. "You're not planning to decamp, are you?"

"What? Of course not," Taylor said, surprised.

"Glad to hear it."

"Hey, I've dealt with harassment before. Maybe not quite this personal, but I'm not so easy to get rid of. Which won't make Dr. Ohlmeyer very happy, by the way, but that's his problem. Of which he has many, I'm sure." Slater raised an inquisitive eyebrow. "We met in the cafeteria this morning. He bought me breakfast and then proceeded to insult me."

Slater sighed. "Ohlmeyer's a bit of a dinosaur, I'm afraid. I'm sorry."

"No need to apologize, Sam. *You* weren't the one who said women were irrational, emotional, naive . . ."

"Oh, dear. That, on top of what happened last night . . ." Sam shook his head. "Well, what I have to say may be coming at a good time." For a brief moment Taylor thought he was about to fire her, but of course he wasn't. "I'd like you to make a trip to New York for me," he said. "To see a prospective patient."

"Why can't the patient come here?" Taylor asked in surprise. "Is she ill?"

"She's perfectly fine," Slater said with a smile. "But Lila Krimm prefers her hired hands to come to her. I see you recognize the name."

"Who wouldn't?" Taylor replied. Married to the head of an old-money investment banking firm, Lila Krimm was as famous for her extravagances as for her well-publicized charity work.

"She wants a discreet—very discreet—face-lift," Slater explained. "Her second."

"Really? How old is she?"

"Forty-nine." Slater pulled an eight-by-ten publicity photo from the file and pushed it across the desk to Taylor. "Doesn't look it, does she?"

"She looks more like early thirties," Taylor said, examining the picture.

"And so she wishes to remain," Slater said, smiling. "Is this retouched?"

"She says not."

"Frankly," Taylor said, "I don't think she needs any work."

"I don't, either. But she wants it. And what Lila Krimm wants . . . Well, if we don't do it, someone else will."

Taylor frowned. "That's no reason to do an unnecessary procedure."

"Come on, Taylor. Elective cosmetic surgery's not like cardiology. None of it's actually necessary. But performed correctly, it's not harmful. And Krimm's money will help pay for the free clinic. Where we do procedures that *are* necessary." Taylor opened her mouth and shut it again. "The surgery will be done here in six weeks," Slater added. "You'll do it, of course."

"Are you sure she'll agree to me as her surgeon?" Taylor asked. "She could have anyone. Daniel Baker. Sherrell Aston. You."

"Not even Lila Krimm could have me," Slater said firmly. "I'm out of the OR for good. No, she'll be perfectly happy with you. Just leave that to me."

Taylor's phone rang, and she answered it. "My eleven o'clock is here," she told Slater, who rose, shoving his hands into the pockets of his medical coat.

"I'd like you to go to New York the day after tomorrow," he told her. "We'll clear your schedule."

"What about Donaldson?"

"The chin reconstruction? Postpone him for a day or two. Thirty-six hours or so won't make a difference. Besides, he's a clinic patient. He'll wait." Again, Taylor began to speak, then bit her tongue. Slater handed her Lila Krimm's file. "Look it over when you get a chance. You'll drive down?" She nodded. "We'll reimburse your expenses, of course. And Donna can arrange your hotel." Donna was the secretary Penny had found for Taylor.

"Hotel? I assumed I'd go there and back in a day."

"You can do that, of course. But there's an AIDS benefit I've been invited to at the St. Regis, and I'd appreciate it if you'd go in my stead. Show the flag. Would you mind?"

"Not at all," Taylor said quickly. She understood the need for cosmetic surgeons to see and be seen. It was an important part of building a high-powered practice. She'd done her share in the past and enjoyed it—another source of tension with her then-husband, who'd disliked socializing and whose discomfort and disapproval at such occasions had been palpable.

"You ought to bring an escort," Slater added. "Less threatening to prospective clients that way. But then, you know that. Shall I send Garrison along?"

"God, no," Taylor said, then flushed. "I didn't mean that quite the way it sounded. It's just that I've been trying to convince Garrison we're just friends, and dancing the night away at the St. Regis could destroy all my good work." She smiled. "Actually, there's someone in New York I'd like to invite."

"Good," Slater said. "Have Donna make the arrangements." He started out of the office. "And have some fun while you're there," he added, turning back. "You look like you could use some."

I certainly could, Taylor thought, reaching for the phone.

"Mrs. Krimm is in the drawing room," the English butler told Taylor, taking her coat. "Please follow me." He led her through the wide marble gallery and along a deeply carpeted hall to an ornately carved door. "Dr. Barnes, madam," he informed the slender blonde woman seated on a damask sofa within.

"Thank you, Thompson," the woman said, waving Taylor to a facing armchair. "You may serve tea now."

"Very good, madam."

Taylor stifled a smile; it was all so self-consciously P. G. Wodehouse.

"So you're Slater's new surgeon," Lila Krimm said, divesting herself of a pair of large tortoiseshell glasses and a copy of *Paris Vogue*. "He's been simply singing your praises. You did Bitsy Merrill, didn't you? It's quite all right to say yes," she added as Taylor hesitated. "Bitsy's an old friend. She told me so herself." But Taylor could see that Lila approved of her reticence. "You did Karen Aiken, too, didn't you? Never mind, I know you did. I like your work. You don't make people look unbelievably perfect, like so many cosmetic surgeons. That's always a dead giveaway, isn't it?"

Thompson entered with a heavy silver tray. "Tea, madam."

"Just put it there," Lila directed, fluttering a be-ringed hand in the direction of the dramatic hand-painted coffee table. "You do take tea?" she asked, turning to Taylor. Thompson set down the tea tray and withdrew.

"Yes, thank you."

"Milk? Sugar? Lemon?"

"Just milk, please."

"Margareta makes the most wonderful cookies," Lila said, filling the delicate china cups. "You must try one." Taylor chose a thin chocolate wafer; it was still warm and smelled delicious. She noticed that Lila didn't touch the sweets herself.

"So now you're at Greenvale," Lila said, sipping. "Do you like it there?"

"Very much," Taylor said. "It's a wonderful facility."

"So I've heard. And the whole concept is so . . . discreet. You simply tell your friends you're off to Greece or somewhere, then pop up to Greenvale and reappear two weeks later saying, 'The islands are so restful. I feel ten years younger.' " She laughed.

Taylor laughed, too, surreptitiously studying the woman. The photo hadn't lied; she looked terrific. A few lines, perhaps a very slight sag around the jawline, but terrific nonetheless.

Lila set down her teacup. "Now, let me tell you what I want done," she said. Taylor drew a pen and a leather-bound notebook from her handbag, surprised that Lila had accepted her so readily. Slater had obviously done his work well. As the woman described the minor flaws she wanted corrected, Taylor made notes, reflecting that if she were still in her own practice, she'd refuse to do any work on Lila Krimm. But you're not, she told herself sternly. You don't have that option.

"I don't need any body work," Lila concluded, tapping her slim, silk-trousered thigh. "I had all that done last year. Your predecessor Harland Ward."

"Body work?"

"Lipo, tummy tuck, thigh lift, the works. I'd been considering the removal of my lower rib, too. Some fashion models do that to achieve a slimmer torso. But Sam talked me out of it," she added doubtfully. "Do you think he was right?"

"Absolutely," Taylor told her, relieved that Slater was capable of drawing the line somewhere. Lila was obviously a surgery junkie, she thought as she slipped the notebook back into her handbag. There was a big difference, in Taylor's mind, between using cosmetic surgery in order to feel better about oneself, and using it in a search for unrealistic physical perfection. People like Lila Krimm made her nervous.

The two women spoke for another twenty minutes or so, tentatively scheduling the surgery for a few weeks hence.

"I suppose you're heading back to Connecticut," Lila said, walking Taylor to the drawing room door.

"Actually, I'm staying in town this evening. There's an AIDS benefit—"

"At the St. Regis?" Taylor nodded. "Why, Martin and I are on the dais," Lila said brightly, then frowned.

Taylor smiled. "Don't worry, Mrs. Krimm. I won't have met you before."

Lila's smile brightened. "I felt sure you would understand," she said.

Taylor pulled her hair back into an onyx clip and inspected herself in the full-length mirror. Not bad, she thought. She'd lost most of the twelve pounds she'd gained during her drinking days, and the black Donna Karan cocktail dress she hadn't worn in months now lay flat against her stomach. She added a strand of pearls and took them off again. She'd known Kip for years; why was she feeling so nervous?

The shrill of the house phone made her jump. "Be right down," she said. She put the pearls back on again, picked up her coat, and went out into the hall.

Kip was waiting for her in the hotel's small but elegant lobby. He stood as she walked toward him, his eyes widening. "Wow," he said.

"Wow yourself," she said, and meant it. He looked even better in his dress clothes than she'd imagined. The butterflies receded, leaving behind a warm glow of anticipation. "It's nice of you to come to this thing with me," she said as he held her coat for her. "I hope you won't be too bored."

"Not at all. I've been living like a hermit the past six months. This'll give me a chance to catch up with a few people."

Catch up? she wondered, then thought, Of course; this is his world.

The St. Regis was only a few blocks from her more modest hotel. As they walked down Madison Avenue under a lowering sky, he took her hand and squeezed it. "I'm very glad you called me."

They checked their coats, found their table assignment, and went into the anteroom, where drinks were being served. The room was packed, the bar even more so. "Why don't you wait here while I brave the crowds," Kip suggested. "Ginger ale? Perrier?"

"Perrier, please."

He started for the bar, and Taylor turned away, idly scanning the crowd. There should be at least one of my noses here, she thought.

"Kip? Is that you? Look, Marty, it's Kip Lawrence."

Taylor swung around. A graying, rotund man was pumping Kip's hand while Lila Krimm looked on, beaming. Neither had noticed Taylor.

"Haven't seen you in months," the man said. "Where've you been hiding yourself?"

"I've been a prisoner of my own device," Kip explained with a smile. "But this beautiful lady rescued me." He reached out a hand to draw Taylor into the group. "Dr. Taylor Barnes, Lila and Martin Krimm."

"A pleasure," Martin said.

"How nice to meet you both," Taylor replied easily. Lila smiled a greeting, her face showing no sign of recognition.

"How's your father?" Martin asked Kip.

"Recovering well," Kip said. "Furious at not being able to go into the office every day, of course."

"He would be," Martin said. "Well, give him my best, will you?"

"Of course."

They moved off. "Is your father ill?" Taylor asked.

"He had a stroke last year, a mild one," Kip said. The crowd had thinned, and he guided her in the direction of the bar. "The doctors wanted him to quit, but of course he refused. They finally said he could go into the office three days a week, so he simply works at home the other two." He turned to the bartender. "A Perrier and a white wine."

"And you know the Krimms," Taylor said. "I'm impressed."

Kip shrugged. "Martin's an old friend of my father's. I've known them for years, but we're not particularly close."

As Taylor sipped her Perrier, she was tempted to tell him she'd met Lila that afternoon, then thought no, a confidence is a confidence. Instead, she linked her arm through his and said, "Shall we go in and find our table?"

Their dinner companions were interesting and amusing. Kip chatted easily with them, and introduced Taylor to several people from other tables who drifted by. He was in his element, obviously enjoying the evening as much she was. How different, how much more fun, she reflected, to be with someone who actually liked this sort of thing.

He looked over at her, catching her staring at him, and winked. She felt herself color. "Trying to figure out where to start?" he asked.

"What?"

"On my face. Trim my nose a little? Work on these bags?" He indicated the smooth skin under his eyes.

"You don't have bags," she laughed. "And I think your face is just fine the way it is."

"So's yours. I always thought so." He smiled. "I've had a crush on you for years. That's why I disappeared from your life when you were working so hard at keeping your rotten marriage going. Sorry."

"That's okay. It *was* a rotten marriage."

"And I always admired your skill with a scalpel. Cutting people up never appealed to me, but I'm in awe of people like you who do it well."

"That's rather funny, coming from you." He cocked an eyebrow at her. "We were all rather in awe of *you*, back in med school," she explained.

"Me? Really?" He looked surprised.

"Sure. Your car was less than ten years old. You'd actually met a Kennedy."

He laughed. "And here I thought I'd succeeded in becoming one of the gang."

"Oh, you did. But underneath, we all knew you

were different." She paused. "Seeing you now, in this
environment, makes me wonder about your choice of
medicine as a career. Why not business? Or investment banking? Especially since your father wanted so
much for you to—"

"Fortunately, there were other influences in my
life," Kip said. He turned away, crumbled a piece of
roll in his fingers.

"Really? What—"

"More Perrier?" Kip reached for the bottle. "Martin's getting up. I think the speeches are about to
start."

After the speeches there was dancing, and Taylor
was pleasantly surprised when Kip took her arm and
led her to the floor. Paul had never liked to dance,
and such functions as she could convince him to attend
they invariably left early.

"If anyone had told me, six years ago, that I'd be
dancing with Taylor Barnes at the St. Regis . . ." Kip
said softly into her ear. He held her close. "I'm glad
you invited me."

"I'm glad you came."

He didn't release her when the song ended, but
whispered, "Shall we leave?"

"Yes," she replied, her body singing. No words were
needed; they both knew what was about to happen.

At the door to the powder room, Lila Krimm
paused to watch them collect their coats. So Kip knew
Dr. Barnes. That would have worried her if Barnes
hadn't been so discreet, allowing Kip to introduce
them as though they'd never met. As it was, she found
their friendship reassuring. Barnes was a class act. Lila
pushed through the door, fumbling in her evening bag
for her lipstick. A thin chain with a flat incised medallion had gotten itself wrapped around the tube. As
she removed the lipstick, the chain fell to the marble
floor. She knelt and scooped it up, shoving it back in
her bag. Pain in the ass, carrying the damn thing
around. But of course she couldn't wear it tonight.

And although she didn't expect to need it for a long,
long time, it was better to be safe than sorry.

The storm broke during the night. A cold rain cas-
caded down the heavily draped hotel windows and ran
in floods through the gutters. In New Chatham, the
rain was icier. It blew into town on a gale untamed
by skyscrapers, freezing power lines and bringing
down small trees.

In Taylor's condo, the phone rang. After three rings
the answering machine clicked on, its green glow
changing to a flashing red. "Dr. Barnes? Taylor? Are
you there? It's Maggie Kay. Maggie McCormick, now.
(pause) I heard you'd come back to New Chatham
and I thought maybe we could meet for coffee, talk
over old times. (pause) Not that we were ever friends
or anything. (pause) The thing is . . . (pause) I need
to warn you about something. It's really important, so
call me back, okay? Here's my number."

Several hours passed. Then the blinking red light
suddenly went dark. So did the porch light. The fridge
went quiet, the hands of all the clocks stopped moving.

This was not an uncommon occurrence, and crews
were out looking for the break as soon as it was reported. Shortly before dawn, Taylor's fridge came to
life again. The porch light lit up. Clock hands recommenced their revolutions. And the message light on
her phone turned a bright, steady green.

Chapter Thirteen

The rain was coming down in torrents, and every passing truck sent a rush of water hard against the windshield, but Taylor couldn't care less that Friday morning. Windows shut tight against the weather, radio blasting, wipers beating a cadence, she sang along at the top of her voice as she drove north.

Sex for the first time in two years could do that to you, she thought happily. And love. She felt sure she was falling in love with Kip, perhaps, had always been in love with him on some secret level. Now the long-standing easiness between them, their mutual trust, allowed her to embrace this new blossoming of their relationship with unquestioning joy.

It had been hard to part from him that morning, and she missed him already, but they both had obligations neither could ignore. Long phone calls, they agreed, would have to do between the times they could manage to be together. There was no question of her returning to New York before her contract was out. It was essential that she put in a year's solid, successful work at Greenvale.

As he'd stood under the sheltering canopy of her hotel and watched her drive away, his face had been serious. It was obvious that he regretted her departure. But unlike Paul, Kip both accepted and approved of her dedication to her work. It was one of the things, he'd told her, that had drawn him to her in the first place, all those years ago.

The radio launched into a series of commercials, and she stabbed at the Select button. Music, she needed music. Soft rock—no thanks. Religious programming—not this morning. Salsa? Its jaunty rhythm suited her mood, and she punched up the volume. Once she'd proved herself, she could move back to New York, reopen her own practice, be with Kip . . .

Slow down, kid, she told herself. You're in a vulnerable place right now. Despite what's just happened, a little distance between the two of you is no bad thing.

More than the usual number of ambulances were parked outside the emergency room entrance as Taylor drove around the side of the hospital to the parking garage entrance.

"What's going on?" she asked the floor nurse as she came off the elevator on two.

"It's the fire," the nurse told her. "Dr. Slater said for you to go up to 'five' as soon as you come in."

"What fire?"

"At the mall. It broke out about four this morning. Some stores were gutted, and there's a lot of smoke damage."

"Anyone hurt?"

"Three firefighters and a security guard. One of the firemen fell through a burning wall."

"That's terrible. I supposed we'll be transferring them to hospitals with burn units?"

"Two of them, yes. The security guard's being treated for smoke inhalation down in the ER."

"And the fourth person?"

"He's the one Dr. Slater wants you for. Broken nose and cheekbone. He was unconscious when they brought him in. He must have hit his head. It's lucky the mall hadn't opened when the fire broke out."

"You bet. Do they know how it started?"

"They're investigating, of course." The nurse lowered her voice to add, "but they seem to suspect arson."

"How awful. I better go up." Taylor hurried downstairs to her office, tossed her coat on a chair, grabbed a white coat from behind the door, and headed back to the elevators.

"You've heard?" Slater said by way of greeting as she emerged on 'five.' He leaned against the counter of the nurses station, a patient chart in his hand.

"Julie told me," Taylor said. "Is he still out?"

"He was when I left him," he said, setting down the chart. "Let's go have a look."

She followed him down the hall. "How's his family taking it?"

"No family," Slater said. "At least not locally. His records say he moved here from Wisconsin four months ago."

"How old is he?"

"Twenty-seven."

A nurse was adjusting an IV line as they entered. Monitors beeped softly. Taylor leaned over to study the unconscious man. "Not pretty, but not nearly as bad as it might have been."

"You'll do the surgery once he's neurologically stable."

Taylor nodded. "How long has he been comatose?"

"About two hours. We did a CT scan of his head."

"Anything significant?"

Slater shook his head. "No intracranial injuries, no subdural." He handed Taylor the patient chart. "The neurologist on call had a look at him. There are no focal signs. Just the facial trauma."

"And his physical condition aside from concussion and trauma?"

"Surprisingly good." As Slater gave her the chart, she noticed his hands were shaking. He was obviously exhausted; the ambulance crew must have woken him when they'd gotten the call. "His heart is strong," he told her, turning away to study the monitor. "Kidneys are working well. He's in excellent physical condition, which is a real help to him now."

Taylor perused the man's chart. "You're a lucky man, James Partrick," she said to the figure in the bed. "I think we can make him look pretty good," she told Slater. "And he'll stand up to the surgery well."

As they left the room, Taylor asked, "Want to scrub in with me on this one? According to the chart, he was admitted under your name."

"Yeah, but I've transferred him," Slater said as they walked toward the elevators. "Partrick's your patient now. And I don't do surgery anymore. I've told you that."

"I know. But to do no surgery at all . . . well, it's an unusual decision."

"People change," Slater said shortly. "So do the things they want to accomplish."

Nothing in the world could make me give up surgery, Taylor thought. But all she said was, "I'm sorry, Sam. I didn't mean to sound critical."

"And I didn't mean to bark at you. I know my decision is incomprehensible to someone like you." He rubbed his eyes. "How about some coffee?"

"Sounds good."

He led the way to his office and ushered her to a seat. She was amused to see Snowball curled up on Slater's desk chair. As he gently moved the dog onto the floor, Snowball blinked, wagged his tail, licked Slater's fingers and promptly fell asleep again. Smiling to himself, Slater filled two mugs from the coffee-maker behind his desk and handed one to Taylor.

"I'm not used to being woken up at four-thirty in the morning, these days," he said, stifling a yawn. "Administrative emergencies tend to happen during normal business hours. And research projects afford one a more civilized schedule than hands-on medicine."

Taylor thought of the hours Kip was putting in, but said nothing.

"I understand you and Lila got on well together,"

Slater said. "She called me as soon as you left. And did you enjoy the benefit?"

"Very much."

"Thought you might. Some people like that sort of thing, some don't. Me, I always enjoyed the socializing. Part of building one's practice, of course, but also fun. With the right companion. I take it you had the right companion?"

"Yes," Taylor said. "Definitely."

"Good." Slater drained his mug. "More coffee?"

"Thanks."

"I know it's hard for you to understand how I could trade surgery for research," he told her as he refilled their mugs. "But I truly love what I'm doing."

"What exactly *are* you doing?" Taylor asked. "You mentioned perfusion solutions when we first met. Organ transplantation's an unusual switch for a cosmetic surgeon."

"Oh, I'm not involved in transplants per se, although there is a connection between that and my work." He sipped his coffee meditatively. "To understand why I'm doing what I'm doing, you need to know something about me personally."

"Really? What?"

Slater leaned back in his chair and laced his fingers behind his head. "I suppose you wouldn't guess it to look at me," he told her, "but in my younger days I was an avid climber. Dangerous for a surgeon, of course—the risk to the hands. But I loved the challenge. And I was damn good at it. Climbed Rainier, Hood . . . I loved the mountains. You couldn't keep me off 'em." He paused, remembering. "And then I got caught in a spring avalanche on Mt. Shasta. Took me a day and a half to walk out, but I made it under my own steam. I was in excellent shape in those days. Like our firefighter friend upstairs. And I was very lucky. I only lost a toe." He drained his mug and set it down. "That's when I became interested in the problem of frozen tissue. Preventive techniques. Cell regeneration." He smiled. "So often, our personal experiences dictate what drives us."

"And that's when you started your research?" Taylor frowned. "I didn't realize you'd been involved in it for so many years."

"No, no," Slater said. "It was only recently that I've had the time and money to—well, look who's woken up." Snowball, tail going a mile a minute, front paws planted firmly on Slater's knees, was gazing earnestly into the eyes of his benefactor. "Hand me a dog biscuit from that tin over there, would you?"

Amused, Taylor watched as Slater fed the dog and tenderly stroked its soft white coat. "He's a very lucky pup," she said.

Slater smiled but didn't reply, continuing to caress the animal. Taylor was about to make her exit—*I really should catch up on some paperwork*—when he turned back to her and said abruptly, "If you've finished with that coffee, perhaps you'd like to see my lab."

"Very much," Taylor said, surprised.

"Come on, then."

Greenvale must be even more profitable than I realized, Taylor thought as Slater threw open the double steel doors.

"I spend as much time down here as I can," Slater told her, ushering her inside the first of three interconnected rooms. Tanks of liquid nitrogen stood against the walls, and she shivered in the cool air.

"Sorry about the temperature," Slater apologized. "Cryobiology's a hot topic these days, but it's cold work."

Taylor smiled at the feeble joke and buttoned her lab coat. "I'm afraid I don't know much about it."

"Don't you? But you've heard of organ cryopreservation?"

"I've heard of it, yes. But that's about it."

"Organ cryopreservation is my area," Slater ex-

plained, leading her deeper into the facility. Workbenches, covered with equipment some of which she
couldn't identify, were scattered throughout the large
space. A number of small blue cylinders, unmarked,
were herded into a small enclosure to one side. There
were no windows, but the halogen ceiling lights were
very bright, making the room feel even colder.

"The aim of cryopreservative research," Slater was
saying, "is to perfect the technique of storing trans-
plantable organs over time. Are you aware that viable
kidneys are now recoverable from temperatures as low
as minus 45 degrees centigrade?"

"I didn't realize that."

"And using intracycloplasmic sperm injections, live
mice have been generated from freeze-dried sperm.
Dead sperm, or so everyone thought."

"No wonder you're in line for a Larrabee."

"Oh, I'm not responsible for that, I'm afraid," Slater
said. "No, my work is focused on the heart."

"You mean heart valves? Like in homograft banks?
Hasn't that been going on for some time?"

"Yes, heart valves harvested for re-implantation
have been stored in homograft banks for some years
now," Slater agreed, his fatigue lifting as he warmed
to his subject. "The banks use a standard cold-storage
technique based on the cryoprotectant dimethyl sulf-
oxide. DMSO works well for heart valves. But you
can't freeze and revive an entire heart that way. No
one's found a way to do that." He paused. "Until
now."

Taylor's eyes widened. "You're telling me that
you *have*?"

"Not a human heart," he said modestly. "At least,
not yet. My work is primarily with hamsters and
rabbits."

"Still."

"And we're at a very early stage. But our results
have been quite promising. We've restored several experimental hamster hearts to beating condition after

cryoprotection and supercooling. Ah, Mary." He intercepted a lab-coated older woman carrying an armful
of printouts. "Mary Quinn. Taylor Barnes. Mary's
been working with me on the heart experiments."
Mary dropped her printouts on a nearby workbench,
and the two women shook hands. "Show her what
we've been doing."

"It's very exciting," the older woman told Taylor
animatedly. "That's our cold room over there." She
indicated a solid-looking blue door stenciled with red
and yellow cautionary warnings. Beside it hung five
long quilted jackets, a padded work glove dangling
from each sleeve. "Come and have a peek."

The two doctors followed Mary to the door, where
she manipulated a large steel handle and pulled.
Slowly, the thick steel slab opened, releasing a cloud
of freezing mist.

"Better put this on." She handed Taylor one of the
jackets and took one for herself. Slater was already
pulling on his own.

The cold room was larger than Taylor had expected.
Several long, wide workbenches dominated its center.
The walls on two sides were lined with steel cabinets,
and tall, frosty red cylinders marked LN—liquid nitrogen—dominated the far wall.

The nearest workbench was covered with a complicated standing network of transparent tubing. Suspended from its center like a large, pale ruby was a
small, still heart.

"This is an artificial circulatory system," Mary explained, "designed like that of a rabbit. We suture a
surgically removed heart into the system here, while
it's still beating"—she pointed with a gloved finger at
the small organ—"we drain the blood, then pump a
blood substitute through it. When that runs clear, we
add our cool perfusion into the tubing up here. It's
been supercooled to seven degrees centigrade, and
when it hits, the heart goes straight into cardiac
arrest."

"And that's what I'm looking at now?" Taylor asked.

"Correct. The process is very much like bypass surgery, except that we keep the rabbit heart much colder. Once it's in this condition, we can hold it in suspension for five, six hours."

"Possibly longer," Slater added, "but six hours is sufficient for our purposes."

"And then?" Taylor asked.

"You'll see."

"Five twelve at seven point two-five," Mary announced, studying the digital readout hooked into the system. "Over five hours at just over seven degrees," she explained, then looked over at Slater. "Shall we show her the beauty part?"

"That's what we're here for."

Mary smiled. "Be right back."

"You're planning to restart it," Taylor breathed, realizing what was planned. "You really think it will?"

"It always has before."

"Artificial blood," Mary explained, rejoining them. The half-filled bag she held steamed slightly in the cool air. "It's been warmed." She fiddled with the tubing. Fascinated, Taylor watched the warm fluid flow into the stilled heart. "Now watch," Mary said, her eyes dancing.

A minute passed. Two. Suddenly the heart gave a tiny convulsive pulse, then another. And another. The heartbeat became more regular, pumping out the artificial blood in small, steady spurts.

"That's . . . that's unbelievable," Taylor said. "A breakthrough."

But Slater shook his head. "It's interesting, of course. But the heart's only been supercooled, not frozen. The real breakthrough is doing the same trick with a frozen heart."

"Can you?"

"We're working on it," Mary said. She led Taylor

to another workbench covered with very different equipment.

"First we cryoprotect the hearts with"—she glanced at Slater, who shook his head—"well, with a cryoprotectant Dr. Slater's invented. It's glucose-based." She frowned. "You do know what a cryoprotectant is."

"It protects the tissue cells from shrinking and cracking during freezing."

"And during the subsequent warming process, too. Once the cells have been thoroughly perfused, we immerse the hearts in liquid nitrogen and we hold them there at minus 196 degrees centigrade for two hours." She indicated a steel drum, its heavy glass lid secured by thick metal bands. The temperature dial set into the lid read "187C." A wire ran from the dial and disappeared underneath the workbench. "I put that one in there about eight minutes ago," she explained. "When it gets down to target temperature, a bell will ring out in the lab and we'll start the timer."

Taylor leaned in for a closer look at the frozen heart deep within the drum. "Careful," Mary cautioned as she bent her head close to the glass lid. "You don't want to touch exposed skin to that thing. Instant frostbite."

Taylor quickly drew back. "Then what?" she asked.

"After two hours, or whatever time we set for ourselves, we gently thaw the heart, de-cryoprotect it, warm it with artificial blood—"

"And it starts beating?" Taylor asked, her eyes wide. "That's amazing."

Slater smiled. "It's only amazing occasionally. Our success rate is about, what? Mary?"

"Twelve percent."

"And even when the heart doesn't actually restart," Slater said, "we can sometimes detect small self-generated electrical impulses in the muscle. Let's get out of here. I'm freezing."

Taylor frowned. "But how can that be?" she mused,

following Slater out onto the lab floor. "If the heart won't beat, it's dead."

"Who says?" Slater replied. "As I mentioned, kidneys have been held at minus 45C, reheated, reimplanted."

"But you're talking about a 150-degree difference," Taylor protested. "And a very different organ." She took off the padded jacket and slung it back on its hook.

"The depth of the freezing process shouldn't matter," Slater said, "except that the deeper the freezing, the better the cryopreservation over time, at least theoretically. As for the difference in organ function, you're right. Which is why our work is so exciting."

Taylor shook her head. "I just don't see how it's possible," she said. "Getting measurable electrical impulses from a dead heart . . ."

Mary and Slater exchanged a patronizing glance. "Who says it's dead?" he repeated.

"Obviously it's dead," Taylor said, brow furrowing.

"There's long been disagreement about the significance of what we call 'clinical death,'" Slater said. "Even among doctors like you and me. Mary? Don't let us hold you up any longer."

Taylor thanked the woman for the brief tour, and she moved off.

"Tell me how were you taught to define clinical death," Slater said, leading Taylor to a seat at a nearby workbench.

"When the heart stops beating and the lungs stop breathing," Taylor replied promptly.

"A fine definition twenty years ago," Slater said, seating himself across from her. "Not so accurate nowadays. At least, I don't believe it is. And I'm not the only one." He paused. "You ever read about that kid who went through the ice into Lake Michigan back in 1983?" Taylor shook her head. "He was in the water for half an hour before the EMS found him and pulled him out. He had no pulse, no heartbeat; he wasn't breathing. He was clinically dead. Fortunately, doctors at the hospital had some experience with hypothermia. They worked on him, wouldn't give up. Two hours later, the kid revived."

"With brain and vascular damage, no doubt."

"Neither one."

Taylor frowned. "A freak occurrence."

"This, from a scientist?" Slater said, amused. Taylor shrugged. "Well then, consider the current ethical debate about when to remove transplant organs from donors. That alone should tell you there's plenty of disagreement about when death can truly be said to have occurred."

"But there it's just a matter of degree," Taylor protested. "A question of timing, not function."

"But sometimes function *is* timing. How long do we wait before declaring that a particular function has stopped? When does it really stop?"

"What are you saying?"

"Are you aware that a number of studies have shown electrical activity continuing in the brains of cats and hamsters for several days after their clinical death?"

"Surely that's just random neural firing."

"Maybe so. But why? Why neural firing in a dead brain? To put it another way, is a brain with demonstrable neural firing really a dead brain? I can see you're not convinced." He thought a moment. "Let me show you something." He rose and started across the lab. As she followed him, his ankle joint seemed to lock, and he stumbled.

"Are you all right?" she asked, catching up with him.

"Perfectly, thank you," he said icily. "I shouldn't wear these leather-soled shoes in here. The tile's too slick."

Unlocking a door marked "RESTRICTED," he led her through a small anteroom into the space beyond. A small surgical table stood in the center; behind it, a counter held a jumble of medical equipment. To the right was a wall of square steel drawers, to the left what appeared to be a walk-in freezer. It looked a lot like a morgue.

"What do you do in here?" Taylor asked, strangely uncomfortable.

Slater turned to her, his eyes bright. "We revive the dead."

Chapter Fourteen

"Dead *hamsters,* actually." A gnomelike man in green scrubs, surgical mask, and heavy black gloves stepped out of the freezer. "Harry Isaacs," he said to Taylor, pulling off his mask. "I'd offer to shake your hand, but you wouldn't like it. Why are you trying to scare the poor girl, Sam?"

"I'm simply explaining what we do here," Slater said defensively.

"What we *try* to do." Isaacs grinned. "Of course, they're not really dead." He stripped off his scrubs, folded them neatly, and set them on the counter beside a tiny respirator. "It's called anabiosis. The reversible cessation of vital activity. Though the reversible part's a little tricky."

"I'll bet it is," Taylor said, smiling. The man's short stature, bright smile and cockney accent reminded her of the English comedian Marty Feldman in his role as the laboratory assistant in *Young Frankenstein.* "I'm Taylor Barnes. I'm a surgeon here. Well, not here. Upstairs."

"Nice to know you, Taylor. I've just put Daisy to bed, guv," Isaacs told Slater. "Don't let him tell you we're the first to do it," he said, turning back to Taylor. "Back in the sixties, a guy named Smith cooled golden hamsters to just below Zero Cee, warmed 'em up, and got 'em going again. *He*"—he gestured toward Slater with his chin—"says some Russian git did the same to a couple of humans. Probably an accident in the gulag, if you ask me. The problem," he continued, taking a clipboard from a wall hook next to the freezer and scribbling briefly on it, "is cellular damage coupled with shock to the system. That's what did for Roger."

"I wish you wouldn't name them all," said Slater petulantly. "And we *are* the first. Smith simply cooled his animals. We perfuse them and hold their de-animated bodies at LN."

Taylor looked from one to the other, feeling somewhat dazed. "De-animated?" she said. "LN? And who the hell is Roger?"

" 'De-animated' because we plan to bring them back," Isaacs explained. " 'De-animated' has a more positive ring than 'dead,' don't you think? Besides, they're not. Dead, that is. So *he* says. Me, I just work here."

" 'LN' represents the temperature of liquid nitrogen," Slater said stiffly. "Minus 200 degrees centigrade or thereabouts. What we do is replace the blood with a cryoprotective compound and cool the animal in ice until the heartbeat and breathing stop. Then we slowly bring the temperature down to about minus ten degrees centigrade in a cold bath for about twenty minutes—"

"At which point, its tiny hands and feet are frozen solid," Isaacs chimed in. "Most of its tiny brain, too."

"We slowly bring the temperature down further," Slater continued, "and we hold the animal at LN."

"In the freezer," said Taylor.

"In a ewer in the freezer," Isaacs said. "And Roger was the first hamster we succeeded in bringing back from the—oops, re-animated, I should say." He chuckled.

"You mean there's been more than one?" Taylor heard herself say, as though freezing and reviving small furry mammals were a normal, everyday occurrence.

"Oh, yes," Isaacs said merrily. "Seventeen."

"You can't really count the first six," Slater told him sternly. "Their vital signs were minimal."

"But we got a heartbeat."

"For about three seconds," Slater scoffed.

"All the same—"

"Hey. Hold it. Wait a second." Taylor took a deep breath. "You mean you perfuse hamsters with DMSO—"

"No, no," Isaacs exclaimed. "Not DMSO. Glycerol-based perfusates are more effective. And now that Sam's come up with his own little cocktail—"

"You perfuse the hamsters," Taylor interrupted. "You freeze them. You warm them again. And they get up and walk around?"

"Right," Isaacs said. "Well, occasionally they do."

"Occasionally." Taylor shook her head. "I don't believe it." She frowned. "What happened to Roger?"

"That's what I've been trying to convey," Slater said tiredly. "If we're very lucky, the occasional hamster does get up and move around a little. Like, uh, Roger did. But eventually, they all lie back down again."

"They die?"

"They de-animate." Isaacs winked at her.

"The physical strain of freezing and unfreezing is simply too great," Slater said.

"We're not sure that's the reason," Isaacs protested. "It could be damage at the cellular level. I mean, your perfusate's terrific, Sam, but there's bound to be some cellular damage."

"I suppose so."

"The point is, Roger kept going for two and a half hours after he was revived. And Petey and Tabitha lasted longer—nearly seven hours."

Petey? Tabitha? Taylor's head was swimming.

"And thanks to Sam's new perfusate," Isaacs continued, "Aretha lived for an entire day. She had a little lunch, went to the potty—"

"I wish you'd just number the damn animals," Slater muttered.

"Oh, let me have my fun," Isaacs said. "All alone down here, night after night, with only the hamsicles for company." He glanced at his watch. "Well, I'm off. Daisy's down for the big sleep, and I could use a little rest myself."

"Daisy's in the freezer?" Taylor asked. Isaacs nodded. "So what are those drawers for?"

"Our filing system." Isaacs went to the steel wall and tugged on a handle. A drawer slid out. On it lay a small, furry creature encased in a clear plastic bag. A large label banded to the bag read *Rodney*. Isaacs pulled out several other drawers at random. Each contained a similar animal occupant: *Brenda, Flo, Colin, Macarthur*.

"Macarthur?" said Taylor.

"Taught me organic chemistry," Isaacs explained. "Hated the old fart." He slid out yet another drawer, removed a coat and woolly cap from inside, and shut all the drawers again. "Toodles," he said. Slinging the coat around his shoulders, he went out.

"What a funny little man," Taylor said.

"Oh, he's a laugh riot," Slater said tiredly. He glanced at the small steel drawers. "Wouldn't surprise me if he kept his lunch in there, too. You do realize," he said, leading her out of the lab and back toward the elevators, "that what I've shown you is highly confidential. The Larrabee people know all about my work, of course—they've actually visited us—but there's an awful lot of competition in research, and not just for awards."

"My lips are sealed," Taylor said. "Besides, I can't imagine whom I would tell, aside from News of The World. Sorry, I guess that was uncalled for."

"You still don't get what I'm doing, do you?"

"Well, it's fascinating, of course. And I can see how your research could inform the treatment of hypothermia . . ."

But Slater shook his head impatiently. "It's the implications for transplant organ storage that are so exciting," he said. "Imagine needing a heart for transplant and being able to simply open up a freezer, choose the one that's crossed-matched for your patient, thaw it out, and plug it in. Imagine storing donor livers that way."

"It would be wonderful," Taylor agreed. "And you did mention a connection with transplants back in your office, so I guess I should have realized. But in that case . . ." She hesitated. "Why the full-body experiments?"

"Because I'm convinced that bodies contain subtle biological information that single organs don't. To my mind, that theory's borne out by the fact that revival rates are higher for my full-body experiments than for the hearts alone. I don't know why that should be, but it's what the evidence suggests. I freeze the hamsters in the hope of learning something that will increase my success rate with the hearts."

"And someday, when every hospital has a freezer full of donor organs," Taylor said, smiling, "we'll be able to say it's all because Dr. Sam Slater lost a toe on Mt. Shasta."

"Funny the way things work out, isn't it?" The elevator stopped and they got in. Slater hit "two" and looked at Taylor inquiringly.

" 'Five,' please," she said. "I want to check on Jim Partrick again." She paused. "Thank you for showing me all that, Sam. I couldn't understand why you would give up surgery for research, but I think now I'm beginning to."

"It's my hope to be able to leave behind a meaningful body of work that will help mankind," Slater said softly, "not just a bunch of face-lifts. Not to diminish what we do here at Greenvale, but it's not much of a legacy, is it?"

"Oh, I don't know," Taylor answered. "There's a lot to be said for quality of life. Anyway," she added as the elevator door opened, "you're too young to be thinking about death."

Slater smiled wryly. "This is where I get off," he said.

The young firefighter was just coming around when Taylor entered his room. "Welcome back," she told him.

"Where am I?"

"In Greenvale Hospital. I'm Dr. Barnes. You're going to be fine," she added with a reassuring smile, seeing the sudden alarm in his eyes. "You're a bit of mess at the moment, but we'll fix you up as good as new."

"What happened?"

"You went through a burning wall. You've got concussion and some trauma. You were very lucky."

"Anybody else hurt?"

"Yes. Two firefighters were transferred to a burn unit. I don't know their names."

"God." Partrick closed his eyes. "Are they gonna make it?"

"I don't know. I hope so." She smoothed the sheet over his chest. "Every person in this hospital is grateful for what you and your partners do for New Chatham. I promise you'll get the very best care we can give you. Now, you rest, and I'll be back to see you a little later."

"Uh, doc? You'll let me know how the other guys are?"

"Yes, as soon as I hear anything."

Taylor made some notes in his chart, then went and conferred with the staff at the nurses station.

"Tell me if you hear anything about the guys they sent to the burn unit," Taylor requested. "Mr. Partrick seems more concerned about them than he is about himself."

Back in her office, Taylor reviewed her hospital messages, then checked her home answering machine. All the messages on it were recent. There was one from Garrison suggesting lunch and a local art show on Saturday (maybe, she thought), one from a local florist wanting to make a delivery of flowers from a Dr. Lawrence (lovely, she thought), and a reminder from Olive Erbach that Taylor had agreed to have dinner at their home that evening (oh, shit, she thought).

Dinner with the Erbachs had been arranged a week earlier, and she'd forgotten all about it. They struck her as well-meaning but dull, and she considered crying off, then thought, no, she'd only have to do it some other time, might as well get it over with. She could use her lack of sleep as an excuse for an early night.

She unpacked Lila Krimm's file from her attaché case and stuck her handwritten interview notes inside. Picking up the phone again, she scheduled OR time for the firefighter's surgery three days hence and reconfirmed the Donaldson procedure. Then, yawning mightily, she rose and went in search of coffee. Sex, flood, fire, and frozen hamsters, she thought; it's been one hell of a day already, and it isn't even noon.

Chapter Fifteen

By the time Taylor pulled into the Erbachs' driveway that evening, she was fading fast. The cold rain was still falling, and the wet ground squelched beneath her shoes as she traversed the small expanse of faded lawn. She climbed the front stairs and rang the doorbell, shifting the bakery box she carried. Maybe some hot food would revive her.

"Taylor!" Olive Erbach greeted her effusively. "Come on in. Taylor's here, Ben," she called over her shoulder. Ben appeared from the rear of the house to take her coat.

"I brought some fresh cookies." Taylor handed Olive the slightly damp box. "From Bonté. I hope you like chocolate."

"Who doesn't," the older woman assured her, smiling. "And Bonté, how grand." Passing the box to Ben, she led Taylor down a narrow hall and into a warm, book-lined living room. A log fire flickered behind a peacock grate.

"Something to drink?" Ben asked, appearing in the doorway. "I make a mean martini."

"Just a club soda, if you have it," Taylor said. "Or a Diet Coke or something."

"We have wine, if you'd prefer."

"No, soda will be fine, thanks."

Ben went to get the drinks, and Olive smiled maternally. "A long day?"

Taylor nodded, aware of the vague beginnings of a headache. "On top of a late night last night and a very wet drive back from New York this morning."

"And then the mall fire," Olive added sympathetically.

"Actually, that was pretty much over by the time I got in. Although I did look in on Jim Partrick, the injured fireman. I'll be operating on his face."

"Yes, I know. Janice told me."

"Janice?"

"Whelan. She's a nurse's aide at the hospital. In fact, she and her husband will be joining us for dinner." A half-formed image of a cheerful red-haired woman came to Taylor's mind. "He teaches at the high school. That's how we know them."

"Oh? What's his subject?"

"Photography."

Ben returned, carrying a small tray on which were a diet soda for Taylor, a martini each for Olive and himself, and a silver dish of mixed nuts.

"So how are you enjoying small-town life?" Ben asked, distributing the drinks.

"It's fine," Taylor said. "Not that I've had much chance to enjoy it, with all there is to do at the hospital."

"Any more voodoo dolls?" Ben asked as he settled into an overstuffed armchair. His tone was light, but his eyes were serious.

Taylor hesitated. She was reluctant to discuss the glove incident, partly because she agreed with Slater about keeping the matter quiet, and partly because of her determination to resist what she was convinced was simply more of the harassment she'd come to expect as a female surgical resident. "No," she said.

Ben looked puzzled. "Really? I thought I remembered hearing something . . ."

Who could he have heard it from? Taylor wondered. Had the duty sergeant mentioned it around? Had Slater? Rather than deny it again, she glanced around at the cozy room. "You have quite a collection of books," she said.

Ben frowned, but Olive gave him a look that clearly said, She doesn't want to talk about it. Leave the girl alone.

The awkward moment was broken by the ringing of the doorbell. "That'll be Janice and Ted," Olive said. Ben rose and left the room. Olive leaned across the coffee table toward Taylor. "Don't mind Ben," she said. "You don't have to talk about anything you don't want to. Janice, dear!" Her voice rose as she stood to greet the new arrivals. "And Ted. Come and get warm. Janice, I think you know Taylor Barnes."

Taylor turned. The pleasant woman who came toward her, hand extended, was one she vaguely remembered seeing on the patient floors. She was about Taylor's age and wore a long silk skirt and matching scoop-neck sweater. Taylor, dressed in the slacks and shirt she'd worn all day, suddenly felt underdressed.

"We haven't officially met," Janice said, "but of course I know who you are."

"And I recognize your face," Taylor told her. "Although you look different out of uniform."

"Don't we both." Janice smiled. "This is my husband, Ted."

In his gray wool trousers and cashmere blazer, Ted looked far more prosperous than one would expect a high school teacher to look. As he came forward to take her hand, he brought with him a whiff of expensive aftershave.

The group settled itself on the sofa and chairs, and Ben went off to fetch fresh drinks.

"I understand you grew up here," Ted said to Taylor, popping a cashew into his mouth.

"Yes, years ago. But with all the changes, I feel like a newcomer."

"Janice and Ted are newcomers, too," Olive said. "Real newcomers, I mean."

"That's the small-town attitude for you," Ted said.

"Been here nearly four years, and we're still newcomers." But he smiled as he said it.

"Oh, dear," Olive said, coloring. "I didn't mean to imply . . . You're both real assets to this town."

"Well, I just love it here," Janice said. "We used to live in Albany. This is so much nicer."

"Janice has a wonderful vegetable garden in the summer," Olive said. "And fruit trees. She even has a root cellar. I didn't think anyone had a root cellar anymore."

"We grow more than we can use," Janice said, "so a root cellar's very useful. Freezing and canning change the flavor and, of course, the texture of food. Root cellars don't. Many of the old ways are coming back."

"Not all of them, thank goodness," Olive said. "I wouldn't want to do without a fridge or a telephone."

"Or antibiotics," Taylor said.

"Living in New Chatham gives us the best of both worlds," Janice said. "Country living and city comforts."

"And rising real estate values," Ted added.

"Ted's a property mogul," Ben said, sounding slightly envious.

"I own a few condos," Ted said modestly, selecting another cashew. Which explains the blazer and the aftershave, Taylor thought. "In a complex on Raven Ridge Road," Ted added. "I rent them out."

"Well, shall we go in to dinner?" Olive said, rising. "We usually eat in the kitchen, but I thought we'd use the dining room tonight, in honor of Taylor's visit."

From Olive's folksy clothes and jewelry, Taylor had anticipated beans, rice, and root vegetables. But she'd judged Olive unfairly. Dinner, consisting of roast chicken, scalloped potatoes, green beans and salad, was delicious. If Taylor hadn't developed a full-blown headache, she would have enjoyed it. As it was, by the time dessert was served, she was feeling very tired and rather unwell.

"Taylor's brought some elegant cookies to go with

my famous Orange Surprise," Olive announced, setting down a large, brightly glazed ceramic bowl. "From Bonté, no less. Hand them round, Ben, would you?" She began dishing out sliced oranges, dusted with coconut and swimming in a pale marinade.

"None for me, please," Taylor said.

"Oh, but you must," Olive exclaimed. "This is one of my party pieces."

"It's really wonderful," Janice told her, reaching over to touch her arm. "You'll love it."

Taylor sighed. "Just a little," she said, then watched helplessly as Olive filled one of the deep dessert bowls to its rim and passed it to her. Head pounding, brain fogged with exhaustion, she lifted a spoonful to her lips. Olive smiled at her in anticipation. Taylor chewed, swallowed. "Delicious," she said. "What's in it?"

"Oh, she won't tell you," Ben said, smiling. "She never does. Her recipes are like trade secrets."

"Have some more and see if you can guess," Janice said.

Obediently Taylor spooned in another mouthful. It really was good. The fruit was tart with an overlay of sweetness; oranges like these in the dead of winter must have cost plenty, she thought hazily. She ate some more. "Oranges, of course," she said. "Sugar, I guess. And I can see the coconut . . ." It really was good. She ate some more.

"And cinnamon," Janice prompted.

"Oh, Janice," Olive said, frowning. "Let her guess."

"And something else," Taylor said, chewing. What was it? An orangey flavor, but with a kick. The spoon dropped from her hand. Her pulse was pounding. "There's alcohol in this," she gasped.

Janice grinned. "Right you are, and plenty of it. Olive soaks the oranges in it and then sloshes it on top. But what kind?"

"No, you don't understand—" How much had she eaten? Judging from the small puddle in the bottom of the bowl, a lot.

"Cointreau? Grand Marnier? Have some more. See if you can tell."

But Taylor shook her head, her eyes on the bowl in front of her. There must have been at least an ounce of booze in her portion; she felt a familiar buzz. "I can't eat this," she said.

"You just did," Ted told her, amused. Then, seeing her face, he frowned. "Is something wrong?"

"I'm . . . I'm a recovering alcoholic," Taylor managed to say.

"But this is just dessert," Janice said, frowning. "It's not like you had a drink."

"It's exactly like I had a drink," Taylor said.

"I had no idea," Olive exclaimed. "I'm so sorry. I never would have—"

"No, of course you wouldn't." Ben put a comforting arm around his wife. "You couldn't have known."

"Are you all right?" Ted asked solicitously.

"Not really," Taylor murmured. "I had a headache when I got here, and it's gotten worse. I should probably just go home."

"Maybe you should lie down on the sofa for a little," Janice suggested. "Come on."

"That's really not necessary," Taylor protested weakly, rising from her chair.

"Go ahead, dear. I'll bring you a nice cup of chamomile tea." Olive bustled off to the kitchen.

"And aspirin, if you have some," Taylor called after her. She leaned back against the pillows. It wasn't the alcohol that was affecting her, she realized. It was the exhaustion and headache. Her spirits rose a little. Okay, so she'd had a drink. The world hadn't fallen apart. Of course it hadn't. Hell, she could handle the alcohol. A chill coursed through her. No, she *couldn't* handle alcohol; that was the whole point. And the fact that the world hadn't fallen apart just now shouldn't make her believe that she could handle it. That was the real danger of that inadvertent drink: the assumption of control. She must never forget that when it came to alcohol, she *had* no control.

"I'm afraid we're all out of aspirin," said Olive contritely, setting down a small tray with a bright yellow mug. "Janice? You wouldn't happen to have any aspirin with you?"

"Sorry, no."

"I ought to be going," Taylor repeated.

"Have some tea first," Olive urged. "It's very relaxing." She removed the tea bag from the mug and stirred. "I put a little honey in. I hope that's all right."

Taylor reached for the mug. "I'm sorry to be so much trouble."

"No trouble at all," Olive assured her. "Careful, it's hot."

"Delicious," Taylor said, sipping cautiously.

"Lean back and rest awhile," Ben said, inserting a pillow behind her back. "We can't have you driving around in the rain in your condition."

Taylor closed her eyes for a moment. The next thing she knew, the room was empty. A knitted afghan was wrapped around her legs, and embers smoldered low in the grate. She frowned and sat up, knocking over the remains of the tea with a clatter.

Olive appeared at the door of the living room. "We were afraid to wake you," she explained.

"Where is everyone?" Taylor asked, rising. "What time is it?"

"A little before midnight. Janice and Ted left about half an hour ago. Ben and I were just cleaning up."

"I've really got to go."

"Who wants coffee?" Ben asked, carrying in a tray with filled mugs.

"Taylor does," Olive said. "No, don't argue. Another ten minutes won't make a difference, and you really do need to revive before you drive home."

Taylor sighed and sat down again, reaching for the steaming drink. It did taste good.

"I can't believe I fell asleep," she said.

"But you feel better for it, don't you?"

"Yes, I do."

Olive came and sat next to her on the sofa. "You've had a difficult time here, haven't you?" she said sympathetically.

Taylor turned to look at her. "Difficult? No, I wouldn't say that."

"Oh, I know your work must be satisfying. But finding that voodoo doll right on your front step. And that disgusting glove."

"How did you know about the glove?"

"Oh, there aren't many secrets in a small town like this," Ben told her.

"It must have been awful for you," said Olive. "Especially on top of your alcohol problem."

"We had no idea, of course," Ben interjected. "I can't apologize enough for the dessert."

"Neither can I," Olive chimed in. She squeezed Taylor's hand. "The stress of being a recovering alcoholic must have made those other things even more frightening to you. Coming back here wasn't such a good idea, was it?"

The coffee was strong and reviving. Taylor smiled. "Oh, I'm used to harassment," she said. "Comes with the territory for female surgical residents."

"But surely this is different."

Taylor shrugged. "Oh, I don't know. Anyway, I refuse to take any of it seriously."

"Maybe you should," Olive said, frowning.

"For heaven's sake, why?"

"You could be in danger."

"You're kidding." She looked over at Ben. "I thought we agreed it was just a prank. That morning in the coffee shop, you agreed with me that it was nonsense. You threw the damn doll in the trash."

"I still feel that way," he said stoutly. "All that stuff about cults and spells. It's just some women acting silly."

"Women?" Taylor frowned.

"He means the members of the cult," Olive told her. "And who says they're all women?" she asked Ben.

"Cult? What cult?" Taylor asked.

"They hold ceremonies near the Rockingham House, so rumor has it," Olive explained. "And despite what Ben says, he won't walk past the place late at night."

Taylor looked from one to the other. "Ben, you're a man of science. You can't really believe any of this."

Ben shrugged. "No, of course I don't."

"But you do avoid the Rockingham House at night," said Olive. Ben looked embarrassed. "Taylor, dear, I know how much you must love this new job of yours, but surely you could get a job somewhere else." She paused. "Are you sure New Chatham is a good place for you right now? Not just the death threats, but—"

"Death threats?" Taylor paled. "I never considered them death threats."

"A scalpel in the back isn't a death threat?"

"Olive, please," Ben said.

"Now, Ben, I'm just trying to help. I mean, struggling with alcoholism is hard enough, but doing it in an unfriendly environment where people are threatening to kill you must make the temptation all the harder to—"

"I really have to get home." Taylor stood. Surely Olive was overdramatizing. Wasn't she? "Thanks so much for dinner. And the use of the sofa."

"Are you sure you're okay to drive?" Ben asked as they moved into the hall. "If not, I could run you home."

"No, I'm fine," she said. She shivered, suddenly cold.

Olive gave Taylor a hug, then peered at her face. "You are rather pale, dear."

"Of course she is," Ben grumbled as he went to retrieve Taylor's coat. "With all your talk about cults and death threats, you've scared the poor thing half to death."

Chapter Sixteen

Kip stepped into the elevator, juggling a fried egg sandwich, a cappuccino, and his overcoat. He pushed the three button with his elbow and was surprised to feel the car descend. The door slid open in the basement, and a man with a tangle of wild hair and an armful of printouts stepped in.

"Morning, Larry," Kip said. "So you're the person responsible for bringing me down to the basement."

"Next time, don't push the down button when you want to go up."

"I didn't," Kip protested.

"Guess I beat you to it, then. Your breakfast smells good."

"It's lunch," Kip said. "I've been in my office since five, doing paperwork." The elevator began to ascend.

"So what's new?" Larry teased. "Find any mascara on the file cabinets? Wigs on the gas jets?"

"I take it you heard about the lipstick incident."

"Yeah. Kind of weird."

"Definitely weird," Kip agreed.

"And whoever it was only wrote slogans in your lab. What do you think that means?"

"That my people are doing stronger work than your people?"

"I'll ignore that," Larry said. "You don't seem very worried about it."

"I have enough to worry about."

"Pushing for that Larrabee, huh? Any idea who your competition is?"

"The only one I know for sure is Sam Slater."

"That society face doctor? No competition there."

"Stranger things have happened," Kip assured him.

Back in his office, Kip dropped into his swivel chair. Mentioning Slater had reminded him that he'd yet to find the time to make his promised visit to New Chatham. It was important that he do so, and soon. Spending time with Taylor was reason enough for a trip to New Chatham. But it wasn't the only reason. The moment Taylor had mentioned Greenvale, that day at lunch, he'd realized how useful it would be to have her in place there. Now that she was, he needed to capitalize on it.

His reverie was interrupted by the arrival of the mail cart. He quickly sorted through the letters and publications, stopping at a white envelope bearing the return address of the laboratory to which he'd sent the vials of coffee. About time, he thought.

Ripping it open, he scanned the contents, then read it through again carefully. Analysis had determined that both samples contained traces of sodium fluoride, the chemical added to drinking water to prevent cavities. The lab estimated the concentration at about 1%.

Kip leaned back in his chair. That sounded right; one gram of sodium fluoride would produce symptoms of poisoning identical to those exhibited by his staff.

And five to ten grams could kill. Had the poisoner known what dosage to use, or had they all just been lucky? Would he or she strike again, changing the concentration—and the odds?

Who would do such a thing? And why?

He thought of the words scrawled on the monitors in his absence. The use of lipstick indicated a woman's hand, yet a man might choose to use it for that very reason.

He stood up, tucking the report into his pocket, then reached for the phone and dialed a number.

"Is Davis there? Good. This is Kip Lawrence. Tell him I'm on my way."

"Are you sure you didn't have words with one of your people?" the security chief asked.

"I just told you," Kip replied testily. "No."

"Maybe something minor? People can take offense at the pettiest things—"

"And poison an entire lab? Sorry, Chris, but I don't buy that."

"Frankly, neither do I," said Davis Leeds.

Davis was Emerson's director of research, and he'd called Chris as soon as Kip had shown him the chemical analysis of the coffee samples. Now the three men were gathered in Davis's office with the door firmly closed.

"If the fluoride attack were directed only at Kip," Davis continued, "it would be different. But nine other people got sick. And what about the lipstick messages on the monitors?"

"Clearly, somebody doesn't like the research Dr. Lawrence is doing," Chris offered.

"We've known that for some time," Davis said. "But who?"

"Those anti-genetics demonstrators were pretty vocal," Kip said.

"That was weeks ago."

"Yeah, but they could have come back," Davis said.

"They did," Kip said. "I saw one of them outside, the day of the coffee incident."

"I read in the paper where they picketed some lab in Boston recently," Davis said. "One of them actually got inside and threw a stink bomb."

"That couldn't happen here," Chris protested.

"I'd like to think you're right," Davis said doubtfully.

"What about that Gaia note I found in my office?" Kip reminded them.

"Anyone could have written that," the security man

insisted. "Listen, our procedures are very tight. I know all the guards personally, and they're completely reliable. Only staffers and escorted guests have access to the building."

"So where does that leave us?"

"It's got to be an inside job."

"A researcher who hates research?" Kip said, frowning. "Working as intensely as we all do, that kind of attitude would be hard to disguise."

"Your team *is* under tremendous pressure at the moment," Davis agreed. "What with the Larrabee and all."

Kip nodded. "We're working flat out."

"People can snap under that kind of pressure," Chris mused. "They just—snap."

"Well, I couldn't slow them down right now even if I wanted to," Kip replied. "They're very excited, very motivated."

"And one of them is very crazy," Chris interjected.

"Hey, you can't assume it's one of my people just because it happened in my lab," Kip retorted. "There are plenty of other teams working in this facility. It could have been anyone."

"So what do we do?" Davis asked. "Chris?"

"We start by interviewing everybody with access, see if anybody noticed anything unusual."

"Like a guy skulking around with a vial of poison in one hand and a lipstick in the other? Come on, Chris," Kip said. "You've already talked to my people about the lipstick incident. You go back to them with this, you won't learn anything new and you'll just make everybody nervous as hell. I can't have my staff distracted just now," he added. "These incidents are bad enough."

Davis sighed. "I tend to agree," he said. "Although I do think a little casual questioning of lab workers in other parts of the building isn't a bad idea. Don't mention the poisoned coffee, though," he warned Chris. "Just ask them about seeing any strangers wandering around, that sort of thing . . . and the messages on the monitors; that's public knowledge. And Kip?"

"Yes?"

"I'd appreciate it if you wouldn't mention the coffee incident to anyone, either. I know I've said this before, but it's especially important now. If word got out, it could be very embarrassing to the university. Probably leave us open to a liability suit, too."

Kip shrugged. "Whatever you say." But his eyes were troubled.

"You're tying my hands here," Chris protested.

"I know," Davis agreed. "But it's a very delicate situation."

"And if somebody dies, it will become even more delicate," Chris told him.

"Oh, I don't think it will come to that," Davis said, eyes widening at the thought. "Do you, Kip?"

"Jesus, I hope not," Kip replied, frowning.

Chapter Seventeen

"It matches your eyes."

Taylor laughed. "It's a painting, not a dress." She moved closer to examine the abstract landscape in its ornate gold frame. "It's beautiful."

"Let me buy it for you."

"Absolutely not. It's far too expensive. Besides—"

"We don't have that kind of relationship?"

"Exactly."

"Well, we could."

"No, Garrison. We couldn't. I thought we'd settled that." She sighed and moved past him to a group of rather crudely painted bathers framed in silver.

"Can't blame a guy for trying," he said, catching up to her. "Sorry," he apologized when she didn't respond. "I thought I'd give it one last try."

" 'Last' being the operative word."

He studied the bathers. "That sucks."

"It does, doesn't it?"

"No, I meant our not having that kind of relationship. Okay, okay, I'm through," he said, laughing and throwing up his hands protectively as she turned around. "Not another word. I promise."

"Good." Taylor smiled at him.

"How about a little air?"

They strolled out of the gallery and meandered through the cobbled courtyard, glancing at the various store windows. Unlike the day before, the afternoon sun shone brightly and the sky was a cloudless blue. The air, freshly washed, smelled crisp and clean. "Sorry I woke you," Garrison said as they stopped to admire a display of collages.

"Glad you did. My clocks were all screwed up."

"Must have been the power outage, night before last. Surprised you didn't notice it before."

"I didn't get home until late last night, and then I just collapsed into bed."

"You *were* out late. I tried calling you to firm up our plans for today."

"I didn't get a message on my machine."

"Didn't leave one. I figured I'd catch up with you in the morning." He paused. "Were you still in New York?"

"No, I was having dinner with my old high school science teacher and his wife."

"Wish I could say it sounded like fun."

"Wish I could say it *was* fun. I went out of a sense of duty, I suppose. Hard to break childhood habits."

"So how come you stayed so late?"

"I didn't mean to. But they served a dessert that was full of alcohol, and I was exhausted and headachy and I ate it, not realizing. I freaked out, and then I felt sick, and then I fell asleep on their sofa."

"The perfect guest."

"Hey, I brought cookies. But somehow I don't think they'll be inviting me back in a hurry." She paused. "Remember when I told you about that voodoo doll someone left under my front step? You mentioned a local cult."

"It's just a rumor," Garrison said, looking uncomfortable.

"Well, Olive thinks the bloody glove was their work, too."

Garrison turned to stare at her. "What bloody glove?"

Oops, Taylor thought. Well, if Ben and Olive knew, it was no secret anymore. Briefly, she told Garrison about what she'd found on the dashboard after their dinner together, and about bringing it to the police.

"I did offer to walk you to your car," Garrison reminded her.

"It wouldn't have made a difference," Taylor said reasonably. "The glove would still have been there."

"Does Sam know?"

"Yes. The chief of police is a friend of his. Sam and I discussed it and decided to keep it quiet. I can't think how Olive and Ben knew."

"Maybe the chief of police is a friend of theirs, too. This is a very small town."

"So everyone keeps telling me. Anyway, after Olive scared me silly with talk about death threats, she carried on about how harassment like this must make it so much harder for me to deal with my alcohol problem."

"Is she right?"

Taylor recalled her visceral craving for a drink as she drove to the police station, the bloody glove on the floor of her car. "Not at all," she lied. "Besides, working is excellent therapy."

"Despite the harassment?"

"It seems I can't have the one without the other." She paused. "It's very important for recovering alcoholics to work. It's part of the recovery program." And no one else will hire me, she didn't say. "No, they'll have to use more than scare tactics to get rid of me. And please don't say, 'Maybe they will.' I don't need to hear that just now."

"I wouldn't dream of it," Garrison said. "How about some food?"

"It's a little late for lunch," Taylor said doubtfully. "Do you think they're still serving?"

"One way to find out." He led her to a café set into a corner of the courtyard. "Looks like we're in luck." Inside, a line of Saturday shoppers waited for seating, but the outdoor tables, their white umbrellas gleaming in the sunlight, were unoccupied. "Inside or out?"

"Outside, definitely. It's not that cold." She settled herself at a nearby table. "I'm glad you got me out of bed," she said, taking in a breath of fresh, cold air. "A day like this is a gift."

"Especially in February."

They ordered frittatas, coffee, and a glass of wine for Garrison. He selected a roll from the bread basket, broke off a piece, chewed, swallowed. "It must have been hard, facing up to your alcoholism."

"It's still hard."

Garrison nodded. "My mother was an alcoholic."

Taylor frowned. "Really? I had no idea—"

"You would if you'd ever met her. She and my dad divorced when I was a teenager. She died of alcohol-related cirrhosis eight years ago."

"I'm so sorry."

"I tried to get her into rehab, but . . . She and my dad had already split up, and I was just a kid." Emotion clouded his face. "What did it for you?"

"I was in denial for a long time," Taylor said. "Then one day I was standing in the OR with a scalpel in my hand, and I couldn't remember what procedure I was there to do. It suddenly hit me that I could kill somebody."

"And you went straight into rehab?"

Taylor shook her head. "I went straight home and poured myself a stiff drink. And then my parents called from Santa Fe, and it all came out. My dad did some research, got in touch with some people, and he and my mom flew in. They held an intervention for me."

"What's that?"

"Painful is what is it." Taylor paused, remembering. "A roomful of people telling you they love you and describing how your drinking is hurting you and them both. It hits home, believe me."

"And then?"

"A lot of soul-searching and counseling. And finally rehab." She paused. "I remember the afternoon I went out to the Caron Foundation. You don't go alone, they send someone from the referral organization to bring you in. It's called a recovery. In my case, it was this tall, gorgeous silver-haired woman, an ex-alcoholic who'd been dry for twelve years. We met at Penn Station—the Caron Foundation is just outside Redding, and we were taking the train—and she looked me over and said, 'You look terrible. I bet you want a drink.' And I said, 'The biggest one they can pour,' and she took me to a bar around the corner."

"A bar?" Garrison looked shocked.

"All part of the program. One last drink before you get on the train. So we're in this bar," Taylor smiled at the memory, "and it's a pretty rough place, full of blue-collar guys who probably never move off their stools except to go to the can. And this tall, striking woman orders a double water with a twist, and a double vodka martini for me. And all the guys are looking at us, going, 'Who are they? Who are these women?' 'What are they doing in here?' And then one of the guys says, 'Are you guys blind or something? It's a recovery team.' And this other guy goes, 'Hey, we're recovering, too. We're recovering from last night.' "

"Is that supposed to be funny?"

"Well, it was funny at the time. I guess you had to be there."

"So what was the treatment center like?"

"Beautiful. Calm. Like a luxury hotel."

"Expensive?"

"It wasn't cheap, no. But the Caron Foundation makes a real effort to be accessible."

Garrison ate another piece of roll. "Have you ever been involved in any foundation projects professionally?" he asked. "I mean, as a physician?"

Taylor shook her head. "Most of my patients are private. Although I certainly know of foundations that fund medical facilities and clinics."

"Ever hear of a private foundation called Saguaro? Based in Switzerland?"

"Saguaro?" Taylor thought for a moment. "Can't say I have, but as I said, foundations aren't my area of expertise. Why do you ask?"

Garrison frowned. "No reason."

"Uh-huh." Taylor eyed him skeptically.

The waiter arrived with their drinks. Garrison took a long pull at his wine and looked up to see Taylor studying him. "Really, it's nothing," he said. "Just me being a control freak."

"A control freak? *You*?" Taylor teased.

Garrison smiled ruefully. "I know, I know. But I *am* the hospital's chief financial officer, and I do need to have control over our funding."

"And don't you?"

"Of course I do. Most of it." He took another swallow of wine. "How much do you know about the funding of Greenvale?"

"I assumed it was funded primarily by patient revenue," Taylor said, "and private contributions. And a grant or two for the clinic."

"And for Sam's research. The majority of our research money comes from foundation grants."

"Foundations like Saguaro?"

Garrison nodded. "Saguaro's a major contributor, and not just to the research program. Our bottom line wouldn't look nearly so good without Saguaro's support."

"And . . . are you having a problem with Saguaro?"

"Not at all. In fact, I adore 'em. It's just that of all our contributing foundations, Saguaro's the only one with which I don't actually have any contact."

"Why is that?"

"Sam deals with them directly. He's the one who brought them on board."

"And that's a problem why?"

"It's not a problem," Garrison said. "It's a question of control. Our other foundations, at least the ones

based in the East, they send a guy out here now and
then, we give him the grand tour, take him to lunch.
And I talk to people at the other organizations at least
three or four times a year, make sure they're planning
to re-up, that sort of thing . . ."

"So Sam does that for you. So what if you don't
get to take the Saguaro guys to lunch?" Their food
was served, and they began to eat.

"It's not about lunch," Garrison said, cutting a forkful of frittata. "Saguaro contributes a lot to our bottom line. Without the normal kind of contact I have
with our other contributors, I have no sense of
whether Saguaro's going to continue its funding, and
at what level. Unlike other foundations, Saguaro pays
us monthly. If they decide to pull out . . ."

"Have you discussed this with Sam?"

"Of course. He says he has a close relationship with
Saguaro's chairman and their funding is assured."

"Well, then?"

"Sam's a scientist, not a money guy. He may be a
little naive about the assurances he's been given."

"Well, if he wins that Larrabee Award, people will
be lining up to fund him," Taylor said. "You won't
have to worry about Saguaro pulling out."

"That's what Sam said. And the Larrabee is looking
very good. But it's not a done deal." He pushed fried
potatoes around with his fork, thinking of the personal
commitment his father had made to New Chatham's
bankers, on his say-so.

Taylor stared at him. "Is Greenvale in trouble?"

"No, no, of course not," Garrison said heartily. "Saguaro gives us a bundle, but so do other foundations
and contributors." He laughed. "Your job is secure, I
promise. No, this is more about me than it is about
Greenvale. We control freaks—" he smiled "—don't
feel comfortable being at the mercy of people we can't
at least *try* to influence."

"So go out and get more funding."

"Once we get that Larrabee—*if* we get the Lar-

rabee—that's exactly what I'll do." He set down his
fork. "Look, I'd appreciate it if you didn't mention
this conversation to Sam."

"Of course I won't," Taylor assured him.

"I wouldn't want him to think I'm second-guessing
him," Garrison continued. "Especially with that damn
Ohlmeyer sucking up to him all the time."

So Sam wasn't above playing the palace favorites
against each other, Taylor thought. But her amusement at the high schoolishness of the situation was
tempered by the concern she saw in Garrison's eyes.
"I wouldn't worry about Ohlmeyer," she told him.
"You've known Sam for many years. He couldn't have
built Greenvale without you. Besides, I can't imagine
he'd have much in common with that sexist jerk, aside
from medicine."

"Me, neither. But that doesn't stop Ohlmeyer." He
frowned. "And Sam listens to him. Oh, he's quick to
agree if you tell him Ohlmeyer's a dinosaur, and that
he has a fierce temper. But that's just talk. The truth
is, Sam's convinced the sun shines out of Ohlmeyer's
ass. He gives him free rein at Greenvale."

"Don't let it get to you, Gar. Sam needs you a lot
more than he needs that bastard. You're the money
man."

"Thanks." He smiled at her and drained his glass.
"More coffee? No? Well, I don't know about you, but
I've had enough culture for one day. How about a
walk on the beach?"

"Sounds good. Chilly, but good."

"Just a short walk. And then maybe a movie?"

"Sure, why not? I haven't seen a movie since I
moved here."

Their route took them past the Rockingham House,
and as Garrison's BMW glided by, Taylor glanced
over at the forbidding Victorian mansion silhouetted
against the early winter sunset. "Olive says the cult
meets near that place," she said. "It does look
spooky."

"That's just because it's in such bad shape," Garrison said. "A coat of paint, new roof . . ."

But Taylor shook her head. "I remember it from when I was a kid," she said. "It was always spooky.

"People do refer to it as the haunted house," Garrison admitted. "Even Sam says he saw a supernatural green glow one night when he was driving past." Taylor raised an eyebrow. "Probably ground fog," he added quickly.

"It seems so strange to me that with all the development around here, that place should just be standing there," Taylor said. "You'd think whoever owned it would tear it down and build a shopping center. Or subdivide it into housing lots." She turned to stare at it through the car's rear window. As they rounded a curve, the view framed in the window changed from the forbidding mansion to the old wrought-iron gates of the cemetery across the road from it.

"Who does own it?" she asked. "Do you know? How can they just let it stand there, crumbling away?"

"The way I heard it," Garrison said, "by the time old Mrs. Rockingham died, her heirs were scattered across the country. Not surprising, really. As you've probably noticed, New Chatham's population consists primarily of newcomers and vacationers. A lot of the former residents, people like you and your parents, left town. And of course most of the Rockingham heirs weren't from New Chatham to begin with."

"All the more reason to sell."

"So you'd think. But they say that some of them wanted to sell and some of them didn't. And of the ones who did, some thought the price they were being offered was too low. When the developers eventually raised their offer to an acceptable level, the heirs that wanted to sell put pressure on the ones that wanted to hold on to the property, even tried to buy them out, but in the end, nobody could agree. Still can't, I guess. So the property just sits there."

"Olive says Ben won't walk by here alone at night."

Garrison shrugged. "Can't think of any reason he'd want to, anyway. Unless you're heading for Duke's, over there"—he jerked his chin at a rough-looking roadhouse they were just passing—"or you've got relatives in the All Saints Cemetery."

"Are people still being buried there?"

"Oh, sure. Especially families who've been here a long time."

Taylor shivered. "Imagine being buried across the road from that old monstrosity."

Garrison glanced over at her, amused. "Somehow, I don't think it would matter."

"I guess not."

He was silent for a moment. "My mother had quite a mordant sense of humor," he said. "When she was in the hospital that last time, my dad came to see her. They'd been apart for many years, but he was still concerned for her." He stared out the window, remembering. "She knew she was dying, talked about it quite openly. My father asked her whether she wanted to be buried or cremated. You know what she said?"

"What?"

" 'Surprise me.' "

Chapter Eighteen

Taylor checked the chart, noting the most recent vitals, then leaned over the supine young man. "How're you feeling, buddy?" she asked. "Ready to rock and roll?"

Jim Partrick grinned up at her, his eyes glassy from the pre-op tranquilizer, and gave a brave thumbs-up, but he looked scared.

"I know you're nervous," she told him. "It's perfectly natural. But I promise you, there's nothing to worry about. Everything will go fine."

"Thanks, doc."

It was Monday, three days since the mall fire, and Taylor was about to operate on Jim Partrick's facial injuries. Ordinarily she'd have preferred doing the reconstruction sooner. But given the head trauma and concussion, the neurologist had insisted on being overly cautious, waiting out the weekend to be sure Partrick remained stable. He hadn't cleared him for surgery until the previous evening.

"We'll get started in just a few minutes." Taylor patted his hand. "See you inside."

Soon after, scrubbed and gowned, she entered the OR, prepared to take the same meticulous care with Partrick's facial reconstruction as she did with her high-paying cosmetic patients. Once she had a scalpel in her hand, the work was the work, and the money she was or wasn't being paid played no part in what she did.

She'd quickly come to like and respect her Greenvale surgical team, and enjoyed working with them. They seemed to like her, too, and had started asking to be assigned to her procedures.

Now they busied themselves around the still figure as Taylor once again checked the roentgenograms in preparation for the reduction of the nasal and zygomatic fractures.

Just under two hours later, a sleeping Jim Partrick was transferred to a gurney and wheeled out to the recovery room. Taylor pulled off her surgical gloves. "Thank you, everyone," she said. "That was fun."

In the changing room, she stripped off her surgical scrubs and sank down onto the bench. She removed her bloody shoe covers and kicked off the molded clogs she wore in the OR. The two procedures she'd done that day added up to seven hours on her feet, tiring despite the comfortable footwear. And the intense concentration of performing complicated surgery was draining. She stretched, then stood and bundled the soiled gear into a red biohazard trash container.

She'd gotten to the hospital around seven that morning for a four-hour facial reconstruction on a clinic car accident victim. Making rounds, signing charts, and consulting with Slater on several prospective cosmetic patients had taken up the brief time between the clinic patient's surgery and Partrick's one o'clock procedure. It was now just after four in the afternoon, and aside from an early morning bagel and coffee, she'd had nothing to eat all day. The adrenaline rush of performing surgery was wearing off fast, and right now she wanted nothing so much as a long, hot bath followed by take-out in front of the television. She was very glad she wasn't on call that night.

Dressed in her street clothes with a standard white medical coat over them, she stopped in Recovery to check Partrick's condition.

"His BP was up a little," the nurse told her, "but we gave him some Demerol per your chart instructions, and it came right down."

"How's it running now?"

"Normal. One-thirty over seventy-five," the nurse said. "And his oh-two sat is good, too."

"Good boy," Taylor told the drowsy figure. "The trauma wasn't nearly as bad as it looked when they first brought him in," she told the nurse. "He'll heal well and fast."

As she turned to leave, Slater came through the wide double doors. "How did it go?"

"Just fine. He's strong as a horse, that one. A walking ad for the New Chatham Fire Brigade."

"Excellent," Slater said. "But you look tired."

"Nothing a food tray and some bed rest won't cure," she said lightly. "Unless you need me for anything, I'm heading home."

"Better use the rear service road," Slater said. "There's a protest rally outside the front entrance."

"Can't Security clear them away? Or the police?"

Slater shrugged. "We've pushed them back to the sidewalk. That's public property, so we can't prevent them from being there."

"What do they want?" Taylor asked, thinking one of the hospital unions might be doing a little softening up in anticipation of contract negotiations.

"Same as always. They want us gone."

"So these are the famous protesters I've been hearing so much about," Taylor said. "The ones who planted that glove in my car."

"We don't know that for sure," Slater objected.

Taylor shrugged. "They're not exactly fans of Greenvale. Or its staff."

"True." Slater sighed. "The town's got this huge celebration planned for Greenvale's fifth anniversary next month, and these people are still demonstrating against us."

"Hard to believe."

"Isn't it? Of course our local bunch of crazies have been reinvigorated by some national anti-genetics coalition. My being nominated for a Larrabee seems to have brought Greenvale to their attention."

"How did they find out about the nomination?"

"Damned if I know." He shook his head in disgust. "All I can tell you is, they apparently heard about it before I did."

"But your work isn't genetics-based."

"Of course not. But I suppose they figure that any research interesting enough for the Larrabee people is research worth protesting."

"So we've got a national group out there as well as our local one?"

"Not really. I gather the coalition funds and advises. It's mostly locals."

"Well, I wouldn't mind having a look at them."

Slater frowned. "Do you think that's wise?"

"Come on, Sam. What are they going to do to me in broad daylight? Besides, *you're* still around, and you're the prime target for them." He shrugged. "Did *you* ever find a voodoo doll on your front step?"

"In my desk drawer, actually," Sam said reluctantly. "I threw the damn thing away, just like you did. It's the only way to treat that sort of thing."

"Why didn't you tell me?"

"It was at least a year ago, maybe longer. Ignore that stuff and it goes away. At least that's been my experience."

"Well, you might have mentioned it. It would have made me feel less . . . singled out."

Slater looked slightly abashed. "Sorry," he said. "I was afraid it might make you feel worse."

"Did Ward Harland ever get one of their little gifts?"

"Not to my knowledge. Of course, he might have ignored it just like I did."

"Well, I'm not driving four blocks out of my way

for those people," Taylor stated. "It's against my prin-
ciples. See you tomorrow, Sam."

Taylor rarely bothered to lock her car doors from
the inside, but when she saw the massed pickets shouting and chopping the air with their large wooden placards, she changed her mind.

GREENVALE = POLLUTION = DEATH!
YOUR GREED KILLED OUR TOWN!
SUPPORT OUR LOCAL STORES!
STOP THE DEVELOPERS!

A little late for that last one, Taylor thought. She
drove slowly toward the protesters, assuming they'd
give way when she got to them. But they didn't. They
crowded around her car, pressing their faces to the
windows, banging on the roof and shouting. Where
were the police? she wondered. She honked the horn
and crept cautiously forward.

As the crowd milled around her, a plump woman
in a worn leather jacket pushed through to the car.
Peering in at Taylor, she knocked on the driver's
window.

Taylor looked straight ahead, intent on not injuring
anyone, but the woman continued to knock. Taylor
flicked a glance at her; I know that face, she thought.

The woman mouthed something and gestured that
Taylor should roll down her window. Taylor shook
her head. The woman nodded and repeated the gesture, then pointed to herself and mouthed something
else. Looking more closely, Taylor realized the woman
was saying "Maggie Kay."

She braked and cautiously lowered the window
one inch.

Maggie pressed her lips to the opening. "Why didn't
you call me back?"

Taylor mimed puzzlement, taking her hands from
the wheel and spreading them in the classic "I have
no idea what you're talking about" gesture.

"I called you." Maggie spoke loudly to be heard over the crowd. "I left a message for you."

Taylor shook her head and shrugged her shoulders. On the other side of the windshield, someone was scrawling a message on the glass in lipstick:

DEVELOPMENT MEANS THE END OF—

Maggie Kay took a quick, fearful look around. "You're in danger," she told Taylor urgently. "I have to talk to you."

Taylor frowned. "What kind of danger?"

"Greenvale's a terrible place," Maggie said, her eyes overly bright. "Crimes against nature. What they're doing is wrong."

"No, Maggie." Taylor spoke gently but firmly. The woman was obviously disturbed. "You're the ones who are wrong, blocking the sidewalk in front of a hospital."

But Maggie shook her head violently. Casting glances right and left, she spoke to Taylor over her shoulder. "There's something I have to tell you—" Suddenly she gasped and broke off.

Following her gaze, Taylor saw Janice Whelan and four security guards pushing their way through the crowd. About time, Taylor thought.

One of the uniformed men peered in at her. "You okay, Dr. Barnes?"

"I'm fine."

Outside, Janice stared threateningly at Maggie, who melted back into the confusion of bodies.

Taylor rolled her window down halfway. "Thanks for bringing the cavalry," she told Janice.

The other woman turned back toward the car. "Happy to do it," she said. "I hate these damn protests. They shouldn't be allowed." Taking a tissue from her uniform pocket, she reached over and began rubbing the lipstick off the windshield. One of the security men went to help her, and Taylor turned her attention back to Maggie's retreating figure. A frown creased her forehead.

Gradually the guards opened a path for the car. With a wave of thanks for the men and a smile of gratitude for Janice, Taylor drove out onto the broad avenue. Well, that was interesting, she thought wryly. Not an experience I'd care to repeat anytime soon.

Amazing the way people change, she reflected, steering the car toward the center of town in search of food. She hadn't known Maggie well back in high school, but she'd always struck Taylor as a dull, unimaginative girl. If anyone had told her little Maggie Kay would turn into a screaming, sign-waving crazy . . . It was all very sad. And what was that about a message?

She pulled into the parking lot of El Pollo Loco and got out of the car, locking the door carefully behind her. There were still some lipstick traces on the windshield, and she fumbled in her handbag for a tissue.

The slogan had been lengthy—the entire glass was faintly smeared with red—but several of the letters were still boldly legible. She started to wipe them off, then froze.

The letters read

DE A TH

"Hello?"

"Taylor? It's Mom. I hope I'm not interrupting your dinner—"

"That's okay."

"—but we hadn't heard from you for a while, and your dad insisted that we call. What are you having?"

"A burrito."

"That doesn't sound like a very good dinner to me."

"Mom, please."

"All right, all right. So how are you doing?"

"Fine. I'm fine."

"You don't sound fine. Is something wrong?"

"Just a long day in the OR. And a clash with a local protest group that doesn't like the hospital being here."

"Why ever not? I'd have thought they'd be grateful."

"Well, the land was supposed to be used for a public park. And also—frankly, I'm too tired to go into it. But do you remember a girl named Maggie Kay? She was in my grade in high school."

"Little Maggie Kay? With the red hair? The one who was so boy-crazy?"

"That's her. She's part of the protest group. Her husband died at Greenvale."

"That's awful. They're not dangerous, these people, are they? Taylor?"

"I was just swallowing. No, they're not dangerous. Please don't worry. How are you and Dad?"

"I've become a golf widow, but aside from that, we're fine. How are things at the hospital? Are they keeping you busy?"

"Very."

"And the people there are nice?"

"Yes, for the most part. Although the chief of cardiothoracic is a real jerk. Actually, I've been meaning to ask you and Dad about him. He practiced here in New Chatham, years ago. I didn't know him then, of course—I was only a kid—but I keep thinking there's something about him I should remember. Something I once knew. Or overheard."

"How curious. What's his name?"

"Ohlmeyer. Peter Ohlmeyer." Silence. "Mom?"

"I suppose you might have overheard me on the phone or something. There was a little talk at the time, but you know how small towns are. Not that he wasn't a strange man. Moody. At least, that's what Millie Varrick said; we didn't really know him. You remember Mrs. Varrick? She lived next door."

"Yeah. She was one mean old lady."

"Oh, she wasn't that bad. She just didn't care for children. Anyway, Mrs. Varrick did volunteer work with Pete Ohlmeyer's wife—he'd been widowed, and this was his second marriage—and Mrs. Varrick just hated him. She was sure he was a secret wife beater."

"A wife beater? How awful. Do you think it was true?"

"Well, Mrs. Varrick was something of a gossip, but she was nobody's fool. Anyway, the Ohlmeyers only lived in New Chatham for a year or so. I'm surprised you remembered the name after all this time."

"Me, too. I didn't notice him wearing a wedding ring. I guess his wife must have left him."

"Well, not exactly. You see, shortly after they moved away, Mrs. Varrick tried to contact the woman. She got a note from Peter Ohlmeyer saying his wife had died. He'd been widowed for the second time. He was still a fairly young man at the time."

"What are you implying, Mom?"

"Not a thing, dear. After all, I barely knew them. But Mrs. Varrick was convinced that Peter Ohlmeyer had murdered both his wives."

Chapter Nineteen

The full moon was bright in the clear midnight sky, coating the ground below in cold, pale light. It whitened the old tombstones and picked out the wrought-iron gates. But beneath the overhanging trees, the shadows were deep.

In stately procession, thirteen robed figures entered the graveyard across from the Rockingham House. The first in line carried a large silver bowl; each of the others held a flaming black candle.

Just inside the gates, they formed themselves into a circle, the bowl carrier in the center. The candles were carefully set down on the wet grass, and bags of powdered chalk in various colors were drawn from sleeves. Chanting, the central figure sprinkled chalk in strange ritualistic designs, invoking the spirits of the North, South, East, and West before offering the silver bowl to the participants. One by one, they drank the drugged potion, their pulses racing, their eyes feverish.

The chanting increased in volume and fervor, reached a crescendo, stopped. The central figure addressed the others.

"Brothers and sisters. The Raising of the Dead is a powerful and dangerous ceremony. It is not one we undertake lightly. But all other methods have failed. *You* have failed," the leader added, turning toward one of the figures. "Others have had to take on your tasks. And at the demonstration, you were seen whispering to one of our enemies."

"But you told me to befriend her," the woman replied, her voice shaky with fear.

The leader approached the woman, looking deeply into the frightened eyes under the dark hood. "What was it you had to tell her? What danger were you going to warn her about?"

"The evil of Greenvale," the woman said. "The danger of her staying here."

The leader stared at her as if trying to read her thoughts. "Never forget, Maggie Kay McCormick," she said at last, "that the punishment for disloyalty is death."

Maggie gasped and drew back. Satisfied, the leader returned to the center of the group. "Raise your candles," she ordered.

A blazing circle of light rose above the cowled heads. The leader intoned the ritual phrases, and the others echoed them.

"We summon the dead to rise from their graves," the leader pronounced, arms aloft. "Rise up and help us in our fight against the evil that is Greenvale. Rise and come to us!"

"Rise and come to us . . ."

"We summon those who died at Greenvale Hospital, two of whom sleep beneath our feet. Rise and avenge yourselves."

"Rise and avenge yourselves."

The leader's gaze swept across the tombstones, came back to rest on the participants. "Those of you who have loved ones buried here, loved ones who died at Greenvale, call them forth." From the sleeve of her robe, the leader took a ritual knife, its bone handle decorated with occult markings.

One figure stepped boldly into the center of the circle. The leader nodded approvingly, then turned and stared at Maggie McCormick. "Come forward."

But Maggie held back. "What are you going to do?"

"You know what I'm going to do," the leader told her. "Step into the circle." Others propelled Maggie toward the leader, gripping her firmly.

The leader went to the first volunteer. The knife flashed in the moonlight, and blood dripped onto the ground. "As your blood was shed, so is mine," the leader intoned, and the words were repeated by the wounded figure.

"Call your grandmother's name," the leader ordered. "Ask her to rise."

The volunteer called loudly over and over, keens and cries gradually subsiding into low moans.

"Now you, Maggie. Give me your hand."

The smaller woman drew back in fear, but the others forced her hand away from her side and held it out toward the leader as Maggie struggled.

"Give her more wine," the leader ordered. Someone took up the silver bowl from the grave on which it had been placed, and held it to Maggie's lips, forcing her to drink.

The leader waited a few moments for this second dose to take effect. "Are you ready now?"

"Yes," Maggie whimpered softly, sagging back into the arms of her captors.

Again the knife flashed, and the blood flowed. Maggie cried out in pain.

"Say the words," the leader ordered.

"As your blood was shed," Maggie intoned, her voice strengthening as the drug coursed through her veins, "so is mine. So is mine!"

"Call him. Call your husband."

Hands released her as she began to keen. Stumbling, she raised her arms and cried out into the night. "Jack! Jack McCormick! Come back. Come back to me." Moaning and calling for her husband, the knife wound still dripping blood, the heavily drugged woman tottered through the wrought iron gates and out onto the road. The others followed after her.

She was across the road now, reeling before the

Rockingham House, calling wildly, the drug running strong. "Jack McCormick. It's me, Maggie," she screamed over and over. "Come back to me, Jack! Oh, God, Jack, I miss you. Come to me, Jack McCormick!"

The leader watched, a satisfied smile on her face. Turning away, she scuffed out the chalk markings. Then, lifting the bowl to each of the four corners of the earth in turn, she drained it. "The ritual is complete," she murmured. "The dead will rise."

She glanced over at Maggie, who was still stumbling blindly around the mansion's facade, wailing for her dead husband. Setting down the silver bowl, the leader started across the road toward the robed figure, then froze. She looked off to her left, listening intently.

"Someone's coming," she warned the group. "Time to go. Hurry."

Again, hands took hold of Maggie and hustled her back across the road. Once inside the cemetery gates, the witches paused only to retrieve the bowl and blow out their candles before drifting back into the woods beyond the graves. Supporting the moaning, tottering Maggie, they vanished into the shadows.

"I saw something, I tell ya. Lights."

"The lights were in your brain, man. You're hammered."

"Hammered yourself."

Three young men approached unsteadily from the direction of Duke's roadhouse. They'd been drinking all evening—nothing new there—and only the need to rid themselves of some of what they'd consumed had forced them out into the cold. Duke didn't like his customers throwing up in the john; they usually missed.

"How you doin', Hank?" A friendly arm dropped around the shoulders of the pale young man in the stained leather jacket, but whether this was for the young man's support or the questioner's was debatable.

Hank shrugged off both question and questioner. "Lemme alone, Rog," he said.

"Nothing like a good chunder, huh?" Roger, a tall, hairy giant of a man, observed.

"What's a chunder?"

"Aussie for what you did in that ditch back there."

"Lights," the first man insisted, ignoring this lively banter. "And yelling." He combed back his greasy blond hair with his fingers.

"Drunk as a skunk," Hank said. "Andy's seein' things."

"Not as drunk as you," Andy told him. Positioning himself on the white divider line, he held out his arms and began inching along it, swaying slightly. "See? Steady as a rock."

"Yeah, yeah," said Hank.

Roger gave Andy a gentle shove, sending him reeling. "Some rock," he commented.

"Fuck you," said Andy mildly, returning to his line. "I seen what I seen." He tottered on for another few yards, then stopped, staring at the spiky Victorian mansion just ahead. "Going back now," he announced, turning sharply and banging into the hairy giant who, having decided that line-walking looked like an interesting challenge, was following close on the heels of his mentor.

"Watch where you're going, for crissake," Roger told him, and then, as Andy wandered past, added, "Where *are* you going?"

"Anywhere else" came the reply.

Roger and Hank regarded their comrade. "He's spooked," Roger said. "Scared of that haunted house over there. Scared of the cemetery. Ain't that right?"

Andy spun around. "Who're you calling scared?"

"You. You're scared the ghosts are gonna get you."

"Am not."

"Are too. Booga-booga."

Hank watched the discussion with growing impatience. "So prove it," he said.

Andy frowned. "What're you talkin' about?"

"Show us how brave you are. Go knock on the door."

"You're crazy."

"Go ahead. I dare you."

"Yeah, me too," Roger chimed in. "I dare you, too."

Andy looked from one to the other. "Okay," he said. "But if I do it, you both have to do it, too."

Roger looked uneasy. "Sure," he said.

Andy stumbled over to the mansion's front door and hammered on the old wooden door. "Come out, come out, wherever you are," he sang before turning tail and scampering back to his friends. "Okay, you're up."

Roger approached the door, then turned and looked back at his friends.

"Go on," Andy urged. "Or are you too chicken?"

"Chicken yourself." But still he hesitated, staring up at the stark outline of turrets against the moonlit sky. Behind him, his friends began making clucking noises. "Stop that, you guys." Heart pounding, he began battering at the door with his fists, whooping and hollering to drown out the clucking.

"What was all that yelling for?" Hank demanded. "You made enough noise to wake the dead."

"I sure hope so," Roger replied, grinning nastily, "because it's your turn now."

"Yeah, go on," Andy urged. "Do it."

But Hank retreated up the road. "Going home," he said.

"Bull*shit*, you're going home." The other two went after him. "Go knock on that goddamn door," Roger said, grabbing an elbow and spinning him around.

"Can't make me."

"Wanna bet?"

"Hey, guys? Look over there."

A wraithlike figure drifted across the uncut lawn.
Swathed in a pale sheet, in turns illuminated by moonlight and concealed in shadow, it flitted around the
old, abandoned house, paused, and started across the
road in front of them.

"Holy shit. What's that?"

"Mother of God, it's a spook."

"I told you I saw something," Andy said, crossing
himself.

"Shut up. It'll hear you."

The three men stood rooted, watching the figure
flow across the road toward the gates of the cemetery.

"You woke it up," Hank told Roger accusingly.

"Maybe it's going home," said Andy hopefully.

But Roger, alcohol working in him, grinned. "Come
on, fellas. Let's go catch ourselves a ghost."

"You nuts or something?"

"Not me, man."

"Who's chicken now?" Roger challenged. "Hurry
up. It's going into the graveyard." But the others hung
back. "Jeez, you guys. There's only one of it and three
of us. We can take it. Come on."

He began running toward the zombielike creature
and, after a moment's hesitation, the others followed.
They entered the graveyard behind it. Now that they
were closer, they could hear the sound it was making,
a sort of high-pitched keening mumble.

"What's it saying?"

"I don't know."

The creature floated among the headstones, turning
this way and that as it moaned to itself.

"It's looking for something," Andy murmured.

"Maybe it's lost."

"You head it off on that side," Roger called to
Hank. "And I'll grab it from behind—"

"Better you than me," Hank replied, moving into
position. The wraith, sensing the movement, spun
away, coming up hard against the side of a small mau-
soleum. Howling, it turned its contorted face toward

its pursuers. Andy, closest of the three, stared into its
face and froze in horror.

What he saw in that brief instant was later hotly
disputed, and even he would come to doubt his own
account. But his two friends were prepared to swear
that at that terrifying moment, he cried out the name
of an old friend.

"Jack McCormick," he gasped.

The zombie turned. Flailing its wrappings and keening, it came straight for him.

Andy feinted to his right, turning the attack into a
glancing blow, and the three drinking pals, suddenly
sober, turned and bolted.

At Duke's, their account was met with hilarity and
disbelief.

"A ghost, you say? Oh, right."

"You sure it was a ghost and not a stray dog or
something?"

"You think I don't know the difference?" Roger
said truculently.

"After the way you were drinking tonight, buddy, I
don't think you know your own name."

"It was a ghost," Andy insisted. "It bumped inta
me."

"It *bumped into* you? Now I *know* you're lying.
Whoever heard of a solid ghost?"

"Somebody was pulling your chain, man."

"Yeah. Someone was messing with you. Got you
good, too."

"Hey, Duke, these guys say they chased a ghost in
the All Saints Cemetery."

"Across from the Rockingham place? All those stories must have gone to their brains."

"What brains? Ha, ha."

"It wasn't talk that went to their brains, Duke. If
you know what I mean."

"Yeah. You guys were hammered."

"Hammered yourself."

"Best story I've heard all week," Duke said, laughing. "Somebody buy these booze hounds a beer."

Chapter Twenty

Days came and went, bringing with them intimations of spring. The temperature warmed to a record sixty degrees that particular Monday, but evening brought a cold front. By midnight, Greenvale Hospital was wrapped in a mantle of mist.

Jim Partrick was dozing fitfully when the door to his room swung slowly open. Light from the hallway stabbed briefly into the darkened room as a white-coated figure stepped inside, syringe in hand. Approaching the bed, the figure bent over the sleeping fireman, then went to the IV stand, bumping the bedside table in the dark. A hardcover novel fell to the floor with a thump.

"Hey," Jim stirred, blinked, looked over. "Who's there?"

"Just me" came the reply. "Time for your meds."

Partrick turned his head and watched the syringe empty into the IV line. "What are you giving me?"

"An antibiotic."

"Oh." Jim frowned. "You're here late," he murmured, watching the figure retreat toward the door.

"It happens."

"I guess. Hey, when can I go home?"

"Soon. A couple of days. Better get some rest, now."

Light from the hallway illuminated the room for a

moment as the figure departed. Within minutes Partrick was asleep again.

The next time he woke, it was to searing pain and a terrible pressure beneath his ribs. Monitors were beeping and someone was banging on his chest. He moaned and gasped for breath. He felt himself drifting away . . .

"Clear!"

Suddenly he was back, and he was moving. What was happening to him? He felt a rush of air and opened his eyes as the gurney on which he was strapped caromed through the double doors of an OR.

He tried to speak but no words came. His brain told him that he was being lifted onto an operating table, but his body was registering no sensations. It was an eerie and terrifying feeling.

A familiar face loomed above him. You're in good hands, he tried to tell himself. You'll be all right. But he felt so ill, so cold. His eyelids drooped.

"Epi . . . Gentomycin . . ." He heard the strange words as if in a dream. Medicines, he thought. Drugs that will save me. He drifted off again.

"It's no good."

"I did everything I could."

"Time of death, one-oh-six."

Time passed. Jim Partrick opened his eyes. He was floating in a dark tunnel, moving forward. Cold air brushed his face. So this is death, he thought. He felt surreally calm, and very, very tired . . .

Suddenly he was jolted back to consciousness. He blinked at the bright, round light above him. Just like they always said, he thought in his preternaturally calm state; a long tunnel and a bright light. Any minute his grandparents would materialize and welcome him to—

A face swam into his field of vision, blocking the light. With a shock, he realized it was a living face.

"So I'm not dead," he murmured.

"No" came the unsmiling reply. A scalpel flashed in the bright, cold light. "Not yet."

As she drove to the hospital that clear Tuesday morning, Taylor was pleased to see that the mist of the evening before had burned off in the bright sunlight. The blue sky matched her mood of happy anticipation. Kip was finally coming to New Chatham that weekend. As she drove, she debated where to take him for dinner, what she'd wear, whether she should get her hair cut. It was fun to have a guy in her life again.

She pulled into her parking space. Enough of that, she told herself. Time to concentrate on hospital business.

She headed for the elevators, deciding to check on Jim Partrick before going to her office. She'd been impressed with the surprisingly rapid recovery the firefighter had made, thanks to his youth and outstanding physical condition, and she sympathized with his growing restlessness. Perhaps she could talk Slater into sending him home today.

In fact, Taylor had been ready to release the young man several days after his surgery, but Slater had insisted they keep him hospitalized until the end of the second week. She'd voiced her surprise at such unusual caution, and also pointed out that the man's health insurance wouldn't cover such an extended stay, but Slater had replied that Greenvale would cover the cost.

"Investigators think that mall fire was set," he'd told her. "They can't prove it was the protest group, but who else would do such a thing? Since the mall fire wouldn't have happened if Greenvale weren't here, we owe it to the town to make sure Partrick gets the best medical care available."

If Greenvale weren't here, there wouldn't be a mall in the first place, she'd been tempted to point out. But hospital beds weren't at a premium at the moment, so all she'd said was "It's your dollar," and had gone to arrange for the pizza Jim had been agitating for.

She sensed the charged atmosphere as soon as she stepped off the elevator on Partrick's floor.

The nursing supervisor rose as Taylor came up to the counter. "We're all so sorry," she said. "Everyone really liked him."

"Liked who?" Taylor said. A chill ran through her.

"Jim Partrick," the nurse said, confirming Taylor's fears. "Didn't they call you?"

"No, no one called me," Taylor replied tightly. "What happened?"

"He died last night. The nurse found him around three-thirty this morning. He was unconscious, with Cheyne-Stokes breathing and decerebrate posturing. She called a code, but as they were responding, he stopped breathing. They could barely find a pulse. They intubated him and started CPR, but they never got him back."

"What was it?"

"Cardiac arrest."

"That's not possible."

The nurse shrugged. "I'm just repeating what the night staff told me. I came on at eight this morning. Maybe you should talk to Dr. Ohlmeyer. He was here."

"The supervisor called Ohlmeyer? Why didn't she call me? Partrick was my patient."

"We're always supposed to call Dr. Ohlmeyer in the case of arrest," the nurse said. "It's a standing order. The supervisor probably assumed he would call you himself."

"Jim Partrick was *my* patient," Taylor repeated angrily. "Is his chart still here?"

"It should have been sent down to Medical Records," the nurse told her, "but maybe it wasn't picked up yet." She went to a wire cart at the rear of the nurses station and shuffled through its contents. "You're in luck," she said, retrieving the metal-covered chart and handing it to Taylor. "They tried everything, Dr. Barnes. Dr. Ohlmeyer even took him to the OR, put him on a heart-lung machine."

"He *what*?"

The nurse shrugged. "Dr. Ohlmeyer said he wanted to give him every chance. We really did do everything we could."

"That's not the point." Taylor took the chart and leafed quickly through the pages. "I should have been called."

"You'd better take it up with Dr. Ohlmeyer," the nurse said. "He took the chart for Room 504 and hasn't returned it, so he's probably still in there."

Taylor spun on her heel and stomped down the corridor. The door to 504 was ajar, and she shoved it open with her palm. "Dr. Ohlmeyer? May I have a word?"

Ohlmeyer was bending over a patient. He looked up, frowning at the interruption. "Please go to your office, Dr. Barnes. I'll see you when I'm through with rounds."

"Why wasn't I called last night? Jim Partrick was my patient."

"I'm busy at the moment, doctor."

"So am I. One of *my* patients d—" She broke off. "I'm sorry, but I need to talk to you *now*."

Ohlmeyer rose, his face flushed and his eyes stormy. Apologizing to his patient, he took Taylor by the elbow and hustled her out into the corridor.

"How dare you interrupt me," he demanded, marching her back up the hall.

"How dare this hospital not notify me when one of my patients dies," Taylor retorted, pulling away from him.

"What's going on here?" Dr. Slater stepped off the elevator.

"I was with a patient," Ohlmeyer told Slater, his face flushed with anger, "when she stormed in and started shouting at me—"

"I did not shout," Taylor retorted. "But yes, I was angry about not being called when Jim Partrick, my own patient—"

"You had no right to interrupt—"

"Stop this right now. The patients can hear you." Slater lowered his voice. "Now, what the hell is this about?"

"It's about unprofessional behavior," Ohlmeyer stated, "and female hysterics."

"How dare you—" Taylor began.

"I'll be happy to discuss this with you later, Sam. Right now I have patients to see." Shooting a fierce look at Taylor, he hurried back toward the patient area.

"Sam, that's completely unacceptable—"

Slater sighed. "The man has a temper. And as I've said before, he's a dinosaur. But he's a helluva doctor, and he has my complete confidence."

"That doesn't excuse what happened."

"You're right." Slater paused. "*Did* you interrupt him with a patient?"

Taylor flushed and nodded. "I shouldn't have barged in like that, but I just heard about Jim. What in hell happened, Sam? He was fine when I left here last night."

"I'm as puzzled as you are," Slater repeated. "I liked the boy. Of course, it proves how right I was to insist that he remain hospitalized."

"It doesn't seem to have helped him any. No, that wasn't fair. I know everyone did all they could. But someone should have called me."

"It happened so fast—"

"Not that fast," Taylor said. "Ohlmeyer worked on him for over an hour, according to the chart. Which I wanted to ask you about—"

"I guess everyone assumed someone else had called you," Slater interrupted. "I know *I* did. In fact, I was kind of puzzled when Pete told me this morning that you never showed up."

"What? He had the nerve to say that after he never bothered to page me?"

An orderly rolled an IV stand off the elevator and over to the nurses station, where the staff was pretending not to listen to the two doctors. "I think we should lower our voices," Slater cautioned.

"The chart says cardiac arrest," Taylor said more quietly. "But his heart was sound as a bell. I don't get it."

"I suspect a delayed intracranial hemorrhage," Slater told her. "We'll never really know."

"The autopsy will tell us."

"Not according to the family it won't."

"You've already located them?"

Slater nodded. "Called them early this morning. They refused an autopsy."

"Poor Jim," Taylor said. "I can't believe this happened."

"We did everything we could."

"Like putting him on that heart-lung machine. Why would Ohlmeyer do that?"

"He wanted to give the man every chance to revive," Slater told her, his eyes serious.

"I never heard of such a thing," Taylor insisted. "And he administered heparin and streptokinase and potassium chloride and methylprednisolone and deferoxamine—what the hell is that about?"

"When it comes to cardiac patients, I give Ohlmeyer carte blanche."

"Partrick wasn't a cardiac patient."

"He became one when he arrested."

"That's nonsense. And so is that protocol."

"I will not be challenged like this," Slater told her, his voice rising. "He was at the bedside, not you."

"And whose fault was that?" Taylor asked, her voice rising to match his.

At the nurses station, heads turned toward the two arguing doctors. Slater grabbed Taylor's shoulders and frog-marched her past the elevators and around the corner.

"Don't you ever argue with me in front of the staff," he told her furiously. "In fact, don't argue with me at all. This is my hospital, and every patient is mine before they're anybody else's. I gave you Partrick when he was a surgical patient, and I reassigned him when his condition changed. Pete Ohlmeyer's worked with me for five years. How long have you been here?" His face was flushed and his breathing harsh. One eye twitched uncontrollably. "I've given you a chance to resurrect your career, Dr. Barnes. It's no secret that Greenvale was the only hospital willing to take a chance on a former drunk—excuse me, a recovering alcoholic. You should be mindful of that fact and act accordingly."

Translation: Argue with me and lose your job, Taylor thought helplessly. And if no one would hire you before you came here, who in hell do you think will hire you if I fire you?

Angry but powerless, Taylor watched him stride away down the corridor. Still clutching the chart, she took a few deep breaths before returning to the nurses station. Frustrating as the situation was, there was nothing she could do about it except quit. Which was not an option if she wanted to continue to practice medicine.

Besides, Slater was just defending the real culprit in all this. And she was damned if she'd let a slimeball like Ohlmeyer drive her away. For a brief moment she was tempted to go after Slater, ask if he knew Ohlmeyer was a suspected wife beater and worse, but stopped herself in time. Talk about unprofessional behavior, she thought.

"Thanks," she told the nurse, handing back the chart. "Sorry if I came on a little strong. I was surprised and upset by Jim Partrick's death."

The woman nodded. "I understand. We all are."

Boarding the elevator, Taylor punched "three." But

when the door opened onto her floor, she hesitated, then thought what the hell, and pushed "B," rubbing her arm where Ohlmeyer had bruised it.

The morgue was located in a corner of the basement near the rear of the building so that transport for the dead could come and go unseen by the general public. This was a fairly usual arrangement; what hospital would want to flaunt its failures?

She pushed through the metal door with its discreet sign. She'd never before had occasion to visit the Greenvale morgue. It was pretty typical, although smaller than other hospital morgues she'd seen. Greenvale, with its high percentage of cosmetic procedures, was obviously anticipating lower-than-normal morbidity.

It was very quiet. She wandered down the linoleum-tiled hallway and past the open door of an empty autopsy room, searching for someone she could talk to.

"Help you?" She jumped. A stocky young man with a round, open face and a blond crew cut stood behind her. He wore a white coat over his jeans. "Sorry to startle you," he said. "I'm Lewis Gamble."

"I'm Dr. Barnes. I was Jim Partrick's surgeon."

"Helluva thing," the young man said, extending his hand.

"You're in charge here?" Taylor asked. His handshake was firm.

"From six in the morning until four at night. Come on into the office." He led her to a small, untidy room containing a desk, several chairs, and a tall file cabinet. "What can I do for you?"

"I'd like to examine the body," Taylor said.

Lewis looked surprised. "Body's gone," he said.

"Gone where?"

"Released to the family."

"How can that be?" Taylor frowned. "His family lives in Wisconsin. Are you sure we're talking about the same patient?"

"Jim Partrick, right?" he said, shuffling through a

tray of papers on the desk. "Let me find the face sheet. I don't know if Wally filed it or not."

"Who's Wally?"

"Wally Gamble, the night guy. He's my cousin," Lewis added as Taylor raised an eyebrow at the name. "No, not filed yet," he said, handing her the paper.

Taylor scanned the face sheet, a copy of the top sheet of the chart she'd already seen. "It's the same man," she said. It was too bad his family had refused the autopsy, she reflected. It would have been interesting to know what had actually caused the sudden cardiac arrest.

Idly, she ran her eye over the time of death and the time the body had been sent to the morgue. There was something about that time of death. . . . Pink traces of pencil eraser clung to the page, and she whisked them away with her hand, then looked more closely. Beside the morgue instructions, someone had scrawled something lightly in red pencil. She tipped the chart toward the ceiling light. By its cool flourescence, she could easily make out the number 37.

"Hey, Lewis? You know anything about this?" She pointed to the barely legible number.

He leaned across the desk. "What?"

"That number. 37."

"I can't see any number."

"Tilt the page toward the light. There, see? Does it mean anything to you?"

Lewis relaxed back in his chair. "Not a thing," he said with a shrug. "Why?"

"Just curious." It probably wasn't important, she decided, returning the face sheet. "So the body's gone? That was fast. What happened to it?"

"Funeral home came and got it," Lewis explained. "The family gave instructions, asked that the body be cremated and the ashes sent to them."

"Who spoke with them?"

"One of the doctors, probably. And then somebody would have called the funeral home, and they would have called Wally. All I know is, everything was taken care of by the time I came on at six."

"By your cousin."

"Right. Wally has the graveyard shift. If you'll excuse the pun." He grinned at his witticism. "He was here when they brought the body down, he signed it in, he signed it out."

"Are you telling me that Partrick's already been cremated? He's only been dead about six hours."

"Well, I don't know about that part," Lewis said, "although Aaron runs a very efficient operation. All I can tell you is, the body was released to Gamble's Funeral Home at—" he consulted a large bound record book on one side of the desk "—five-ten this morning." He pushed the book toward her. "See right there? That's Wally's signature. And that's the transport driver's signature."

"Gamble's Funeral Home . . . Gamble is *your* name, isn't it?"

Lewis nodded. "Aaron Gamble is my father."

Chapter Twenty-one

The rest of the week flew by in a flurry of procedures, consultations, and rounds. Slater's attitude toward Taylor remained cool, and she found herself avoiding him whenever possible. She'd been wrong, she knew, to barge in on Ohlmeyer the way she had, but he'd been wrong not to make sure someone reached her the night Jim Partrick died. While she conceded that she might have overreacted in the heat of the moment, each time she recalled Slater threatening her with the loss of her job, she became furious all over again. In her former practice, she had been highly respected, a star. She wasn't used to being treated in such a cavalier manner.

Going to her AA group on Friday evening helped put things back in perspective. Blaming Slater for her current situation was unproductive and unfair. If she hadn't become an alcoholic, she'd still have her own practice. What he'd said to her in anger on Wednesday morning was no less true for the tone of his voice. Greenvale *had* been the only hospital willing to take a chance on her. If anything, she should be grateful to Sam for giving her a way back.

Meanwhile, she prepared for Kip's arrival on Saturday, filling the apartment with fresh flowers and the fridge with interesting tidbits.

The only thing she hadn't been able to fit in was picking up her dry cleaning. She rectified that right after Saturday morning rounds, during which she was pleased to note that Slater's attitude toward her had softened. She returned home to find a message on her answering machine: *Running a little late, I'm afraid. See you around two. I'm counting the hours.*

It was now a little after noon. She made herself a cup of tea, reached for a medical journal, and settled down to wait. But she couldn't concentrate. She felt nervous, and wondered why. Aside from the hiatus during her marriage, Kip had been her friend for years. And their recent evening in New York had proved that they were as good together as lovers as they had been as pals.

Still, they'd only had that one evening together, plus the lunch near his lab. Would Kip's appeal be as strong this time? Had it been a onetime thing, built on the past? No; she'd felt so comfortable in his arms, on the dance floor, and afterward. So comfortable with their conversations and their silences. Yes, things had happened kind of fast, but given their history, you could also say things had happened kind of slowly. Either way, it had felt like the real thing, that night in New York. She hoped it still would.

The two men shook hands, studying each other. "It's good to see you," Slater said. "It's been a long time." The other man nodded, thinking how strange it was, given their past relationship, that they should be so formal with one another. "You'd better come in."

He led the younger man past a large, formal living room and into a paneled den. "Can I get you something? A drink?"

"A little early for me, Sam. Maybe some coffee?"

"I just put on a fresh pot. Won't be a moment."

The man wandered around the room, glancing at photos: Sam at Greenvale's groundbreaking ceremony. Sam with various celebrities. There were several framed watercolors along one wall, unschooled but powerful.

He was admiring them when Sam returned with a tray. "You're still painting?"

"Not anymore. Those are old."

"You were good. Why'd you stop?"

Slater shrugged and set the tray on the large glass coffee table. "My interests changed." He held out a filled cup to the man who took it and settled himself in a leather club chair across from Slater's sofa.

"I read about you in the *Times*," Slater said gruffly. "You've done very well, thanks to me. My interest, my encouragement."

"I owe you a great deal," the man acknowledged.

"So in a sense, your success is mine."

Startled, the man looked up from his coffee. "In a sense," he repeated slowly. "But you've been very successful in your own right. Greenvale Hospital is quite . . . remarkable."

"Oh, come now," Slater said with a sardonic smile. "We all know what they're saying about Greenvale. Cosmetic surgery for the rich and a little clinic work to justify it." He sipped his coffee. "No, founding Greenvale means nothing to me. It's the recognition of my peers that's important." His eyes sparkled. "And I believe their recognition is coming my way at last." He set down his cup. "I've been nominated for a Larrabee. Not for my surgical work, of course. For my research. What's the matter?"

"Nothing," his companion said, frowning. "I'm very happy for you. Really, you deserve it. It's just . . . I'm afraid I've been nominated, too."

Slater's face darkened. "You? Well, that's wonderful," he said quickly, struggling to hide his obvious disappointment. "Congratulations, Kip."

"Thanks." Kip hesitated. "Ever since I heard you were up for the award, I've been thinking about withdrawing my name from consideration. I'd be happy to see it go to you."

"And you think it won't go to me anyway?" Slater

asked angrily. "You think the only way I can win it is if you give it up?"

"Of course not," Kip stammered. "I just thought one less competitor—I'm sorry if that's how it sounded, Sam. All I meant was that I'd be happy to withdraw if it would help your chances."

"Is that what you think of me?" Slater demanded, furious. "That I want to win it that way? What value, what meaning would the award have for me then?" He slammed his cup onto its saucer.

Kip sighed and set down his own cup. "I can't seem to say anything right. Look, let me buy you lunch. We can talk over old times—"

"I can pay for my own lunch, thank you. I may not be as rich as you, I may not have gone to Harvard Medical School—"

"Please don't start all that again. I only meant—"

"I think you should go now." Slater stood, shaking with anger. "Good luck with the Larrabee."

"Dammit, Sam—" Kip was angry, too, now.

"I'll walk you to the door."

Kip rose. "I can't believe I was actually hoping we could . . ." He trailed off.

"What were you hoping?" Sam asked, his tone scathing.

Kip shrugged. "Nothing. It doesn't matter." He followed Slater down the hall in silence. "I hope you win the Larrabee," he said at the door. "I really mean it."

"Strangely enough, I think you do."

"And I'm sorry I offered to withdraw my name. I didn't mean to insult you. Sure you don't want to go have lunch somewhere?" He smiled weakly. "You can pay."

"I don't think so."

"Well, I guess that's it, then." Kip held out his hand. "May the best man win."

Slater gave the hand a perfunctory shake. "I intend to."

The nervousness she felt when the bell rang disappeared the moment she opened the door and saw him smiling at her, cheeks pink with the cold, a trench coat thrown over his well-cut blazer and pressed jeans, flowers in one hand, overnight bag in the other.

"It's good to see you, too," Taylor said a few minutes later. "But you'd better come inside." She grinned at him. "I do have a reputation to protect."

Inside, they embraced again. For Taylor, it was like water in the desert. Aside from the night in New York, it had been a long time since she'd felt such passion, or felt good enough about herself to allow anyone else to feel such passion for her.

"Traffic or work?" she asked when they came up for air.

"What do you mean?"

"You look a little . . . harried," Taylor told him, holding him at arm's length. "And you were late. I figure it had to be one or the other." She smiled into his handsome face.

"A little of both," Kip replied, pulling her close again. "As my personal physician, what course of treatment would you recommend for someone in my condition?"

"Well," Taylor replied, snuggling against him, inhaling his scent, "there is a protocol I can suggest. It's kind of experimental, but they've had excellent results with it in the field."

Later—much later—they showered and dressed, and went in search of sustenance.

"What sort of food do you feel like?" Taylor asked. "Italian, Japanese . . ."

"I've become rather fond of classic Chinese cuisine lately," Kip said. "I don't suppose . . ."

"Not unless you consider a poo-poo platter classic Chinese cuisine. But that does give me an idea."

"I'm in your hands."

She led him to a small, elegant restaurant on a cobblestoned street. "I think you'll like the food," she said. "French, with an Asian twist."

"Sounds interesting."

It was still early, and they were able to snag a corner table not far from the front window. "You certainly look a lot more relaxed than when you arrived," Taylor teased as he slid into the banquette beside her.

"And you look even more beautiful," Kip said, "if that's possible." Taylor flushed with pleasure. She'd chosen the long skirt and sweater with care, and blow-dried her hair carefully, something she rarely bothered to do on workdays. He smiled at her. "I've been looking forward to this. Seeing you. Spending more than just a few hours together."

"Me, too."

"You're a very easy person to be with."

"You wouldn't have said that a year ago."

"I'm not so sure. We've known each other a long time, off and on. We've always been easy with each other, even in stressful circumstances."

As they ordered drinks, Kip surveyed his surroundings approvingly. The polished wooden tables, placed far enough apart for private conversation, were set with crisp napery and flickering candles. Brocade draperies framed the tall French windows at the front of the room; in the rear was a garden, closed now but dotted with fairy lights. Beyond the front window, a few light flurries floated past under the yellow glow of an antique streetlight, illuminating the Saturday night crowd that sauntered along the cobblestone street.

Conversation flowed effortlessly and in many directions, but it wasn't until they were finishing their main course that Kip brought the conversation around to Sam Slater.

"I still find it hard to understand why a renowned surgeon would give up the practice of surgery," Taylor said. "It's not as though he's given up medicine. He still makes rounds, consults on patients, even treats a few. He just won't operate." She sipped her Perrier.

"I asked him to scrub in with me recently, and he refused."

"Maybe he didn't want to cramp your style."

"That wasn't it. Although it didn't keep him from taking a patient away from me the other night," she added, an edge to her voice.

Outside, a figure in a dark overcoat stood in a pool of shadow, muffled against the cold, his hands shoved deep inside his pockets. Scowling, he stared in through the window at the two doctors.

"What happened?" Kip asked. Neither was aware of the watcher outside the window.

Briefly, Taylor told Kip about Jim Partrick, how Ohlmeyer had taken over during the nighttime emergency, how no one had thought to call her, how she'd barged in on Ohlmeyer and a patient. "I admit I overreacted," she said, "but can you blame me? I was furious." She sipped her Perrier. "And then Sam got mad, too. He said all patients were his first, to reassign at will. He was so angry, he was shaking." She hesitated. "At least, I thought that's what it was at the time, anger or fatigue. He'd been up most of the night." She paused. "But later I wondered if he was ill."

"Really? Why do you say that?"

"Because it wasn't the first time I've seen him shake." She paused while their plates were removed and the dessert menus presented. "It seems to happen when he's upset about something," she continued, "but a couple of times I've noticed muscle tremors during a perfectly calm conversation."

"That sounds worrying." Kip looked troubled. "Has he seen anyone about it?"

"I have no idea," Taylor said, surprised. "I don't think it's the kind of thing he'd tell me. And I certainly have no intention of asking. I don't think he'd exactly appreciate it."

"Does he tire easily?" Kip asked. "Has he been complaining of headaches?"

"Not that I'm aware of." Taylor stared at him. "Why this sudden interest in my boss?"

"Old habits die hard," Kip told her, laughing. "I trained as a physician, remember? Don't get much chance to use my diagnostic skills these days."

"Well, here's something you can use them on. When Jim Partrick coded, Ohlmeyer took him to the OR and put him on the heart-lung machine."

"He what?"

"Weird, huh? Then he administered epi—"

"Epinephrine's standard practice."

"Yeah, but he also gave him potassium chloride."

"You mean calcium," Kip corrected her.

"Nope. Potassium."

"But that would—"

"Kill him. Right. And he gave him methylpredniso-lone and a shitload of heparin. And gentamicin."

"Gentamicin? An antimicrobial agent?"

Taylor nodded. "It doesn't make sense."

"Did you ask him about it?"

"I didn't get the chance. But I did ask Slater. At least, I started to, but he bit my head off. Told me Ohlmeyer had carte blanche. When I said the protocol was nonsense, Slater got furious. He said not to challenge him, and that nobody else would hire me, especially if he fired me. He's right about that, of course. And I have to admit he's been very proactive about resuscitating my career." She sipped her mineral water thoughtfully. "He was also right about keeping Jim Partrick in the hospital so long. I was ready to send him home days before he arrested, but Sam was more cautious."

"Well, Slater's not an easy guy, so I've heard," Kip said. "But his heart's in the right place." Taylor looked over at him questioningly. "The low-cost clinic. The professional support he's giving you." He drank off the last of his wine and set down the empty glass. "Hell, he might even win the Larrabee. Not bad for a society doctor. How's his research going? Does he ever mention it?"

"He not only mentioned it, he showed me his lab last week."

"Did he? I'm jealous." He turned to grin at her. "I bet mine's bigger."

"It *is* his lab we're talking about, isn't it? And no, it's not bigger."

"So what's his setup like?"

"He asked me to keep what I saw confidential. But I can tell you it seemed very impressive."

"I'm sure it is, if the Larrabee committee is interested," Kip said. "Good for Slater."

"Good for Slater?" Taylor repeated, amused. "You don't even know the man. And aren't you the one who was crowing about how a cosmetic surgeon would be so easy to beat?"

"Did I say that?"

"You did. At lunch that day, when I told you I'd been interviewed by Sam." She laughed.

"Guilty as charged," he admitted, smiling. "But I didn't drive all this way to talk about Sam Slater."

"I should hope not."

He reached for her hand. "Maybe tomorrow you can give me the grand tour. I'm serious about finding a weekend house. God knows when I'll find the time to use it, but I'd sure like to spend as much time up here as I can. With you."

A loud beeping made both doctors jump and reach for their pagers. They looked at each other and laughed.

"Mine, I'm afraid," Kip said, then frowned as he read the calling number. "I have to answer this."

"The phone's back there near the rest rooms."

"Thanks. Order me something chocolate, and an espresso, okay?"

Taylor watched him go, then turned back and reached for one of the small dessert menus. As she did so, a figure at the window caught her eye. She turned toward him, and for a moment they stared at each other. Then he spun on his heel and hurried away. Taylor sat looking after him for a moment, frowning. The man's face had been in shadow and partly hidden by the muffler he wore, yet she was certain his eyes had been fixed on her. But that was silly; why would anyone be spying on her? She turned away and signaled the waiter.

"I ordered us one chocolate mousse and two forks," she told Kip as he slid in beside her again, then saw his face. "What's the matter? You look like you've seen a ghost."

"Close. That was the Security Office at Emerson. Somebody got into my lab and turned on all the valves."

"What valves?"

"The flame valves. They release the gases we light when we need to heat stuff."

"My God. How far did the fire spread? Was anyone hurt?"

"We were lucky," Kip said. "Whoever opened the valves didn't light them, so there wasn't any fire. But the toxic fumes had spread all through the lab space. Fortunately, one of my researchers went back to retrieve some papers he'd left. He began to feel dizzy, realized what had happened, and went straight to Security, who turned everything off."

"But . . . that's so odd. Was it done deliberately, or was it accidental?"

"Oh, it was deliberate, all right," Kip said darkly. "It's not the first time we've had trouble."

"Really? You never told me."

"You had your own problems," he said. "No need to burden you with mine."

"Well, tell me now."

Kip sighed. "Someone fed a bunch of my researchers poisoned coffee. Somebody wrote slogans all over the computers in lipstick."

"But who would do stuff like that?"

"Someone who doesn't like the subject of my research. We've been picketed by an anti-genetics protest group; I suppose they could be involved. Or else . . ."

"Or else what?"

"Someone's trying to disrupt my research for . . . other reasons."

"But why would—you mean because of the Larrabee Award?" Kip nodded. "But no one's supposed to know who any of the contenders are."

"*You* knew," Kip pointed out.

"True. But only because you and Sam Slater both happened to tell me." She thought for a moment. "I suppose it wouldn't be that difficult to find out who else was up for it if someone really wanted to."

"Now that all the nominees have been notified, no, it wouldn't."

"But . . . you're not really implying that Sam Slater broke into your lab tonight and turned on the valves?" She gave him an amused smile.

"No, of course not," Kip said. "He didn't even know until I—he probably doesn't even know I'm a competitor."

"That anti-genetics protest group sounds much more likely," Taylor said. "It's quite frightening, the lengths to which people will go when they feel threatened by scientific progress." Kip looked at her questioningly. "We have a local protest group here in New Chatham. They've been picketing the hospital ever since it was built."

"You'd think they'd have given up by now."

"Yes. But rumor has it they've been taken up by some national group and reinvigorated." She sipped her mineral water. "I assume the police are checking into the people that picketed Emerson."

"Of course. But the thing is," Kip added thoughtfully, "mine's the only lab being targeted. It feels personal, somehow."

The dessert was served, tasted, and declared delicious. "Maybe I'm being paranoid about the Larrabee," Kip conceded, taking a second forkful. "It could be a disgruntled employee, someone who doesn't like me, or has a problem with Emerson."

"Well, it's very scary, whoever's doing it," Taylor said. "Poisoned coffee, lethal gas. What are you doing about it?"

"We've already beefed up security," Kip told her. "Aside from closing down the lab, I'm damned if I know what else we *can* do."

Taylor reached over and touched his arm. "This is serious stuff, Kip. Be careful, okay? Now that I've found you again, I'd like to keep you awhile."

Kip covered her hand with his and leaned over to kiss her. "My sentiments precisely," he said.

Chapter Twenty-two

The man known as Cheng was very angry. He rode the small mirrored car of his private elevator down to the basement of the building that housed the offices of the Formosa Trading Company, cursing quietly to himself in Mandarin. How could it have happened? How could it have been allowed to happen?

He stepped out onto the concrete floor, blinking as his eyes adjusted to the gloom, then went forward toward the glow of a low-wattage bulb dangling from the ceiling. Faint street sounds reached him; somewhere a cracked pipe dripped rhythmically.

Beyond the light was a painted steel door. He knocked once and the door immediately swung inward, revealing Fong's bulky figure and beyond him a small, filthy, windowless room. The girl lay on the concrete floor, her ankles shackled together, her arms bound in front of her. Her eyes were closed. Blood spotted the white medical coat she wore, and a dried crimson smear ran from the corner of her mouth.

Fong went over and kicked her lightly. She opened her eyes, staring at the mute bodyguard. He jerked his chin toward his master. The girl turned, her eyes big with fear. Manipulating her bound body as best she could, she prostrated herself before Cheng.

"Mercy," she whispered in Mandarin, her head bowed. "I beg mercy."

"You have failed in your duty," Cheng told her harshly.

"Yes, master," she replied softly. "I have failed you. But how could I know? You must believe—"

"I believe nothing. You are no longer useful to me. You will be replaced."

"What will you do to me? What will happen to my family?"

"Your family will be sent back to China."

"No!"

"As for you . . ." Cheng strode back and forth before the woman, studying her. She was fairly pretty and not too old. "You will go into one of my brothels. There they will teach you to obey orders."

"No," the girl gasped. "I will kill myself first."

"You may not kill yourself," Cheng told her. "You are my property, and I do not allow my property to kill itself. Only I may kill you." He paused. "Today, I do not choose to do so. Tomorrow I may change my mind. As long as you are alive and working for me, your family will be spared."

"But . . . you will send them to China?"

"Yes. They, too, must pay for your failure. But they will be allowed to go on living."

"Mercy, please, generous master." The woman groveled before him, weeping. "I beg you to be merciful."

Cheng gazed dispassionately down at her. "I have already been merciful," he told her. "I have allowed you to retain your miserable life." He turned to Fong. "The car will come in three hours to collect her. You will accompany her to Madame Jade. Until then, she is yours." The bodyguard smiled and leaned over the girl. He reached under the white jacket and ripped away her blouse, clouting her across the ear as she screamed and tried to roll away.

"Please remember," Cheng cautioned, "that she has to be able to work. Other men must make use of her. Keep the damage to a minimum."

Fong nodded and reached for the shrieking woman again as Cheng spun on his heel and walked quickly away. Violence was necessary, of course, but he had always found it personally distasteful.

"This just in. Lynda North, the popular Oscar-winning film actress and star of Blue Dusk, is in grave condition after the car she was riding in skidded off the road tonight and hit a concrete barricade just south of Malibu. Ms. North was returning from a party at the home of producer Toby Scott. The West Coast has been experiencing heavy rains recently, and the road was wet and slippery with mud. The car was being driven by Anthony Crewes, an attorney who has been romantically linked with Ms. North. The Mercedes was demolished, and Mr. Crewes was pronounced dead at the scene . . ."

The ambulance sped along the dark, wet road. It took the curves fast, its tires hissing, while medics dripped fluids into Lynda North's veins and tried to raise a pulse.

The nearest hospital was twenty minutes away, but Lynda's personal physician, reached at a dinner party and apprised of her condition, immediately ordered the ambulance to head for Cedars-Sinai in Los Angeles, instead.

He met the ambulance at the emergency entrance, pushing past the reporters and TV crews who had somehow gotten word of the change of direction.

As soon as he saw the nature and extent of her injuries, he knew it was too late. It had been too late the moment the Mercedes had collided with the barricade. Her face was untouched, but she had suffered a terrible blow to the head as well as serious internal damage. Even if Lynda survived physically, which was extremely doubtful, her mind would be gone. Still, they continued to work on her far longer than made any medical sense.

At last they accepted the inevitable, recorded the time of death, and sank back, exhausted. Her physician went out to face the crowd of reporters.

The immediate outpouring of grief at the death of Lynda North was remarkable, spurred by both the popularity of the actress and the late-night feeding frenzy of the media. Cameras recorded her doctor, flanked by the Cedars-Sinai administrator, as he made his emotional announcement of her death. A short time later, reporters filmed the transfer of her body from the hospital to a fashionable funeral home. There, crews shot footage of the funeral director announcing the schedule for public viewing of her closed casket, and the date and time of the funeral mass. On the street in front of the funeral home, people were already lining up to pay their last respects, and the media dutifully recorded their memories of Lynda and their sadness at her passing.

The front of the funeral home, bathed in light, was abuzz with activity. The rear exit was deserted, and cloaked in darkness. It was from this rear exit that three men emerged, wheeling a pale body on a stretcher. IV lines depended from plastic bags hung on a portable stand and snaked down beneath the sheets. A private ambulance stood ready, its motor turning over, its lights doused.

The men opened the rear doors, quickly collapsed the stretcher's wheeled legs, and slid the pallet and its occupant inside. One man remained there with the stretcher; the other two got out and closed the doors. Its siren mute, the ambulance sped away into the night.

Just before dawn, a small private plane landed at a remote airstrip in the Arizona desert. The runway lights that had been turned on for the plane's arrival illuminated a barren landscape of dry, cracked earth. Giant cacti, their arms outspread, stood like sentinels beyond the perimeter of the field.

The plane taxied toward the wooden shack that passed for a terminal. Beside the shack, an unmarked ambulance waited, its occupants watching the plane's approach. As the pilot shut down his engines, two men emerged from the car, jacketed against the coolness of the desert night.

Together with the pilot, they unloaded a rectangular box from the cargo hold and carried it the few feet to the waiting ambulance. As soon as the ambulance was loaded, the pilot revved up his engines, eager to be off again.

The ambulance left the airport, driving fast, and turned onto a potholed dirt road leading into the scrub. Half hidden by the tall cacti, the ambulance drove through barren landscape, crossing a dry river-bed and winding around several large rock formations.

"Hate to run out of gas around here," the young man in the passenger seat told the driver.

"It's only seven miles," the driver replied with more than a trace of bravado.

"Yeah, but what a walk. Snakes and shit." The young man paused. "I guess it wouldn't be so bad if it was during the day. Or if there was a moon. In the dark, you could really get lost."

The driver smiled. "You get used to it. You start to recognize certain rocks and stuff. Landmarks that tell you where you are."

"I guess." The passenger looked out of the window. A faint pink glow lit the eastern sky, silhouetting the tall forks of vegetation that lined the road. "What do you call those things again?"

"What, the cacti? Saguaro. One of the biggest cacti in the west. Old, too. Some of them have been around for hundreds of years."

"Spooky-looking things."

"You think so?" the driver said. "I kinda like them."

The road became a narrow track. Several miles on, it curved left and continued for some five hundred feet, then ended abruptly at a small complex of low concrete bunkers.

"Home, sweet home," the driver said.

Outside, several men in jeans and leather jackets stood sentry.

Inside, an operating room stood ready.

Chapter Twenty-three

All weekend, the media played with the story of Lynda North's demise, and at the hospital cafeteria on Monday, people were still talking about it. Taylor had a brief conversation with one of the nurses about the event as they went through the service line, another with the cashier. She was heading for a vacant table by the window and a little relief from the subject when Slater called out to her. "Looking for a seat?"

"Thanks. It's crowded in here today." She set down her tray and took the chair across from him.

"It just seems that way because you rarely eat lunch." He smiled at her. "At least, not here."

"That's true."

She took a bite of her sandwich, glad that things seemed to be okay again between them. She'd recently replied affirmatively to a hand-lettered invitation to a party at his home, some four weeks hence, in celebration of the hospital's fifth anniversary. The fact that the handwriting was his secretary Penny's did nothing to diminish her pleasure at being included.

For a moment neither spoke. Then, "So sad about Lynda North," Slater said.

God, him, too? Taylor thought, then remembered he'd met her. "Did you know her well?" she asked.

"Fairly well," Slater replied, toying with a dish of half-eaten macaroni and cheese. "Harland did her surgery, but I'd met her before that, through mutual friends." He sighed. "She was a lovely woman. Smart, too."

"Mind if I join you?" Garrison asked, putting down his tuna salad and fruit cup.

"Sure," Slater told him. "We were just talking about Lynda North."

"Yeah, a tragedy," Garrison said feelingly. "I really liked her."

"You knew her, too?" Taylor asked, surprised.

"Met her through Sam. When she came in for her procedure." The two men were silent for a moment, and Taylor felt something unsaid hanging in the air between them. Then Slater spoke. "Garrison gets to meet lots of nice women through his work, don't you? Like that research assistant you were living with, back in Boston. And now the charming Mrs. Goodbody."

To Taylor's amusement, Garrison blushed. "Come on, Sam," he protested. "Her name's actually Dolores Goode," he explained to Taylor. "She came in to see Sam this morning."

"I gather she's attractive," Taylor said, smiling.

"Gorgeous," Slater said. "But I brag."

"You worked on her?"

"Some years ago, yes. Anyway, I thought Gar here needed a little excitement in his life, so I introduced the two of them. He's taking her to dinner tonight."

Good, Taylor thought.

"She's divorced," Slater continued, "lives in Boston, has lots of money, some of which she spends with us from time to time. I know you and Garrison have become friends," Sam continued, "but I got the impression your romantic interests lie elsewhere. Am I right?"

"Yes," Taylor said uncomfortably. How had he known that? For a fleeting moment she wondered whether he'd been the figure staring at her and Kip through the restaurant window. But no; of course not.

"Someone in New York," Slater said.

"That's right," Taylor replied shortly. Her relationship with Kip, solidified by their weekend together, was still too new for her to feel comfortable discussing it with Slater or anyone else.

"A gentleman named Kipling Lawrence, I believe," Slater said. Garrison's head jerked up. "Lila Krimm called me from New York this morning. She mentioned the two of you looked rather chummy." He smiled, but there was no warmth in his eyes.

"And I thought *New Chatham* was a small town," Taylor said, forcing a laugh.

"There are no small towns anymore," Slater said. "And certainly not New Chatham."

"Oh, I don't know," Garrison said. "New Chatham is still a typical New England town in many ways."

"Well, witchcraft is an old New England tradition," Slater said, "I'll give you that."

Taylor started to laugh, then noticed that Slater wasn't. "You're not serious?"

"Oh, it definitely exists," Slater told her. "That damn cult has cast spells against Greenvale, against me, against Ward Harland, probably against Potter, here. And you, of course."

"Hey, you were the one who told me not to justify that nonsense by pursuing the incidents," Taylor protested. Slater frowned and said nothing. "Come on. You're not saying you believe in that stuff."

"Well, Ward Harland's gone."

"He went to L.A." Taylor frowned. "Didn't he?"

"Sure," Garrison said. "But he left pretty damn fast."

Taylor stared at the two men. "If you talk to plants, they grow better. People used to think this was because of some psychic energy, a kind of witchcraft if you will. Now we know that it's the carbon dioxide you exhale at the plant when you talk to it that makes it flourish."

"You're right, of course," Slater said. "The fact that the cult exists doesn't mean they actually make things happen psychically or whatever. I didn't mean to imply that." He hesitated. "Although there is the matter of that ghost that was sighted near the Rockingham estate."

"Please," Taylor exclaimed. "I heard the whole story at the coffee shop. Those guys were ripped. Daring each other to bang on the door. We used to do that as kids, Sam."

"But this time, something came out."

"Oh, right. Three drunks on a country road at night? I know about drunks, Sam. Those guys could have been chasing a plastic bag, for God's sake."

Garrison forked up the last of his tuna fish. "Whatever did or didn't happen down there," he said, "I wouldn't go near that place on a bet." Taylor stared at him. "Except in a car," he added. "Your friends the Erbachs are right."

"Things happen because people make them happen," Taylor said. "I mean, physically make them happen. Like the mall fire. I understand they think it was arson." Slater nodded. "Well, whoever set that fire didn't rely on spells and incantations. They drenched the place in kerosene." She shook her head. "I sure hope they catch those bastards."

"Me, too," Slater said. A sudden sweep of his hand knocked the half-filled coffee cup from his tray onto the floor. "Shit." He dabbed at his white coat with a paper napkin.

"Here." Taylor thrust her own napkin toward him.

"Thanks." Flushing, he wiped the coffee from his sleeve as Garrison bent and mopped up the coffee from the floor.

"About Jim," Taylor said. "I noticed something funny on his chart. Not the chart itself, the face sheet down in the morgue."

Sam looked up, frowning. "What were you doing in the morgue?"

"I wanted a look at the body, but it was already gone. Anyhow, the number 37 was written very lightly in red pencil next to the morgue instructions."

"So?"

"It's probably not important, but I was wondering what it meant."

"Beats me," Sam said. "Did you ask Wally Gamble?"

"He'd already left. His cousin Lewis was on duty. He had no idea."

"Well, neither do I," Sam said. "Maybe someone was jotting down a phone number on the face sheet and forgot to erase it. Or maybe Wally was writing on a form or something, and the face sheet was next to it and he wrote on it by mistake. It must have been something like that." He rose abruptly. "Well, I'm going back to work," he said. "You coming, Garrison? I want to go over those figures with you."

"I'll just be a minute, Sam," Garrison said, attacking his fruit cup.

Slater scowled and stalked off, leaving his empty tray on the table. Taylor looked after him. "Looks like you're in for a rough afternoon," she said.

"Oh, Sam's all right. He gets a little edgy sometimes, that's all. It's because he works so hard."

Taylor nodded. "It's hard to imagine Sam just kicking back," she mused. "I never think of him as having a personal life. He seems so . . . 'of the hospital.' Has he ever been married?"

"Not as long as I've known him. He's always lived a rather solitary private life. I think that's why he's so attached to that damn dog of his."

"Snowball? It *does* seem a little . . . strange"

"It's *very* strange." Garrison set down his spoon beside the empty bowl. "I think Sam's gotten even more reclusive the past few years, despite Pete Ohlmeyer's attempts to get close to him. Probably comes from having to do so much professional socializing as part of his cosmetic surgery practice. Was it that way for you, when you were in private practice? Did you grow to hate the social side?"

"Not me," Taylor said, "but my ex-husband—Never mind. Nothing's more boring than someone else's divorce." She smiled. "Don't feel you have to stay," she added as Garrison shot a glance toward the door. "I know Slater's waiting for you."

"I guess I should be getting back," he apologized, rising.

"Oh, and have fun tonight."

"Thanks." Garrison hesitated for a moment as though about to say something, then turned and went out.

Taylor sat there a little longer, sipping her apple juice. Why, she wondered, should Sam go to such trouble to explain away some random numbers Peter Ohlmeyer had scribbled on a face sheet? And why would a man of science, a serious contender for the Larrabee, suddenly propose the existence of ghosts?

Patients and paperwork kept her in the hospital until after nine that evening, and she was grateful for the cafeteria lunch. Slater's office was dark as she passed his door, and Garrison was long gone, too. The parking garage beneath the hospital was nearly empty, and her footsteps rang on the cement floor as she approached her Lexus, fumbling in her handbag for the car door remote.

As she came around the side of the car, a bulky figure loomed up in front of her, barring her way. She screamed and stepped back before recognizing the intruder.

"Dr. Ohlmeyer? You scared the hell out of me."

"I think it's time we had a little talk." His eyes were dark, his body language threatening.

"It's late," Taylor replied, her heart knocking in her chest.

"It is. I've been waiting for you since seven." He took a step toward her.

Was old Mrs. Varrick right? she wondered nervously. Had the man really murdered two women? "Come to my office in the morning," she said with more confidence than she felt. When he didn't reply, she added, "Please move away from that door. I want to go home."

"Gamble tells me you've been inquiring about my patient," he said, not moving. "I'm afraid that just won't do."

"He was my patient first," Taylor replied. "I had every right to question what happened to him."

"I don't agree." He stepped toward her again. "It's called meddling, and I will not have it." His icy eyes bore into hers. "Understand?"

"Don't threaten me," Taylor retorted. "I'm not your wife." The words slipped out before she could stop them, and she gasped as they echoed in the deserted garage.

Ohlmeyer studied her. "So you finally remembered. Well, you shouldn't believe everything you hear."

"The jury's still out on that."

"Is it?" He reached forward and grabbed her shoulders, squeezing hard.

"You're hurting me," she protested, struggling.

"Good." He smiled grimly. "Isn't that what they said? That I like hurting women?" Releasing his grip, he shoved her hard against the side of the car. "You listen to me, Dr. Barnes. I'm happy here at Greenvale, and I plan to stay awhile. I will not have you interfering with my patients or undercutting me with Sam by questioning my professional judgment." His eyes bored into hers.

"I don't need to undercut you," Taylor retorted. "You're doing a fine job of shooting yourself in the foot right this minute."

"Your word against mine, doctor; a respected cardiologist against an hysterical ex-drunk. Oh, and if you're thinking about regaling Sam with rumors about my past, don't bother. He already knows. I told him myself." He smiled cynically. "Sam hates rumor-mongering every bit as much as I do."

"How does he feel about homicide?" Taylor shot back without thinking.

Ohlmeyer stared at her. "Manslaughter isn't—" he began, then broke off. "Don't push it."

"Get out of my way."

He held her eyes for a long moment, then brushed past her. As he stepped clear of the car, he paused and looked back. "Stay out of my affairs. You've been warned." He spun on his heel and hurried away, losing himself in the shadows.

Pulse racing, Taylor stared after Ohlmeyer's retreating figure, then yanked open the door and slid onto the leather seat. Why was he so worried over an old rumor? she wondered, turning the ignition key with a trembling hand. Especially if he'd already told Sam. It didn't make sense.

She drove slowly out of the garage. Unless there was more; something he *hadn't* told Sam. Something he thought she knew. "Manslaughter isn't—" he'd begun. Isn't what? She turned onto Main Street, rolling to a stop at the traffic light as she reviewed the conversation in her mind. Manslaughter isn't homicide; that's what he'd been about to say. Manslaughter.

The light turned green, and the car behind her honked loudly as she sat there, the light dawning.

As soon as she got home, she called Slater and described what had happened in the parking garage, but Ohlmeyer had obviously gotten to him first. Although Slater apologized profusely for the cardiologist's lack of social skills, he was adamant that Taylor had misinterpreted, perhaps overdramatized, what had actually occurred. His word against mine, and Sam believes *him,* Taylor fumed as she slammed down the phone. And in her current, professionally vulnerable position, there wasn't much she could do about it except quit.

And telling Slater about the suspicion that had come to her at the traffic light would do no good, not without proof of some kind. Sam was too committed to Ohlmeyer to listen to vague accusations.

The man's deranged, she thought; surely Sam must sense it. What kind of hold could Ohlmeyer have over Sam that would make Sam choose to defend him?

Chapter Twenty-four

February gave way to March. Crocuses sprang up in Taylor's front yard, purple and yellow and white. In anticipation of bathing suit season, well-known women were quietly booking into Greenvale for tummy tucks and thigh lifts as well as for the usual face-lifts. She'd never worked harder in her life, and she thrived on it.

Despite the limitations her OR schedule put on her personal time, she managed to steal a weekend in New York with Kip. He was genuinely delighted with her visit, but he seemed tense, popping those little white pills he carried everywhere. The pace of his work, coupled with the stress of the mysterious disruptions, was making everyone in his lab edgy. An important piece of research had been botched; one of his assistants had quit.

Taylor's initial impression that Greenvale Hospital enjoyed a lower-than-normal mortality rate was borne out by personal observation. The preponderance of cosmetic procedures did skew the odds. But not all procedures were cosmetic, and people did die. Several of the clinic patients Taylor worked on had suffered additional injuries that were far more serious than the reconstructive problems she was called in to deal with. Like every doctor, she grieved to lose a patient, but none of the losses were totally unexpected. And none of those patients had the number 37 penciled in red on his or her chart.

Then late one night, her beeper went off. A teenage football player, concussed in a scrimmage, had coded. Though not his admitting doctor, Taylor had been scheduled to fix his broken nose early the following morning. Since prudence dictated that his surgery be postponed, the hospital paged her in order to inform her of this change in her schedule. A perfectly normal occurrence, if an unfortunate one. During the night, however, the boy coded again, and this time the team was unsuccessful in bringing him back.

The following day, Taylor, conferring with Slater about another patient, remarked on the case. Any loss of life was sad, but the loss of such a young and promising one was particularly tragic. Perhaps the young man had had a history of heart disease? No. Well, perhaps the autopsy would reveal a hidden heart or circulatory defect. Yes, perhaps it would. Now, about Mrs. Harvey . . .

Taylor had always had a deep respect for nurses: their skill, their experience, and their instincts. Evening rounds took her to the nurses station on the floor where the footballer had died. When the conversation turned to the young man, Taylor noticed that the nurse seemed unusually troubled.

"It just didn't feel right," she said under Taylor's probing.

"How do you mean?"

"I'm not sure. I know head injuries can be like that, but . . ."

"Were you here when he coded?" Taylor asked.

"The first time, yes. Not the second."

"Anything strange about the response to the first code?"

"No, although I understand they put him on the heart-lung machine the second time."

"The heart-lung machine? But why—"

"Look, I'm sorry I said anything," the nurse said quickly. "Let's just forget it, okay?"

"I'd like to see the chart."

"It was sent downstairs, along with a copy of the face sheet. Listen, I'm not saying Dr. Ohlmeyer didn't do his best for the Rogers boy," the woman added emphatically. "I'm sure he did."

"I'm sure he did, too," Taylor replied, frowning at the mention of the cardiologist's name.

She returned to her office to collect her coat. If the nurse hadn't said anything, she probably wouldn't have given Jason Rogers's death another thought. But now she sat down at her desk and reflected. A strong young man in excellent physical condition. A blow to the head. No abnormalities in the CT scan. Fatal cardiac arrest. And a heart-lung machine. Although the boy had arrested prior to surgery and Jim Partrick afterwards, the scenarios sounded very much alike. And Ohlmeyer had been involved in both cases.

Picking up the phone, she dialed the morgue, then hung up quickly. It might be more productive to go down there in person.

Lewis's cousin Wally was coming out of the autopsy room carrying a clipboard when she arrived. "They doing Jason Rogers in there?" Taylor asked. "If so, I'd like to scrub in."

"No, they finished him this afternoon," Wally told her. "Who are you?"

"Sorry, I'm Dr. Barnes. Cosmetic and Reconstructive Surgery."

"Oh, yeah." Wally frowned, shifting his clipboard from one hand to the other.

"May I see the autopsy report?"

"Dr. Ohlmeyer had it sent to Dr. Slater. You can get it from him."

If I dare ask for it, Taylor thought. Rogers wasn't her patient, and given their run-in over Partrick's death, Slater would consider it meddling. She'd pull the report after it had been sent to Medical Records. "Has the body been released yet?"

"Yes, to Gamble's."

"Your uncle."

Wally smiled. "That's right."

"I'd like to see the face sheet."

Wally looked surprised. "He's Ohlmeyer's patient."

"Yes, but I'd like to see it anyway. Is that a problem?"

"Guess not," Wally said. "Except it's not here."

"Where is it?"

"Medical Records."

"Really? That was fast. I mean, when Jim Partrick's body was released, Lewis still had the face sheet in his office."

Wally shrugged. "Guess I'm more efficient than Lewis."

"Guess you are." Taylor turned away.

"If you're heading for Medical Records, I can spare you the trouble," he said. "They're closed now. They open at eight in the morning."

Next morning, Taylor was waiting outside the records office at 7:55. Having responded to a call from the ER around seven, she was in the hospital anyway and now had half an hour to spare before morning rounds. It was probably a wild-goose chase, but the mention of the heart-lung machine had been suggestive. In addition, Wally's attitude, just this side of disrespect, had both offended and puzzled her.

"You're here early," the clerk observed pleasantly as she retrieved Jason Rogers's papers. "You can use this table over here. Anything else you need, just holler."

Taylor started with the chart. There it was: they'd put the boy on the heart-lung machine during the second code. But the notes were all in Ohlmeyer's handwriting, not the code team leader's. Had the code team even been there, or had Ohlmeyer taken over? Her eyes flicked over the time of death, then stopped. Was it her imagination, or was there the very faint indication of an erasure? Yes, it appeared to have been rewritten. A simple correction, or a later revision? She turned the page, looking for a listing of the medica-

tions that had been given during this final stage. She
began reading, then stopped, flipping back and forth
between the two pages. It was obvious that a page of
the chart was missing. The page that, on Jim Partrick's
chart, had listed the unusual medications given him:
the streptokinase, the deferoxamine, the gentamicin,
and the rest. . . .

Hmm.

She reached for the face sheet.

"I'm sorry, Dr. Barnes. I'll have to take those." The
records clerk stood above her, her hand on the chart

"I'll be finished in a moment," Taylor said, scanning
the face sheet.

"Dr. Slater needs these records immediately," the
clerk said, pulling the face sheet from Taylor's fingers.
"If you'd care to come back another time—"

"That's all right," Taylor said, thinking quickly. "I
won't need to come back." Jason Rogers was dead,
his body autopsied and released. There was absolutely
no reason Sam would need those records now. "I was
just curious about the cause of death. I realize now it
was just one of those things that can happen with head
wounds. Sorry to have troubled you."

"No trouble at all."

Taylor rose and went out into the hallway, heading
for the elevator. So Sam had known she was planning
to look at Rogers's chart—Wally must have called Ohlmeyer after her visit to the morgue last night, and
Ohlmeyer must have complained to Sam. If she'd gotten to Medical Records five minutes later, the clerk
would have already heard from Sam, and Taylor
would have been refused the charts. Or told that the
records weren't there.

Just five minutes later and she'd never have gotten
a look at those papers. She'd never have known that
a page had been removed from the chart. And she'd
never have seen what she'd glimpsed as the clerk
pulled the face sheet from her hand: the number 37,
written faintly in red pencil.

Was that what Ohlmeyer didn't want her to see? Or was it the unusual code protocol and the missing chart page? Surely the latter, Taylor decided, recalling Sam's angry reaction to her questions when Jim Partrick died. Sam might not even know about the 37, whatever it was, but he sure hadn't wanted to talk about the medications Ohlmeyer had ordered. And she wasn't about to tackle him on them again, especially since Rogers wasn't even her patient.

But what about the penciled 37? Should she mention that to Sam again, or was she making too much of it? The number appeared only on the face sheet, not the chart itself, so it could be a morgue notation of some kind.

But no other face sheets she'd seen had had that sort of notation.

And just how many face sheets of deceased patients have you actually looked at? she asked herself. Cosmetic surgery is a low-mortality specialty, kid.

One of the many things Taylor had always liked about surgery was the sense of control, coupled with the immediacy of the decision-making process. Running her own practice had extended that sense of control to the administrative end. At Greenvale, things were different. While she did enjoy a certain autonomy inside the operating theater, outside of it she answered to Slater. And she answered to him in ways and to a degree that a less vulnerable cosmetic surgeon would never have endured.

Reclaiming her career meant nonconfrontation. She understood this, and she accepted it. But that didn't mean she had to like it. Or that she had to give up thinking for herself. She simply had to keep her own counsel.

Was there a long-term file storage room she could check, or were all the old charts kept in the Medical Records office? Could she get back inside Medical Records once the clerks changed shifts? *Did* the clerks change shifts? 8:00 A.M. to 8:00 P.M. she thought; surely someone different would be working there this evening.

Mentally making her plans, she went off to morning rounds.

It was five of eight in the evening when she appeared again at the entrance to the Medical Records office, prepared to say she'd left something behind that morning should the same clerk be on duty.

She wasn't. A young man was hurriedly putting on his coat as Taylor went in.

"Can't it wait until tomorrow?" he asked anxiously. "I'm about to close up." He glanced at his watch nervously. "I can't stay late tonight."

"There's no need for you to stay," Taylor said easily. "I'll lock up when I'm finished."

"And you are?" He fidgeted with his gloves.

"Dr. Taylor Barnes. I'm on staff here." She put her handbag down on the table. "Can you set the door to lock when it's closed from the outside? I'll pull it shut when I leave."

"And turn off the lights."

"Of course."

He hesitated. "Okay, I guess so." He went and fiddled with the buttons on the side of the door. "You're all set. Just don't leave your bag in here and go get coffee, or you'll lock yourself out."

"I won't."

"Well, good night."

"Good night. And thanks."

Taylor quickly explored the office. The main room held the most recent files. Beyond it was a smaller room, empty save for metal racks of older files. She closed the door to the corridor and doused the lights in the front room. Leaving the light on in the rear room, she closed its door and surveyed the effect from outside. The light that leaked from beneath the door frame was barely noticeable. A casual passerby would assume the office was closed for the night.

She retreated to the rear office, and behind its

closed door skimmed through the first rack of files, looking specifically for deceased clinic patients. She worked fast; her AA meeting, at a church half an hour away, started at nine.

Twenty minutes later, she checked her watch, then replaced the chart she was holding. She hadn't gotten through more than a third of the files in the back room, but she'd already seen enough.

She turned off the light and retrieved her handbag and coat, berating herself for having come here. If she'd only left well enough alone, she could have remained in blissful ignorance. But no; she had to go looking for trouble. And now, having found it, she had to figure out what to do about it.

Because there was definitely something odd going on. On nine different face sheets over the past three years, she'd found a faint red 37 penciled beside the morgue instructions. Other clinic patients had died, but only these nine had been numbered. The times of death had all been altered, although only on one chart was the original time legible: nearly an hour earlier than the amended time. All nine patients had been relatively young, healthy people. All had been put on heart-lung machines. All the charts were missing medication lists.

And all the bodies had been released to Gamble's Funeral Home.

She went over and over it, during the drive to Hamden and throughout the AA meeting. What was the connection? What could it all signify?

She was still puzzling over it when she braked for a tight curve and the car kept going, skidding and swerving as she hauled on the hand brake, gasping with terror. The car bounced off a guardrail and slid across the road before coming to rest with its front left wheel in a ditch.

Shaken, she sat for a moment, collecting herself. Her elbow was bruised, and her stomach hurt from the sudden grip of the seat belt, but otherwise she was okay.

She turned off the engine and got out, trembling. Just beyond where the car had stopped, the shoulder fell away steeply. If she hadn't wrestled the car to a standstill as quickly as she had, she'd have gone right over the edge. She pulled out her cell phone, took several deep breaths, and began dialing.

The all-night mechanic towed the car to a nearby garage and put it up on the lift.

"It's your brakes," he told her.

"But the car's new."

"Someone's been messing with 'em. And see there?"

Taylor looked. A section of the undercarriage had been wiped clean of grime and grease. On the shiny metal the words

GREENVALE OUT!

had been spray-painted in red. Nearby were strange markings in colored chalk.

"If I was you, lady," the mechanic told her, "I'd call the police."

"Absolutely," Taylor agreed. And someone else, too, she thought. Her first thought had been Peter Ohlmeyer. But seeing the markings had reminded her that the cardiologist wasn't the only person in New Chatham who wished her ill. Unless she was planning to decamp, which was suddenly a distinct possibility, it was time to have a serious talk with Maggie Kay McCormick.

Chapter Twenty-five

"I didn't think you were coming."

"I'm sorry I'm late."

The two women studied each other in the dim light of the empty church. Aside from the brief face-to-face during the demonstration, it had been many years since they'd seen one another. Maggie thought Taylor looked very sophisticated in her tailored suit. Taylor thought Maggie looked scared.

Maggie had insisted on their meeting place being somewhere other than New Chatham, and Taylor had suggested Hamden as being the only other town she was familiar with in the area. She'd offered to buy lunch but Maggie had rejected restaurants and coffee shops as being too public, so the two women sat in the rear pew of the church in which Taylor's AA group met.

"Voodoo dolls are one thing, Maggie," Taylor said without preamble. "Tampering with my car is quite another. I could have been killed." She paused. "I knew you when we were both little. I can accept that you have a problem with Greenvale, but I can't believe you'd actually want to kill me."

"I didn't," Maggie said, twisting her fingers. "I don't. It wasn't me."

"But it *was* the protest group."

"It wasn't."

"Then, who was it?"

"I don't know."

Taylor noted Maggie's smeared lipstick, the hair coming loose of its worn clasp, the fingernails bitten down to the quick. The woman was obviously under severe strain. Taylor sighed. "That day in front of the hospital, you said you'd called me. That you wanted to warn me about something. What was it?"

"That the hospital is evil. Sam Slater is evil."

"In what way is Sam Slater evil?"

"He's brought evil to New Chatham."

"Gee, Maggie," Taylor said, "I look around and I see a new high school, a shopping mall, old buildings being restored, the waterfront being developed, a new library, a movie theater. Doesn't seem so bad to me." She sighed. "You didn't agree to drive twenty miles just to say something you've already said."

Maggie was silent. At last she spoke. "I remember you from when we were in school. You were smarter than me, and more popular. All the boys liked you. I was real jealous." She paused, remembering. "But I also remember you were nice to me. We didn't say much to each other. We ran with different crowds. But whenever we happened to meet—in the cafeteria or someplace—you were always nice."

Taylor waited.

"The protesters . . . well, I agree with them. The hospital was built on land that should have been a park. And they have special permits for bio-trash disposal."

"But Greenvale's been here for, what is it? nearly five years now. There's a big celebration next week, a ceremony at the town hall. Isn't it time to let go?"

Maggie shook her head. "We'll never let go. Especially now that we're part of a national group."

"But why? Why spend all that energy on something that's a done deal? Surely there are other worthy causes."

"It's personal," Maggie said. "My husband died at Greenvale."

"Tell me about it."

"Jack went in for bypass surgery, at least that's what they said. There were complications. He never came out again."

"That could have happened anywhere."

"But it didn't happen anywhere, it happened here. And the group took care of me. I was a real mess when Jack died, and they got me back on my feet. They made me realize . . ."

"Realize what?"

"That the hospital is evil. It's against nature. We believe in Gaia, the spirit of the earth. We try to live in harmony with Gaia."

"There's nothing inharmonious about good medical practice," Taylor said, wondering whether the woman was all there. "Did you know that many of our most effective medicines come from the rain forest?"

"Really? I didn't know that." Maggie frowned. "And I don't care."

"Let me understand this," Taylor said. "The protesters believe in Gaia—"

"No, not all of them. Just some of us."

"The some of you who wrecked my car."

"No, I told you. We wouldn't do that."

"But you *would* put a bloody glove inside my car, isn't that right?"

"How did you know that was us?"

"Oh, come on," Taylor said impatiently.

"Okay, I knew about the glove. And the doll. They were supposed to scare you away. But I don't know anything about what happened to your brakes."

Was it possible the woman was telling the truth? But who else could have been responsible? A vision of Peter Ohlmeyer and the deserted parking garage flashed through Taylor's mind, but she shook it off. "Maggie, you're involved in something that could really hurt you. The police are investigating the car incident, and they're taking it very seriously. If they find fingerprints, whomever those prints belong to could go to jail for a long time."

"I didn't do it, I swear." Maggie began to weep. "I didn't know anything about it."

"Well, now you do," Taylor said sternly. "People say you're one of the leaders of that Gaia group. If you have any influence at all, you better get them to stop before someone is seriously hurt. Like I could have been."

"I don't have any influence," Maggie said. "Not anymore. They don't trust me anymore."

"Why not?"

"I was supposed to do some things, and I refused. Please don't ask me what. I can't tell you." She pulled a tissue from her handbag and wiped her eyes. "Anyone could have made those chalk markings you told me about," she said. "Anyone could have written the words. But if it was the Gaias, there's not a thing I can do about it."

"You can warn me," Taylor said dryly, "the next time they decide to try and kill me."

"That's what I wanted to do," Maggie said. "That day outside the hospital. But I was too scared. And I thought they'd just try and frighten you again. I didn't know about the car." Maggie hesitated. "I know it's hard for you to understand, but the Gaias have been very good to me. I was a wreck when Jack died. I had no anchor. They got me on my feet. I owe them a lot." Taylor was silent. "I thought you, of all people, would understand."

"I do understand," Taylor assured her. "They helped you through some bad times, and you feel gratitude and loyalty. But the Gaias aren't the same as a rehab center or an AA group. Besides, it sounds like you're in over your head. What would happen if you wanted to break with them? If you decided you'd had enough?"

"I wouldn't do that."

"Wouldn't? Or couldn't? You were very nervous

about meeting me today, wouldn't even take the chance of being seen in a coffee shop twenty miles away. What's the penalty for disloyalty in that little group of yours?" Naked fear shone in Maggie's eyes. Taylor nodded. "I see. Well, I guess that's that." She rose.

"Will you leave town now? Go back to New York?"

"Why? You want to report it at the next protest meeting?" Maggie's eyes filled with tears again. "Please don't cry," Taylor told her. "We both know what's happening here. You came to spy on me, didn't you? See how I'm doing. See if the Gaias need to step up their campaign."

"That's not true."

"No? Then prove it," Taylor said, sitting down again. "Tell me something useful."

Behind them, a door creaked open. Maggie spun around. An old woman limped slowly down the aisle to a front pew and knelt down.

"Let's get out of here," Maggie whispered, her eyes wild.

Taylor stared at her. "You don't really think—"

"Who knows? Come on."

Across the street from the church was a large park. The wind was cold, and Maggie hugged her cloth coat tight around her body as she headed toward it. She chose a path that led into the trees, not speaking until they were hidden among the oaks and maples.

"I'll tell you two things," she said. "Number one, you're in a dangerous place."

"Tell me something I don't know."

"I don't just mean the Gaias." Maggie paused. "I told you: my husband went into Greenvale, and he never came out."

"And I told *you*: that could happen anywhere." An image of Peter Ohlmeyer bending over the recumbent figure of Jim Partrick flashed through her mind, but she willed it away.

Maggie shook her head. "They talked me into a closed casket. Said I wouldn't want to see Jack looking the way he did. But heart surgery wouldn't make him look bad. I mean, his face would look normal, right?" Taylor nodded. "So why would the funeral home say that? I think they did something to him."

"Who? The funeral home?"

"No, the hospital. I think they killed him because he knew too much."

"Wait a minute," Taylor said. "Didn't you identify him? The hospital would require a formal ID to release a body. You saw him then, didn't you?"

"Well, he looked okay on the television," Maggie said, "but the picture was kind of blurry."

"What television?" The light dawned. A number of police departments had moved to closed-circuit TV identification as being less stressful for family members, but Taylor was surprised Greenvale had adopted it. "You identified him on closed-circuit TV?"

"I guess. Anyway, after Jack's funeral, I got to thinking about it, and finally I went to the police. I told them something wasn't right, and they should dig him up."

"What did they say?"

Maggie scowled. "They thought I was crazy."

Was she crazy? Taylor wondered. All evidence to date pointed that way. Then again, there were those numbers penciled on the face sheets. "What did your husband know that would make someone want to kill him?"

Maggie looked around fearfully as though expecting someone to drop down on her from the trees. "Jack worked construction," she said. "He helped build Greenvale Hospital, isn't that ironic? He wasn't an architect or anything, but he was used to looking at building plans in a general sort of way. He told me something was strange about the plans for Greenvale."

"Strange how?"

"The plans and the building didn't exactly match up."

Taylor frowned. "Building plans often change. Maybe he only saw the preliminary plans."

"No, he saw the plans in the construction trailer, while the work was going on. He was in charge of a crew," she added proudly.

"But . . . why would someone kill him for that? I'm afraid I—"

"Maybe there's a secret part of the hospital nobody knows about," Maggie said, her eyes wild, her hair swirling around her face.

"You've been seeing too many B movies," Taylor said.

"Have I? The Gaias believe—"

"The Gaias also believe medicine is inharmonious with nature. Their opinions are not exactly disinterested."

"They're—what?"

"Never mind. I don't suppose you'd care to tell me any of their names?"

"Oh, I couldn't," Maggie breathed, eyes wide. "They'd . . . hurt me."

"If they found out."

"Oh, they'd find out." Maggie kicked at the decaying leaves with the toe of her boot. "They're everywhere. You'd be surprised."

"What was the second thing you were going to tell me?"

"They got rid of Ward Harland. You're next."

"Who got rid of Harland? The Gaias?" Maggie nodded. "How?"

"Spells. Ceremonies. Psychic powers."

"You've got to be kidding," Taylor scoffed.

"He's not around anymore, is he?" Maggie demanded.

And he doesn't seem to be anywhere else, Taylor thought, remembering the calls she'd made to various medical associations, trying to locate him. The wind suddenly felt colder. "What really happened to Harland?"

Somewhere nearby, twigs snapped loudly. "I just told you," Maggie said, spinning away. "I have to go." But Taylor grabbed her arm. "One more question. What funeral home did you use for Jack?"

"Gamble's." The word floated back over Maggie's shoulder as she broke free and ran up the path, her hair streaming in the wind.

Taylor trudged slowly after her. Maggie Kay might be nuts but she was no liar. The question was, how much of what she'd told Taylor was the truth, and how much was simply the ramblings of a disturbed mind?

Printed schematics of the hospital complex were available to the general public at the lobby desk, and that afternoon Taylor hunched over one of these, reconciling it with her personal knowledge of the hospital layout. Greenvale was relatively small, and while she hadn't been to every corner of every floor, she'd walked through enough of the building to feel fairly certain that the schematic was accurate. The walls were where the schematic showed them to be, and the positions of the rooms and facilities were correctly rendered. Despite whatever Jack McCormick had thought he'd seen, the building and the schematic matched up with no mysterious bits left over.

But of course, they would, wouldn't they? The schematic would have been prepared after the building was functioning. It was the actual blueprint she needed to see.

But the schematic also matched what Taylor had observed of the outside landmarks. It didn't matter when it had been drawn; she was certain it was accurate. There was simply no space in which to hide a secret section of the hospital.

Just listen to yourself, she thought. She reached for the schematic and balled it up in her hands. Surely you're not taking the imaginings of that disturbed woman seriously.

Slater entered her office as she was tossing the crumpled paper into the wastebasket.

"Chief of police just called me," he said. "They found no fingerprints on your car, I'm afraid. Same as with that glove you gave them, as you'll recall. The paint's from an ordinary spray can, sold everywhere." He lowered himself into her guest chair. "What have I gotten you into?"

"A lot of surgery and a shot at a comeback," Taylor said. He didn't look at all well, but she refrained from saying so.

"You mean, you're staying?"

"Even if I weren't enjoying my work here at Greenvale, which I *am*, I don't really have a choice."

"I could write you a glowing reference."

"Yeah, and when people ask why I left, I could explain that a bunch of witches were trying to kill me. I'd sound real stable, wouldn't I?"

"People could ask me. I'd back you up."

"We both know you wouldn't dare. If people really thought some weird cult was taking potshots at Greenvale's doctors, you couldn't get one of your rich-and-famous patients within miles of here. Thanks, anyway."

Slater shrugged. "The police are very curious about those chalk marks," he said. "They think your car was targeted by two different groups."

"At the same time? Please." Taylor pushed her hair back out of her eyes. "No, the protesters and the cultists are the same people, at least some of them are. Surely you know that. Writing those symbols just gave them a little extra bang for their buck."

"You're taking this rather lightly, aren't you?"

"Not at all. I take the brake tampering extremely seriously. But I don't buy that mumbo-jumbo crap, Sam. There's only one way that kind of stuff works, and that's through fear—the fear that it works."

"I used to believe that, too," Slater said slowly. "But with some of the things I've heard . . ."

"Like what?"

". . . it's no wonder people stay away from the old Rockingham place," he finished, ignoring her question.

"What I can't understand is why real estate agents stay away from it," Taylor said dryly. "Why don't the heirs unload the place?"

"But who would want to buy it?"

"Any good property developer," Taylor retorted. "It's prime real estate."

Slater shrugged. "Perhaps. But would people want to live in any housing built on that land?"

"Of course they would. Why wouldn't they?"

Slater sighed. "Old buildings acquire a certain . . . atmosphere. An aura, inside and out. Haven't you ever noticed that? You get a gut feeling: good or evil. You grew up here. Didn't that place seem spooky to you?"

"Yes, when I was ten years old," Taylor replied, determined not to play into his hand by telling him it still did.

"Well, it feels spooky as hell to *me,*" he said. "It's no wonder everybody says it's haunted. Now, I'm not saying I believe that, exactly." He put up a hand to ward off Taylor's protest. "But I do believe there are some things that science simply can't explain."

As Taylor sat there openmouthed, Slater got up, went to her small window, and looked out. "By the way," he said, "what did you want to see Jason Rogers's chart for?"

Thrown for a moment by the conversational whiplash, Taylor gaped at him. Then, "Pure curiosity, I'm afraid," she improvised. "The case reminded me of Jim Partrick. And since Partrick's family refused an autopsy, I thought Rogers might give me a clue as to why Partrick arrested like that."

"The Rogers autopsy showed the same thing Ohlmeyer and I suspected with Partrick," Slater said, turning to face her. "A delayed intracranial hemorrhage." His eyes dared her to argue.

"Mystery solved," Taylor said, smiling. Yeah, sure. Again, she wondered about the hold Ohlmeyer obviously had over Sam. Her mind went back to her run-in with Ohlmeyer in the parking garage, and his cryptic remark about manslaughter not being homicide. If her suspicion was correct, and if she could prove it, she might be able to give Slater the leverage he needed to resist whatever pressure Ohlmeyer was putting on him. Not that it was any of her business, she reminded herself. Especially now that Ohlmeyer was avoiding her.

She realized Sam was studying her. "You were right, of course," she told him brightly.

"Yes," Slater agreed, the tension leaving his face. He gave her a big, open smile. "I usually am."

Chapter Twenty-six

The lights were still on as Taylor drove past the town hall that evening, and on an impulse, she pulled into the small parking lot.

"You're working late tonight," she observed to the clerk, an ascetic-looking middle-aged man in jacket and tie.

"Town meeting," the man said, gesturing toward the double doors that stood open at the end of the short corridor. Folding chairs had been set up facing the shallow stage, and coffee and cookies were laid out on a paper-covered trestle table along one wall. The clerk peered at her over wire-rimmed glasses. "Doesn't start 'til seven. You can wait in the hall or come back in half an hour, your choice."

Thursday seemed to be the day for meetings in New Chatham, Taylor reflected. The hospital's board of trustees was meeting tonight, too. "I'm not here for the town meeting," she said. "I was wondering if I could have a look at a building blueprint."

"You want the Town Planning Office," the man said. "They're gone, but maybe I can help."

"That's very kind of you," Taylor said, thinking, Ah, the courtesies of small-town living.

"What do you need?"

"I'd just like a quick look at the Greenvale Hospital plans."

The man's smile faded. "The hospital? I took you

for a realtor selling a house. What do you want the Greenvale plans for?"

"I . . . work at the hospital," Taylor said. "For Garrison Potter," she added, instinctively knowing his name would carry greater weight than her own. She'd square it with him later. "We're planning an historical display in the lobby, and—"

"This is for Potter? Why didn't you say so?" The smile returned. "Just come through here; we'll go the back way." He opened the half door and led her through a series of small offices into a room lined with file cabinets and pullout blueprint drawers. "Any particular section?"

"I'm not really sure. Garrison said to get an overview and then, uh, decide."

The clerk shrugged. "Suit yourself. You'll find everything in these two drawers. You an architect?" he asked as she began to pull out the large sheets.

"No."

"Well, you might want to come back during the day, talk to someone in the Planning Office. They can explain those blueprints to you."

"I might do that. Or I suppose I could talk to the builder." She glanced at the set of names printed in a corner of the topmost print. "John Roche."

"Oh, that's not possible. Mr. Roche is deceased."

"Well, perhaps his office. Where was he based?"

"Based? Why, right here in town. Local man; worked out of his home. The council encourages the hiring of local people. Greenvale was most cooperative in that respect. Of course, with all the new people buying homes out here, there's been a lot of new talent to choose from." He glanced at his watch. "I'm the recording secretary, so I'd better get going. Just put everything back before you leave."

"Will do."

"Oh, and don't go back the way we came; the meeting will be going on. Go through the next office, make a left, go through the door and you'll come out in the main hall near the front entrance."

"Okay. Uh, what happened to Mr. Roche?"

"Happened? Oh, you mean . . ." The clerk thought a moment. "Surgical complications, I believe. Very sad. He died not more than two months after Greenvale opened, in the very hospital he built. Oh, and turn off the light when you leave, will you?"

When Taylor had opened her New York practice, she'd hired an architect to help her turn an old New York maisonette into a modern medical office. He'd taught her how to read a blueprint, but the Greenvale plans were more complicated. She'd taken another copy of the hospital schematic from the lobby desk, and now she spread it out on the table, referring back to it as she scanned sheet after sheet, looking for any glaring inconsistencies and finding none. Intent on her work, she didn't notice one of the telephone extension buttons light up.

To get a better picture of the overall design, she started laying out the blueprints in a rough approximation of their relative position. The table wasn't big enough, and she moved it to one side and transferred the plans to the gray-carpeted floor. Again, everything looked accurate. The plans had been stored in no particular order, and it wasn't until she'd nearly completed the layering of drawing over drawing that she realized the plan for one section of the basement was missing. She checked the drawer—nothing. Still, everything around it fitted together and echoed the schematic.

With a mental shrug of her shoulders, she put all the drawings back and prepared to leave. Glancing at her watch, she was surprised to see it was nearly eight o'clock.

She went through to the next office as directed, turned left, and found herself in a small room. It was quite dark, and as she moved forward, she tripped over a chair and fell against the corner of a desk.

Fumbling in the dark, she found a desk lamp and switched it on. Ahead was the wooden door leading to the corridor. Between the door and the desk was a pink horizontal file cabinet bearing a large hand-lettered sign that read: "TAX ASSESSMENTS."

Who were those mysterious heirs who were so unaccountably unwilling to unload the Rockingham estate?

She went to the cabinet and began rifling through it. Properties were filed by address. The Rockingham place was on Stevens Road, but its file was missing from the Stevens Road section. She looked under "Rockingham." No luck. She put her hands behind the small of her back and stretched. It was late; why was she bothering with this? If the Rockingham heirs wanted to sit on their valuable land, surely that was their business. Still, she was here . . .

Perhaps the tax assessment had been misfiled. She decided to go through the S's from the beginning and then quit. She shoved the files back in the drawer to give her room, and began flicking them forward one by one. She'd barely started when the name on a label caught her eye. Saguaro. Where had she heard it before? Oh, yes; that day with Garrison. She pulled the file from the drawer and opened it, wondering why a philanthropic foundation was paying New Chatham property taxes.

But this Saguaro wasn't a foundation. It was a real estate partnership with a San Francisco address. And it had been paying the property taxes on the Rockingham estate for the past six years.

She replaced the file and closed the drawer. It was perfectly likely, she told herself, that the Rockingham heirs could have formed a partnership to manage the property. According to Garrison, they were scattered around the country; why shouldn't one of them be based in San Francisco? The Rockinghams had been rich; why shouldn't they have formed a philanthropic foundation called Saguaro? And didn't it make perfect sense that they would use foundation money to support a new hospital in their old hometown?

It did.

What didn't make sense was the fact that neither Sam nor Garrison knew about the connection between Saguaro and Rockingham. Or if they did, they weren't telling.

But why should that be a secret?

She turned off the desk light and made her cautious way across the room to the wooden exit door. There are too many damn secrets around here, she thought. I wouldn't mind a few answers.

She unlocked her car and drove off. As she rounded the corner onto Main Street, a fast-moving dark blue sedan came up the road behind her and turned into the town hall parking lot.

Chapter Twenty-seven

"You finished?" the first woman asked, swallowing the last of her tea. "It would be nice to get home before midnight, for once."

The second woman smiled ruefully. "What? And spoil our perfect record?" But she drank off the last of her coffee and reached for her purse.

"On me," her companion said, picking up the check. "For a coffee, a tea, and a piece of pie, I can be a sport."

They put on their coats and went out of the warm, bright diner into the cold, dark night. "What time is it?"

"Around ten."

"Not very nice around here after dark, is it?"

"No. But the lab's not far."

They hurried down the street and around the corner, giving a wide berth to two figures rooting through some large black garbage bags that had been dragged to the curb for pickup the next morning.

"I'll be glad when this part of the project is over," the first woman said. "Don't get me wrong; I can use the overtime. But these hours."

"It's not the hours that bother me so much," her friend replied. "It's the lab."

"You mean, being down here late at night?"

"No, I mean the lab itself" came the reply. "All that weird stuff going on. Like the gas jets."

"They said that was an accident."

"Right." She raised a cynical eyebrow. "And the poisoned coffee?"

"That was months ago."

"Yeah, but who's to say it won't happen again?"

"Which is why you wanted diner coffee tonight."

"No, I just felt like some fresh air. But it *is* why most of us have been sending out for coffee. You, too, I noticed."

They came through the plate-glass doors and showed their identification to the guard even though he'd seen them leave not half an hour before. Emerson's already tight security was now even tighter.

They took the elevator upstairs and went along the silent corridor to the lab. On the main door was a handwritten note from Kip saying he'd gone home with a headache. The two women looked at each other.

"You want to go home, too?" the first one asked. "It's awfully lonely up here."

"Just give me half an hour," her friend said, using her key card to unlock the door, "and we can share a taxi."

"Okay." She followed her companion into the lab space, then paused. "I'll be in in a minute. Pit stop." She disappeared down an interior hallway as the other woman went through the common space toward her workbench.

The scream came not more than two minutes later, so startling in that silent space that she dropped an expensive piece of equipment. She was debating whether to call Security or investigate matters herself when her companion came running out into the work area from the direction of the bathrooms. "Get out of here," she shouted. "Let's go, let's go."

"What is it? Are you hurt?"

"Come on." She grabbed her friend and hustled her out into the hallway. "Move."

"What happened?"

"On the mirror," the woman gasped. "They're going to kill us."

"Who's going to kill us?" They were in the elevator, heading down. "This is all about some words on a mirror?"

"Not just words. Security!" The guard came running. "Kip Lawrence's lab," the woman gasped. "There's blood all over the bathroom. And words on the mirror."

"Anyone hurt?" he asked, pulling out his pager.

"I don't think so. We were the only ones up there."

"You'll have to wait until the police get here," the guard told them.

"Okay, but I'm not going back up there," the woman said.

Her friend put an arm around her. "You're safe now," she said.

"What exactly did you see?" the guard asked.

"The first thing I saw was the blood," the woman said, her voice low and shaky. "It was smeared on the walls, the stalls . . . And then the words on the mirror. 'Quit your job or next time this blood will be yours.' "

"Jeez."

"I'm not going back there," she said again. "In fact, I *do* quit. Right now."

"Hell, me too," her friend agreed. "Enough is enough." She shivered. "Having your name associated with a Larrabee Award is a wonderful thing, but not if you don't live long enough to enjoy it."

Chapter Twenty-eight

"A little more Darjeeling?"

"Yes, please."

"Such a nasty day," Mrs. Roche murmured, refilling the delicate porcelain teacups. "I always think tea chases the chill better than coffee, don't you?" She added more brandy to her cup and smiled brightly.

Anything would chase the chill with that stuff in it, Taylor reflected. She sipped her tea, spiked only with milk, and smiled at the elderly blonde woman in the pink cardigan. "Oh, I agree."

"You said on the phone that you wanted to talk to me about Greenvale." Mrs. Roche peered at Taylor through her glasses. "The anniversary celebration, wasn't it?"

"That's right," Taylor said. She'd been getting a lot of mileage out of that one lately.

The morning after her Thursday night visit to the town hall, Garrison had dropped by her office and she'd told him a story about having gone there to choose a blueprint to frame as a gift for Slater; she wanted to give it to him at the anniversary party he was hosting at his home the following week. It sounded flimsy to her but it was the best she could think of, and he seemed to buy it.

She'd been tempted to mention the Saguaro tax assessment—she wouldn't have recognized the name if he hadn't mentioned it to her that day at lunch—but something stopped her. Despite Garrison's openness, there was no question that he was Slater's boy. And Slater had made it quite clear that he didn't like her asking questions. Still, she felt a little guilty about holding back.

She hadn't slept well Friday night, tossing and turning as she ran various scenarios through her head, one more lurid than the next. She fell into a light doze toward dawn and woke determined to ferret out the truth.

Greenvale was her comeback job and, protesters aside, there was an undercurrent here that worried her medically and ethically. If whatever was going on were to blow up in her face, she could end up more vulnerable than before. She really needed this job and wanted to stay, but if she had to bail out, she would. The only way she could protect herself was to learn the truth and then make her decision.

She didn't like having to lie to people. But, recalling the Records clerk plucking Jason Rogers's face sheet from her hand, she knew it was essential that she conceal her real intentions.

"It's about the anniversary, yes," Taylor told Mrs. Roche. "And I really appreciate your letting me intrude on your Saturday morning like this."

"Oh, not at all, dear." The birdlike woman beamed. "I'm always happy to meet people from the hospital. I'm ever so grateful to you all for what you did when John died." She dabbed at her eyes and took another deep swallow of her tea-flavored brandy.

"Actually, I'm new at Greenvale," Taylor said. "I wasn't there when your husband—"

"So very grateful," the woman continued, unheeding. "When I think of the distance we used to have to travel to get first-rate medical care. When John became ill, I was so relieved that Greenvale was here for him. And, of course, they treated him like royalty. Which he was, in a way, having built the place." She drained her cup and refilled it straight from the brandy bottle. "Nothing like tea on a chilly day," she proclaimed.

I'd better get to the point, Taylor thought, while she's still capable of speech. "Did Mr. Roche leave any papers relating to Greenvale? Building plans, maybe? Drawings?"

"Why, I believe so," Mrs. Roche said vaguely. "But why on earth would you need them now?"

"We thought it would be nice if we could make a display showing the original building plans and photographs of the actual building itself and then—" She broke off as Mrs. Roche drank off the rest of her brandy and refilled it again, humming softly to herself. Obviously, long-winded explanations would not only be unnecessary, they'd be downright risky. "Can I see them?" she asked.

Mrs. Roche frowned. "See what?"

"Your husband's plans and drawings for the hospital."

"Well, I suppose you can. I'm not sure where they'd be. Most of them are on file at the town hall, you know. Did you try there?"

"Yes, but I thought you might have something more . . . personal."

Mrs. Roche considered. "I might, I suppose. In the attic, maybe. Or the cellar. Yes, I do believe there's a box or two of John's papers in the cellar. Or the attic. I threw a lot of things away when he died. No reason to keep them, but who knows what we may find? Let's just have another cup of tea, shall we, and then we'll go and look."

Forty-five minutes later, Taylor was sitting cross-legged on the attic's unfinished floorboards, poring through the contents of the second of two dusty cardboard cartons. The attic was chilly and damp, and rain drummed heavily on the low roof. Mrs. Roche, having climbed the narrow stairs with some difficulty, had immediately declared the place much too cold and quickly retreated below.

Both cartons contained papers and blueprints, and

she'd been excited until she'd realized that they were all copies of material already on file in the town hall. Some of papers were stuck together; all smelled of mildew. Still, she carefully pried them apart, studied each page, and set it down on the floor beside her, trying not to let her impatience cause her to miss something. She had one more call to make that day, and she'd hoped to get there by noon. That hope was now gone, thanks to Mrs. Roche's fondness for her "tea," and Taylor was ready to declare the morning a total waste when she came upon the torn blueprint. It was folded neatly near the bottom of the carton, and although it took some coaxing, she opened it at last and spread it flat on the dusty floorboards.

It was the blueprint for the northwest section of the basement, the only section she hadn't found a drawing of in the Planning Office. Three of the sides were cleanly cut; the fourth had a ragged edge. Taylor examined the heavy paper, turning it over in her fingers. It was obvious that a piece had been torn off.

She searched through the papers still in the carton and checked the pages already laid out on the floor, but could find no hint of what had been removed. All she could tell for certain was that whatever the missing piece represented, it abutted the morgue.

Had Jack McCormick been right?

Of course not; she'd been down there herself. And she'd walked around the outside of the hospital, too. There was simply no space between where the morgue ended and where the outer wall of the hospital began to hide some mythical "secret part." But she folded up the blueprint and slipped it into her purse.

Mrs. Roche was waiting at the bottom of the narrow stairs as Taylor came down. "Did you find what you needed?"

"Actually, there wasn't anything I could use," Taylor told her. "But thanks for letting me look."

"That's quite all right," the widow replied, taking her arm. "Only I do hope you'll put something in your celebration about John anyway. He was such a good man."

"I'm sure he was."

"Always thinking of others," Mrs. Roche continued, listing slightly to port as she led Taylor down the hall. "He certainly took good care of me. And I never even knew about it. Can you believe that? Married forty-five years, and I never knew about the life insurance."

Taylor stopped. "What life insurance?"

"Half a million dollars, that's what I got when he died. Such a thoughtful man. I was so surprised when they told me. Now, you drive carefully," she added, opening the big front door. "These roads get very slippery in the wet."

"Thank you for your time, Mrs. Roche," Taylor said, stepping out into the rain. Why would a man neglect to tell his wife he'd insured his life for half a million dollars? She turned back. "Do you remember the name of the insurance company?"

"The company? I have no idea, never had. Sam Slater handled the whole thing. He said John had asked him to arrange for the insurance payment if anything happened to him. Now, I hope you'll come and see me again, dear. You can try the oolong. I have a friend who sends it to me all the way from Hong Kong."

She watched from the bay window as Taylor climbed into her car and drove off. Such a nice young woman, she thought. I must remember to mention her visit to Sam.

One down, one to go, Taylor thought as she rang the doorbell. Then I can get out of this damn rain and into a hot bath. Her mind still swirling with thoughts of insurance payments and torn blueprints, she huddled under the umbrella and rang again. The wind was blowing sideways now, and despite the Burberry she wore over her jeans and sweater, she was feeling uncomfortably damp. Maybe the super didn't work on

Saturdays. But he did live here, she reminded herself. Surely he'd answer the door if he were home. And who would choose to go anywhere in this awful weather if they could help it?

She was about to head back to the shelter of her car when the door opened. A short, squat man in a paint-smeared turtleneck and corduroys peered out at her. "Yes? What you want?" He spoke in a guttural mittel-European accent.

"Uh, I understand you have a vacant apartment."

"No apartment."

"I meant Ward Harland's apartment," Taylor said. Harland's phone still hadn't been disconnected, so there was a chance no one else had moved in. It was worth a try, anyway.

"Dr. Harland sell you his apartment?" The super scowled.

"Not me. It's for a friend of mine who's relocating here. Dr. Harland told my friend he could rent his apartment."

"When he say this?"

"Last month, I think. My friend called and asked me to look at it for him. Uh, can I come in? It's very wet out here."

The super shrugged and stepped back. Taylor followed him into a tiny hall reeking of paint fumes. Beyond was a small living room, its furnishings covered with stained drop sheets. "You know Dr. Harland?"

"Er, yes."

"You tell him for me please he must send me a letter about your friend."

"Yes, absolutely."

The super shook his head. "Dr. Harland is not good at this."

"How do you mean?"

"First he disappear in the night. One day here, next day gone. Two weeks go by, finally a letter. 'Dear Darius'—that is me. 'Here I am in San Francisco.' "

"San Francisco? But he went to Los Angeles."

"I thought you say you know Dr. Harland."

"I do."

"Then why you say Los Angeles? The letter comes from San Francisco. He say he will send someone to pack up his things, that he is going to sell the place. But months go by, and nobody comes to pack him up. No real estate agent. No more letters." He paused. "And now you."

"That's right."

"You are going to pack him up?"

"Uh, no. He wants to rent the apartment furnished. To my friend."

"Okay. You tell Dr. Harland send me letter." He reached for the door handle.

"I will. But first I need to look at the apartment. For my friend."

"I am very busy. You come back."

"Please," Taylor said. "I'm a doctor, too. I don't have much time. Can't I see it now?"

The man sighed. "I take you. You stay." He disappeared into the apartment, returning shortly with a tagged key. He pulled the door open, looked out into the rain, looked back at the unfinished living room. "You have doctor ID?" he asked.

"What? Yes, of course." Taylor fished in her bag for her hospital badge. He examined it closely.

"Okay. You take key, go look. Number 22, over there. You bring key back."

"Thank you very much."

Holding the umbrella in front of her, she ran through the rain to the unit and unlocked the door. Inside, it was overly warm, with a dank, fusty smell. The place needed a good airing out.

And a cleaning, she realized as she flicked on the light. Several dirty plates stood in the sink, food rotted in the fridge, four-month-old newspapers were stacked in one corner. She wandered through the small, well-furnished living room and down the hall to the bedroom.

Clothes hung in the closet, crisp shirts were stacked in the dresser drawers.

Back in the main living space, the dining area had been arranged as a study. Taylor went through the small desk, scanning papers and bills and canceled checks. She found nothing to indicate a recent move to the West Coast or anywhere else.

So where in hell had Harland gone? Sam had claimed Harland had relocated to L.A., but the super had gotten a letter from San Francisco. Saguaro was in San Francisco; was Harland connected with the foundation in some way? Were they funding a West Coast rival to Greenvale? Had they tapped Harland to head it up?

But why had he left his clothing and furniture behind? And dirty dishes in the sink?

She wandered over to the window and raised the shade. The view was to the woods that bordered the complex. She pulled the shade back down again and went to the narrow built-in bookcase. Novels, history, biography. She took several volumes out at random. Maybe she should call the Saguaro Foundation in San Francisco, see if they know where Harland went.

And maybe she should mind her own business.

But Harland had been her predecessor; whatever had happened to him could happen to her. It was a very unsettling thought.

As she began replacing the books, she noticed a thick volume protruding beyond the line of spines. She tried to shove it back into place but it wouldn't go. There seemed to be something behind it. She removed it and, without thinking, reached into the opening, then pulled back with a startled cry. Blood dripped from a tiny but deep cut on her finger.

Wrapping the cut in a tissue, she tumbled out the books to either side of the blocked space and peered in. Something was wedged against the back of the bookcase. She went and got a fork from the kitchen and coaxed it out, gasping as it tumbled onto the floor at her feet.

It was all too familiar, a male doll this time, but dressed in the same surgical greens she remembered. The figure had brown hair, and its facial features had been skillfully drawn. She'd never met Ward Harland, but she'd seen his photograph in the Greenvale literature. And this doll looked very much like him.

A scalpel had been stuck so deeply through his back, its silvery point had penetrated the chest. Clinging to the tip of the blade was a bright drop of her own blood.

Chapter Twenty-nine

"They're all terrified," Kip said. "We were down four people on Friday, and I thought, well, the weekend's coming up; they'll get over it. But only two guys showed for work this morning." He paused. "I'm shutting the project down."

"But you can't," Taylor exclaimed. "The Larrabee—"

"I don't have a choice," Kip said morosely. "Not without a research staff."

"That's awful. I can't believe your security people haven't found out who's been doing all those things. Or the police."

"Well, they haven't."

"What about the anti-genetics group?"

"They're still looking into that. Right now, all they can tell me is, the blood smeared all over the ladies' room wasn't human."

"What was it?"

"Chicken blood," he said disgustedly. "Rooster blood, actually. I thought that would make people feel better—I mean, it's sort of humorous in a way—but it didn't seem to help. They refuse to come back to work until the culprit is caught."

"Can't say I blame them." Taylor frowned. Rooster blood smacked of voodoo. Could the national group that was now backing the Gaia cult be the same group that had picketed Kip's lab? Could the Gaias have repaid that debt in blood?

"Anyway," Kip was saying, "what with the lab smeared with animal entrails and my research at a standstill, I could use a little sanity. How would you feel about a visitor, day after tomorrow?"

"I'd love it," Taylor said. "But I should warn you: New Chatham isn't any saner than New York. In fact, you might suggest the police look for a connection between your protest group and ours." Briefly she told Kip about the brake tampering, Slater's seeming belief in witchcraft, the torn blueprint, and the voodoo doll in Ward Harland's apartment.

"Jesus," he said. "I never should have urged you to take that job. But who could have imagined . . . Maybe you should think about quitting."

Taylor was silent for a moment. "I have thought about it," she conceded. "But I'm doing good work here, and I'm making excellent contacts. The longer I can hang on, the stronger my position will be when I leave."

"I guess." Kip sounded doubtful. "But be damn careful, okay?" Then, "You really think there could there be a connection between my problems and yours?"

"It's tempting to think so, especially with that rooster blood. Although how they'd get past your security people—"

"Actually, I was thinking of Sam Slater."

"Because you two are competing for the Larrabee, you mean? Hey, Sam's a little strange, I grant you, but I can't see him sneaking into your lab at night and rubbing dead chickens all over the walls. Besides, he was at a hospital board meeting Thursday night."

"Well, we can work on it together when I get there."

"Come tomorrow, and I'll take you to a party Sam's throwing for the hospital's fifth anniversary."

"I would if I could," Kip said regretfully, "but Wednesday afternoon's the soonest I can manage."

"Your loss. How long can you stay?"

"Two or three days, if that's all right. Can you suggest a nice hotel in town?"

"Don't be silly. You'll stay with me." She laughed. "It's not as if you won't be sleeping here anyway."

"I think it's your shyness I like best."

"Ho, ho. Call my office when you get in, and I'll get a key to you." She hesitated. "Kip, have you ever heard of a Saguaro Foundation? They fund medical research among other things."

"Doesn't ring a bell. Why?"

"Apparently they're big supporters of Greenvale. And it turns out they—or a real estate partnership of the same name—own the Rockingham estate. The place Slater insists is haunted."

"Sorry. The only Saguaro I ever heard of is a cactus."

"A *cactus*?"

"Arizona's state flower, as a matter of fact." He thought for a moment. "Maybe you should discuss it with that guy Potter. Slater's financial honcho."

"I considered that, but . . . Potter belongs to Slater, and Slater's already threatened to fire me for challenging him about the Partrick case."

"Slater's also given you the chance to rebuild your career. A chance no one else would give you. If he's in over his head, maybe Garrison can protect him."

"You're suggesting I put my job on the line to protect *Slater*?" Taylor asked incredulously.

"Absolutely not. But if you and Garrison combine what you know, the picture might become a lot clearer. Which might help everybody."

"That kind of depends on what it's a picture *of*, doesn't it?" Taylor said tartly. And where does Ohlmeyer fit in? she wondered. "I'll think about it."

"Hey, don't do anything you're uncomfortable with," Kip said quickly. "Trust your instincts."

"Those instincts didn't keep me from marrying Paul. Or accepting Slater's job offer, for that matter."

"Well, they were working overtime when you called

me after you saw that article in the paper," Kip said.
"I've been thinking a lot about—"

The buzz of Taylor's intercom interrupted. "Sorry.
Hang on a minute," she told him, and hit the hold
button. "Go ahead, Donna."

"Tannenbaum's starting to close," her secretary
told her.

"Thanks for the warning. I'll be right down."

She manipulated the buttons again. "Gotta go," she
told Kip. "The guy I'm following in the OR is wrapping up. Uh, you were saying?"

"It can wait. No, actually, it can't. I've been thinking
a lot about us, and there's something I think you
should know."

"What's that?" she asked with some trepidation.

"I, er, I think I'm in love with you." Click.

Taylor sat there, stunned, the receiver dangling
from her hand. You think you're in *love* with me?
You *think* you're in love with me?

"Let me know when you decide," she might have
said if he'd still been on the line.

Or, "Aren't you rushing things a little?"

Or, "I think I'm in love with you, too, Kip. In fact,
I'm sure I am."

It was probably just as well he'd hung up, she decided. The first two responses would have been wrong,
and as for the third, well, just because he'd said the
L word didn't mean she wouldn't scare him into the
next county if she said it, too.

She replaced the receiver and headed down to the
OR, her heart banging away in her chest.

"You're glowing," Garrison observed, smiling.

Taylor looked up. "Flushed is more like it," she
replied, blushing. "I've been rushed off my feet all
morning. I came down here to escape for a minute."

"Tell me about it," he said, shifting a sheaf of papers and a wrapped sandwich from one arm to the
other. "I think we'll all be ready for a little R and R

tomorrow night. Should be quite a scene." He paused. "You *are* going, aren't you?"

"Yes, I guess I should."

"You definitely should. Why don't you come with Dolores and me?"

"Dolores . . . ? Oh, yes; Mrs. Goodbody."

"Don't *you* start."

"Sam's expecting quite a crowd, I gather."

"You bet," Garrison said. "The three B's: board members, bankers—you'll get to meet my father—and benefactors. We'll pick you up around eight, okay?"

"It's nice of you, but I'd rather drive myself," Taylor answered, "so I can leave if I have to. I'm on call tomorrow evening."

"Well, we'll keep an eye out for you." He rose and put his hand lightly on hers. "Whatever you're glowing about, I'm glad it's working out for you."

"Thanks." She watched him walk away. Maybe Kip had the right idea about taking Garrison into her confidence. After all, he'd already taken her into his, that day at lunch, when he'd asked her not to mention their conversation about Saguaro to Sam. The more she thought about it, the more inclined she was to give it a whirl. Perhaps tonight at the party, if she could pry him loose from Mrs. Goodbody.

Chapter Thirty

Taylor drew up in front of Sam's elegant, porticoed colonial, and a parking attendant hurried over to take her keys. The house was ablaze with lights. Dozens of cars had been herded into an adjoining field, and the pulse of a live band floated out of the partly opened front door.

Inside, the crush of people was intense. Someone took Taylor's coat, and someone else pointed her toward the rectangular double living room in which waiters circulated with trays of champagne. For those philistines who preferred soft drinks or hard liquor, a bar had been set up in one corner. A small dance floor had been laid in one section of the huge room, and eight or nine couples were gyrating enthusiastically. Two long tables held a lavish buffet, and logs blazed in the twin Adams fireplaces. Beside one of the hearths was a small basket in which Snowball, Sam's small white dog, was dozing.

An elegantly attired Slater was holding court by the window. Framed in the drawn-back drapes behind him was an elaborately landscaped garden illuminated by outdoor spotlights. Taylor started toward him to make her hellos.

"You missed Sam's speech," said a voice in her ear. "But I won't tell on you."

Taylor turned to smile at Garrison. "Couldn't be helped," she said. "I'm on call tonight, remember?"

She turned to the buxom middle-aged brunette with perfect skin who stood beside him. "And you must be . . ." Damn, what was the woman's name?

"Dolores Goode," Garrison said smoothly. "Dolores, this is Taylor Barnes."

"Dolores, of course. Garrison's—" told me so much about you, she was about to say, then realized Garrison hadn't told her a damn thing. "—lady," she finished lamely.

"Dr. Barnes." Dolores extended a plump paw. "Garrison's told me so much about you."

Well, one of us had to say it. "Nice to meet you," Taylor replied. "So what did Sam say?"

" 'Thank you for five wonderful years, here's to the future, yadda, yadda, yadda.' " Garrison grinned. "Come on, let's get you a drink." He bulled his way through the crowd, the two women following close behind.

"Club soda and lime, please," Taylor requested when they arrived at the bar. "This is some crowd. Do you know all these people?"

"Most of them. That's my father, talking to Sam. I'll introduce you later. The tall blond guy in the blue blazer over by the buffet is Calvin Mayhew, head of the bankers association. I feel like I'm shouting."

"You are," Dolores told him. "If you weren't, we couldn't hear you. Let's move away from the bar." She led them toward the fireplace, where the crowd was a little thinner. "That's better. By the way, I love your outfit, Dr. Barnes."

"Thanks. And call me Taylor." Taylor was wearing an elegantly simple navy silk suit she'd bought on her recent visit to New York. Its designer label had been expensive, but she'd decided she was worth it. Which was a nice change from the way she'd gotten used to feeling about herself. "I like your outfit, too," she said graciously. She wouldn't have been caught dead in the beaded cocktail dress Dolores wore, but somehow it suited the woman.

"Ooh, a dog," Dolores cooed, spotting Snowball in

his basket. "I just adore dogs. My husband never liked them, but Gar's just crazy about them." She knelt down and began petting the small white terrier.

"Really? Just crazy about dogs, is he?" Taylor said, giving Garrison a wicked smile. "Any particular breed?"

"Dolores and I are planning to visit a breeder friend of mine who raises corgis. She's thinking about getting a dog, now that, um . . ."

"Now that she's alone so much?" Taylor said innocently.

"Exactly," Garrison agreed solemnly, but his eyes twinkled.

"Hey, I think there's something the matter with this little guy," Dolores told them. "He can barely lift his head." She took the dog up from the basket and held him against her. He gave her hand a tentative lick and then lay listlessly in her arms.

"He's just tired," Slater said, arriving with Donald Potter in tow. "Been chasing caterers all day." But he eyed the dog with grave concern. "Glad you finally made it," he said, shifting his attention to Taylor. "You missed my speech," he said, slurring the final word badly. A little too much to drink, Taylor guessed; the effect was all too familiar to her.

"I was on call," she apologized. "Garrison said it was brilliant."

Slater raised a cynical eyebrow. "He would. He wrote it."

"Well, it's all in the delivery, isn't it? This is a really great party," she added hurriedly. "And you have a very beautiful home."

"Thank you," Slater said, somewhat mollified. "Oh, do you know Donald Potter?" The introductions were made, Slater moved off to shake some more hands, and Donald took Dolores to the dance floor.

Thought Taylor, If I'm going to do it, now's the time. "You have a minute?"

"Sure," Garrison said, his eyes on the dancers. "What's up?"

"Is there somewhere quiet we could talk? I have a few things to tell you."

He eyed her curiously. "The den." He led her back through the crowd, passing Peter Ohlmeyer, who pointedly managed not to notice them, and down a wide hallway to a comfortable book-lined study with leather-upholstered furniture and a colorful kilim on its polished wood floor. A home computer sat on a pine table under the window.

"Take a pew." Garrison settled into a club chair and sipped his drink.

"This is confidential," she said, seating herself on the sofa. "I'm only telling you because you might have some insights. And also because you asked me about the Saguaro Foundation."

"What about Saguaro?" Garrison asked cautiously.

"I happened on some information, that night I went looking for a blueprint for Sam."

"Hey, did he like it?"

"I decided it wasn't a very good gift. But while I was at the town hall, I learned a few things."

"Shoot."

Briefly she told him about the Rockingham tax assessment and the missing blueprint. "You've been at Greenvale from the beginning," she finished. "What do you think it means?"

She had expected Garrison to be surprised, puzzled, perhaps even alarmed. She'd certainly never expected him to be indifferent.

"Oh, I wouldn't worry about the blueprint," he said, relaxing back in his chair. "The hospital's gone through numerous accreditation inspections that are quite thorough. If anything were amiss, it would have been found years ago. As for the Rockingham connection . . ." He thought a moment. "If the Rockingham heirs formed a real estate partnership, which is perfectly likely, they could call it anything they wanted."

"But . . . Saguaro? The same name as the foundation?"

"Maybe it's their foundation."

"I thought of that too, although I would never have guessed the Rockinghams had so much money. But in that case, why all the secrecy? Why is Sam the only person at Greenvale who deals with them? Why not you?"

"I'm sure Sam has his reasons," Garrison said placidly. "And it's a private foundation, after all. Perhaps they prefer it that way."

Taylor stared at him. "Not four weeks ago, you came to me very concerned about—"

"I wasn't concerned, I was curious. You remember I told you it was a control issue. Since then I've decided I was wrong to try and second-guess Sam. I trust him. And once we get that Larrabee—"

"That's another thing. Sam mentioned the name of the guy I've been seeing, that day in the cafeteria. Kip Lawrence. Remember?" Garrison nodded. "Well, Kip's a strong contender for the Larrabee. At least, he was."

"Why 'was'?"

"His lab's been systematically vandalized, and his research has stopped. In the latest incident, someone smeared blood all over the ladies' room. Two-thirds of his research assistants are women. They're terrified."

Garrison frowned. "What does that have to do with—"

"Maybe nothing, I don't know. I just thought if I could combine what I know with what you know . . ."

"But I don't know a thing. I mean, I'm sorry your friend's work has been disrupted, but I don't see how—"

"Do you think Sam could have done it?"

"Sam? You're joking."

"I don't mean personally, of course. But I know how badly he wants that Larrabee." Kip was wrong, she thought; I should never have told Garrison any of this.

"Sam would never do such a thing." Garrison leaned toward Taylor. "I know him a lot better than you do. He wouldn't want to win by eliminating the competition; the award wouldn't mean anything to him. If he couldn't win the Larrabee fair and square, he wouldn't want it."

"I'm sure you're right," Taylor said quickly. "I never should have suggested it."

She hesitated. "By the way, since you know Sam so well, maybe you can tell me what's the matter with him." Garrison looked at her questioningly. "Surely you've seen the way his hands shake. How tired he looks."

"I haven't noticed him looking tired," Garrison said. "If he is, it's because he's been working so hard. But I did notice the tremors. In fact, I asked him about it. He says it's a chronic neurological tic and has no medical significance."

"Well, that's a relief," Taylor said. "As long as you're sure that's all there is to it."

"I know you have Sam's best interests at heart, but you have to trust me on this. Sam's fine, Greenvale's fine. Everything's just fine."

"Not everything." Garrison's smile faded. "That day we went to the art show, you mentioned how chummy Peter Ohlmeyer had become with Sam, that Sam gave him free rein at Greenvale. It sounded as though you didn't like him very much."

"I don't."

"Well, neither do I," Taylor assured him. "For one thing, I'm concerned about the patients who've died under his care; Jim Partrick, for one. His methods are . . . unorthodox, to say the least."

"You think we'll get sued?"

Taylor sighed. "How should I know? Anyway, my concerns go deeper." She sipped her soda. "Did Sam tell you about my run-in with Ohlmeyer in the parking garage?" Garrison frowned and shook his head. "He jumped up from behind my car, grabbed my shoulders, and threatened me if I told what I knew about him."

"My God." Garrison leaned forward. "What *do* you know about him?"

"Then? Only that he'd been suspected of beating his wife, years ago. Last night—" She broke off. "When I told Sam, he took Ohlmeyer's part. He said I was overdramatizing things, even though I had the bruises to show for it. No, Gar," she added, seeing his face, "*I'm* not going to sue Greenvale, either. The point is that Slater refuses to see how nutty Ohlmeyer is, on duty and off. The man has some kind of hold over Sam."

"What is it?"

"I don't know. But Ohlmeyer said something in the garage that night that got me thinking. Something about manslaughter not being homicide. It took me awhile to get around to it, but I finally did a little Internet snooping last night, and—"

Garrison's face had gone pale. "You're saying Ohlmeyer's hold over Sam involves murder?"

Taylor frowned. "No, I'm not. In fact, what I learned last night sort of confuses everything." She set down her glass. "My mother said a neighbor of ours, years ago, was convinced Ohlmeyer had murdered his wife after they left town. It turns out she was right."

"What?"

"Accidentally. At least, that's how the jury saw it. They convicted him of manslaughter. This was many years ago."

"Does Sam know?"

"I have no idea. But if he does, it wouldn't put him in Ohlmeyer's debt, would it? I mean, it should be the other way around."

"And if he *doesn't* know?" Garrison rose. "We can't have a murderer on the staff of Greenvale Hospital."

"It was manslaughter, not homicide. Accidental death. And before you say anything to Sam, we have to think this through. There's something here I don't understand."

"But Sam should know—"

"It's possible Sam already knows. Look, he gave me a job despite my history of alcoholism. Maybe he's doing the same for Ohlmeyer."

"But that would put Sam in the driver's seat, not Peter."

"Exactly." Taylor frowned. "I don't like Ohlmeyer any more than you do. But I think we need to be careful about what we say to whom. If Ohlmeyer really does have some hold over Sam that we don't know about, well, he *is* a violent man. Sam could get hurt." And so could I, she thought.

"I suppose you're right," he said reluctantly. "As long as the hospital's not at risk."

"I think the hospital's more at risk from Ohlmeyer's medical procedures than from an ancient manslaughter charge."

"That's reassuring." He gave her a weak smile.

Taylor shrugged. "We need to think about all this some more before anyone mentions it to Sam. Promise me, Gar."

"Okay. I promise." He picked up his glass. "And now I'd better go rescue Dolores. Coming?"

"You go ahead," Taylor told him. "I need to find the powder room. Uh, Garrison? Please don't mention the rest of this conversation to Sam, either."

"I wouldn't dream of it," he assured her. He patted her shoulder and gave her a reassuring smile. "I'm grateful that you confided in me. Anyway, we're buddies, remember?"

When he'd gone, Taylor wandered around the room, trying to regain her composure. She'd put herself in a very vulnerable position and learned nothing in return. Well, maybe one thing: no banker, board member or hospital executive had any intention of rocking Sam's boat. They were all making too much money.

She felt like a fool. Why had she listened to Kip

when her instincts had told her to keep the information to herself? Well, Kip had also suggested she listen to her instincts, so she couldn't really blame him. God, she wished she could wipe out the last ten minutes.

At least she hadn't told him about her visit to Mrs. Roche or her search of Ward Harland's apartment.

Photographs in silver frames were grouped together on a side table, and she scanned them idly. Sam at Greenvale's groundbreaking ceremony, Sam with several celebrities. A young, robust Sam in climbing gear. A thirty-something Sam with his arm around a pretty, fiftyish woman. A boy of ten or eleven appeared in several of the older photos; she had the feeling she'd seen him somewhere before. She looked more closely; the boy bore a faint resemblance to Leonardo DiCaprio; that must be it.

She really did need to use the bathroom now. A small door beside the bookcase looked as if it might lead to one. She went through and found herself in Sam's bedroom.

Oops.

Directly across from where she stood, a bathroom door stood open. She started to retreat, then thought, What the hell; I'll just be a minute.

Her business done, she came out again casting an eye over the bedroom, attractively furnished in masculine Ralph Lauren plaids and stripes. The door to the hall stood partly open, and rather than going back through the den, she made for it. As she passed the bedside table, she noticed a well-thumbed Chinese language text. Another lay beside it, on top of the latest popular business tome. It appeared that Sam was teaching himself Mandarin. A curious choice of language.

She was nearly at the door when a flash of gold, half buried in the deep pile carpet, caught her eye. Without thinking, she bent down and retrieved it. It was a medical alert necklace, its medallion inscribed with the familiar staff-and-serpent symbol.

". . . push 50,000 U Heparin IV and do CPR—"
she read.

Voices in the hall made her look up.

". . . lend it to you," Sam was saying. "Every creative businessman should read it."

Although using his bathroom was no crime, she
somehow felt Sam wouldn't be too pleased to find
her in his bedroom. Especially with his medical alert
necklace in her hand. What sort of medical alert was
this, anyway? Fifty thousand units of heparin? That
would be lethal. And doing CPR was standard emergency procedure; no physician or EMT would need a
medical alert to tell them that.

"Thanks, Sam," she heard Calvin Mayhew reply.
"I've been meaning to pick it up. You really think it's
that good?"

Frowning, Taylor dropped the gold disk on a nearby
dresser. It flipped over as it landed, and she caught a
glimpse of the reverse just before she hurried through
to the den and closed the connecting door behind her.

Sam and his guest were just disappearing into the
bedroom as she stepped out into the hall. It was true
that this little interlude hadn't produced any answers,
she reflected as she headed back to the party, but it
sure as hell had posed an interesting new question.

Kip had said saguaro was an Arizona cactus.

Garrison had said Saguaro was a private philanthropic institution.

The town hall tax assessment had defined Saguaro
as a real estate partnership.

So why was the outline of a giant cactus inscribed
on the back of the medical alert she'd found in
Sam's bedroom?

Chapter Thirty-one

The demonstrators arrived just after ten. They massed on the front lawn, shouting and brandishing placards. The chief of police, who'd been a guest at the party, had left a quarter of an hour earlier. They'd somehow known that, and waited for his departure before making their presence known.

When Sam went to the phone to call the station house, he found nine separate messages on his answering machine, all left within the past hour, threatening violence to him and his guests.

Furious, he strode out onto the grass and began shouting at the demonstrators to remove themselves from his property or risk arrest. Calvin Mayhew and Donald Potter followed after him, more to persuade him to return to the safety of the house than to mix it up with the rowdies outside.

Frightened guests watched from the living room windows. Garrison put a protective arm around Dolores. "Police'll be here any minute," he reassured her. "Nothing to worry about. I wish Sam would come inside, though," he added, brow furrowing. "It could get nasty out there."

"It's already getting nasty out there," Taylor told him, surprised that Garrison was more concerned about Sam's safety than that of his own father. She watched with trepidation as Donald Potter wrested a placard from a demonstrator's hands and smashed it on the ground. The man took a swing at Potter, who promptly dropped the sign and punched him in the stomach. The protester sat down heavily. Potter took Slater by one arm, Mayhew grabbed the other, and together they hustled him back inside as two police cruisers came screaming up the tree-lined drive.

As the officers burst from their cars, the protesters fled into the woods that bordered the house on three sides, one young man pausing to hurl a rock through one of the side windows.

Calvin Mayhew was fuming. "How dare they?" he repeated, wrapping a handkerchief around the cut on his palm. "Greenvale is this town's bread and butter." Donald Potter was equally angry, and Slater nearly incoherent. "This is private property," he sputtered. "This is my home." His body shook uncontrollably. Garrison found a blanket and tried to wrap it around Slater's shoulders, but he shoved it away.

Fortunately, no one had been standing near the side window, all the action taking place in front of the house, so there had been no serious injuries. Several people had been scratched by flying glass, however, and Taylor was doing some impromptu cleaning and bandaging when several police officers came around the side of the house with three handcuffed miscreants.

The guests looked at each other, at the mess of glass on the floor, at the lights of the police cruisers on the lawn, and began making their farewells.

The crowd of cars and their owners was such that Taylor, having retrieved her coat, decided to wait awhile before venturing in search of her vehicle. She came back into the living room, where the caterer's assistants were sweeping up the glass and dismantling the buffet. Slater was on his knees by the dog basket, a plate of food in his hand.

"Chasing caterers is hungry work," Taylor said with a smile, then realized the lethargic animal was ignoring the piece of roast beef Sam held out. "Is he sick?"

Slater turned to her and nodded, his face filled with anguish. Setting the plate on the floor, he took Snowball gently from the basket and cradled him against his dress shirt. The dog licked his hand torpidly. "He's dying," Slater murmured, rocking the dog in his arms. "He's dying." When he looked up at her again, his face was streaked with tears.

With the arrival of the squad cars, the demonstrators had scattered. Several had hidden their vehicles down the road from the house when they'd arrived, and were already heading home. Others had walked in, and were now making their cautious retreat along the darkened roads.

Well back among the trees, they'd watched the cruisers pass them, moving fast. Once the police cars were out of sight, they'd moved onto the road itself. Several hugged the shoulder, but others strode boldly down the center of the road, the better to converse with their pals.

They were dressed in black and carried no lights, so Taylor, coming around a sharp curve, didn't see them until she was very nearly upon them. She braked hard and swerved away.

The day had been warm enough to thaw the light, late snow that had fallen the evening before. But the night had brought a cold wind and plummeting temperatures, and the runoff on the roads had turned slick.

Her car skidded across the road, sideswiped a tree, spun halfway around, and banged into the guardrail on the opposite side. The rail ballooned but held, and the Lexus slued along for another ten yards before coming to rest against a section of railing.

Dark figures approached the car. "Hey, it's that woman doctor from the hospital."

"So what should we do?"

Faces peered in at Taylor. "Is she dead?"

"Maybe. Or maybe she's just unconscious."

"Shouldn't we call someone?" a woman asked.

"Absolutely not."

"But she might die."

"Yeah, she might. Save us the trouble." The others started off down the road, but the woman stood staring in at Taylor's still form.

"You coming?" a man called.

"We can't just leave her."

"Move it, Maggie." A tall figure came toward her, raising a heavy placard threateningly. "Unless you want to join her in there."

"I'm coming," Maggie said quickly. "I'm coming." She trailed after the group, falling farther and farther behind. Some thirty yards past the smashed car, she ducked into the trees and began to run.

Chapter Thirty-two

Kip steered with one hand and held the car phone to his ear with the other. "It's okay, Davis," he said. "You can read it to me."

"You sure? It says confidential on the cover sheet."

"They sent a goddamn fax," Kip said. "How confidential could it be?"

"Okay," Emerson's research director said doubtfully. "If you're sure."

"Hey, we all know what it's going to say," Kip told him. "Just give me the gist of it."

There was silence while Davis read and digested the contents of the fax. Then, "They say your project isn't far enough along. Maybe next year."

"What a surprise," Kip said bitterly. "Whoever decided to disrupt my work sure did a bang-up job." He paused. "Let me guess who the front runner is now: Sam Slater."

"Nothing's official, but . . ."

"You've heard something?"

"Well, you two were the top runners."

"So it's Slater."

"Looks like it. I'm sorry."

"Me, too."

"Look, go see your girl, give yourself a break. You always insisted the lab disruptions were connected with the Larrabee. Assuming you're right, they'll stop now that you're no longer a contender. All you have to do is wait a few weeks, recruit some new staff, and pick up where you left off."

"Sure."

"Hey, I'm really sorry, Kip."

"Thanks, Davis. Look, I'll give you a call in a day or two, and we can put a game plan together."

"Good."

Kip disconnected. He was disappointed and angry. All that work, for nothing. But of course it wasn't for nothing. He didn't do research in order to win awards. And he didn't need a Larrabee to get funding; he had all the funding he needed. Still, it would have been awfully nice . . .

Well, Davis was right; there was always next year. He suddenly felt the need to hear Taylor's voice. Put things in perspective, he thought.

He picked up the car phone again and dialed her office number, identifying himself as a personal friend from New York and explaining that she was expecting him.

"I have a key for you, Dr. Lawrence," Donna, Taylor's secretary, told him. "But . . . I guess you haven't heard. Dr. Barnes was in a car accident."

"What? When? Is she all right?"

"She was very lucky. A mild concussion, a bruised shoulder. They admitted her last night."

"My God. Did the CT scan show anything?"

"I really don't know."

"Well, if it's possible, would you please let her know that I'll be there in a couple of hours?"

"I'll try. But Dr. Slater isn't allowing her any visitors."

"Why on earth not?"

"You'll have to take that up with him."

"I sure will. I'll be there around two." He broke the connection and stepped on the gas.

Slater stood by the window, his eyes wet. The small dog lay in his arms, fighting for breath, its tiny body quivering. The sky was a brilliant blue, and the sun shining through the glass was warm on his face. Spring was coming, a time of new beginnings. But not for Snowball.

He stroked the soft white fur with shaking hands. Don't die, he breathed. Please don't die. Our lives are intermeshed. But as he watched, the animal gave one last convulsive shudder and lay still. Slowly Slater knelt down and laid the dog on its cushion under the window. Is this really how it ends? he thought bitterly. After everything I've done? Unconsciously he fingered the disk of the medical alert under his shirt. What's the use, he thought despairingly, if this is how it ends.

Come on, man, he told himself angrily. Pull yourself together.

He stood and went to the phone. "It's over," he said into the receiver. "You can come and get him."

A white medical coat was slung over the back of his desk chair, and he put it on. He looked down at the dog, his eyes filling again. Will I ever see you again?

Don't give way now, he told himself firmly, forcing himself to turn away. There's too much to do. You don't have time for self-indulgence. He went out into the hall. "I'm going up to check on Dr. Barnes," he told Penny as he passed her cubicle.

It's a problem, he conceded, his thoughts going back to the small ball of fur. But I've solved other problems. Given time, I can solve this one, too. Given time.

But time was precisely what he didn't have.

Taylor lay in the cool white room, her mouth slack, her eyes closed. An IV feed dripped fluids into her arm.

"What are you doing here?" Slater asked as he came through the door.

Garrison straightened up. "Just wanted to see how she is."

"And how is she?"

"You tell me."

Slater leaned over, lifted an eyelid, felt her pulse. "She's still out."

Garrison frowned. "You mean she's been unconscious since they brought her in last night?"

"When she came to in the ER," Slater said, "she was in a lot of pain, so Ohlmeyer sedated her."

"Ohlmeyer? Why was he called in?"

"She was having some arrhythmia, too." Slater took the chart from the end of the bed, scanned it, put it back. "I've asked Peter to stay involved in her case."

"Is she going to be all right?" Garrison asked worriedly.

"Probably. Eventually." He eyed Garrison suspiciously. "I thought you were involved with Dolores. Why are you hanging around here?"

"The health of the lady who brings in the money," Garrison replied, "is not something I take lightly."

Slater's eyes flashed. "I suppose my benefactors and foundation grants mean nothing?"

"Come on, Sam. You know I didn't mean that. Hey, you hired her yourself, said she'd bring in the big bucks. And you were right."

Taylor rose up through a thick sea of nothingness. Ignored by the two men, she fluctuated between consciousness and sleep. Where was she? Who was speaking?

Garrison eyed Slater critically. "You don't look well."

"I'm fine." He sighed. "Snowball died this morning."

"Oh, hell, Sam. I'm sorry. I liked the little fella." Garrison hesitated. "If you decide to get another dog, I have a breeder friend. I'd be happy to—" Slater shook his head. "Too soon?"

"It's not that. Snowball was special."

"I understand."

"You don't, but it doesn't matter."

"Sure, Sam. Anyway, I just heard some news that'll cheer you right up. It's about the Larrabee."

Her awareness flickered and grew. Her head hurt. The voices were clearer. She sensed daylight beyond her closed eyelids.

"Kip Lawrence is out of the race," Garrison said triumphantly, dropping into a visitor's chair. "Looks like you're the front runner."

Slater stared at him. "That's terrific. Wonderful." He frowned. "What happened?"

"His research was continually disrupted, and his project had to be put on hold. The committee decided he wasn't far enough along and disqualified him. Good news, huh?"

"Great news." He studied Garrison. "You wouldn't happen to know who disrupted his research?"

"Not a clue."

"You're sure?"

"Hey, you wanted the Larrabee, and you've got it. That's all I know."

The figure on the bed moved, rustling the crisp sheets, and both men turned toward her. "Taylor? Dr. Barnes?" Slater said, but she made no reply, and her eyes remained closed.

"Is he very disappointed?" Slater asked.

"Who, Lawrence? I'm sure he is. But he has next year." Garrison hesitated. "So tell me: what's the story with you and this Lawrence guy?"

"Nothing that concerns you," Slater said firmly. "It goes back years. Don't you have work to do?"

"Sure, Sam," Garrison said, rising. "We can talk later about how to spin this Larrabee thing."

"Isn't it a trifle early for that? The award isn't officially ours yet."

"It's never too soon to plan."

When Potter had gone, Slater leaned over Taylor, listening to her breathing. He spoke her name several times, but she didn't respond. Was she really still out? How much of their conversation had she heard, and what had she made of it? No matter, he decided; whatever she might say could be explained away as the

ramblings of a concussed, sedated mind. A heavily sedated mind.

He took out his pen and increased the dosage on
her chart.

"What room is Taylor Barnes in?"

"I'm sorry, miss," the receptionist said. "No visitors allowed."

"Just tell her it's Maggie. I know she'll let me in."

The receptionist shook her head. "Doctor's orders."
She took in the woman's scattered appearance and
flushed face, and raised an eyebrow at a nearby guard.
The guard moved closer.

"Who's her doctor?" Maggie demanded.

"Dr. Slater's taking care of her personally. She's
had a bad knock on the head, and she needs her rest.
Why don't you come back tomorrow?"

"Dr. Slater?" Maggie breathed. "But he's . . .
he'll . . ."

"Mervyn? You want to give me a hand here?"

The guard approached and took Maggie firmly by
the arm. "You'll have to leave, miss," he said.

Maggie pulled free. "Get your hands off me."

"Please, miss," the guard said. "You have to leave
now."

Maggie looked from him to the receptionist. The desk
blocked half the main corridor leading to the elevators; the guard stood squarely in front of the other
half. Muttering under her breath, she turned away.

She pushed through the revolving door and started
down the cement walkway that led from the hospital
entrance to the sidewalk. Her steps slowed, then
stopped. She was deeply worried. Who knew what
would happen to Taylor in there? People died in
there; her husband had. Slater was an evil man. She'd
known Taylor since they were children, and Taylor
had never hurt her or anyone she knew.

But it wasn't just the thought of Slater that was
bothering her. Her growing doubts about the Gaias,

and her resentment at being used by them, had finally come together at the crash site. The Gaias—her so-called friends—were only indirectly responsible for the accident that had put Taylor in the hospital, but they tried to turn it into murder. And they forced her to be a part of it, or so they believed.

No, she didn't like the hospital being built on what should have been a nature preserve. Yes, she felt strongly about the hospital bio-trash issue. Of course she blamed the hospital for her husband's death. Sure, Taylor brought in money that kept Greenvale operating. But protests, even spells, were one thing; murder was quite another. And it was finally clear to her that standing with the Gaias meant embracing the idea that one terrible evil justified another.

People pushed past her, but she stood there, unseeing.

The Gaias had been there for her when her world had fallen apart, and she'd bought into everything they told her, all that stuff about living in harmony with nature and the spirit of the earth. She'd drunk their potions and let them slash her with the ritual knife, and joined in the orgies that were supposed to raise their spiritual energies.

It was time to ask herself what she really believed.

Did she believe it was in harmony with nature to tamper with someone's brakes, hoping they'd be killed? To walk away from a car crash, not even report it? If she hadn't given them the slip and called the police from a nearby house, Taylor might have died, and the Gaias would have rejoiced. Was that really how she wanted to live her life?

No, Maggie thought; it wasn't.

Her thoughts still far away, she started walking down the path again. People hurried past her in both directions, but she didn't notice them until she walked into one.

"Whoops. Careful, there," a voice said. Maggie

turned. Olive Erbach stood in front of her, a slightly
dented bakery box in her hands.

"Sorry," Maggie apologized. "I didn't see you."

"You weren't looking," Olive replied tartly. "I hope
these aren't damaged. I baked them for Dr. Barnes
when I heard about her accident."

"What are they?"

"Orange-yogurt cupcakes."

"Sounds delicious," Maggie said. "Only I was just
in there, and she's not allowed any visitors. Or solid
food."

"Well, I'll just send them up to the nurse's station.
They can keep them for her until she's well enough
to eat them." Olive glanced at her watch uncertainly.

"Aren't you supposed to be at the school?" Maggie
asked. "I can take them in for you."

"Would you? But you said they turned you away."

"Yes, but I know who to talk to," Maggie said. "I'll
make sure she gets them." She reached for the box.

"Well . . . all right," Olive said a little doubtfully.
"Be sure to tell them to keep these safe for her."

"I will. Don't worry." Maggie took the box, and
Olive hurried off. As soon as the older woman was
out of sight, Maggie lifted the lid and looked in. Five
elaborately iced cupcakes were arranged on a paper
doily. She studied the cakes carefully. Then she replaced the lid, carried the box to a nearby trash bin,
and tossed it in.

Chapter Thirty-three

Kip strode through the lobby toward the reception desk. "Can you tell me the number of Dr. Barnes's room?"

"She's not allowed any visitors."

"So I understand. I want to send her some flowers."

"Oh." The receptionist consulted her computer. "Four-oh-nine," she told him. "All messengers have to stop here first, so be sure and tell them that. Excuse me," she called after him as he started past her toward the elevators. "You can't go up there."

Kip turned back. "I wouldn't dream of it," he assured her. "I've got an appointment with Dr. Slater."

"Oh, sorry. Second floor. Turn left when you get off the elevator."

"Thanks." He'd told Taylor's secretary that he'd take up the "no visitor" policy with Sam, but he had no intention of doing so, not after their last meeting. He stepped into the car and pushed "four."

On the fourth floor, he stepped off the elevator and started down a corridor, but the numbers were too high and getting higher, so he turned and went the other way. Several nurses looked at him curiously, but he smiled, nodded, and continued walking.

The door to 409 was slightly ajar. He pushed it open and went in. A very pale Taylor lay on the bed, a white hospital blanket drawn up to her chin. A red-

haired woman in a pink uniform was fiddling with the
IV drip, a filled syringe in her hand.

"How is she?" Kip asked, startling the woman, who
dropped the syringe. It skidded along the floor, coming to rest under a chair.

"Who are you?" she asked, dropping the IV line.

"Sorry to startle you," Kip said quickly. He bent
and retrieved the hypodermic. "I'm a friend of Dr.
Barnes. I'm Dr. Lawrence." He handed the syringe
back. "You're going to need a fresh one of these,
I'm afraid."

"No, no," said the woman, smiling brightly. "All
finished."

"How is she?"

"As well as can be expected. Excuse me, doctor."

Kip watched the woman leave, then went and closed
the door firmly behind her. The nurses he'd seen in
the corridor had been wearing white uniforms. And the
syringe he'd retrieved and handed back had still
been full.

He studied Taylor's chart with troubled eyes, then
went to the IV stand and carefully clipped one of the
plastic leads shut. Saline continued to drip from the
larger of the bags hanging from the metal stand, but
the other lead was now blocked.

He was rehanging the chart on the end of the bed
when Slater burst into the room. "What the hell are
you doing here?"

"Visiting," Kip said mildly.

"You've already been told," Slater said. "No visitors. Get out."

"Why? Your Dr. Ohlmeyer"—he nodded toward
the chart—"has got her so doped up, she won't even
know I'm here. Why is he doing that, by the way?"

"What do you know about treating concussion?"

"I know that you don't usually prescribe what
you're giving her, and certainly not in that dosage."

"I don't need you to tell me how to practice
medicine."

Kip went to Slater and placed a hand on his shoulder. "When did we become enemies, Sam? What have I ever done to you?"

"You sent her here," Slater replied, jerking his chin toward Taylor. "To spy on me."

"You're nuts. I advised her to take the job if you offered it, that's all."

"I saw the two of you with your heads together," Slater said accusingly. "In a restaurant, that day you came to see me. Why didn't you tell me you and Taylor were lovers?"

Kip shrugged. "I probably would have, if you hadn't bitten my head off. Look, part of my wanting Taylor to work for you was that I thought it might provide a way of bringing us—you and me—together."

"And the fact that we were competing for a Larrabee had nothing to do with it," Slater scoffed.

"Hey, you're the one who's getting the Larrabee," Kip said angrily. "I'm the one whose research project is in the toilet, or haven't you heard?"

"I heard."

"So if anyone should be accusing anyone of sabotage, it ought to be me accusing you."

"Screw you, Kip. I had nothing to do with it." The two men scowled at each other.

"Kip?" Taylor's voice was weak, her words slurred. "Is that you?"

"Taylor?" Kip moved quickly to her side. Taylor blinked and opened her eyes. Seeing Kip, she smiled and murmured his name again before lapsing back into sleep.

Slater frowned. "She shouldn't be awake," he said.

"Why? Because Ohlmeyer's pumping her full of sedative?"

"Because she needs to rest."

"Bullshit. You don't sedate a concussion patient. I'd like a word with this Ohlmeyer guy."

"I'm afraid Dr. Ohlmeyer has been called away." Slater's face was flushed, and his right eyebrow jerked spasmodically. "But he left very specific instructions, and I intend to follow them."

"Even if they're not in your patient's best interest?"

"You're a researcher, Kip, not a practitioner. And you're leaving this hospital. Now."

"No way."

Slater stuck his head out into the hall. "Stacy? You want to get Security up here?" To Kip he said, "We can do this the hard way, or we can do it the easy way. Either way, Taylor is my patient, and this is my hospital."

Kip sighed. With a covert glance at the IV stand and its clamped tube—he'd circumvented the sedation, at least for now—he crossed to the door. If he left the hospital with Slater, he might be able to fake his way back in later on. If he forced Security to escort him out, he wouldn't stand a chance. "Okay," he said. "You win."

"I'll walk you down to the lobby," Slater said, "to make sure you don't get lost."

Kip allowed Slater to lead him down the hall. He hung back slightly, smiling at the nurses and trying to look like a consulting physician.

They rode the elevator down to the lobby. Slater held the door open as Kip stepped out, watching grimly as he went past the reception desk and out through the glass door. Then he took the elevator back upstairs.

Kip took six steps and did a U-turn. The elevator door was closing as he came back into the lobby.

"Thanks for your help finding Dr. Slater's office," he told the receptionist, who looked slightly surprised. "I guess I should have introduced myself. I'm Dr. Lawrence, Kip Lawrence. I'm consulting with Dr. Slater on the Taylor Barnes case."

"You are?"

"Yes. So I'll be in and out fairly often."

"Dr. Slater didn't say anything to us about it."

"No, he asked me to. Which is what I'm doing

now." He smiled his most ingratiating smile. "By the way, where would I find Dr. Ohlmeyer?"

The woman frowned. "Second floor. Most of the doctors' offices are on 'two.' But he's not in today."

"Are you sure? He signed Dr. Barnes's chart early this morning."

The receptionist shrugged. "Dr. Slater said for me to tell any patients who asked for him that he wouldn't be in all week. I suppose you could leave a message on his voice mail."

"Good idea. Well, I'll be back a little later"—he leaned in to read her badge—"Heide."

"You'll need an ID badge."

"Dr. Slater's getting me one. Meanwhile, *you* know who I am, right?"

"Right." She smiled at him. "Welcome to Greenvale, Dr. Lawrence."

"*Kip* Lawrence?" Kip turned. A dark, elegantly dressed man with an air of self-importance stood beside him. "I'm Garrison Potter."

"Nice to meet you," Kip said, drawing him out of earshot of the reception desk. So this was the famous Garrison.

"I heard Heide say 'Lawrence,' and I took a chance. You came to see Taylor?"

"That's right. She's still sedated."

"Yes, and I hope she wakes up soon. We've had to postpone all the procedures she had booked for this week. I didn't mean that the way it sounded," he added quickly. "I consider Taylor a friend as well as a colleague. Hey, I'm sorry about your losing out on the Larrabee."

"Not as sorry as I am, but thanks. And congratulations to you guys. It looks like you're it."

"Yes. Sam's delighted, of course, as am I. Too bad it had to be at your expense, but there's always next year, isn't there? Well, I just wanted to say hello. You'll be around for a while?" Kip nodded. "Where are you staying?"

"I was supposed to stay at Taylor's place, but when I heard she'd been hospitalized, I booked a room at the Post House."

"You'll like it there. Hey, maybe we could have dinner. I'm busy tonight, but how about tomorrow?"

"Nice idea, but I hope Taylor will be better by tomorrow."

"We all hope that."

Kip left the hospital and headed for the public parking lot. He'd drive to the Post House and check in, he decided, wait a few hours until the sedation wore off, then come back and try to talk to Taylor. He ought to give Davis Leeds a call, too. It looked like he'd be here longer than he'd planned.

It was after six when Kip smiled his way past the reception desk and took the elevator upstairs. Dinner trays were being collected, and visitors were saying their good-byes. Taylor's door was closed. Cautiously he turned the handle and slipped inside. The room was dark. Closing the door behind him, he went to the bed and stared down at the still figure.

"Taylor? Are you awake?"

Taylor blinked at him in the darkness. "Kip? What happened?"

"Your car is totaled, and you've got a concussion," he said. "Mild, I think, but Slater's making it into a big deal. And that guy Ohlmeyer has been keeping you sedated. I came by earlier and blocked most of it."

"Ohlmeyer? He's a cardiologist." Her eyes were cloudy, and her voice slurred. "Why is he treating me?"

"Good question," Kip said.

"Don't let Ohlmeyer treat me."

"I won't. Sam says he's away for the rest of the week." He studied her. "I'd like to get you out of here. Can you walk? If not, I can carry you."

"I'm feeling kind of rocky," Taylor said. "My head

hurts, and . . . I'm woozy. I think maybe I need to be here."

"You're drugged," Kip said. "You're not a good judge."

"And you specialize in research, not medicine. Have you seen the CT scan?" Her words ran together, and Kip was having difficulty understanding her. "Never mind. Greenvale's a good hospital." She closed her eyes.

"Taylor, listen to me. Sam's keeping you doped up. I don't like it."

"For me or for you?"

"What are you talking about?"

"I heard Sam talking . . . they thought I was asleep. You and Sam . . . a long time ago. Garrison asked . . . what was with you two?" Taylor opened her eyes again. "Did you know Sam once? Is that why you told me to come here?"

Kip was silent for a moment. "Sam and I . . ." He paused. "It's . . . a long story, and I don't think you're in a state to hear it right now."

"Try . . . tell me."

"Sam's always been jealous of me," Kip said sadly. "He's resented what I had and he didn't. Money, an Ivy League education. I admit that I had hoped your being here might bring about a rapprochement. But that wasn't why I told you to accept his job offer. I really believed it was a good way back for you."

"Sam was jealous? Is that why you thought he was doing those things to your lab?"

Kip nodded. "It was very unfortunate that we both were up for the Larrabee. If I'd known he was being considered, I would have withdrawn my name. But once he knew I was up for it, too . . ."

"I still don't understand . . . What was there between you? Why would—"

The door banged open. "They told me you were back."

Kip rose. "Sam, I'm taking Taylor home."

"The hell you are." Behind Slater stood two beefy security men. "Remove him, gentlemen, please."

Kip glanced over at Taylor as they frog-marched him out of the room. Her eyes were closed, her body slack. She's faking, he exulted, then thought I hope she's damn careful when she decides to "wake up."

Slater bent over her inert body. He thought he'd heard the murmur of voices before he'd burst in, but she certainly seemed comatose now. It must have been Kip's voice, trying unsuccessfully to wake her. How could it be otherwise, with the stuff they were giving her?

He'd talk with the night staff, make sure Kip wouldn't be able to get up here again. Then he'd go home and get some rest. He felt lousy.

He went out into the hall. His hands were shaking badly, and sweat stood on his forehead. He leaned against the wall for a moment, gathering his strength. Taylor would be no problem, but Kip . . . He knew what he had to do if Kip persisted.

Chapter Thirty-four

As the hours went by, Taylor's mind began to clear, although she was careful to hide the fact. When she felt strong enough, she sat up and had a look at her chart. Kip was right; she was being kept heavily sedated. Ohlmeyer had signed the original orders, but Sam had continued the sedation and was now signing the chart as doctor of record.

She got up and walked a few steps. Her headache was nearly gone. Curiously, the results of the CT scan hadn't been noted on the chart, but she'd take a chance on their being normal. More normal than the treatment she'd been given, she thought. She sat on the edge of the bed and withdrew the IV needle from her arm, using gauze and a Band-Aid she found in the small bedside cabinet to stanch the bleeding.

Why should Sam want to keep her sedated? Whatever was going on at Greenvale, she was no threat to him.

Unless Garrison had gone back on his promise, the night of the party, and told Sam everything she'd told *him*. And Sam then assumed she knew a lot more than she did.

Thanks, Gar, she thought bleakly.

So, now what?

Well, she could put on her clothes and walk out. Sam couldn't actually prevent her from leaving. She could walk out on Greenvale, her job, the whole damn mess.

And have Sam tell everyone whatever he thought would best kill her career. He could blame her concussion on drunken driving, for example; he seemed chummy enough with the chief of police. Well, she'd just have to take that chance, wouldn't she?

Maybe not. It was nearly midnight. Surely Sam would have left the hospital hours ago. If she could get inside his office, she might discover a bargaining chip. God knew the man seemed to have secrets aplenty: Saguaro and blueprints and something to do with Kip . . .

What was there between Sam and Kip? Jealousy and resentment, Kip had said, but he hadn't told her the cause. Well, that was personal; she could deal with that later. Right now she could concentrate on only one thing at a time, and saving her career came first.

But to do that, she needed a little time, so the longer she could make people believe she was comatose, the better. She buried the needle tip-first in the mattress, about where her arm would be if she were still lying in bed. If a nurse came to check on her before she'd left, she'd leap back under the blankets and position her arm so the needle would appear to be in place. She noticed one of the IV lines had been clipped shut. Kip must have done that, she thought as she opened it again. Sooner or later it would be noticed, and since the fluids were now draining into the mattress, she ought to make it look kosher.

She went to the closet and surveyed her designer suit and heels. Not the best disguise for prowling a hospital at night, she thought. And no good if she had to move fast. She kept a pair of clogs in her locker on the floor below. And surgical scrubs and mask made a good disguise if you kept moving.

The corridor lights had been lowered, and the hall was empty as she made her quiet way down the stairs, feeling a little woozy. Midnight in Greenvale was a lot

quieter than in a municipal hospital, and she met no
one. She was inside the changing room in an instant,
grabbing the clogs and a scrub suit and heading
through to the bathroom in case anyone came in. The
locker room might be empty now, but an ER case
could send a surgeon racing to scrub in at any hour.

In the stall, she shucked her hospital gown and
pulled on the green shirt and pants, then tied a surgical mask around her face. She bundled the gown into
the trash and went through the locker room and out
into the corridor, heading for the stairway again.

On "two," she went straight to the common administrative area, dark at this hour, that led to both their
offices, and tried his door. Locked, of course, but
Penny would have a key. She hit pay dirt in the back
of his secretary's second drawer. Unlocking Slater's
door, she went in and switched on the light, closing
the door behind her. The glow could be seen
through the frosted glass, but the rare passerby
would assume the cleaning staff had left the light on
or that Sam was working late. At least Taylor hoped
so; she couldn't search his office in the dark.

The tall red-haired aide came around the corner and
started down the hall. She was not happy.

"Janice? What are you doing here at this hour?"

Janice turned toward the fourth-floor nurses station.
"Night shift," she replied, forcing a smile.

"But you're not on my schedule."

"I'm a replacement."

The nurse frowned. "For whom?"

"I haven't the foggiest," Janice replied. "I got a
message on my machine and came on in."

"Let me call the supervisor . . ." The nurse reached
for the phone.

"Actually, I'm working on 'three.' "

"Oh." The nurse looked in the direction Janice had
come, from the patient rooms. "Then, why—?"

"I came up the stairs," Janice said quickly. "I

thought I'd say hi, see if you wanted coffee when I go on break."

The nurse dropped the receiver back into its cradle. "Well, thanks. That's very nice of you."

"My pleasure. I'll be back up in half an hour. Uh, you want a Danish with that?"

"Cinnamon."

"You got it." With a friendly wave, Janice hurried to the elevators and stabbed the button fiercely. How the hell had Taylor Barnes managed to get out of her room, and where had she got to?

Taylor turned the small plastic medicine containers over in her hand. Neurological tic my ass, she thought. The man's dying. She replaced them in the desk drawer, wondering whether Garrison knew. No, she was positive Slater hadn't told him. If he had, there wouldn't have been quite so much rejoicing at that anniversary party. Slater's death would definitely be bad for business. And wasn't that really what the party had been about?

She turned back to the desk, replacing the meds carefully in his top drawer and shutting it. She pulled open the second, but found only a mess of blank hospital forms and prescription pads. Wedged among them were several pieces of lined paper, folded in half. Curious, she drew them out. Sam's signature, written over and over, line after line. And not written very clearly. Doctors' scrawls were legendary for being indecipherable, but this looked almost as if the man were learning to write all over again.

The bottom drawer was filled with files in Pendaflex folders. She did a quick survey of their titles, but found no Saguaro, no Rockingham.

She turned her attention to the computer, booting it up and combing through his files. Opening one titled *Greenvale Board,* she found the most recent financial report, distributed via e-mail to all the trustees. She scanned it; the hospital was in excellent financial

shape. Garrison obviously had no need to be concerned about Saguaro's contribution, which was less,
proportionately, than she would have expected from
Garrison's conversation. But in no file could she find
any other reference to Saguaro, or any reference at
all to Rockingham. She was disappointed but not surprised; Slater wouldn't leave his secrets so accessible.

On the other hand, he wouldn't be expecting anyone to come in and rifle through his things, either, the
proof of that being that his desk had been unlocked.
No, Slater obviously felt safe here, and why shouldn't
he? New Chatham ran on Greenvale money, and in
Greenvale, Slater was king.

She stared at the screen in frustration. She'd opened
every file on the desktop except the applications: *Nor-
ton, Virex, QuickTime . . .* Wait a minute. There were
two *QuickTime* application files; that wasn't right.
And now she noticed one of them didn't have a trademark symbol. That was curious. She clicked on it and
it opened, revealing the icon for another file.

Her headache had come back, and she was feeling
a little muzzy, so it took her a moment to recognize
the icon that had appeared: the stylized outline of a
cactus. She clicked on it, and two document icons appeared. She chose one, opened it, and began reading.

She'd checked almost all the fourth-floor patient
rooms before the nurse's curiosity had made her retreat. The third floor was both easier and harder:
fewer patient rooms but more places to hide. She
checked supply closets and changing rooms, even the
OR itself. With a smile for a passing orderly, Janice
headed toward the recovery room. She wasn't very
hopeful. Taylor had probably left the building by now.
Still, she had to be able to say she'd done her best.
She pushed through the double metal doors.

Taylor stared at the screen, trying to digest what
she was seeing. The Saguaro Foundation, registered in

Switzerland and with a business address in San Francisco, had indeed contributed a great deal of money to Greenvale over the past five years. Far more, in fact, than the board of trustees had been told. Greenvale's true financial picture, hidden away in one of the cactus files, was very different from the one that had been e-mailed to the trustees.

Greenvale wasn't turning a profit at all. It was running at a loss. And contributions from the Saguaro Foundation were covering the shortfall. Saguaro was also paying the cost of Slater's hugely expensive research. Taylor frowned. From what she'd seen of Sam's research setup, it shouldn't cost nearly this much.

She ran her eye down the columns of figures again. Even if Sam's research were eliminated, the hospital was barely making it. Without Saguaro's contributions, Greenvale would have defaulted months ago on the exorbitant building loan interest payments that were making the local bankers so happy.

Garrison's instincts had been correct. If Saguaro pulled out, Greenvale was out of business. Unless new funding could be found, and fast. A Larrabee would certainly help there. In fact, handled correctly, a Larrabee could probably save Greenvale, and keep the bankers from going under.

Of course, such replacement funding would have to be spendable against general expenses, the way the Saguaro grant was. And that was unlikely. Most foundation grants were restricted. A research grant could only be used to pay research costs; a grant underwriting the clinic could only be spent against clinic expenses. Still, creative accounting could do wonders; witness the two very different financial reports she'd just read.

A glance at the small digital clock on Sam's desk read 12:54; she'd been away from her room for almost an hour. The nurses would be making their next rounds at one. If she wanted to be gone before they came looking for her, she didn't have much time. She switched on the printer.

The second document was a set of driving directions to some undefined rural location. She had no idea what it meant, but decided she might as well print it along with the contradictory sets of financial records.

So the Rockingham connection had been a blind, she thought. The action, whatever it was, was somewhere else: in San Francisco, perhaps, or at the end of some country road. Well, she had what she needed to ensure an excellent reference from Slater. Whatever else was going on at Greenvale—Ohlmeyer's number 37 and Sam's medical alert necklace and the source of Ohlmeyer's influence over Sam—she didn't need to know about it.

Her headache had worsened, and she was anxious to leave. She'd tried to reach Kip at her condo before starting her search but gotten no answer. Now she tried again, with the same result. Strange, but no time to worry about it now. She took the pages from the printer and switched it off. Where could she conceal the papers? Feeling slightly melodramatic, she folded them twice and bound them against her stomach below the line of her panties using surgical tape from Slater's cabinet. Then she turned off the light and opened the door.

Janice had scoured the third floor, gone upstairs to bring the nurse on "four" her coffee and pastry, and then come down here to "two." She'd searched most of the second floor, and was ready to give up. The woman wasn't anywhere, dammit. From her position in the hall as she started past the administration area, she could see Taylor's office but not Slater's. Taylor's was dark, so Janice's last hope—that Taylor had taken refuge in her office, although surely the woman wasn't that stupid—was gone. She continued past the open area, noticing that Slater's light was on. Unusual for

Sam to be here so late, she thought. Then as she watched, the light went out.

She cursed under her breath and backed away. The last thing she needed was for Sam to find her here. He knew she worked the day shift. An offer of coffee and cake wouldn't fool *him*. There was a supply closet just down the hall. Using her key, she unlocked it and slid inside, sneaking a peek behind her.

But it wasn't Slater who came out into the hall, it was Taylor. Gotcha! she exulted. She slipped a syringe from her pocket and waited for Taylor to approach her hiding place, then uncapped the needle and stepped out into the hall.

Taylor heard the creak of a door, felt the sudden movement of air. She spun around, her eyes widening as she recognized Janice and saw her raise the hypodermic.

Janice moved toward her. "They're looking for you upstairs," she said with a reassuring smile. "They asked me to find you, give you your sedative."

Taylor circled away. "You're not a nurse. They'd never—"

"You're right," Janice said. She lunged, but Taylor, her head beginning to pound, deflected the attack and retreated. Janice advanced, herding her toward the open closet.

"I don't understand," Taylor said. "Why are you doing this?"

"You shouldn't have come here." Janice reached out and grabbed Taylor's arm with her free hand, spinning her around. Taylor shoved hard with shoulder and elbow, putting her body into the blow, and Janice dropped to the floor of the storage closet, taking Taylor with her. They wrestled together on the cold linoleum as Janice raised the syringe again. Taylor grabbed her hand, and they grappled for control as Janice tried to jab the needle through Taylor's scrub suit and into her side. Taylor was fit, but hours of heavy sedation had sapped her strength and her head was exploding with pain. She felt the needle brush the cloth of the scrub suit and gave a final, desperate twist of her body. At the same moment, Janice punched the hypodermic downward, sending its point into her own thigh. Janice stared at Taylor, her eyes wide with shock. A guttural cry rose in her throat. Taylor pulled free of Janice and knelt by her side. "What's in it?" she said. "Tell me, and I can help you." But Janice's eyes were already closing.

Her head buzzing, Taylor leaned over her. She felt for a pulse and was relieved to find one. Still, who knew what was in that syringe? The woman needed help.

She managed to pull herself erect, strength ebbing from her arms and legs, and tottered out into the hall. She'd come down from the locker room via the rear stairs so she wouldn't have to pass the nurses station, but she knew they weren't far away. "Nurse!" she called out. "I need help. Help me!" She leaned against the door for support, and it swung shut behind her. She suddenly felt faint.

Two nurses came around the corner.

"Dr. Barnes? Is that you?"

"They're looking for you upstairs."

"What are you doing in those scrubs?"

"And her IV's out."

"Poor woman's delirious."

"Uh-oh, she's going down."

"Call for a gurney. We'll take her back to her room."

Chapter Thirty-five

Although he'd slept for nearly ten hours, Sam Slater was still feeling rotten as he approached the nurses station, a CT scan in his hand.

"Well, don't you look nice," the nurse greeted him. "What time is the ceremony?"

"Ten o'clock," Slater replied, forcing a smile. Usually he looked forward to events such as the public service award and breakfast the local political machine was mounting at the town hall this morning. Right now he could have done without it. "How's Dr. Barnes? Did she have a good night?"

"An active one," the nurse said. "They found her wandering in the hall near her office around one in the morning, apparently delirious."

"How did she get out of her room? She was heavily sedated." He glared at the nurse. "Who was on last night?"

"Maura Henson. But I hope you don't think—"

"Tell me exactly what happened."

"I only came on duty half an hour ago," the nurse said defensively. "Apparently Dr. Barnes woke up and pulled out her IV. Dr. Cohen, the senior resident, left this note for you."

Slater scanned the proffered paper. Given Taylor's state when she'd been found, Cohen wrote, he'd been concerned about the effects of the heavy sedation, and despite the instructions on the chart had decided not to continue it. Instead, he replaced her IV line, instructed that she be given only a saline drip for hydration, and injected her with a mild soporific.

"Dr. Cohen kept saying he hoped you'd approve of his decision," the nurse said. "He felt strongly she should be reevaluated when she wakes up."

"She's not awake yet?"

"No. Dr. Cohen thought she'd be out until ten or eleven."

"Well, he made a good call," Slater said slowly. "I've had another look at her CT scan. She's got a subdural hematoma. I'll be scheduling her for surgery to relieve the pressure on her brain."

Just for a moment the nurse had the fleeting impression that Slater was planning to do the procedure himself. But of course that was impossible; it was the neurosurgeon's job. "Shall I call Dr. Thomas?" she asked.

"Thomas?" Slater looked puzzled. "No, I've arranged—"

The ringing of the phone interrupted them. "Four West. Yes, he's standing right here." The nurse passed the instrument over to Slater saying, "Lobby reception."

Slater listened, his expression darkening. "Hold him there," he ordered. Slamming down the phone, he strode briskly to the stairs.

Kip, wearing a tailored shirt and chinos, a navy sweater tied around his neck, was arguing with the receptionist as Slater entered the lobby some five minutes later with a chart under his arm. "This is ridiculous," Kip said as Slater came up to him.

"You're right," Slater replied. "I've been thinking about it all night. I want to apologize for my actions yesterday. I was way out of line."

"Yes, you were."

"And I was wrong to accuse you of spying on me." He shook his head regretfully. "I was wrong about a lot of things, Kip. I want us to be friends again. Do you think that's possible?"

"It's what I want, too."

Slinging an arm around Kip's shoulders, he led him toward the elevator. "Let's go somewhere where we can talk."

"Sure. But first I want to see how Taylor is."

"She's fine, I assure you. There's plenty of time for that afterward." Slater punched the second floor button. "I want to make up for lost time," he said as the elevator ascended. "I hope you'll give me that chance."

"I'm happy to, Sam. You know that. I just—"

"This isn't easy for me," Slater insisted as they emerged on "two." He led Kip down the hall to an empty examination room. A transport gurney stood along the wall outside. "If I don't say this now, I don't know if I'll have the courage to say it later." He held the door open. "Please."

"All right." Kip stepped inside and Slater followed, closing the door. "You look ill, Sam. And your hands are shaking."

"Actually, I'm dying. But it's only temporary. Come, sit here next to me." Slater dropped the chart on a nearby chair and hoisted himself up onto the examining table.

Kip hesitated, then followed suit. "Have you seen a doctor?"

"Several. It seems my only option is 'physician, heal thyself.' "

"I don't understand."

"How could you? I'm referring to my research. My illness is the reason for my research."

Kip looked confused. "Your frozen heart work? You need a heart transplant?"

"I wish it were that simple," Slater said regretfully. His hand dropped casually into his jacket pocket. "No, I need the perfusion solution."

"I still don't get it."

"Oh, you will," Slater said grimly, withdrawing a

syringe from his pocket and jabbing it through Kip's shirt into his arm.

Kip's eyes widened in surprise, but the drug acted quickly. Slater slid off the examining table and eased Kip down onto his back. He recapped the hypodermic and shoved it back in his pocket, then reached for the phone.

"Send an elevator to Two North R and wait for it," he instructed. "Do it now."

He wheeled in the gurney, positioning it alongside the table, then rolled Kip onto it, tied him in, and pulled the sheet up to his neck. Trembling with physical exhaution, he leaned against the examining table and took several deep breaths before retrieving the chart he'd prepared. As he picked it up, his arm shot sideways of its own accord, sending the sheaf of papers flying. Cursing, he retrieved the chart and placed it across Kip's legs. In the pocket of his medical coat were the admission papers; he'd file them later.

He peered out into the hallway. Much of the second floor was physician and administrative offices, and didn't get a lot of traffic. That was why he'd chosen it. He wheeled the gurney out into the hall, prepared to shout "Code Blue" if he had to, although that would make things a little trickier. But he didn't have to; the corridor remained empty.

Quickly he rolled the gurney to the rear elevator. The door opened as he arrived, and he pushed Kip inside. Holding the door open with his foot, he picked up the chart and reviewed the story he'd created. Had he forgotten anything? Ah, yes.

He took a red pencil from his shirt pocket and lightly wrote the number 37 on the face page. Then he set the chart down again, pushed the button for the basement, and stepped out. The door closed, and the car descended.

Back in his office, he dialed the number for Emerson and asked to speak with the director of research.

"A heart attack?" Davis Leeds exclaimed. "That's not possible."

"I understand he's been under a lot of strain lately. That could have contributed."

Davis was silent a moment, absorbing the news. "Can he be moved? I'd like to have him transferred to New York Hospital."

"His condition's extremely grave. I wouldn't want to risk it."

"Excuse me, Dr. Slater, but I'd like to talk with his cardiologist. That's not you, is it?"

"No, I'm the doctor who admitted him. I'm also in charge of this hospital, and I can assure you that I will vigorously protest any attempt to move Dr. Lawrence. In fact, I forbid it."

"I'm afraid you can't do that," Davis replied hotly. "You have no right to keep him there."

"According to his admitting form, I have every right," Slater replied calmly. "I'll fax you a copy if you like. Oh, and he's not allowed any visitors. His condition's much too serious."

He hung up and checked his watch. Time to head over to the town hall. He hoped the ceremony wouldn't take long. Maybe he could duck out of the breakfast part, he thought. Slinging his coat over his shoulders, he stepped out of his office, nearly colliding with Penny and Donna. In the hallway beyond, people were shouting.

"What's going on out there?"

"I don't know," his secretary said. "We were just coming to get you."

Together they went to investigate. A crowd was gathering around the door to a nearby storage closet. As they watched, a crash team and cart came flying down the corridor.

To one side, an hysterical aide was being tended by several nurses. "I just opened the closet," she kept repeating, "and there she was on the floor."

"Who is it?" Slater pushed through the crowd to where the crash team had set up.

"Janice Whelan," a resident told him. "I'm afraid she's dead. Been dead awhile, too."

"Cause?"

"Can't tell. Although there's a small puncture wound on her right thigh."

Slater frowned. That was odd. He stepped back out of the confusion. The closet was just a few yards from the anteroom that led to his office. And to Taylor's. Wasn't this where she'd been wandering, supposedly delirious, at one in the morning? That was nine hours ago. They could have been here around the same time. Was that a coincidence? If not, what did it mean?

He turned to Penny. "Damage control," he ordered, drawing her aside. "Call Chief Randolph, tell him to be discreet. And have them keep the press away if possible. People?" He turned back to address the crowd around Janice's body. "For Janice's sake, please try and keep a lid on this until we know what happened. We don't want the press jumping to the conclusion that she OD'd on something."

People turned toward him. "OD'd? Not Janice." "She wasn't a druggie."

"Of course she wasn't," Slater agreed. "And we don't want anyone implying that in the press. So please, everybody. Let's keep this among ourselves— and the police—until we find out what happened."

His mind was whirling as he strode through the lobby. Was there a connection between Taylor's delirium and Janice's death? Or had Taylor been faking delirium in order to snoop around? Good Lord, had she been in his office? Had she found anything? Maybe Janice surprised her in there, maybe they'd struggled.

But why should Janice have been in the hospital in the first place? She worked the day shift.

Maybe Janice had been the one snooping in his office, and Taylor had found her. That made sense, except that Taylor wouldn't have fought with Janice, she'd have called Security.

Well, he didn't have to worry about anything Janice might have discovered. But if the snooper had been Taylor . . .

Shit.

He made a sharp reverse and took the elevator up to "four." "Get a security guard on Dr. Barnes's door," he told the startled nurse. "It's for her own protection. No one goes in or out."

"Why? What's wrong?" the woman asked, but Slater brushed the question away. She'd find out about Janice soon enough, he thought as he hurried to Taylor's room.

She was still asleep. Good. He went to the foot of the bed, unhooked the chart, and scribbled in the CT-scan result. It was really too bad, he thought; she was a wonderful surgeon. Still, these things happen. He took out the red pencil and wrote 37 lightly in one corner.

Chapter Thirty-six

". . . A man whose personal vision has brought pros-
perity and fame to New Chatham," Calvin Mayhew
was proclaiming loudly. "Because of that vision, our
educational and cultural institutions, not to mention
our tax base, have been revitalized." The chanting of
the protesters on the town hall steps was louder now,
and Mayhew was almost shouting in an attempt to
drown them out. "And so it gives me great pleasure
to present this plaque in appreciation of his . . ."

"Why are those crazies still out there?" Slater whispered to Garrison, seated beside him on the dais.
"Where the hell is Randolph?"

"On his way to Greenvale, probably," Garrison replied tautly. Like Slater, he was hoping the news of
Janice's death wouldn't come out until this ceremony
was over and the press had dispersed.

Sam graciously accepted the public-service award
and spoke briefly. The hundred or so carefully selected
attendees munching croissants and forking up the
scrambled eggs applauded vigorously. The first select-
man spoke. The high school chorus sang a medley.

Finally it was over, and Slater and Garrison made
their way through the congratulatory crowd, smiling
and shaking hands. Gradually the stream of people
flowed out onto the steps of the town hall, where the
noisy demonstrators were shouting protests through
bullhorns and arguing with police officers.

"How's Dr. Barnes?" Slater turned. A dramatic-looking dark-haired woman, a colorful silk scarf at her throat, stood before him. "I'm Olive Erbach," she said, offering her hand. "I don't think we've met."

Slater started to reach for her hand, then stopped abruptly.

Olive looked startled. "Is something wrong?" When Slater didn't reply, she withdrew her hand, frowning. "I heard about what happened to Dr. Barnes. How is she?"

Slater's face turned solemn as, with great effort, he managed to pull back his rigid arm and shove it into his coat pocket. "She's not very well, I'm afraid."

"Oh, no," Olive said, a concerned look on her face. "What's wrong?"

"I'm afraid I can't discuss it," he told her firmly and moved away.

Garrison frowned. "I thought you said Taylor was going to be okay."

Slater paused in mid-step. "I'm no longer sure she will be."

"What do you mean?"

"I had another look at her scan. She's got a sub-dural hematoma, and it's in a bad place. She'll need surgery, and soon. Frankly, it doesn't look very good." Slater sighed. "Right now I'd characterize her condition as grave."

"Jesus," Garrison breathed. "That's terrible. Does she know?"

"Not yet. I'll—" He broke off, suddenly aware of listeners all around them. "Not here," he told Garrison quickly. "I've got some business to take care of, outside the hospital. I'll give you a call later on."

Once Slater's car had driven off, the demonstrators abandoned their position on the town hall steps and grouped on the sidewalk.

"When we get to the hospital," a man in a red anorak was saying, "we start distributing the flyers.

And don't use the bullhorns there, or you'll give them an excuse to move us away. Are you listening, Maggie?"

"Uh, yeah. No bullhorns." Maggie turned back to the demonstrator beside her. "He said she needs an operation?"

"Yes" came the reply. "Apparently her condition's grave. I got the impression he didn't think she'd survive the surgery."

"My God."

Her companion stared at her suspiciously. "You seem upset."

"Oh, no," Maggie said quickly. "It's what we wanted."

"That's right. Our spells are finally working. Although," the protester frowned, "Janice should have acted by now."

"What was she supposed to do?"

"Kill her, of course."

Maggie paled. "I didn't know that."

"There was no reason you should. Especially after your behavior at the crash site."

"Maybe Janice knew about the surgery and decided to wait," Maggie said quickly.

"That's not what she was told to do, but . . . maybe you're right. There's a certain justice in letting Slater do our dirty work for us."

"Uh, when will he operate on her?"

"Soon," he said. And if the surgery doesn't fix things, Janice will. This time tomorrow, Barnes will be history. Hey, where are you going?"

"I came here in my car. I'll drive over and meet you in front."

"No need to do that. My car's here, too. We'll all be coming back together." But Maggie was already running toward the town hall parking lot.

Her green Ford soon came barreling out onto the street, tires squealing as she turned the wheel toward Greenvale. She parked in the outdoor lot at the rear of the building and slipped in at the kitchen entrance.

Several workers stared at her as she hurried through the two-level food-prep area, but she kept moving and no one stopped her.

She pushed through a door marked EXIT and found herself in a corridor. She looked around. She gathered she was somewhere in the basement, since the door numbers all began with B. She walked up the hall, wondering where Taylor was and how she would find her.

The door to the Radiology Department was open. A sleepy young resident sat staring at images on a large light box mounted on the wall. "Excuse me," Maggie said, stepping through the doorway. "Can you tell me Dr. Barnes's room number?"

The resident turned around. There were deep circles under his eyes. "Doctors' offices are on 'two,' " he told her tiredly.

"No, I'm looking for a doctor who's a patient. Taylor Barnes. I'm, uh, her sister."

"What in the world are you doing down here?"

"I got lost," Maggie said. She smiled apologetically. "I just came in from, uh, Chicago, and I didn't get much sleep last night. The family's been so worried."

The doctor nodded sympathetically. "Let me see if I can help." He went to the computer on a nearby desk and hit some keys. "Barnes, Barnes . . . There it is: Room 409. But it says she's not allowed any visitors."

"That's okay. I'll go up and talk to the nurses. Where's the elevator?"

"Make a left out this door and go all the way down until you come to Pathology, then make a right. But maybe you should stop at the lobby first."

"Okay," Maggie said. "I will." Like hell. He turned back to the light box display, and Maggie headed down the hall to the elevator.

The doors opened on "four," and she rushed out, nearly running down a passing nurse.

"Help you?"

"Uh, 413," Maggie told her.

"Mrs. Hendershot, right?" Maggie nodded. "That way."

Maggie scurried up the corridor in the direction the nurse had pointed. 417, 415 . . . A uniformed security guard was seated on a chair in front of 409, reading a newspaper.

"You can't go in there, miss," he said. "Oh, hi, Maggie."

"Alvin? Aren't you working at the garage anymore?"

"I quit there a couple months ago." He put down his paper and leaned back in the metal chair. "I like this better." He frowned. "What are you doing here?"

"I'm a volunteer."

"You don't look like a volunteer. Where's your uniform?"

"I forgot to put it on," Maggie told him. Alvin had never been the brightest bulb in the package. "How come you're sitting in front of Dr. Barnes's door?"

"Dr. Slater's orders. After what happened to that aide Janice Whelan, he didn't want to take any chances. I mean, first someone messes with her brakes, then she's—"

"Back up a minute," Maggie said. "After *what* happened to Janice?"

The guard glanced down the empty hallway. "They found her in a closet this morning," he told her. "Dead."

Good, Maggie thought. "Poor Janice. How terrible. Well," she said, placing her hand on the doorknob, "I better go on in."

"Whoa," Alvin said, rising. "Nobody goes in or out. That's why I'm here."

"Of course," Maggie agreed. "Nobody except hospital people."

"Nobody except *nobody*."

Maggie gave a theatrical sigh. "Come on, Alvin. You want me to get fired?"

"Volunteers can't get fired."

"Well, un-volunteered, then. Look, you're doing a great job. I'll tell them that when I go back to the, uh, office. But right now, I have to give Dr. Barnes a message."

"Who's the message from?"

"Dr. Slater, of course." Maggie cracked the door. "I'm going in now, okay? Don't shoot me."

Alvin sighed. "I'm not gonna shoot you, Maggie. I don't even have a gun. Just make it snappy, okay?"

Unlike the day before, Taylor came awake quickly, her head clear, the pain and muzziness gone. Still, it took her a minute to realize she was back in her hospital room, and several more to remember the events of the night before: Slater's office, Janice coming at her with the syringe . . . The aide's words came back to her: "You shouldn't have come here." Where was "here"? Slater's office? Had Janice followed her there? Were she and Slater in league? Had Janice seen her using the computer?

In a sudden panic she reached under the blanket. The top of the scrub suit was gone, and a hospital gown covered her chest. Her fingers scrabbled at her stomach, and she sighed with relief when she felt the scrub suit pants and found the papers still taped to her stomach beneath them.

Her IV had been reconnected, and she sat up and removed it again, pressing on the site with gauze until the bleeding stopped and applying a Band-Aid. Then she stood and untaped the papers, placing them in the handbag she retrieved from the closet along with her designer suit, bra, and shoes.

She was untying the hospital gown when the door to her room opened and Maggie slipped in, her finger to her lips.

"Maggie?" Taylor exclaimed. "What are you doing here?"

But Maggie shook her head. "I came to warn you,"

she said softly, taking Taylor's elbow and leading her away from the door. "Slater's going to operate on you."

"What? Why?"

"They heard him telling somebody about it at the town hall just now." Quickly she told Taylor what Slater had told Garrison.

"But that's not possible," Taylor said. "There's nothing like that in my chart. At least, there wasn't yesterday."

"Look again."

Taylor started for the chart, then stopped. "Why are you telling me this, Maggie? Why did you come here?"

"I'm leaving the Gaias," Maggie said. "I've thought a lot about it. It's wrong, what's going on here at Greenvale. But the Gaias are wrong, too." She studied Taylor for a minute. "You do believe me, don't you?"

"I want to believe you," Taylor said doubtfully, lifting the top page of the chart as she stared at Maggie. It was true that the woman's appearance was neater, her manner more focused and controlled than the last time she'd seen her. She sighed; maybe it was true. She hoped so.

"Go on and look."

Taylor glanced down at the chart. "My God," she breathed. "Sam's right about the hematoma." She sank into a chair. "They must have done another scan after I collapsed last night."

"He's going to kill you," Maggie insisted. "Just like he killed my husband. Like he killed Janice Whelan, I bet."

"Janice is dead?" Taylor looked up at Maggie in horror.

"They found her this morning. Just as well," she added. "She was—"

"Sam didn't kill Janice," Taylor interrupted. "I—" She closed her mouth again. If Maggie thought Sam had killed Janice, then she didn't know that Janice had tried to kill *her*. Maybe Maggie *was* telling the truth about leaving the cult. "Why would Sam want to kill me?" she said instead. "Why would he kill your husband?"

"I told you: Jack worked on the building," Maggie said impatiently. "He knew something was wrong." She hesitated. "I don't know why he wants to kill you. But he does."

"You're being fanciful."

"Fanciful?" Maggie retorted. "Is it fanciful that there's a security guard sitting outside your door?

"There is?"

"His name's Alvin. I've known him for years. Luckily, he's not too smart. I told him I was a hospital volunteer, and he let me in."

"Why would Sam put a guard on my door?" Taylor's mind was reeling.

"For your own protection, he *says*. But you just try leaving and see how far you get."

"That's ridiculous. They obviously ordered another scan after I collapsed last night, and they found a hematoma . . ." She glanced down at the chart in her hands and frowned. There was no indication of a second scan. Now, that *was* strange. She let the top page fall back, and gasped. There in the corner of the face sheet, in light red pencil, was the number thirty-seven.

"Oh, shit. I don't believe it."

Maggie stared at her. "What is it? You're white as a sheet."

"You wouldn't understand. I don't understand it myself."

"Try me."

"See that number?" Taylor pointed. "When it's written on someone's chart, they die."

"I told you," Maggie breathed.

"No, that's not strictly accurate. Every time I've seen that number written on a chart, the person was *already* dead."

Maggie's brow wrinkled. "What's the difference?"

"Well," Taylor explained, her heart pounding, "I only saw the charts after the patients had died, so it doesn't mean . . ." She broke off, started again. "Jim Partrick, the fireman that was hurt in the mall blaze. He was doing fine, and then suddenly he died, and I saw 37 written on his chart."

"They marked him for death!"

"And then in Medical Records I found some other charts with 37 on them. The patients were all deceased. And all the bodies had been sent to Gamble's."

"Like Jack's. Did you see my husband's chart?"

"No, I didn't. But let's not—"

"Be fanciful? You still think all this is my imagination? Slater killed him, just like he wants to kill you. Oh, sure, he said they did everything they could, even put him on some heart-and-lung gizmo for a half an hour, but—"

"What?" Taylor put a hand on Maggie's arm. "What did Slater tell you about a heart-lung resuscitator?"

"Just that they put Jack on some heart-and-lung thing to try and bring him back." She stared at Taylor. "What is it?"

"Everyone with a 37 on their chart was put on the heart-lung resuscitator. Ohlmeyer did it."

"And they don't do that for everyone?"

"No. In fact, in the cases I saw, it didn't make sense to do it at all." She collapsed heavily into a nearby chair.

Maggie stared at her. "Jack had a 37 on his chart, didn't he?"

"I told you, I didn't see his chart."

"He must have. Oh, God, poor Jack." Her eyes filled with tears. "He was only thirty-two years old. And Dr. Slater murdered him."

But Taylor shook her head. "Ohlmeyer's the one who's been writing 37 on the charts, not Slater. Besides, there's something here that doesn't make sense. I mean, let's say Slater did think that your husband knew some terrible secret about Greenvale and wanted him dead. At least theoretically; I still can't picture Sam as a murderer. But Jim Partrick didn't know any secrets. Hell, he'd only come to New Chatham a couple of months ago, and he had no connection with the hospital at all. And he was Ohlmeyer's patient." She frowned. "Besides, if Sam really wanted Jack dead, why hook him up to a resuscitator? It's not exactly common practice." She stood and paced to the window. "Let me think a minute."

Through the pane, she idly surveyed the parking lot that abutted the north side of the hospital. All young and fit, she thought. All sent to Gamble's within hours of their deaths. Sent from the morgue. The morgue at the northwest corner of the building. The morgue where the blueprint had been torn.

She swung around. "Where is Gamble's Funeral Home?"

"Chestnut and Belkin," Maggie said. "Over near the mall. Why?"

"I had an idea for a minute," Taylor said, her shoulders slumping. "But it's wrong. The mall's to the east of the hospital. The morgue's on the west."

"I don't understand." When Taylor remained silent, Maggie added, "If you think you know what happened to Jack, please tell me."

"I don't know a thing," Taylor said. "I wish I did." She turned back from the window. "What I do know is, it's time to leave this place."

Maggie went to her, tears filling her eyes. "If Jack and the others were murdered, someone should answer for it. Won't you help me find out?"

"Find out what?"

"How he died. What happened to him. Please, Taylor. I need to know."

"But—I wouldn't know where to start."

"Yes, you would—thirty-seven—it must mean something, right? I mean, why not write one or five or ten? Why thirty-seven?" Taylor shrugged. "Well, think!"

Maggie insisted. "You said something about the morgue. Could thirty-seven have something to do with the morgue? Please, Taylor. Let's go look."

"It's too dangerous. If Sam finds us—"

"But Dr. Slater had something to do outside the hospital. That's what he told that man he was talking to. He's not even here."

"At least let me bring in some reinforcements." Taylor went to the phone and dialed. "There's a man I've been seeing, a doctor from New York. He's staying at my place, at least, I thought he was. But he never answers the phone."

"Maybe he went home."

"Still no answer." She hung up, frowning. It wasn't like Kip to just take off without a word. She looked over at Maggie's anxious face. "Okay, we'll give it a shot. But not in this," she added, surveying the dressy designer suit. "Have a look in that cabinet, see if they put my scrub suit top and clogs in there."

"These?" Maggie held up the green top and shoes.

"Bingo. I'll go get dressed, and you see if you can find a patient bag I can put my good clothes in."

"What about Alvin?"

Taylor smiled. "Don't worry. They can't hold me here against my will."

"Yeah, but if they know you're leaving, that you don't want the operation, they might find Dr. Slater and tell him."

"Good point," Taylor conceded. "Well, you talked your way in here. See if you can talk us out."

Chapter Thirty-seven

He staggered slightly as he approached the first of the three patients. The stethoscope flashed in his trembling hand as he bent to examine the semi-comatose figure strapped to the first bed.

"No change?" His Mandarin left much to be desired, but the young woman in the white uniform seemed to understand, and shook her head. He studied the monitor readout for a few moments and checked the transparent bags of fluid that hung from the IV stand, then turned back to study the patient's pale face. "Can you hear me?" he asked loudly in English. "Can you understand me?" The man's eyes opened, and his mouth moved in a semblance of speech, but only a low moan emanated from his dry lips.

Slater sighed. He'd done his best. Better scientists than he, with knowledge not yet discovered and equipment not yet invented, would have to do the rest. For his sake as well as his patients', he hoped they would succeed.

The other two were even less responsive, but he examined them thoroughly. He straightened up, massaging the small of his back. Clearly it wasn't the unqualified success they'd hoped for, but it was still better than anyone else would have believed possible.

Barking an order at the young Chinese nurse, he went through the gracious, high-ceilinged room to a

smaller one beyond. A blond man, groggy with sedation, lay strapped into a hospital bed. A second nurse
was adjusting his IV lines.

Slater's eyes filled with tears as he approached. He
hadn't planned for it to happen, but maybe it was
better this way. He dragged a chair over to the bedside
and lowered himself painfully into it.

"Sam?" The man in the bed looked up at him questioningly. "What's happening?"

"If only you'd stayed in New York, where you be-
longed," Slater told him regretfully. "If only you hadn't
come meddling."

"Meddling? I never—"

"You and Taylor Barnes. Not a happy combination,
at least not for me. What she knows, what you know."

"I don't know anything, Sam."

"But once you talk to her, you'll understand, and
then . . . 'The time is out of joint,' Kip. But someday,
years from now, it will all come right."

"What do you mean?"

Slater smiled. "I'm rambling, a dying man's preroga-
tive. And yet my death is only temporary. As your
death will be, too."

Kip's eyes registered his alarm. "You're going to
kill me?"

Slater smiled sadly. "I was afraid you might see it
that way. But you must admit you've had some very
good innings. Better than I have."

Kip struggled against the straps holding him to the
bed. "Whatever innings I've had, I worked for. Sure,
I was born to money, but I never had anything you
couldn't have had." He tried to sit up, but the straps
prevented any movement, and he fell back against the
pillow. "You've always resented me," he said morosely. "Even back when you pretended to care
about me."

"I did care," Slater protested. "If not for me—"

"I'd be a businessman, not a doctor, yes, I know.

But was that really because you cared about me? Or was it just a cheap shot at my father?"

"It was for you, Kip. Your father was—"

"My father was rich, yes, and yours was poor. But that wasn't my fault. Besides, you could have had everything I had, including a degree from Harvard, but you turned it down."

"Of course I did," Slater said angrily.

"I've never understood why you hated him so much. And that hatred grew, didn't it, Sam? It festered and festered. And see where it's led you."

"Where it's led *me*? You're the one tied to a bed."

"And you're the one who destroyed my research to get himself a Larrabee."

"I never did any such thing," Slater exclaimed, looking shocked. "I wouldn't want to win that way. The award wouldn't be worth anything to me."

"So you keep saying. But why should I believe you? You've always been jealous of my success, furiously jealous. We both know it."

"God help me, it's true," Slater said softly. "You had the best and I had the leavings, and I hated you for it."

"You only had the leavings because that's all you would take. It was your own doing."

Slater was silent. "I suppose it was."

"So why hate me, Sam? I was as much a pawn of circumstance as you."

Slater shook his head slowly. "I don't hate you, Kip. Not anymore. I want us to join forces. Work together. Go forward together."

Kip looked puzzled. "Good," he said slowly. "Let's do that."

"I'm so happy you feel that way," Slater said, his face lighting up.

"But first you'll have to release me. Then we'll find a really good doctor for you—"

"No, you misunderstand," Slater said, his voice strangely calm. "I told you: I'm dying. There's no cure

for what I have. But it's going to be all right, you'll
see. I'll take you into the future with me. Many years
from now, when the time is right, we'll do great
things together."

He's mad, Kip thought despondently. He's crazy,
and he hates me, and he's going to kill me.

"We could telephone and say Slater wants him
upstairs."

"He'd find out pretty quick that Slater doesn't,"
Maggie objected. The two women stood in the hall
just beyond the morgue entrance. "And he'd come
right back."

"So we need to think of something else."

"Yeah. And once we do get rid of Lewis, how're
we going to keep other people from going in?"

"That one's easy," Taylor said. "You put on a scrub
suit and mask—they're in the Autopsy Room—and
stand near the door and tell people there's a biohazard
problem inside."

"A bio—"

"Hazard. Problem." Taylor studied her. "Can you
remember that?"

"Yeah, I'll remember. And you'll find out what happened to Jack?"

"I'll try. I can't promise anything. But first we have
to get Lewis Gamble out of there."

"I'll do it," Maggie said. "Be right back."

"How?" Taylor asked, but Maggie was already disappearing inside.

What the hell am I doing? Taylor wondered as she
waited. Why am I standing here, waiting for a slightly
crazed ex-cultist to get rid of a morgue attendant who
just might be involved in murder so I can inspect a
place I've always hated in the hope of discovering I
have no idea what?

Well, Sam *was* away, and she *was* about to leave
this place forever. It would be her last chance to try
and figure out what the man was up to.

And what do you care what he's up to? she argued with herself. You've got the two sets of financial records. Why don't you just walk away?

But the financial records might not be enough to save her reputation. What if Slater refused to play ball? What if he wiped them from his computer and denied any knowledge of them, blamed Garrison for everything? What if he publicly accused her of being a computer thief? She *had* stolen the reports from his computer, after all.

But that wasn't it, either; the financial records would probably stand.

No, it was the thought of Jim Partrick, who'd been her patient, and Jack McCormick, and all the others who'd had thirty-seven scribbled on their charts, just as she had, and had probably died because of it. She owed it to them to learn what she could before she left Greenvale. And it was really no biggie. All she was planning to do was to take a fast look around the morgue.

Maggie came rushing into the hall, her face flushed, a scrub suit covering her clothes. "All set," she said breathlessly. "Did I put these on right?"

"Yes, only you should be wearing shoe covers."

"What?"

"Never mind. The pants are long, no one will notice." She started for the morgue, then stopped. "I didn't see Lewis come out."

"He's locked in the Autopsy Room."

"There's a phone in there," Taylor exclaimed. "He'll call someone."

"No, he won't. I locked him in a closet."

"You . . . how did you get him into a closet?"

"I remembered what happened to Janice. How they found her in a closet? So I told Lewis there was somebody dead in the Autopsy Room closet."

"And he believed you?"

Maggie shrugged. "I said I was a volunteer, and they'd sent me down to get some papers and I heard someone screaming. When he opened the door to look, I shoved him in." She smiled. "Lewis is almost as dumb as Alvin."

Well, it was better than my idea, Taylor thought. She headed into the morgue, and Maggie took up her position in front of the double doors.

It's not a file, Taylor decided, as she rifled through the messy records cabinet in Lewis's office. These files were named, not numbered.

And it wasn't a room number, she thought as she hurried through the various sections of the small morgue. The room numbers all had triple digits.

What else could it be? she pondered, then suddenly realized, Of course, dummy. What took you so long?

The body room was cold, and Taylor shivered in her thin scrubs. She looked around at the large stainless-steel drawers, each neatly numbered on a small metal plate just above the handle. How many of these drawers contained bodies, waiting for identification or autopsy or pickup? If Maggie hadn't come to warn her, she would have become one of them.

Drawer number thirty-seven was on the lowest tier, down near the floor. She put down the patient bag with her clothing, took hold of the handle, and tugged. The drawer rolled out smoothly, taking the frontages of several adjacent drawers with it. The slide-out base was a steel slab similar to but larger than a normal morgue slab, and covered with thick removable padding. She stared at the space in front of her. It was big, high enough to sit up in, and wider than a hospital gurney. The facade around drawer thirty-seven had been incised to look like the rest of the wall so as to disguise the large space within.

Leaving the drawer open, she pulled out another one halfway down the room and compared the two. The inside of this second drawer was maybe a third the size of drawer thirty-seven. She pushed it back in and examined drawer thirty-seven again, peering into its dark interior. She ran her hand along the near side wall as far as she could reach. There seemed to be a sort of cable lying flat against the wall. Curious.

It was too dark in there to see the end wall clearly. She climbed onto the padding and moved forward on her knees toward the far end of the slab. With the drawer standing open like this, the gurney-like slab extended out into the room, and there was a wide space at the back of the drawer between the head of the slab and the rear wall. She leaned out over it and reached her hand to the end wall. A vertical crack ran straight down the center. They're doors, she hazarded; the drawer's a tunnel. But how do they open? And where do they lead?

The second question would be answered by the first. Leaning farther over, she tried to pry the two halves apart with her fingers. No luck. There must be a switch or a button or something, she decided.

She backed out of the drawer but remained kneeling on the slab as she examined the metal facade around and beside the opening. Nothing. Lying back on her side, she reached out a hand and felt the flat outer surface of the drawer. Aside from the number plate, it was smooth. Her fingers returned to the number plate; it was raised a good inch above the surface. What the hell, she thought, and keeping her eyes on the far wall, she pressed the plate hard. With a faint buzz of machinery, the slab slid back into the dark interior. Taylor barely had time to pull in her hand as the drawer slammed shut, trapping her in utter darkness.

Chapter Thirty-eight

For a moment she lay there, heart pounding, too stunned to think clearly. Then the slab fell away beneath her and she realized it wasn't a tunnel she was trapped in. It was an elevator.

Hyperventilating, trying to control her panic, she descended slowly and inexorably into the ground. Was this how Ohlmeyer disposed of his mistakes? But no, the slab was covered with padding; he wouldn't bother to pad the dead.

With a low whine, the elevator slowed, then stopped. For a terrible moment, nothing happened. Then the doors beyond her feet slid apart, a faint glow flooded the compartment, and the slab shot out of the drawer into the light. Gasping with relief, Taylor scrabbled off and looked around.

She was in a low, narrow, roughly finished tunnel, its walls and ceiling covered with some sort of black insulating foam. Low-wattage bulbs depended from an industrial-looking metal strip running along the ceiling. Behind her, the drawer compartment stood agape. A call button and a lock light were set beside the opening, the light glowing a reassuring green. Running off into the darkness in front of her were two monorail tracks, one of which began at the entrance to the elevator. A tiny raised catwalk ran along the right-hand track, separated and partly screened from it by a solid metal guardrail.

Part of her wanted to go on, another part wanted to go back. What if someone came down the track? Was the guardrail high enough to screen her if she lay down behind it? What if the elevator doors closed, trapping her down here? Would the call button open them again? The tracks ending at the elevator doors gave her an idea. She tugged at the pallet and it rolled forward, blocking the elevator opening. With her escape route thus secured, she climbed the two stairs to the catwalk and started down it, wishing for sneakers instead of the awkward clogs she was wearing.

The air was dank and chilly, and she hugged her body for warmth as she hurried along. I'll give it ten minutes, she thought, then I'll turn back.

The tracks continued straight, with no curves. She tried to work out what direction she was heading, visualizing the schematic she'd studied so closely. The morgue was on the west side of the hospital, and west was the direction she'd been facing when she'd entered the morgue. The body room had been at the end of and left off the morgue's interior hallway, which ran westward. That put the body room to the south, and its far wall to the south, too. The wall containing drawer thirty-seven was catty-corner to the far wall and to its right—to the west. So the slab had moved westward when it carried her inside the drawer, and westward when it shot her out again. Therefore, the tracks stretching out in front of her were heading west, too. What of significance lay to the west of Greenvale?

The tunnel dipped slightly, and she saw a faint glow far ahead. It looked like she was about to find out.

She estimated she'd traveled the equivalent of some ten city blocks when the track rose, the glow blossomed, and she found herself at the end of the line. Ahead was a low yellow-and-black-striped barrier. A roofless two-seater cart snuggled up to the barrier on the left-hand track, a small open-bed platform sat beside it on the right-hand track, grappled to the cart along one side. The catwalk widened, dropped to track

level, and continued around the barrier to form a
small off-loading platform for the cart. A set of solid-
looking double doors were set into the wall to the
right of the tracks.

Well, she was here, wherever "here" was. Hesitating
a moment, she pushed one of the doors open and
stepped inside.

The change in light level was nearly blinding. The
tile walls were a brilliant white; blazing arc lights depended from the ceiling. In the center of the room,
surrounded by monitors, a defibrillator, and various
equipment stands, stood a full-size operating table. A
heart-lung machine and a blood exchanger used in
open-heart surgery dominated one long wall.

She moved slowly around the room. Space suits
with spooky-looking helmets hung along one wall.
Tall pressurized cylinders were grouped in a corner.
Built-in cabinets were filled with an assortment of
medications and instruments. And there was other
equipment, too, the use of which Taylor couldn't begin
to fathom. A rubberized holding tank. A high-efficiency heat exchanger. A closetful of sleeping bags.
Suddenly she knew exactly what it was he was attempting to do. Not Ohlmeyer—Slater. Maggie had
been right; it was Slater all along. No wonder his research costs had been so high.

She'd read it wrong from the start, just as Slater
had intended everyone to do. Ohlmeyer had no hold
on Slater. It was Slater who controlled Ohlmeyer,
Slater who threatened Ohlmeyer with exposure and
the loss of his career if he didn't do precisely as he
was told. Or maybe Ohlmeyer hadn't needed much
persuading; maybe he believed in Sam's research.

He's insane, she thought, shivering. He's certifiable.
Then another thought struck her: had he succeeded?
At the far end of the room were two closed doors.
There was no doubt in her mind that the answer lay
behind them. Yes, she thought, and if you open either
one of them, you're as crazy as he is.

*   *   *

"Don't be afraid," Slater crooned, placing a trembling hand lightly on Kip's shoulder. "It's not really death."

"The hell it isn't. You loved me once, Sam. Please. Let me go."

But Slater shook his head. "I can't. Not after what you've seen here. Oh, don't get me wrong; I've wanted to show it to you for years. I've wanted you to see what I've achieved, wanted to prove to you that despite all your honors and your reputation, I'm still your scientific superior." He sighed. "I never thought I'd *have* to prove that, never thought you'd rise so quickly. It's been a long time since I was your mentor, Kip. The one you turned to for encouragement and advice. But the world turns, and once again I've become your guide. And you'll go where I take you."

"Please, Sam. I promise I won't tell anyone what I know."

Slater smiled sadly. "No," he said. "You won't. And neither will Taylor."

"Taylor?" Kip's eyes widened in alarm. "She doesn't know anything."

"She knows more than she thinks she does. And once you've disappeared, she'll bring others, dig deeper . . . No, Taylor will join us."

"No!"

"I thought you loved her," Slater said, puzzled. "Don't you want her with you?"

"I do love her," Kip exclaimed. "Very much. That's why I'm begging you, for the love of God, to leave her out of this." He struggled against the restraining straps, his face torn by emotions.

"I'm afraid I'll have to sedate you again if you keep that up," Slater warned. His beeper sounded, and he glanced at the readout. "Shit." He stood and pulled a cell phone from his jacket pocket. Walking away from the bed, he stabbed in a number.

"Penny, it's Sam. This better be important." He listened a moment. "Barnes and who else? Maggie

McCormick, the protestor? What the hell is *that* about?" Another brief pause. "Well, find them, dammit." He listened again. "Of course it's for her own good. The woman's ill; she's not responsible."

He broke the connection. "Help me get him to his feet," he called to the hovering nurse in Mandarin. "No, keep him bound, you understand?" Without waiting for a reply, he dialed another number. "I need a private ambulance, as fast as you can get one here," he ordered into the phone. "Back it up to the morgue door, and I mean right up. Twenty minutes? Okay. Oh, and book me a Medevac plane. I'm accompanying a patient to Arizona."

Taylor came out onto the catwalk, anxious to be away. The cart was a lot more appealing than another long, dark walk. Could she get it to start? She walked over and examined it. The controls on the dashboard were simple and clearly marked. A key was in the ignition.

A key . . . something had been tickling in the back of her mind ever since she'd arrived at this secret lab, and now it swam front and center. If the morgue drawer was the secret passageway to this place, the cart should have been back at the other end of the tracks. Unless someone had driven it to this end. Unless that outside business Sam had was down here.

With a nervous glance at the door she'd just come through, she climbed in and turned the key. The electric motor began to hum softly. With a sigh of relief, she pushed the button marked FORWARD. Nothing happened.

Why? Was there some other control she hadn't found? A lock on the system she couldn't open? Her pulse was racing as she glanced again at the door she'd come through. If Slater was here, he could come through it, too.

Calm down, she told herself. Think logically. She

took a deep breath, thought for a moment, and then
pressed REVERSE.

"Where the hell's the cart and pallet?" Slater barked.
The Chinese nurse, pushing the gurney through the door
onto the catwalk, stared at him in incomprehension.
He repeated the question in Mandarin, but she didn't
answer, her eyes wide with wonder at the sight of
the tracks.

Beside the door was a flat metal panel, like a fuse
box, painted the same black as the surrounding wall.
He yanked it open and stabbed at the call button,
then went and stared anxiously down the tracks.

"Where are we going?" the nurse asked softly.

"This man is sick. You will help me take him in an
ambulance and then an airplane." It was a risk bringing her along, but in his deteriorating physical condition, Slater knew he couldn't handle Kip alone, even
sedated as he was.

And where the hell was Lewis? He'd called him and
beeped him, but the man hadn't responded. Without
Lewis in place to pull Kip off when the slab surfaced
in the morgue, he and the nurse would have to ride
up with him. It would be a tight fit, especially if the
woman panicked in the dark.

Nearly twenty minutes passed before the cart and
pallet emerged from the darkness. Together he and
the nurse strapped Kip onto the platform and set off
in the cart.

"What took you so long?" Maggie stared at Taylor's
disheveled figure. "You found something, didn't you?"

"You wouldn't believe what I found," Taylor said.
Then, glancing behind her, she added, "We have to
get out of here."

"What about Lewis?"

"Leave him. We'll call Security later, tell them
where he is."

"You're shivering."

"I'm freezing. Hungry, too."

"We'll go through the food-service entrance, grab you something on the way out."

Fresh air never felt so good, Taylor thought as she gobbled a tuna fish sandwich and followed Maggie to the visitors parking lot.

"Did you find out what happened to Jack?" Maggie asked anxiously as she unlocked the Ford's doors.

Taylor popped the last of the sandwich into her mouth and slid into the passenger seat, slinging the bag with her clothes into the backseat. She chewed and swallowed while Maggie waited impatiently. "I can't be sure," she murmured, "but I have a pretty good idea."

"Tell me."

"I need to be sure of something first," Taylor said. "To do that, I need your help. And . . . you may not like it."

"What do you want me to do?"

"I'll tell you when we get there. Start driving."

What with stoplights and traffic and one way streets, the drive to All Saints Cemetery took nearly fifteen minutes. All the way, Taylor kept turning things over in her mind. If she was wrong, then what she was about to ask Maggie to do was pretty horrific. But if she was right . . .

They pulled over just outside the cemetery gates, and Taylor glanced over at the Rockingham House. "Such a weird-looking place," she said idly. "Always was. I can see why your cult meets there."

Maggie looked surprised. "We don't meet there," she said. "We meet at different people's homes. Sometimes we hold a special ceremony out in the field behind the Rockingham place or in the cemetery. The house itself means nothing to us."

"But what about those reports of mysterious moving lights?"

Maggie shrugged. "Beats me."

"And the rumors about the place being haunted? Something must have started them."

"It wouldn't take much." Maggie smiled, amused. "The place does look pretty scary. Always did, even when we were kids. Did it used to scare you?"

"You bet."

"Me, too. Even after I met Mrs. Rockingham, it still looked creepy."

"You met her?"

Maggie nodded. "You remember how we kids used to bang on her door and run away? Well, one time she caught me. She was pretty old and kind of ugly; I guess she did look kind of like a witch. But she was really nice. She gave me tea and chocolate chip cookies." Maggie paused, remembering. "She died a couple of months later. It's funny."

"What is?"

"How we were all afraid of the place when we were kids because of the way it looked. But adults were never scared of it back then. Not like now."

"How do you mean?"

"Well, you said it yourself. These days, people talk about witches meeting at the Rockingham House. How do stories like that get started?"

"The activities of your cult might have something to do with it," Taylor replied tartly.

"No, I told you. We don't meet there."

Taylor frowned. "When did the rumors start?"

Maggie thought. "Around the time the hospital was being built. I remember when I joined the Gaias, I assumed people had been talking about us. Then I realized they couldn't be." She put a hand on Taylor's arm. "I wish you'd tell me what you found. I can take it."

"We have to do something first." Taylor got out, and Maggie followed. "Which is your husband's grave?"

"Back there." She led Taylor toward the rear of the bleak, deserted burial ground. "Poor Jack. Slater killed him, didn't he? I've always known it. That's one of

the main reasons I joined the Gaias. For revenge."
Her eyes grew moist. "I knew it couldn't really work,
but I wanted to believe it. Even when I let them cut
me with the ritual knife that night—" She held out
her arm so Taylor could see the pink scar. "We stood
right over there and chanted and called." She sighed.
"I knew we couldn't really raise the dead, but part of
me desperately wanted to believe we could."

Taylor was staring at her. "You tried to raise the
dead? Here?"

"The Gaias did, yes." She turned around. "Over
there, by the gates."

"Was that the night those drunks from Duke's told
everybody they'd seen a ghost?"

"Yeah, but they were ripped." Maggie's eyes grew
large. "You believe them?"

"Which direction is the hospital from here?"

Maggie thought for a moment, then pointed. "Over
there to the east. The other side of those trees."

"That's east? How do you know?"

"I told you, we hold ceremonies in the graveyard
sometimes. We invoke the spirits of the cardinal directions, so we have to know."

If the hospital was to the east, Taylor reckoned,
then the cemetery was due west of the morgue. And
so was the Rockingham House.

"This is Jack's grave," Maggie said, stopping before
a small, simple headstone nearly hidden by overhanging branches. "What do you want me to do?"

"First, I want you to trust me," Taylor said. "I
wouldn't ask this if it weren't terribly important. Second," she hesitated, "see if you can find us a couple
of shovels."

Chapter Thirty-nine

An ambulance bearing the logo of Gamble's Funeral Home sped past the gates, siren wailing, as they stared down into the empty coffin. "I don't understand," Maggie whispered. She wiped at her eyes, leaving a streak of mud across one cheek. "Where is he? Is he alive?"

Taylor put an arm around the trembling woman. "Don't get your hopes up," she said softly.

"But there's a chance?" Maggie said, hearing the ambivalence in Taylor's voice.

"Not a very good chance. I think we both better sit down." Taylor led the woman back to the car, where Maggie collapsed heavily onto the front passenger seat. "I found a tunnel going west from the morgue," Taylor explained. "It led to a secret operating room, with two doors. I didn't dare go through either of them, but I guess it's possible—barely—that Jack could be down there somewhere. Wait," she urged as Maggie started to get up. "That doesn't mean he's alive."

"The ghost those guys from Duke's saw. It was Jack!"

"I don't know, Maggie. It could have been the booze."

"Or it could have been him." Maggie fumbled in her handbag for the ignition key. "Let's go back to the morgue."

"No," Taylor said. "I think there's a more direct

route." She paused. "I wondered why Slater kept repeating those witchcraft rumors. Why he insisted there were things that science couldn't explain. Now I understand. He wanted to scare people away from the Rockingham House."

"You mean . . . Jack's in *there*?" Maggie stared across at the crumbling Victorian structure.

"Tell me about the ritual that night," Taylor said. "Raising the dead. What did you do?"

"We drank the sacred potion, we let our blood fall on the ground, we called on the dead to rise . . ."

"Where? Here?"

"Yes. Well, I'm not sure. The potion was drugged; it always is. I remember running . . . Jack must have heard me calling. Oh, God, I know he's alive." She turned to Taylor. "Let's go get him."

"If he really *is* in there, he won't be alone. We'll need help." Taylor got her handbag from the backseat and retrieved her cell phone. "I'll call the police." But Chief Randolph was one of Sam's buddies; they all were. She looked over at Maggie. "That man I'm seeing, Kip Lawrence. He's sort of a big deal back in New York. He'll know what to do and who to call to get it done." She dialed her home number and listened to it ring. "Maybe he did go back to the city." She felt terribly sad as she dialed his office number. She'd really believed Kip cared for her.

"Come on, come on." Maggie paced around the car impatiently.

"Dr. Lawrence is out of town," Emerson's research department secretary told her. "Is this, uh, business or personal?"

"Personal."

"I'd better let you talk to Mr. Leeds, then. Hold on, and I'll transfer you."

"Dr. Barnes?" Davis Leeds sounded puzzled. "I thought Dr. Lawrence was visiting you."

"He was, but I was hospitalized with a concussion, and now I can't seem to find him."

Leeds was silent for a moment. "Then you don't know."

"Know what?"

"Dr. Lawrence had a heart attack this morning. He's at Greenvale Hospital."

Taylor reached out to the car door to steady herself. "I can't believe it. How is he? How did you find out?"

"A Dr. Slater called me. I told him I wanted to transfer Kip to New York, but he refused. He said Kip was too ill to—"

But Taylor had already broken the connection and was frantically dialing the CCU. "This is Dr. Barnes, calling about Dr. Kipling Lawrence," she told the nurse. "What's his condition? Who's his cardiologist and can I speak with him?"

"Just a moment." Then, "We have no Dr. Lawrence in the CCU."

"He has to be."

"Wait a sec, and I'll check the computer. Oh, I see what happened. He was admitted to Greenvale but immediately transferred. He was never brought up here."

"Transferred where?" Taylor asked. Strange that Slater would say Kip couldn't be moved and then go ahead and move him.

"Well, that's odd," the nurse said. "It doesn't say."

"But . . . he has no family in town. Who approved the transfer?" If they'd reached Kip's parents, that would mean New York General; Kip's father had recently donated a wing.

"All the forms were signed by his next of kin," the nurse said. "Dr. Lawrence's brother."

"That's not possible. Dr. Lawrence is an only child."

"Not according to the records. The computer says the papers were signed by his brother and—well, what do you know? Sam Slater signed them."

"Sam? Why would Sam sign?"

"Because Dr. Slater *is* his brother," the nurse explained patiently. "It says so right here. I suppose if

you're going to have a heart attack, what better place
than in your brother's hospital?''

But Taylor was no longer listening. She was thinking
of the silver-framed photos in Sam's study, of Sam
and a young, vaguely familiar blond boy.

So Kip was Sam's brother. Half brother, she corrected herself. Of whom Sam was deeply jealous.
Whom he bitterly resented. Whom he'd first refused
to transfer and then moved to points unknown.

Filled with apprehension, Taylor called several major
New York hospitals, starting with New York General.
None of them had admitted a Dr. Kipling Lawrence.

The CCU nurse was wrong, Taylor thought. There
were a hundred better places to have a heart attack
than in Sam Slater's hospital.

Or to *not* have one, she thought. Slater claimed she
needed surgery for a mythical hematoma. He'd said
Jim Partrick died of an intracranial hemorrhage, then
sent his body to Gamble's without an autopsy. And
then there was Jason Rogers. Could Kip's heart attack
be yet another fable?

Sam had personal business to take care of outside
Greenvale today. And the cart had been at the wrong
end of the tracks. Oh, shit.

"I was hoping Kip could help us," she told Maggie,
her voice shaky with emotion. "But it seems we have
to help him."

"What are you talking about?"

Taylor looked over at the forbidding mansion, her
face tight. "Kip Lawrence is in there, too."

"Let's go, then," Maggie said. "How do we get in?"

"We don't. Sam Slater's there."

"I don't care," Maggie exclaimed, and started across
the road, but Taylor went after her and grabbed her
arm.

"Give me a minute," she urged. "Maybe I can draw
Slater out." She dialed yet another number. "Penny?
It's Taylor Barnes. They have? Well, I decided I was
well enough to leave. No, I didn't know about the

surgery. I want to discuss it with Sam first. Please tell him I'll meet him in his office right away. Well, try and find him. Tell him I won't come in until I know he'll be there. Okay, I'll call back in five minutes to make sure he's on his way." She disconnected.

"Can we go now?"

"Five more minutes. Although it could still be risky with Slater gone. We don't know who else is there." She watched the second hand creep around the dial, trying to control her impatience and dread. The thing the drunks had chased that night had been zombielike and incapable of speech. Whatever had been done to Jack McCormick had been done long ago, and delaying his rescue for a few hours wouldn't make much difference. But for Kip the slightest delay could be disastrous.

"How are we going to get in?"

"Any way we can," Taylor said. "Do you have a jack in your car? A flashlight? Any tools?"

"I think so." Maggie went around and unlocked the trunk. "There's a crowbar, too," she said, pulling things out, eager to get started.

"Good," Taylor said, turning back to her phone. "I'll just call Penny back, make sure Slater's—"

But Maggie's patience was at an end. She gathered up the equipment and headed across the road.

"Wait," Taylor called after her, but Maggie didn't even turn around. She slammed the trunk shut and chased after the stocky figure, the phone to her ear. Penny's line was busy. Let's hope she's talking to Slater, she thought. Let's hope he bites. Maggie disappeared around the side of the house, and Taylor followed. If Slater was still in there, backup would be imperative. But who could she call? Yes, of course, she thought. She dialed once again, spoke briefly, and disconnected, shoving the phone into the pocket of her scrub suit.

She ran around to the rear of the building. Maggie

had swung back a peeling shutter and was attempting
to pry thick boards off a window.

"Don't waste your time," Taylor told her. "They're
probably bolted on." She looked around. If Jack
McCormick really had gotten out, whatever exit he'd
used would no doubt have been secured by Slater
after the escape. But it did indicate that security might
not be all that tight.

She tried each of the two back doors in turn, not
surprised to find them permanently sealed with steel
strips. The tunnel, cart, and flat-bed pallet provided
the usual access to the house, not the doors. She hurried around the far side of the house toward the front.
The side door was sealed, too, but its steel strip
seemed shinier than the others. She paused for a
closer look; part of the wooden frame was splintered
and rotting. Had Jack come through here that night?
Had the metal strip been added after his recapture?
Not that it mattered, she thought; nobody was going
through that door today.

At the back of the house, Maggie had given up on
the window and was trying the crowbar on one of the
doors. "Come help me."

Ignoring her, Taylor stepped back and stared at the
back wall of the house. Something was bothering her
about all those sealed doors and windows. She pictured the morgue tunnel, the secret surgical suite.
There was a lot of large-scale equipment in that OR
that wouldn't have fit through the morgue drawer.
There had to be another way in. A more straightforward way. A large-scale way.

She began circling the house in the other direction,
her eyes on the facade, and tripped over a low bush.
She steadied herself and looked down. A large azalea
plant was lying on its side. She looked more closely;
its roots were encased in a large black plastic pot.
Frowning, she examined the shrubs that stood beside
it. They were all potted.

The Rockingham estate had been professionally and

extensively landscaped with specimen plantings. Why would the gardener lay down a rectangle of wood chips and stand a bunch of potted plants on top? Then she thought, What gardener? The grounds hadn't been cared for in years. She kicked at the wood chips with the toe of her clog. There was something solid under there. She knelt and cleared a small section with her hands. Underneath the chips were clean wooden boards.

"Maggie? I think I've found something."

Excitedly, the women dragged the plants away and cleared the chips. Set flush into the ground below were two large rectangular wooden doors, their hasps secured by a small, simple lock.

"Get the crowbar," Taylor ordered. "Bring the flashlight, too."

As quietly as possible, they broke the lock and opened the doors, lying them back against the surrounding shrubbery.

It had once been an old-fashioned storm cellar. The cement steps that had led down into it had been ripped out and replaced by a wide, smooth cement ramp. Cautioning Maggie to silence, Taylor started down into the huge, reconstructed cellar. Still grasping the crowbar, Maggie followed.

They moved away from the entrance into darkness, guided only by Maggie's small flashlight. Some interior walls had been removed, others left in place; thick structural columns loomed in the faint light. The long rectangular space fell away to the right and rose up to the left. As her eyes adjusted, Taylor was able to make out two sets of doors, one at each end. Motioning Maggie to stay back, she went quickly down the slanting floor to the right and eased the door open an inch. A thin shaft of bright light shot out into the gloom.

"Is Jack in there?" Maggie whispered urgently.

"It's the operating room I told you about," Taylor said. "It's empty." She slipped through the door, Maggie following, and went toward the tunnel entrance. Standing to one side of it was something that hadn't been there on her previous visit: a camcorder on a tripod. So much for closed-circuit identification of the dead, she thought. Jack McCormick would have been long gone from the mortuary by the time Maggie'd been shown the video of his "body." She shivered; did that camera now contain Kip's image?

The door to the tunnel was ajar, and she peeked out at the empty tracks. No cart, no pallet. She sighed with relief. "Slater's gone back," she told Maggie, turning. "Maggie?"

"Are these coffins?" Maggie called anxiously. The second of the two doors Taylor had resisted opening on her previous visit to the OR was now open. Frigid vapor boiled out into the OR as Maggie peered inside.

"Don't go yanking doors open like that," Taylor scolded, hurrying over. "And keep your voice down. You want to get us killed?"

Maggie gave her a startled look and stepped back, and Taylor went through the doorway.

The sudden cold was a physical thing, like falling into an ice bath. Tall metal canisters lined the tile walls. In the center, two seven-foot silver ewers wreathed in freezing mist were laid horizontally on plastic sawhorses. Labels were secured to the sides of the ewers. Names, Taylor thought. Kip's? Terrified of what she would see, she moved through the misty chamber, teeth chattering.

Jim Partrick's body was in the first ewer, Jason Rogers's in the second. The relief she felt was immediately overwhelmed by terrible sadness for the brave firefighter and the young athlete. Why would Slater do such a thing?

"Are there people in them?" Taylor turned. Maggie stood beside her, her eyes wide with horror. "Is Jack?"

"Not Jack," Taylor said. "Other people." Through the swirling vapor she caught sight of a dark shape huddled against the far wall. Cautiously she approached and looked down at the body of Peter Ohlmeyer, his eyes wide, his body rigid with frost. Automatically she knelt and felt for a pulse, knowing it was no use. Had he become too much trouble? she wondered. Or had Sam decided it was too risky to have a doctor with a manslaughter conviction as his coconspirator? She felt a chill that had nothing to do with the temperature of the room as she wondered whether it was possible that Sam hadn't known about the cardiologist's manslaughter conviction until Garrison had told him what Taylor had discovered. If so, she was responsible, at least to some degree, for his death.

"What's in the little one?" Maggie asked, her voice quavering. "Is it a child?"

Not a child, Taylor prayed. Please, no. She looked in the direction Maggie pointed. A much smaller ewer stood on its own miniature sawhorse beyond the others. Taylor bent down and read the label. "It's a dog," she said softly. "A sweet little white Scottie."

Maggie came over and frowned at the plastic label. "A Scottie? How can you tell?"

"Because it's Slater's dog. Don't touch it," she warned as Maggie reached out a hand. "Your skin will stick to the metal." She bent closer to read what was printed beneath the name. "This is his second time around," she said softly.

The two women stared at the canisters for a moment. Then, wordlessly, Taylor led Maggie from the room.

With shaky steps they went through the OR and back into the cellar. "The patient rooms must be that way," Taylor said, indicating the opposite set of double doors at the top of the rising floor.

"Patients?"

"It's best to think of them that way," Taylor said softly. She inched open one of the doors and put her eye to the crack.

Chapter Forty

She was looking across the mansion's central hall, a wide paneled corridor lit by fluorescent light strips crudely attached to the molded plaster ceiling. The deserted corridor ran left and right of where she stood.

Maggie jostled Taylor's arm impatiently. "Go on," she whispered.

Taylor turned and gave her a fierce stare, holding a finger to her lips as she tried to decide which way to go. Jack would have had to come from somewhere near the front of the house, she decided; otherwise he wouldn't have heard Maggie calling, or the drunks beating on the door. She thought for a moment, mentally retracing their way into the house. The front of the house should be left of where she now stood. She stepped out into the hall, then looked back. Both she and Maggie were wearing green scrubs, albeit dirty ones.

"If we run into anyone," she murmured, "pretend you're a doctor."

"But—"

"Just follow my lead."

The interior of the old house smelled of wood and mold and dust, overlaid with the familiar scent of hospital antiseptic. Faintly Taylor heard the sound of a passing car, the call of a bird.

The hallway ran straight for about thirty feet, then turned sharply right. Signaling Maggie to follow, she inched her way along. A board creaked beneath her feet and she froze, heart pounding, then crept forward again.

At the end of the hall, she stopped and sneaked a look around the corner. The corridor beyond was wider, and ran parallel to what looked to be the main staircase. The sound of music drifted toward her; someone was playing a radio. She moved toward the sound, which seemed to be coming from an open door near the end of the hall. Approaching cautiously, she turned and indicated that Maggie should wait, then peeked around the door frame.

A Chinese woman in a nurse's uniform sat at a makeshift counter, listening to a small portable radio. Her eyes were closed. Off to one side were two narrow metal cots topped with floral comforters. A hot plate and mini-fridge were set up nearby. Beyond the nurse's counter, surrounded by various life-support machines, lay two men in hospital beds.

It was hard to control the impulse to dash over and see if one of the two patients was Kip, but if she could win the nurse's confidence and cooperation, what they had to do would be a lot easier. With an assurance she didn't feel, she stepped into the doorway. "Good afternoon," she said loudly.

The startled nurse leapt up, turning to stare at Taylor, her eyes wide.

"I'm Dr. Barnes, a colleague of Dr. Slater's. He asked me to check on the condition of your patients."

The nurse continued to stare, her face devoid of comprehension.

Taylor frowned; was the woman deaf? "Please tell me the names of these patients. Do you have their charts?"

The woman shook her head, turning her hands palm-up in the international gesture of Huh?, and murmured falteringly in a very foreign language.

Mandarin, Taylor guessed, recalling the textbook beside Slater's bed.

"Dr. Slater," Taylor repeated, pointing to herself. "I work with Dr. Slater."

The nurse gave no indication that she recognized the name. Perhaps, Taylor thought, she'd never been told it. "Doctor," she said slowly. Ah, that got a flash of recognition. "We are doctors."

"Ah, doc-tor," the woman repeated, her expression serious but accepting.

At which point Maggie burst into the room, crowbar in hand, shrieking, "Where's Jack? Is Jack here?"

The nurse sprang in front of her, but Maggie shoved her aside in her rush to the beds. The nurse staggered but righted herself, and ran for the phone on the counter.

Furious with Maggie, Taylor grabbed the nurse's arm. The phone went flying off the counter onto the floor as the nurse spun around, attacking Taylor with fists and feet and screaming curses in Mandarin.

Gasping, Taylor tried to defend herself. Behind her, she heard Maggie shout, "It's him. It's Jack. Taylor, it's Jack."

Then suddenly Maggie was behind the nurse, lifting the crowbar. "No," Taylor shouted, too late, as the nurse went down.

Taylor knelt by the unconscious woman, but Maggie grabbed her arm and pulled her up again. "Leave her," she urged, dragging Taylor over to the patient beds. "You have to help Jack."

"She's hurt," Taylor protested.

"So's Jack, and he's the one we came for." Maggie stared hard at Taylor through narrowed eyes, the crowbar still in her hand, giving Taylor no choice.

Taylor shot an anxious glance at the dark-haired figure in the other bed—not Kip, thank God—and began examining the pale, wasted figure of Jack McCormick.

Maggie watched intently, kneading Jack's shriveled hand. "Jack? Can you hear me?" The man moaned and opened his eyes. "It's me. Maggie."

"Mag-ee." His voice was thick and guttural, his eyes dazed.

"Do something," Maggie begged tearfully.

"He needs to be hospitalized," Taylor said, straightening up. "It's a miracle he's alive at all."

"Not Greenvale."

"Of course not. New York General. We'll call a private ambulance. I'll set it up."

"What happened to him? What did Slater do?"

"He froze him."

"What?"

"He froze him and then revived him. Or tried to."

"Why?"

"Research," Taylor said, moving to the second bed, "although I can't imagine the purpose of—" She looked down and gasped.

Maggie watched her. "Is it Kip?"

Taylor shook her head. "I don't believe this," she said softly. "It's Ward Harland."

"It can't be," Maggie said in surprise. "We made him go away. With chanting and spells."

"*Slater* made him go away," Taylor told her impatiently, "and he didn't use spells." Fighting for control, she examined the comatose figure. Despite the brain damage Jack McCormick had obviously suffered, he was in better shape than the vegetable-like Harland.

So this had been Slater's reply to Harland's boast about opening a competing practice, she thought.

Behind them, the nurse groaned and tried to rise. Leaving the insensible surgeon, Taylor went to the woman, her fury at Maggie returning. Even without a common language, the nurse could have been made to understand they were seeking yet another patient. Ordering Maggie to help, she lifted the woman onto the cot. The nurse opened her eyes. To Taylor's surprise, they were full of tears.

"It's all right," she told the woman. "We won't hurt you." Although the words would be meaningless, she hoped the tone would reassure.

The nurse shook her head. Murmuring words the meaning of which Taylor would never know, she closed her eyes in resignation.

"Are there any others?" Taylor asked, although she knew the nurse couldn't understand her. Her eyes, too, were filling. "Stay here with her," she ordered Maggie. "Don't let her get up. I'm going to look for Kip."

She dashed through the decorative archway into a small room beyond. A mussed hospital bed stood alone in the room. The nearby monitor screens were dark, the IV leads clipped off and dangling. She lifted the blanket and felt the sheet with her hand. The room was cool but the sheet was still slightly warm. A hint of scent floated on the air, subtle, masculine, distinctive. Kip's cologne. Kip had been here, and recently. Where was he now? Where had Slater taken him?

She ran through the empty mansion, opening and closing doors. Only one other room showed signs of occupation. It was across the hall from the room with the radio, and held three patient beds, all stripped and empty.

She returned to the first room. "Kip's not here," she said tensely.

"We have to get Jack out."

"Yes, and Harland, too." She pulled out her cell phone and dialed Garrison's number. Be there, she prayed.

"Potter here."

"Garrison, it's Taylor."

"Taylor? Where are you? Everyone's looking for—"

"Shut up and listen. Everything you and your banker buddies have built up is about to go down the drain, big time."

"What do you mean?"

"You know those hamster experiments Sam's doing? The ones the Larrabee Committee thinks are so terrific? Well, he's been running a secret extension of it in the Rockingham House. With people."

"What?" Garrison sounded genuinely astonished.

"He's been killing and freezing clinic patients and then trying to revive them. Occasionally he sort of succeeds."

"But—that's not possible."

"Wanna bet? He's been falsifying medical records and death certificates. Gamble's Funeral Home's in on it, too. So was Ohlmeyer. He's dead."

"Christ," Garrison breathed. "Are you sure about all this?"

"You remember Maggie Kay McCormick's husband? He died after surgery at Greenvale? Well, I'm standing right next to his bed. Oh, and if you want to know what really happened to Ward Harland, I can tell you that, too. It isn't pretty."

"*Ward*? But he went to California. At least, that's what Sam—"

"He never left town," Taylor assured him. "And ever wonder why Sam's research costs are so high? He's built a tunnel between Greenvale and Rockingham, and a secret surgical suite." She paused. "But maybe you already knew that."

"God, no," Garrison breathed. "You have to believe me."

"I'd like to, but I'm reserving judgment."

"Please, Taylor. I'd never be a party to anything like that. I'd never allow—"

"Slater brings in the big bucks. You'd allow whatever he wanted."

"Within reason, yes. Nothing like what you're describing. Murder? Fraud? Jesus, no."

"Then prove it. Find Slater and restrain him. Call the cops; they'll listen to you."

"Not the police. I'd like to handle this discreetly. With damage control."

I don't think that's possible, Taylor didn't say. She needed Garrison's help to find Slater; only Slater could tell her where Kip was. If Garrison thought she'd support damage control, he'd be a lot more helpful. "Okay," she said, "but the first priority is Sam."

"I agree. I'll deal with him as soon as he returns."

"Returns from where?"

"He's on his way to Arizona with, er, a patient."

"What patient?" Taylor asked, knowing the answer.

"Slater said we shouldn't tell you in your concussed state," Garrison said. "It's your friend, Kip Lawrence."

"Kip's no patient," Taylor snapped impatiently. "Sam kidnapped him, the way he tried to do to me. He wrote *coronary* in Kip's chart, but he brought him to Rockingham instead of the CCU."

"Then you know Kip had a heart attack."

"I just told you: that's what Sam wrote, but I'm sure it's not true. Did you know they were brothers? That Sam—never mind, I'll explain it all on the plane."

"What plane?"

"The one you're about to charter to fly us to Arizona. Try and find something fast enough to get us there ahead of them."

"Sam left forty minutes ago. He phoned me from the airport to cancel a meeting, said he was waiting for a Medevac. We'll never catch him."

"Then book a helicopter to meet us when we land. If Sam's got Kip sedated and on a stretcher, which is the only way he'd get Kip on a Medevac, they'll go the rest of the way by ambulance."

"The rest of the way?"

"Don't be dense, Gar. He's taking Kip to Saguaro, isn't he?"

"Not exactly. I mean, it's funded by Saguaro, but . . . you don't understand. If they're going where I think they're going, it means . . ." Garrison trailed off.

"What? What does it mean?" But Potter was silent. "The New Chatham police may be in your pocket," Taylor declared, "but the New York and Boston police aren't. One call, and I can have a hundred officers and press people here within a couple of hours."

Garrison sighed. "It means Kip's dead. Or dying."

"I don't believe it. Sam does a lot of lying about the condition of his patients. Me, Jack McCormick, Jim Partrick . . ."

"What about Jim Partrick?"

"I'll explain on the plane. You do know where they're going?"

"Vaguely."

"Somewhere remote, right? Somewhere in the desert?" Taylor asked, remembering the directions she'd printed out in Slater's office.

"Yes, but I've never been there. I don't know how to get to it."

"I do. Can a corporate jet get into Stillwell Field?"

"Yes, I've flown charters out of there before."

"Then that's where I'll meet you. Twenty minutes. And Garrison? I have a witness to all this: Maggie Kay McCormick is standing right here next to me."

"Shit," Garrison said forcefully. "That woman will go tell those crazies of hers, and the whole town will be up in arms. There's no way in hell I can contain—"

"Don't worry about her. She'll be on her way to New York General within the hour, along with her husband and Harland. Anyhow, she's broken with the cult. I promise you that neither of us will say anything until you've had a chance to protect yourself." Maggie started to protest, but Taylor put a finger to her lips and shook her head.

"Do I have your word on that?" Garrison pressed, wanting to be convinced.

"Absolutely," Taylor told him. "As long as you help me find Kip. But if you screw this up, you and your dad are going down."

She disconnected and glanced at her watch. It was nearly three-fifteen. Quickly she dialed a New York internist friend and arranged for Jack McCormick and Ward Harland to be picked up by a private ambulance and taken to New York General for treatment. If treatment were possible.

"I have to leave now," she told Maggie. "You wait

here with Jack." But Maggie shook her head. "It's only for a few hours, until the ambulance gets here."

"It's too spooky." Maggie glanced over at Harland and shivered.

"Well, Olive and Ben will be here any minute. They'll keep you company."

"Olive? Ben?" Maggie paled.

"Yes, I left a voice mail message for them at the school to meet us here, give us some backup. I explained how you'd rescued me and—"

"No. Oh, no."

"What's the matter?"

"They'll kill me," Maggie breathed, backing away.

"A chemistry teacher and an art instructor? I hardly think they're involved in Sam's research."

"You really don't know?" Maggie's face was a mask of terror.

"Know what, for heaven's sake?"

"Who do you think made that surgeon doll you found?" Maggie whispered. "Who put the glove in your car?"

"Olive and Ben?" Taylor shook her head in disbelief. "They couldn't have."

"They did. Janice took your car keys from your handbag at the hospital and made a copy for them."

"*Janice?* But she *worked* at the hospital. I thought the Gaias hated Greenvale."

"We—they do. Janice was a spy. How do you think they knew you were an alcoholic?"

"But they didn't know. Olive felt terrible about—"

"—putting all that liquor in the dessert. Right."

Taylor stared at Maggie. "They're cult members."

"Very important ones. They don't go out and picket because they don't want to lose their jobs. But Ben's the one who makes up the potions. And Olive cut me with the ritual knife. When you were in the hospital, she brought you cupcakes. I promised to give them to you, but they were poisoned. I could tell by the icing designs on top. So I threw them away."

"Why didn't you tell me this before?"

"I was scared. Olive said the punishment for disloyalty was death."

"I thought you broke with the cult."

"Yes, but they don't know that," Maggie wailed.
"I can't believe you called them." She rushed to her
husband's bed and reached for the IV lines. "Let's
take out the tubes. We have to get out of here."

"Don't touch those," Taylor ordered. "Without
them he'll die. We can roll the bed down into the
cellar, the IV stand and monitor, too. I'll close the
doors from the outside. The Erbachs won't know
you're still here."

"What about *her*?" Maggie shot a glance at the
nurse, whimpering on the bed.

"I'll take her out with me," Taylor decided. "Garrison can figure out what to do about her. Oh, and I'm
borrowing your car to get to Stillwell. It's just as well.
If Olive and Ben don't see it, they'll think we've left."

"I don't want to wait down in the cellar."

"It's the safest place for you right now," Taylor
insisted. "There's probably a light switch down there.
There's no time to argue about this, Maggie. I'll call
the internist from the car, make sure the ambulance
driver knows how to find you."

Taylor took the car keys from Maggie's reluctant
hand and hurried to the cot. "Time to go," she told
the nurse, tugging at her arm. The woman looked at
her with frightened eyes. Taylor smiled reassuringly
and pointed at herself. "Doc-tor. You understand?"
The woman nodded. Still smiling broadly, Taylor
pointed toward the hospital beds. "Come and help
the doctor."

The woman hesitated, then allowed Taylor to pull
her to her feet and hustle her to Jack's bed. All the
fight seemed to have gone out of her. Docilely she
helped them roll the moaning figure of Jack Mc-
Cormick out into the hall, down the cement ramp and
into the cellar.

"I told you there'd be a light," Taylor said triumphantly as the flashlight picked out a commercial
switch. She flicked it on, flooding the cellar with cool
greenish light. So much for the supernatural glow
Slater had pretended to be so impressed by, she
thought. Something must have started the haunted
house rumors, she'd told Maggie earlier, but she'd
been wrong. Not something—some*one*.

She quickly checked Jack's IV lines to make sure
nothing had pulled loose during the trip downstairs.
"All set. Show the ambulance people where Harland
is," she said, turning to Maggie, "and they'll bring
him down." She hesitated, then embraced her. "Thank
you," she said. "You saved my life. I hope they can
do the same for Jack."

Pushing the nurse gently before her, she hurried up
the ramp onto the scraggy lawn. With a final wave to
Maggie, she shut the double doors and scattered chips
and potted plants over them. When she turned
around, the Chinese nurse was gone.

No time to look for her, and no reason to, she decided. She ran across the road to Maggie's car and
slid behind the wheel, stabbing the key into the ignition. As she sped away, a white Volvo station wagon
came around the bend behind her, slowing as it neared
the Rockingham House. Taylor floored the gas pedal,
praying that Kip was still alive, and that Slater had
once again been lying about the condition of his
patient.

"I realize it's short notice," Garrison repeated. "But
we've done business for years, Roy. You've got to
help me out." He held the receiver slightly away from
his ear in anticipation of Roy's reply. The charterer
always spoke as though trying to be heard over the
roar of aircraft engines.

"It'll cost you," Roy boomed.

"I thought it might," Garrison said. "How soon can
you be here?"

"If I pull a plane out of Logan, it can be at Stillwell in half an hour."

"Do it."

"You're the boss," Roy roared. "Bring your checkbook."

Garrison disconnected, then hit the intercom button for his secretary. "Helen? Cancel everything on my calendar for this afternoon and tomorrow."

"But you've got the Board Finance Committee at six this evening," she protested, "and breakfast with—"

"Cancel 'em. I've got some important business out of town. Oh, and you can tell everyone to stop looking for Dr. Barnes. I found her, and I'm taking her with me."

He slammed down the receiver, cutting off Helen's surprised exclamation, and stared out the window, trying to control his panic. Damage control, he thought; was it even possible? Meditatively he fingered the incised silver medallion that lay concealed beneath his blue-striped, French-cuffed, lightly starched shirt.

Olive tugged at the sealed doors as Ben cursed under his breath. "We're too late," she told him. "They've gone."

"They can't have gotten far."

"Where would they go?"

Ben shrugged. "Who knows? Maggie's house? Taylor's condo?"

"You wish," Olive spat. "They're probably halfway to New York by now."

"She'll talk," Ben said as they stomped back to their car.

"And we'll deny. Janice is dead. They can't prove a thing."

They drove off in silence, neither one believing it.

Behind them, the faint sound of an ambulance siren floated on the wind.

Chapter Forty-one

"Well, he's definitely alive," Garrison said without preamble as Taylor slid into the plush leather seat next to him, still wearing the muddy green scrubs she'd left the hospital in, her wool coat thrown over her shoulders, and the patient bag with her party clothes in her hand. "I called Gamble's," he continued. "One of their ambulances took three people to Stillwell to wait for a Medevac."

"Three?" Taylor clicked her seat belt closed as the plane rolled down the runway.

"Sam, a nurse, and a cardiac patient. Blond. Male. Sedated."

"Kip."

"I'm so sorry." Garrison patted her hand.

"I keep telling you," Taylor exclaimed, shaking him off. "Kip didn't have a heart attack. Sam's got hold of him for some reason, and— Wait, let me back up a little. Kip told me Sam's been jealous of him for years; I don't know why. So it seems pretty obvious that when Sam found out Kip was up for the Larrabee too, he sabotaged his lab. He poisoned the coffee, scared the women lab workers away with threats . . ."

Garrison looked deeply troubled. "I'm sure he didn't."

"Don't defend him, Gar. We're way beyond that sort of thing. I got into Sam's computer the other night. Greenvale's financial picture isn't nearly as rosy as the Board's being told. Saguaro's funding is vital to your survival."

"My God. I had no idea."

"Of course you did," Taylor snapped. "You were worried about losing Saguaro's funding that day we went to the art show."

"I was concerned, yes, but I never—"

"Whatever," Taylor said tiredly. "The point is, Sam knew how desperately Greenvale needed the additional funding the Larrabee could bring in, and he was determined to win it. The idea of getting back at Kip personally was icing on the cake."

"Okay," Garrison said. "Even if I could buy the idea of Sam scrawling slogans on computer monitors, Kip's out of the race now. Why kidnap him?"

Taylor sighed. "I don't know."

"Would either of you care for a drink? Coffee?" A male steward stood beside them. "There wasn't time to arrange for hot food," he told Garrison apologetically, "but we have sandwiches and fruit."

"I'm ravenous," Taylor said. "A sandwich and some fruit would be great, thanks. And coffee."

"For you, sir?"

"Just coffee."

"I do know that Slater is sick," Taylor resumed as the steward moved away. "Physically and probably mentally. You're in denial about it, but it's true."

"He said the tremors were just a—"

"—neurological tic, yes, you told me. He's been lying about a lot things."

"So you're saying Sam grabbed Kip because he's mentally unstable?"

"Maybe. Or maybe he just wants Kip out of the way. Maybe Kip knows what Sam's doing over at Rockingham."

"I don't see how he could. Even *I* didn't know." He hesitated. "You're sure about what you saw? It couldn't have been legitimate research?"

Taylor raised a cynical eyebrow. "Not unless killing

your patients, falsifying their records, smuggling them to a place you keep telling people is haunted, putting them in ewers of liquid nitrogen—"

"Stop," Garrison begged, paling. "It's too appalling." He turned to stare out of the window. "That crazy bastard," he muttered.

"A choice of sandwiches for the lady," the steward announced, unloading the food from his rolling cart. "Fruit basket. Milk? Sugar?"

"Just leave it," Garrison said tightly.

"Of course. The captain said to tell you we'll be landing at about five-thirty local time. Ring the call button when you're ready for a refill on that coffee."

They were silent until the man had gone back toward the galley. Then, "Greenvale's board will make restitution to the families, of course," Garrison said. "And we'll pay for any medical care." He was gripping his coffee cup so hard, his knuckles were white.

"Damn right you will." Taylor took a bite of her sandwich, chewed, swallowed. "How far ahead of us do you think Sam is?"

"An hour, maybe more, depending on how long it took the Medevac to get to Stillwell."

"The road into the desert will be bad," Taylor murmured. "That'll give us a little time." She turned to Garrison. "You have a helicopter meeting us?"

"Yes, but . . . Taylor?" He hesitated. "I think you need to prepare yourself for the worst. You say Sam's lied about his patients before, but that doesn't mean he's lying about Kip. I know where Sam's headed, and believe me, it only makes sense to take Kip there if he's gravely ill."

"It makes *no* sense," Taylor retorted. "You don't fly a cardiac patient thousands of miles and then drive him into the desert—"

"You do if he's dying. In fact, that's the whole point." He sighed. "It's possible that Sam's doing what he's doing not because he hates Kip but because he cares for him."

Taylor stared at Garrison. "Are you hinting at some miracle cure?"

"I'm afraid not. At least, not today. Years from now, who knows?"

Taylor shook her head in frustration. "Are you doing this on purpose, or are you just naturally maddening? Put down the damn coffee, Garrison, and tell me what the hell Saguaro's up to out there in the desert."

"It's not Saguaro," Garrison said. "It's TransLife. The Saguaro Foundation is their primary financial backer."

"And TransLife is? Come on, Gar, don't make me strangle you."

"It's a cryonics facility."

Taylor frowned. "What's that?"

"Think of it as long-term cold storage of the deceased."

"You mean, like what Sam's been doing at Rockingham?"

"I don't know what Sam's been doing at Rockingham," Garrison insisted, "but TransLife is a completely legitimate not-for-profit foundation. People arrange to have their bodies frozen when they die so that years from now, when a cure is discovered for whatever killed them, they can be revived and cured."

"You're talking science fiction."

"Men walking on the moon was once considered science fiction. So was gene therapy. Hell, so was the microbe theory, and the idea that the Earth revolved around the sun. Until we do it, or prove it, or discover it, all of science is science fiction."

Taylor shook her head as if to clear it. "You think that's why Sam's taking him to TransLife? To freeze him?"

"Assuming he's dying, yes."

"And people actually do this? I mean, people other than Sam."

"Absolutely, although most don't talk about it. Other people tend to look at you funny." He gave her a crooked smile. "Sort of how you're looking at me right now." He sipped his coffee. "Remember Lynda North, the actress? She's a TransLife resident."

"Resident? Garrison, she's *dead*."

"De-animated," Garrison corrected her. "One day she'll be revived."

De-animated . . . where had she heard the term before? That funny little man in Sam's lab, the one who looked like Marty Feldman and talked about hamsicles. Understanding dawned. No matter what Sam had told the Larrabee people, his frozen hamster experiments had had nothing to do with the preservation of transplant hearts, and everything to do with human cryonic preservation. "Why didn't you tell me about TransLife back when we talked about Saguaro?" she demanded.

"I didn't know about it then. It was only after I talked to Slater, the night of the party. I was worried about what you told me—" He flushed and broke off.

"You told him about the Saguaro tax assessment and the missing blueprint? After you promised me you wouldn't?"

"He already knew about your trip to the town hall," Garrison protested. "And your visit to Mrs. Roche—"

"He *knew*?"

"New Chatham's a small town. So you see, it wasn't me who—"

"He may have known where I went," Taylor said hotly, "but he didn't know what I found until you told him. You told him about Ohlmeyer, too." She slammed her fist on the food tray, sending an apple bouncing into the aisle. "You're a bastard, Garrison. Don't you realize that's why he killed Peter and then came after me?"

"Surely you're exaggerating."

"He put a guard outside my hospital room, for chrissake. He kept me sedated, then falsified my CT scan results so he could kill me during surgery I didn't need."

"The guard was for your own protection. As for the surgery, you can't be sure."

"He had Ohlmeyer write thirty-seven on my chart. Everyone with thirty-seven on their face sheet dies. I checked the back records."

Garrison's eyes widened. Then, "Jesus, Taylor, I feel terrible. I had no idea." He touched her shoulder, but she shrugged him off. "Look, the only reason I went to Sam that night was for reassurance. If the Rockinghams were behind Saguaro, that gave them a personal stake in the town, made them less apt to withdraw funding."

"What did Sam tell you?"

"That the Rockinghams had quietly sold out to Saguaro six years ago. That Saguaro funded a cryonics facility in the desert. That I shouldn't worry about Saguaro withdrawing their grant because some of Sam's research directly benefited them."

"The hamster research? Or the people research?"

"The hamsters, of course. I swear I had no idea he was experimenting on people." He shuddered.

"Sam tell you anything else?"

"Yeah." Garrison fumbled with his collar button. "He told me about the cryonics facility, explained what they were trying to do. He said he was a suspension member." From under his shirt Garrison withdrew a small metal disk on a long chain. "He made me one, too."

"What's a suspension member?"

"Someone who's arranged to be cryonically suspended—that's what we call long-term freezing—when they die. This medallion instructs medical personnel to take certain steps, in case of death, to preserve my body until the cryonic suspension team arrives."

"Like injecting 50,000 I.U. of Heparin?" Taylor

asked. "Putting you on a heart-lung resuscitator?"
Garrison nodded. She reached over and took the disk,
turning it over in her fingers. There was the cactus
imprint, just as she'd seen it in Sam's bedroom. The
only difference between this medallion and Sam's was
that this one was silver. "Kip doesn't have a necklace
like this," she said. "I'd have seen it."

"That doesn't matter. Sam will make the necessary
arrangements with TransLife."

"Assuming Kip really *is* dying."

"Yes."

"But he's not. Look, I have no objection to cryonics
as long as the people being frozen—sorry, suspended—
have agreed to it beforehand."

"Of course."

"Not like Jack McCormick, frozen against his will
and probably while he was still alive. And Rogers and
Partrick and Harland. Human hamsicles."

"Human what?"

"Never mind."

"You could be wrong about Kip," Garrison said.

"No, I couldn't." *Was* she wrong? Were those
"ulcer pills" Kip kept popping actually nitroglycerin
tablets? No, she was a physician. She and Kip had
spent several weekends together in intimate proximity.
If he'd had heart problems, she'd have known.

"I hope we can resolve all this without involving
the police," Garrison was saying.

Maybe she *should* get the Arizona state police involved, she thought. Even with a chopper, she and
Garrison might not get there in time. But who knew
what a cornered Sam might do to a captive Kip? No,
involving the police was too risky. It would be safer
to rely on Garrison's sense of self-preservation. Sam
obviously trusted Garrison. If anyone could convince
Sam the game was up, that if he released Kip everything could be smoothed over, it would be Garrison.
But Garrison would do that only if he really believed
he could save his own skin.

Apparently, Garrison was having similar thoughts. "There's no reason the hospital shouldn't continue under a new medical director," he pointed out. "The tunnel can be sealed up, certain patient records destroyed. Greenvale does do a lot of good for the community. It would be a shame for all that to go down the tubes because of a madman like Slater. Don't you agree?" Biting her tongue, Taylor nodded. "After all, only you and the McCormick woman know the truth, and she can probably be bought."

"There's Kip, too."

"Yes. But you can handle him." He eyed Taylor speculatively. "How would you like to be the new chief of staff?"

Taylor forced herself to smile. "My present job will do just fine," she said. Like I'd really set foot in that place again. She leaned back and closed her eyes, physically and emotionally exhausted. Within minutes, she was asleep.

The ambulance pulled away from the plane, its siren silent. The driver had been assured there was no hurry since the patient was still alive. The doctor accompanying the dying man had insisted on caring for him alone, relegating the attendant to the passenger seat up front. He and the driver marveled at the foresight of the doctor's arrangements; the sooner after death a suspension was performed, the less the ischemic damage and the better the chance for a successful reanimation some day. Of course, the patient was the doctor's brother, so you could understand his desire to do the best he could for him. Still, there was something a little macabre about allowing a man to observe the preparations for his own death. True, the doctor had assured them that his patient was barely conscious, but they could hear the murmur of the doctor's voice through the Plexiglas panel. Who could say how much of the situation the patient was taking in?

"He calls me Forewing," Slater said. "He calls her

Lop-yen, which she hates. He means it as an insult, I
think, or a way of reminding us of his power." He
leaned closer to the sedated man, adjusting the cotton
blanket around his shoulders. "Not that we're in any
danger of forgetting," he added. "Me, I find it amusing. Of course, I'm low man on the totem pole. Arnold
runs Century Entertainment, has more money than
God. And the princess . . . Frankly, the only reason I
was included in that august group was my research.
But then, without my research, the Society couldn't
fulfill its mission." He leaned closer. "If he knew that,
do you think my stepfather would be proud of me
at last?"

The ambulance left the perimeter road and turned
onto a busy four-lane highway, past shopping malls
and fast food restaurants. Traffic was heavy but the
road was good, a situation that would be reversed
once they got to the small turn-off leading into the
desert.

"The Saguaro Society," Slater mused. "Philanthropic foundation and tong." He smiled at Kip. "An
interesting combination, isn't it? Kip? Are you listening?"

Kip murmured something, and shifted restlessly on
the padded slab.

"Wheels within wheels and nothing what it seems,"
Slater said, brushing the hair back from Kip's forehead
with a trembling hand. "The Saguaro Society funds
the Saguaro Foundation, which, in turn, funds me and
the TransLife facility. Of course, most of the money
comes from Cheng, with donations from Lop-yen and
Arnold—I mean, Kung Wu. My own contribution is
purely scientific.

"The Society also owns a real estate partnership,
which in turn owns a prime piece of property in an
overdeveloped town called New Chatham. The partnership refuses to replace it with a shopping mall or
condominium complex, preferring to preserve the past
instead of wantonly destroying it. Unusually high-

minded of them, don't you think?" He smiled cynically. "And then there's the Formosa Trading Company, and probably a hundred other ways Cheng
disguises his money and his intentions.

"I wish you could meet him, Kip. He's quite an
experience, he and that bodyguard of his. He left
Hong Kong a few years before the Brits pulled out,
but he's still a major player back home. To think the
man started life selling plastic flowers on the
street . . ." Slater shook his head in awe.

"Cheng kindly supplies me with nurses for my special research. They don't speak a word of English, but
they're very well trained. He has some sort of feudal-
like power over them. God knows what he did with
the one who let Jack McCormick get out. It doesn't
do to inquire too deeply into anything Cheng does.
He's a ruthless bastard." Slater smiled. "But he's *my*
bastard, my ticket to eternity. And yours, too, Kip.
Someday you'll thank me."

Kip stared at Slater through blurry eyes. His mouth
moved, but no sound came out.

"Don't try to speak," Slater told him gently. "With
the drugs you're getting, you wouldn't make much
sense."

The ambulance bumped onto the rough track and
slowed. An inexperienced driver had broken an axle
out here some months back, and no one wanted a
repeat of that. Tall dusty cactus dotted the landscape
ahead. The man in the passenger seat uncapped two
sodas and handed one to the driver.

"Preserving the past," Slater murmured, "funding
scientific research, backing a community clinic, aiding
Chinese emigrants. And the sole purpose of it all is
to send the members of the Saguaro Society into the
future." He patted Kip's hand. "Cheng's nearly eighty.
Arnold's sixty-eight and has a heart condition. And I
doubt I have more than six months left at the outside.
So you see why I was under pressure to perfect the
perfusion solution.

"Cryonics, Kip. Reversible, full-body suspension, with a perfusion solution that protects the cells from freeze-and-thaw damage. Ultimately, my cryoprotectant will also allow donor organs to be stored and retrieved for transplant. I'll probably win a posthumous Nobel for it. But for me, the benefits are far more personal."

He sighed and turned away. Snowball and the hamsicles and Jack McCormick had all proved that with his perfusate, freeze-and-thaw was occasionally possible. Their re-animations had raised his hopes, but they'd also shown him how flawed the process still was. As Sam had watched the small dog shudder and die, it was like watching his own death. Well, the work would continue; Cheng would make sure of that. Others would come, new cell repair techniques would be developed.

"Nanotechnology," he said, turning back to Kip. "Molecular robotics. Manipulation of cells at the atomic level. That's what you should have worked on. That's the kind of research that would have been of benefit to you."

The attendant slid back the panel. "How's he doing?"

"It won't be long now."

The man nodded sympathetically. "You want a soda?"

"Why not?" Slater took the proffered can and popped the lid. "To life."

"You betcha." The attendant closed the panel between them and turned around to stare at the empty landscape ahead.

Slater lifted the can to his lips. It would be like an anesthetic, he thought. I'll wake up with no sense of how long I was sleeping. Years, centuries; it wouldn't matter. At the temperature of liquid nitrogen, all biological processes ceased.

He looked down at Kip. And you'll have the best

chance of any of us, he thought. You'll be suspended while you're still alive.

"Don't think of it as death," he crooned. "Think of it as resurrection. We'll go into the future together."

A yellow airport jeep drove them to the helipad at the edge of the airfield where the small jet helicopter was waiting, its rotors idling.

"They said you have directions to where we're going," the pilot said to Taylor as she and Garrison climbed in.

"Only driving directions, I'm afraid," Taylor told him, pulling the folded paper from her handbag and passing it over.

"Won't be the first time I've navigated by road signs," he told her with a grin.

"Landmarks are more like it," Taylor said.

"Same difference." He studied the page. "These directions . . . they don't start from here. Lone Pine Road's way out in the boonies."

"Can you find it?"

"Yeah. I seem to remember a small private strip somewhere out there. You probably could have flown there directly."

Taylor looked over at Garrison suspiciously. "Why didn't you tell me?"

"I didn't know. Damn it, Taylor. I'm as eager to find that bastard as you are."

"Runway might not have been long enough for us, anyway," the pilot told them diplomatically. "It's real small."

"Could a Medevac get in there?" Taylor asked.

"Depends on the size."

"He wouldn't have had the Medevac land out there," Garrison said. "How could he explain it? You bring a cardiac patient *out* of the desert, not into it."

"Let's hope you're right."

"Strap in tight," the pilot said. "The thermals can get a little bouncy. Oh, and better put these on." He handed them each a set of headphones. "Once the rotors get going, it's the only way we can hear each other."

Some tower cross talk, a brief delay for an incoming commercial flight, and they were airborne, lifting straight up into the sky, then heading east. Garrison seemed deep in thought, his eyes closed, so Taylor sat back and stared at the 360-degree view, praying they'd be in time.

Chapter Forty-two

The chop of rotor blades brought the sentry out of his guardhouse, his lean body casting a long shadow in the dying sunlight. He stood just out of range of the small dust storm as the helicopter set down, then moved forward to intercept the doctor and the businessman who emerged from its belly.

"This is a private facility."

"We know what it is," Taylor said, moving toward the door.

The guard grabbed her arm. "Excuse me, ma'am," he said, his tone polite but firm. "If you'll just step over here, I'll call inside—"

"Get your hands off me." Taylor pulled free.

"My name's Potter," Garrison interrupted as the guard's hand went to his holstered sidearm. "Taylor, stand still a minute. I'm a TransLife suspension member," he continued, turning back to the guard. "I work with Dr. Slater at Greenvale Hospital, and I understand he's bringing a patient here. Has he arrived?"

"He has," said a voice. They turned. Slater stood at the entrance to the cinder-block building, dressed in spotless blue scrubs. On his head was a surgical cap. In his hand was a pistol.

"Where's Kip?" Taylor demanded. "Is he all right?"

"Your lover's resting comfortably," Slater told her, "although I'm not optimistic about his prognosis. As

Garrison may have told you, he's had a heart attack, a serious one."

"Bullshit," Taylor said. "I'm taking him out of here. You coming, Garrison?"

"Hold it right there." The guard went after her, pulling his gun from its holster.

"No, let her come," Slater told the guard. "Since you've honored me with this unexpected visit, Dr. Barnes, the least I can do is show you around. You, too, traitor," he told Potter over the roar of the departing chopper, its pilot having caught sight of the guns.

Slater waved his pistol in the direction of the steel door, standing aside as first Taylor, then Garrison, went in. At a gesture from Slater, the guard went back to his sentry post.

"First you released her, then you brought her here," Slater snarled. "Smart."

"It didn't happen like that," Garrison protested as the door closed behind them, "but it doesn't matter. Sam, we know what you're doing at Rockingham." Slater froze. "It's okay. We can cover it up and save Greenvale. You'll have to resign, of course, but Taylor's agreed—"

"You're a fool," Slater spat. "As for you," he turned to Taylor, eyes blazing, "I gave you a chance no one else would, and you repaid me by spying on me. You and Kip."

"Where's Kip?" Taylor said, fighting for calm in the face of the gun.

"You'll see your collaborator soon enough," Slater told her grimly. "First, since you have such an inquiring mind, let me show you what we do here. You might as well come, too, Garrison, see what you signed up for."

Garrison shuddered. "I don't actually need to see it."

"Move," Slater ordered. "Through there." He ges-

tured with the gun toward a door festooned with biohazard signs and followed them through it.

They came out into a cinder-block corridor painted
white. "Go left," Slater ordered. "Into that empty surgical suite. Kip's in another one just like this," he
added as they entered the spotless, well-equipped
room. Keeping the gun aimed at them, he went to a
wall phone and dialed. "Send the team to OR Two,"
he ordered. "We'll be starting in a few minutes."

"Starting what?" Taylor asked.

"Come, now," Slater said, hanging up. "You're a
bright young woman."

Taylor gasped. "But you can't," she protested.
"He's alive."

"There's far less ischemic damage that way," Slater
said. "But if you insist, I could kill him first."

"Hey," Garrison protested. "Don't talk like that.
We can still save Greenvale if you—"

"I don't give a damn about Greenvale," Slater interrupted. "I'm dying. She's guessed. Haven't you,
Taylor?"

"Yes. You have Huntington's chorea. That's why
you had to stop performing surgery."

"You're a fine physician. Too fine for your own
good."

Garrison looked from Slater to Taylor. "Huntington's chorea?" He repeated, stunned. "Is it treat-
able?"

"The symptoms are, to some extent," Taylor said,
"but there's no cure. Sam's in the final stages. Choreiform movements, cogwheel rigidity, a variety of neurological tremors. Eventual dementia. Tell him, Sam."

"It's true," Slater agreed. His shoulder shrugged uncontrollably. "I'll soon follow Kip into the deep
freeze. A relief, in a way. It's terrible to watch yourself
disintegrate." His face clouded, and his gun hand
drooped. "Still, they'll have discovered a cure by the
time they revive me. Don't try it," he added, raising
the gun again as Taylor started forward. "At this

range, I can't miss. And I'm damned if I'll pay for *your* suspension."

"Talk to him, Gar," Taylor urged. "Make him understand that he has to let Kip go. Everything you've built—"

"She's right," Garrison told Slater. "There's too much at stake to let Greenvale go down."

"Yes," Slater agreed. "Too much money. Well, that's your problem, yours and your father's. Greenvale's given me all it can. Oh, I would have liked to have improved the resuscitation technique, but I don't have time for that, not in this life."

Garrison unbuttoned his collar and removed the silver chain. "I thought this place was legitimate," he said. "I thought this"—he brandished the medallion at Slater—"was on the level. It sounded so good to me. A chance to live again. Hope in the face of death." He tossed it on the floor. "Fuck you, Slater."

"But it *is*." The older man looked nonplused. "TransLife is completely legitimate. It's registered with the state of Arizona."

"Then why's it hidden way out here in the desert?" Taylor demanded.

"Where should we have built it?" Slater sneered. "Downtown Scottsdale?"

"Why not?"

"Our situation is . . . unusual. First of all, we need to have complete control over our environment. We can't run the risk of civil disturbance or a loss of electricity or anything else interfering with our ability to care for our patients, year after year."

"Your 'patients,' as you call them, are dead."

"De-animated," Slater insisted, "someday to be revived, so 'patients' is an accurate term. Second, secrecy *is* important, but not for the reason you think." He sighed. "I'm afraid that cryonics is a bit of an embarrassment, even to many cryonicists. Do you know, of our four hundred suspension members, only something like fifteen percent have agreed to let us publish their names in our newsletter, or list them in our membership directory? Did *you* agree to it, Garrison?"

Garrison flushed. "No."

"Exactly. Public figures fear people will think they're kooks. Statesmen—we have a congressman and a state legislator—are afraid of losing their constituencies, serious actors their audience, scientists their funding. I'm as guilty as anyone. And yet, I believe in this wholeheartedly. I'm proud of it. And as you put it"—he nodded at Garrison—"it gives me hope in the face of death."

Hope in the face of death, Taylor thought bitterly. Right. "I saw Jack McCormick," she said. "And Ward Harland. It didn't look very hopeful to me."

"It's early days yet," Slater told her. "Who knows what discoveries they'll make, fifty, a hundred years down the line?"

"You can't be sure," Taylor said. "Besides, this facility could go broke, the power could fail, new laws could put it out of business. And it could be a century or more before science is capable of even attempting to revive you. Assuming anyone wants to bother."

"Everything you say is true. There are no guarantees, and yes, the odds against re-animation are high. But in a coffin six feet under, you have no chance at all, that's for dead sure."

Garrison nodded slowly. "You're right," he said. "If it doesn't work, you're no worse off. But if it *does* . . ." Moving beyond Slater, he bent and retrieved the medical alert, dropping the chain over his head.

"Please," Taylor said, edging back toward the door. "Let me take Kip out of here. Why come back to life a century from now with your brother's blood on your hands?"

"What do you know about it?" Slater demanded. "Stand still, dammit."

"Not much," she replied as calmly as she could manage. A chorea-induced twitch of his finger on that trigger and she was a dead woman. "Why don't you tell me?" Slater was now positioned between herself and Garrison. If she could just keep him talking to her, facing her, Garrison could slip away and get help. She tried to signal Potter with her eyes, but he seemed not to understand.

"I suppose he made her happy," Slater said. "But we were happy, too, before he came. It was a struggle financially, but we had each other."

Taylor frowned; had he and Kip argued over a girl? "Who was she?"

"Marion? She was wonderful. A strong, beautiful, wonderful woman. I loved her very much."

"And she and Kip . . . ?"

Slater nodded. "He loved her, too. And she loved him."

"I'm sorry. It must have been very hard for you. But these things happen, Sam. People fall in love, and then they meet someone else—" She broke off in alarm as Slater's face turned purple with rage.

"How dare you?" he roared. "I was talking about my mother."

Taylor stood speechless. Behind Slater, Garrison rolled his eyes. "I'm sorry," she managed to murmur. "I misunderstood." It would have been hard not to, she thought.

"I was six when my father walked out," he said, struggling for composure. "He left us with nothing. I was only a child, but I ached for Marion just as I ached for myself. I was determined to take his place, to make her happy." He paused, remembering. "Things were very difficult. We had very little money. But we had each other. We were each other's world. And then *he* came along."

"Kip?" But that couldn't be right. Kip was fifteen years younger than Sam. Again she tried to signal Garrison, but he was oblivious.

"Kenneth," Slater said. "Kenneth Lawrence. With his money and his charm, he swept Marion off her feet. Did I say she was a beautiful woman?" Taylor nodded. "His first wife had died childless, and he wanted to adopt me, make me into the son he'd never had. Offered to send me to Harvard after high school, and then to Wharton. Said he'd take me into his investment firm, make me a partner someday." Slater's lip curled with scorn. "Imagine."

"Doesn't sound so bad to me," Garrison said.

Slater swung around. "Come stand where I can see you," he told him, waving the gun. Taylor was so angry with Garrison, she refused to look at him as he came and stood beside her.

"I wanted to be a doctor," Slater continued. "I'd known it since I was ten, and the cost notwithstanding, Marion had always been very supportive. We often talked about what my specialty would be; it was like a game for us. But when Kenneth started in about Wharton and investment banking, she suddenly changed her mind, and she urged me to change mine. She said I should do what Kenneth wanted, that it would be good for me to have a father again."

"And you didn't agree."

"I was fourteen," Slater said, "and I hated him. He'd stolen my mother, and now he wanted to steal my dream. I refused, and I kept refusing. I wouldn't let him adopt me, and I wouldn't let him pay for college; I worked my way through. Even when he finally accepted my decision to become a doctor, I wouldn't let him pay for med school. I didn't want a penny from him."

"But Kip felt differently," Taylor commented.

Slater smiled. It was not a nice smile. "Yes," he said. "And no." His right hand had begun to tremble, and he switched the gun to his left. Taylor considered rushing him, then remembered the page of signatures on Slater's desk. She wasn't about to bet her life on his not being able to use his left hand efficiently enough to kill her.

"Kipling Colwell Lawrence was born a year into

the marriage. *K* for Kenneth," he added scornfully.
"Kipling for Kenneth's grandfather."

"And Colwell?"

"My mother's maiden name. So now Kenneth had
a son, a real one, and he had Kip's future all mapped
out. But while he was filling Kip's head with talk of
debentures and leveraged buyouts, I talked to Kip
about medicine."

"And you won."

"I did." Slater smiled. "Kenneth was furious with
both of us. But I was happy. Not just because I'd given
my stepfather one in the eye, but because of the way
Kip worshiped me. He did, you know. And I loved
him. I was proud of him. It took guts for Kip to stand
up to Kenneth, to tell him he wanted to study medicine." Slater's expression darkened. "He took Kenneth's money, though. Let him send him to Harvard
and all the rest."

"Why shouldn't he? He didn't have the same issues
with Kenneth Lawrence that you did."

"He lapped up the wealth and privilege," Slater
continued, oblivious. "Just lapped it up. He wore the
right clothes, met the right people. No wonder he did
so well."

"He worked hard," Taylor reminded him. "And he
has a brilliant mind."

"He was lucky," Slater said bitterly. "He had all
the breaks. I had to work for everything I got while
Kip was hailed as some kind of genius. People belit-
tled my work, called me a celebrity chaser, while Kip
had awards, prestige, the respect of his peers. But I'll
show them." He looked challengingly from Taylor to
Garrison. "It may take a century or two, but I'll
show them."

"Be reasonable, Sam," Garrison said. "None of that
was Kip's fault. You can't blame him for an accident
of birth."

With Slater's attention fixed on Garrison, Taylor

began edging away from them. "You said yourself that he worshiped you," Garrison was saying.

"He did," Slater replied. "And he will again, once he realizes the full grandeur of my achievement."

"Please let him go," Garrison begged. "Help me save what we've worked so hard to build."

Taylor shot a look around. Just a few more yards . . .

"I've already told you," Slater said. "I don't give a damn about you or Greenvale. Now, why did we come in here?" One eyebrow twitched convulsively as he looked around, momentarily disoriented. "Ah, yes," he said, refocusing. "The grand tour." He glanced over at Taylor, just feet from the door, and lifted the gun. "Dr. Barnes? Join us, won't you?"

Chapter Forty-three

"Let's use Kip as a hypothetical example," Slater said. Ashen and trembling, he gripped the pistol in both hands. "As I said, this is a legitimate cryonics facility. All our patients have legally chosen to be cryonically suspended when they die. And believe me, the paperwork is voluminous."

"Everyone except Kip," Taylor objected.

"I have chosen *for* him," Slater said, "as his next of kin."

"It doesn't work that way."

"I have the gun, and I say it does. Now ordinarily, Kip's body would be wrapped in ice and cooled before the surgical team begins its work. But because of the rather unique circumstances of his suspension, that part of the procedure won't be necessary."

Thank God, Taylor thought; as Slater had spoken, she'd been terrified that Kip was already dead of hypothermia.

"No, Kip will be handled a little differently," Slater continued. "We'll begin the process while he's still awake, so that I can explain what we're going to do, just as I'm explaining it to you now. I want him to appreciate the trouble I'm going through to take him with me." Taylor paled, and Garrison looked as if he were going to be ill. "Of course we'll anesthetize him as soon as he understands," he added mock-reassuringly. "We can't have him thrashing around on the table during surgery. Then we'll administer a slow calcium channel blocker—I like to use nimodipine—and an anticoagulant such as—"

"Heparin."

"Very good, Dr. Barnes," he said coldly. "All your work in the Medical Records Office has paid off. We'll also give him free radical inhibitors and other meds, pack him in water ice—"

"But he'll still be alive," Garrison exclaimed, horror showing on his face.

Slater frowned. "Oh, I doubt it. Not by that time."

"He's nuts," Potter murmured to Taylor.

"No shit."

"We have an excellent surgeon here," Slater continued, unheeding. "You'll enjoy watching him work."

Garrison stared at him. "I won't. You can't force me."

Slater just smiled and waggled the gun at him. "He'll access the femoral vessels," he continued, his speech slurring, "and attach the blood pump and membrane oxygenator to core-cool the body—sorry, the patient. I use a high-efficiency heat exchanger at Rockingham, and they've got a similar one here. They also use the same artificial circulatory system I do. Best on the market. All the major hospitals use it during open heart surgery. They'll crack Kip's chest, stick a cannula in the upper right chamber of his heart and another in his aorta, and replace his blood and at least sixty percent of the water in his system with my very own cryoprotectant. Yes, that wonderful perfusion solution the Larrabee people got so excited about when I showed them the experimental hearts and Harry Isaacs's hamsicles. Pity they can't see how well it works on, er, larger animals.

"But I can see you're eager to know what happens next." He smiled grimly at their white faces. "He'll make a burr hole in the cranium and expose that brilliant mind that's won so many prestigious awards. He'll check the brain tissue shrinkage as an indicator of water replacement, and he'll put in a monitoring probe. Then he'll close up all the incisions, stick a dab of bone wax on the cranial opening, and slide him into a vinyl body bag for deep cooling."

Using the pistol, he prodded them toward a large rubberized bath similar to the one Taylor had seen in the Rockingham surgical suite. "We'll fill this with dry ice," he said, "and take him down nice and slow. You won't be here for the final steps, so I'll walk you through them." Garrison and Taylor glanced at each other in alarm. "When he gets to about minus eighty degrees," Slater said, enjoying their fear, "we'll unwrap him and make him nice and cozy in a couple of precooled sleeping bags. Then we'll take him through there."

He indicated a small door at the far end of the operating room. "Go on," he ordered, and followed them through into a high, white-tiled chamber, much larger than the vapor-filled room Taylor and Maggie had explored at Rockingham and just as cold. A high yellow crane towered over one corner of the room. To the left were a series of pod-like metal containers, to the right, a collection of sturdy red-painted tanks filled with what Taylor guessed was liquid nitrogen. Ahead stood an army of seven-foot-high vertical aluminum canisters, wreathed in vapor.

"One of our two pod rooms," he explained. "The patient goes into one of those single pods, which is put into a cool-down vessel of nitrogen vapor. Down, down, down to the temperature of liquid nitrogen he goes. Is it starting to look familiar?"

"It's like your hospital lab," Garrison said shakily, "only bigger."

"And slower. We take five days to bring a human patient down to minus 196°C," Slater said. "Then the pod is dunked in liquid nitrogen, and the crane lifts it up and drops it into one of those final storage canisters, also filled with LN. The canister's sealed, the tem-

perature alarm set. It's quite a dramatic moment. I'm
sorry you'll miss it. Go on. Take a closer look."

Trailed by Potter, Taylor moved forward, her arms
wrapped around her body for warmth. In place of the
plastic labels at Rockingham, metal nameplates had
been soldered to the sides of the giant aluminum
ewers. She walked slowly past, reading the names of
the people preserved inside: Lynda North, a beloved
old sports figure, a well-known captain of industry,
and a host of other names, many of which she didn't
recognize.

The plate on the final canister was engraved with
the names of Kipling Lawrence and Samuel Slater.

"It's four to a capsule," Slater said. "There's room
in there for you and Gar, too." He smiled brightly,
raised his gun, and advanced.

Taylor looked around frantically. To one side of the
tank room, a door stood partly open, its interior just
visible from where she stood. Bright lights, the edge
of a gurney. As she watched, gloved hands moved an
instrument stand into position. It was an OR, she realized, and it was ready for action. Kip would be in
there.

He's going to kill us whatever we do, she realized,
and ran for the opening. Behind her, Slater began firing wildly, his gun hand whipping around uncontrollably. She heard the ping of bullets hitting the giant
ewers, heard Slater shout and Garrison yell, and then
she was through the door, banging it shut behind her
and flipping the lock.

Kip lay strapped to the operating table, his eyes
huge and frightened. Around him, a gowned and
masked cryonic suspension crew stood ready.

"Taylor?" Kip murmured as she took his hand.
Then the realization hit him. "Get out of here," he
whispered hoarsely. "Sam's gone crazy. He'll kill you,
too."

Behind them, a door swung open. "Out of the frying
pan," Slater said, pushing Garrison before him, "and

into the surgical suite. No, stay where you are, Taylor. What better way for Kip to die than surrounded by his loved ones? Dr. Evans? Ladies and gentlemen?" He turned to the suspension team, now staring at him in apprehension. "Let's get started, shall we?" He moved around to the foot of the operating table.

"You told me he was de-animated," the TransLife surgeon protested angrily. "What the hell is going on?"

"It's only a matter of hours," Slater said, his slur worsening. "His condition's quite hopeless. But if you insist—" He turned to one of the OR assistants who was pulling medications from the surgical cabinet. "Give me 40 cc of potassium chloride," he told her.

"Don't," Evans told her firmly. "It'll kill him."

"Shut up." Slater raised the gun. "Hurry," he told the assistant. Slowly, she opened a drawer and withdrew a hypodermic. "Believe me," he told Kip softly, "I'm doing this out of love."

"I won't be a party to murder," the surgeon announced. He ripped off his mask and stepped back from the operating table. The rest of the team also moved away.

"Murder? Not at all. It's transplant surgery. A time transplant." Slater smiled at his witticism. "But if you won't do the suspension, Evans, I will. Dr. Barnes, here, will assist me."

"Like hell," Taylor told him.

"Then you'll be next." Slater raised the gun, switching it from his right hand to his left as he held out a hand for the hypodermic. In that instant, the surgeon launched himself across the operating table at Slater, who fired, hitting him in the chest. Evans fell back, bouncing off the counter before sliding onto the floor. Stunned, the team stared at the surgeon's body, the red froth on his lips, the fountain of blood spouting from his chest.

Taylor bent down and felt for a pulse. "He's gone," she said heavily. "I think you hit his heart."

"That was the idea." Still holding the gun in his left hand, Slater extended his right toward the assistant at the counter. "It'll be messy," he said, "but I can do the suspension myself. Give me the syringe."

"No!" Taylor cried, rising.

Slater raised the gun to point at her chest. "Keep away." His face twisted into a bizarre grimace. "Hurry up," he croaked, extending his hand toward the woman at the counter.

The assistant went forward, slapped the filled hypodermic into his palm, and quickly retreated. "I filled it with saline," she whispered to Taylor as she brushed past. Behind them, two members of the suspension team were pulling bags of ice from a wall freezer and packing them around the dead surgeon's body.

His facial spasm abating, Slater came around the side of the table and looked down into Kip's terrified eyes. " 'Good night, sweet prince,' " he murmured, his thumb on the syringe plunger, " 'and flights of angels—' " Suddenly the hand gripping the hypodermic shot up over his head. His eyes widened in alarm as the arm jerked spasmodically forward, then sideways. He stared at his flailing hand in horror. Dropping the gun onto Kip's legs, he grabbed his right hand with his left, cursing in frustration.

"Now!" Two team members launched themselves at Slater from the side, driving him into the instrument tray. It fell to the floor with a crash, and the three men followed. The hypodermic skittered away across the tiles as, pinned beneath the pair, Slater howled in frustration.

"What happened?" Garrison murmured, ashen-faced.

"Choreiform movement," Taylor said. "It comes and goes." She picked up the gun, turning it over in her hands, then aimed it at the floor, away from the pile of men. "Let him up," she said, "but keep hold of him. I've never shot a gun before," she told Slater as the three men rose from the floor, "but how hard can it be?"

"What will you do with him?" Garrison asked, frowning.

"What do you think?" Taylor replied grimly. "Someone untie Dr. Lawrence, please." The woman who'd filled the syringe with saline hurried over to help. "Can you sit up?" she asked Kip gently.

"I think so."

Together the two women helped Kip off the table and onto his feet. "Get him a robe," Taylor said, "and then call the police."

"Not the police," Garrison said. "You promised."

Taylor turned to stare at him. "That was before he shot and killed Dr. Evans. We don't have a choice now." She paused. "We never really did."

"You can't save Greenvale if you let her turn me over to the police," Slater told Garrison, his arms pinioned behind his back. "You'll lose everything, you and your father."

"Forget it, Sam," Taylor said. "There's no way Evans's death can be covered up. Tell him, Gar."

The shaken Potter shook his head.

Slater's shoulders sagged. "So this is how it ends," he said softly. He took a step toward Kip, but the two men pulled him back. "I didn't really want to hurt you." Slater regarded his half brother sorrowfully. "I just wanted you there with me when they woke me up a hundred years from now." He paused. "And I didn't mean to kill Dr. Evans. My hand spasmed."

"He's dead just the same," Taylor told him.

"I know, and I'm sorry. But don't call the police, not yet. There's another way to handle this." Slater turned to the cryonics team. "I'm dying. This time it's the truth; not like what I told you about Dr. Lawrence." He jerked his chin toward Taylor. "She knows it."

"Don't expect any help from me," Taylor said. "You're a murderer many times over."

"I'm also a suspension member of TransLife," Slater said, turning back to the cryonics staff. "And TransLife's charter guarantees every member the right to be suspended. You don't make personal judgments about people's worthiness."

"Maybe we should," someone murmured.

"So I'm claiming my right to suspension. And I want you to do it right now, while I'm still alive. Don't worry about the legalities. I'll sign anything you like." No one replied. "I developed the perfusate you use here. I did the research that'll let us all live again, someday. Use it on me. You owe me that."

"No," a woman said firmly. "It's against the law." Above her surgical mask, her eyes were ice. "Besides, I don't want to share the future with you." She glanced over at the surgeon's body. "Dr. Evans is a suspension member, too." She looked at Taylor. "You're a doctor, right? Will you help us?"

Taylor turned toward the staff member, lowering the gun. "I'm not sure I—"

"Look out!"

Taylor swung around in time to see Slater twist free of his captors. Kicking the fallen instrument stand out of his path, he ran through the door into the pod room. "Stay here with Kip," Taylor ordered the assistant. She charged after Slater, the gun still in her hand, TransLife staffers close behind.

Slater was halfway across the room, heading toward the red cylinders. He stumbled as his ankle spasmed, but managed to regain his balance and half ran, half limped to the nearest cylinder. Grasping its dangling hose in one hand, he twisted open the valve with the other. A thick, freezing mist spewed out.

"Stop!" Taylor ran toward him as he thrust the hose down his throat, filling his body with killingly cold nitrogen vapor.

"Don't touch him," a staffer warned, grabbing her by the shoulder and spinning her around. "The LN will kill you, too." They stared in horror at the frozen, contorted figure on the white tiles.

"Get back," he called to the others as he guided Taylor toward the surgical suite. "Somebody call maintenance, tell 'em what happened. They'll need protective gear to shut that valve. Oh, and page David Posner. He's our backup doc today." He turned back to Taylor. "My name's Brad Wrightson," he said, pulling off his surgical mask.

"Taylor Barnes." She glanced back over her shoulder. "So Sam got his wish. He's frozen, suspended. Someday they can bring him back."

Brad shook his head. "Not like that, they can't. Without perfusate to protect his cells, the damage is already irreversible."

Garrison leaned against the pod room wall and vomited onto the floor.

"Better come inside," the man advised. "You'll freeze out here, with that valve open." He helped the shivering Potter into the surgical suite behind Taylor, and closed the door.

Taylor hurried to Kip. "How do you feel?"

"Alive," he said, taking her in his arms. "Thanks to you."

Her arms went around him, and tears filled her eyes as they held each other close.

"I'm sorry I wasn't completely open with you about Sam," Kip murmured. "I thought your being there might help bring about a rapprochement between us. I never meant to put you in danger. Can you forgive me?"

Taylor nodded. "You had no idea, then, that Sam was . . . the way he was. And when you did realize . . . well, if you hadn't stopped the IV sedation, Sam would have killed me on the operating table."

He took her face in his hands and looked deeply into her eyes. "I love you, Taylor," he said. "I always have. I wanted to tell you, years ago, but the timing wasn't right, and then you were married . . ."

"I love you, too."

Behind them, the cryonics team was tucking more ice around the dead surgeon. "We need to suspend him as soon as possible," Brad told Taylor. He turned to a hovering medical assistant. "Any luck finding Posner?"

"On his way."

Brad turned back to Taylor. "I heard Sam Slater call you 'doctor.' Will you help us until David gets here?"

Reluctantly, Taylor drew back from Kip. "I can't." She looked around at their anxious faces. "Dr. Lawrence needs care."

"I'll be all right," Kip insisted shakily. "I could use some clothing, though."

"And a place to lie down," Taylor said, "while the sedative wears off. You're still pretty wobbly." She studied him. "Can you handle a telephone?"

"I think so."

"Then call the police. And see if you can get us some transportation out of here. She turned to the medical assistant. "Is there somewhere he can stretch out?"

"There's a sofa in the on-call room. I can show him where it is."

"I'll come, too," Brad offered. "He can borrow my clothes. And I'll bring a death certificate. We can't suspend Dr. Evans without a signed death certificate. Will you sign it?" Taylor nodded.

"Should we put *him* in there, too?" The cryonics assistant indicated the green-faced Garrison.

"I guess you'd better," Taylor said slowly, then gave a sharp intake of breath. Something Garrison had told her on the plane from New York suddenly made unpleasant sense to her. "And stay there with them, okay? Don't leave them alone." She turned to Kip. "You sure you're all right?"

"I'll be fine."

"Okay, then." Taylor turned to Brad. "You'll have to tell me what to do."

"Don't worry. We'll talk you through it," Brad assured her.

"And I can't stay long. Just until our transportation arrives."

"I understand. The scrub room's through here."

"One more thing. Before we get started, I need to talk to whomever's in charge. I have a few . . . nonmedical questions that need answering."

"You can talk to me," Brad told her. "Let's get those two settled, and then I'll tell you anything you want to know."

Chapter Forty-four

"We're over Ohio now," Kip told her. "Almost home."

Eyes closed, head lolling against the upholstered seat back, Taylor nodded. "I wish I could change out of these filthy scrubs," she murmured. "And wash my hair. I'm a mess."

"You look beautiful," he told her.

She smiled and opened her eyes. "You've been out in the desert too long." She reached over and squeezed his hand.

Beneath the small private jet, towns glided past, pinwheels of light in the velvet darkness.

"Maybe the sedative hasn't worn off yet," Kip murmured, "but it all still seems . . . dreamlike. Unreal."

"It's real, all right," Taylor assured him.

"Believe me, I know," Kip sighed deeply. "Sam was always . . . odd," he said slowly, "but it's hard for me to understand how he could have done what he did."

"It might have been the Huntington's. The mental deterioration is relentless."

"That would account for some things," Kip agreed, "but we both know it wouldn't explain the really bad stuff. No, his problems went way back: the sudden loss of his father, his abnormal attachment to our mother, his awful jealousy, his driving need to prove himself . . ."

"Capped by the discovery that he was dying. Around

the time he founded Greenvale would be my guess.
Probably *why* he founded Greenvale."

"You're right," Kip said. "In the ambulance he told
me his illness was the reason for his research."

Taylor nodded. "He knew he was dying. He'd risk
anything for a chance to be revived, once a cure was
discovered."

"The whole concept of cyronics is scientifically un-
sound," Kip said. "Even if you could repair the cell
damage in some way, the spark of life would be gone."

"Today, you're right. A hundred years from now,
who knows?" Taylor sighed. "It all comes down to
hope, doesn't it? Whatever gets you through the night."

"I guess."

She studied the dark circles under his eyes, the new
lines on his cheeks. "That's enough talk for now," she
told him. "You should rest. You're exhausted."

"I am, but I need to talk. You've had more time to
absorb it all."

"At least eat something." She glanced at his untouched dinner tray.

Obediently he speared some roast beef with his
fork, carried it to his mouth, chewed, swallowed. "I'm
still wrestling with the fact that Sam was capable of
murder. Sabotage, sure. I mean, he was the first person I thought of when my lab was vandalized, but to
kill his patients, to shoot Evans, to try and kill *me* . . ."

"Killing you was his way of taking you with him
into the future," Taylor said.

"I know. He told me that in the ambulance, too.
And in the OR, he said he loved me."

"I'm sure he did. And he hated you, too."

They were silent for a while, picking at their food.

"I sure wouldn't want to be in Potter's shoes tonight," Kip said, consciously changing the subject.
"Having to tell his father what's about to happen to
his investment."

"Don't waste your sympathy on him," Taylor said
shortly.

Kip looked over at her, puzzled. "I thought he was one of the good guys," he said, frowning. "He came out here with you to try and talk Sam into releasing me."

"To save his own skin, yes." Taylor paused. "It wasn't Sam who sabotaged your lab. It was Garrison."

"What?" Kip stared at her. "Why?"

"Think about it. Garrison was the financial guy. His dad put the investment package together, brought in all his banker buddies. Anything Sam knew about Greenvale's balance sheet, Garrison knew first. And he was in a better position to understand its significance than Sam was. Hell, he knew the Board wasn't seeing the real figures."

"You can't be sure."

"He *had* to have known. Months ago, he spoke to me about his fear of losing Saguaro's funding. And then there was Sam's illness. Sam told him the tremors meant nothing, but Garrison's not stupid. And he knew that if Sam *were* seriously ill, they were really in the shit. If Sam went, Saguaro's money went with him; Sam was the only contact they had with Saguaro."

"But what use would the Larrabee be without Sam?" Kip asked. "Potter couldn't fund-raise on it once Sam was gone."

"True. But as long as Sam hung on for a few months, Garrison could probably raise enough money for Greenvale to pay off its bank loans. After that, if Sam died and the hospital went belly-up, at least his father and the other bankers would be whole. Also," she theorized, "he may have figured he could attract another star researcher to take Sam's place. The Larrabee carries a lot of clout. No, Garrison saw the award as vital to Greenvale's survival, and his own. He was desperate for it."

"Makes sense," Kip conceded. "But it's just conjecture."

"No, it's not. When Garrison and I were talking on the plane, I accused Sam of sabotaging your research.

That's what I believed then. He said something to the effect that he might be able to buy the idea of Sam writing slogans on computers but he couldn't understand why Sam would kidnap you, now that you were out of the race."

"So?"

"So," Taylor said. "I'd only mentioned the blood on the mirrors. I hadn't said a word about writing slogans on computers. But Garrison knew."

Kip frowned. "I wonder what he meant by that strange word."

"What word?"

" 'Gaia.' It was scrawled on a piece of paper in my office, the day the computers were vandalized."

Taylor turned to stare at him. "You sure it said 'Gaia'?" Kip nodded. "That's the name of our local cult, the one that's been picketing the hospital."

"Then . . . it wasn't Garrison after all?"

"Oh, it was Garrison all right. Writing 'Gaia' was a blind. He must have known the Gaia cult had been taken up by a national anti-genetics group; Slater mentioned it to me some time ago."

"You're saying the Gaias were involved with the same group that picketed Emerson?"

Taylor shrugged. "Maybe, maybe not. The point is, Garrison knew that the word 'Gaia' would lead investigators to a national anti-genetics organization. It didn't matter which one."

"Our security people did suspect the group that had picketed us. But they couldn't prove anything." Kip was quiet for a moment. "How did he manage it?" he asked at last. "Our security was very tight, we ran checks on all our people." He frowned. "Ronnie Leong. She was the one who made the coffee that day everybody got poisoned." He sighed. "I hate to think it was Ronnie, but I guess it all fits: Cheng, the nurses . . ."

But Taylor shook her head. "This was Garrison's scheme, not Cheng's. Before he came to New Chatham, Garrison lived in Boston, same as Sam. He had a relationship with a medical researcher there. Any of your new staff members happen to come from Boston?"

"Lisa Kemp," Kip said, relieved that the perpetrator wasn't the congenial Ronnie. "But Lisa's an excellent researcher. Why would she do such a thing?"

"Love. Money. Maybe both. Garrison's the hospital's CFO. He could keep throwing money at her until she said yes." Taylor sighed. "You'll never prove it, of course. You have no physical evidence, right?"

"If we had, Security would have asked for an arrest months ago."

"Well, there you are, then."

"How about the Rockingham experiments? Did Potter know about those?"

"Oh, I'm sure he didn't." Taylor replied. "He'd have been horrified. He'd never have allowed the hospital to be put at such risk."

"What about Gamble's Funeral Home? How did the Gambles get involved?"

"They were probably bought, same as Roche. God knows what story Sam told that builder about needing a secret tunnel. Whatever it was, Sam must have had second thoughts about how well it would hold up because—surprise, surprise—Roche died during bypass surgery in Greenvale Hospital, and his wife received a mythical insurance payment from Sam to keep her quiet." Taylor sipped her tea. "It's amazing what people are willing to believe if you wrap it in lots of cold, hard cash."

"And Ohlmeyer?"

"We'll never know for sure, but my guess is that Ohlmeyer was having a tough time holding a job when he applied to Greenvale. He must have moved around a lot. Each time he'd be okay for a while, and then the manslaughter conviction would come to light and he'd be fired. But with Sam, it was different. Sam knew he could use the manslaughter conviction to co-opt him." She set down her cup. "When I found his body, I thought I'd killed him." Kip looked startled. "By telling Garrison about his past, I mean. I was sure Garrison had told Sam, along with everything else I said that night, and Sam decided Ohlmeyer had become too big a risk. But when I thought about it, I realized Sam must have known all along. He'd have reveled in the hold it gave him over Ohlmeyer. Of course, Sam made it look as though things were the other way around, quietly setting up Ohlmeyer to take the fall if things went wrong."

"Which they did, big time." He drank some water. "So what happens now?"

"To Greenvale? I don't see how it can survive, once all this comes out. It's a shame, in a way. Aside from Sam and Ohlmeyer, it was a pretty good hospital. And it did help the community."

"And TransLife?"

"They're legitimate," Taylor said, "and low-profile. As long as they can convince the media that what happened there today was the result of Sam's mental condition, they should be fine. Sure, they benefited from Sam's research, but I had a serious talk with Brad Wrightson, and I came away convinced that nobody at TransLife had the slightest idea of what Sam was up to at Rockingham." She paused. "Whether or not one agrees with them, they're ethical people. That surgeon gave his life trying to keep Sam from killing you. And the medical assistant filled the syringe with saline instead of potassium chloride. If Sam had noticed . . . I think TransLife will be okay. I hope so; none of this was their fault." She paused. "The Saguaro Society's a very different matter. I'll be glad to see the end of them."

"Don't hold your breath."

"You're kidding. With what we know—"

"It's all hearsay," Kip reminded her, "and from a deranged and dying man. No, Cheng will throw up his hands in horror, dismantle the Rockingham lab, claim no knowledge of Sam's research. And no one will be able to prove anything different. A man of his power and wealth will have made damn sure to distance himself from the dirty work nine ways from Sunday."

"You said there were others involved."

"The princess and the movie mogul? All they gave was money. All they got were medical alert medallions." Kip shrugged. "Try and prove otherwise." He took a sip of orange juice.

"What about the nurse who went with you in the Medevac?"

"Sam put her on a plane to San Francisco. Cheng will deal with her."

"I don't like the sound of that," Taylor said. She frowned. "There was another nurse at Rockingham. I took her out with me, but she ran away."

"She'll go to ground. You'll never see either of them again." He put an arm around her. "I'm more concerned about what happens to *you*. How will you . . . cope?"

"No guarantees," Taylor said, "But if everything I've been through lately hasn't put me back on the sauce, I don't think the fallout from it will. In fact . . ."

"Yes?"

"I'm thinking of reopening my New York practice. Irene Lacey and Lila Krimm are excellent references. It's worth a shot."

"So you're coming back to New York?"

"Fast as I can pack my clothes." She grinned.

"That's good," Kip said, "because I hate commuting." She eyed him quizzically. "You don't think I'm going to give you up a second time, do you?" He kissed the tip of her nose.

"You really think I'm ready to run my own practice again?" she asked, suddenly unsure.

"There's only one way to find out." He smiled at her. "I have high hopes for you. For us."

Hope, Taylor thought. It was all about hope, wasn't

it? Cryonics, love, staying sober. The whole business of living.

She knew what it was like to watch a marriage fail. To drink oneself into oblivion. To destroy a career that had taken years to build.

But she also knew what it was like to take the first, halting steps toward sobriety. To pick up a scalpel for the first time in months. To feel loved again.

Hope allowed you to believe that tomorrow might be better. And sometimes it was.

She was suddenly very tired. She leaned her head on Kip's shoulder and closed her eyes. Sometimes hope is the only thing that keeps you going, she thought. Sometimes hope is all you have.

Kip reached over and touched her hand.

Sometimes it's enough.